WAR OF MONSTERS

ABERRATIONS
BOOK ONE

RUTH YORK

ISBN: 979-8-9936306-0-1 (paperback)

ISBN: 979-8-9936306-1-8 (ebook)

This is a work of fiction, and the views expressed herein are the sole
responsibility of the author. Likewise, certain characters, places, and incidents
are the product of the author's imagination, and any resemblance to actual
persons, living or dead, or actual events or locales, is entirely coincidental.

Cover design by Shannon Velazquez.

First printing edition 2026.

For my parents,
who never stopped believing in me

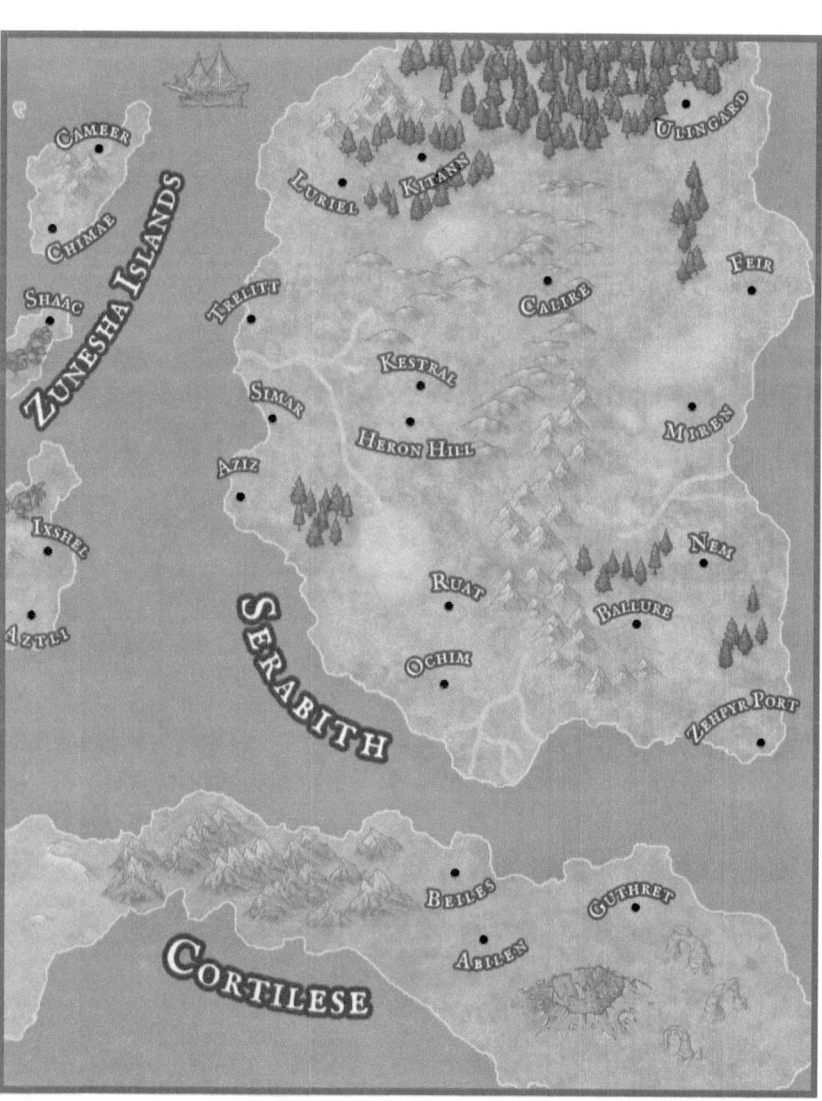

CONTENT WARNINGS

This book contains graphic violence, blood and gore, adult language, explicit sexual scenes, on page sexual assault, and drinking.

Your mental health matters. Please take these warnings seriously.

If you or anyone you know has dealt with sexual assault, you are not alone. If you need help, there are many free resources available.

National Sexual Assault Hotline: 1-800-656-4673 (HOPE)

Domestic Violence Hotline: 1-800-799-7233 (SAFE)

Victim Hotline: 1-855-484-2846

CHAPTER
ONE

The stench from the bodies is overwhelming.

The mage lowers her hands, turning to us with exhaustion creased into the soot-stained lines of her face. The flames behind her leap over the piled corpses, devouring tunics stained red, torn flesh and gaping mouths and eyes sightlessly still denying reality.

We built the pyre far enough from the shoreline to avoid high tide, but roils of dark smoke glide over the murky waters, swept away by the salt-tinged breeze that is the one constant of this place.

The breeze, and the waters, and the death.

"Would you like to say any words over their souls?" The mage's voice is bone-tired, the words rote, a script to say as they burn.

Faaris curls his lip and spits next to me. "No one is here to guide them to the afterlife. If there was, they would have stopped this light forsaken bloodbath months ago."

I agree, but I don't have the energy to reply aloud. We were up most of the night gathering the bodies from yesterday's skirmish, a short but bloody massacre that barely came out in our favor. We lost many good people. Too many. Our numbers are dropping rapidly, and I've heard whispers of letters begging the king to send reinforcements from the initiates.

Initiates. They haven't finished their training, don't even know what it truly means to give life and honor to the crown by taking on the mantle of knighthood.

I despise every soul for daring to ask for their lives. I despise myself for agreeing with the damning reality of how badly we need them.

The tide surges, white-capped waves cresting onto the beach, darkening the sand already stained with our blood. I watch the sea, watch as the water retreats, leaving divots in the wet mud, erasing whatever bootprints were there yesterday, erasing the death until only the living can speak their memory.

This war has gone on too long.

The heaviness drags me down, threatening to drown me just as effectively as the water now once again lapping almost at my feet. Waves lick the edges of the pyre.

No. That's not right.

I turn, exhaustion muddying my thoughts, only to jerk back as an arrow sprouts from Faaris's eye, hot blood spraying across my face. The stench is a familiar companion.

The world explodes into shouts and screams as the scrubby hills beyond the beach elongate into the shapes of men, soldiers with the elegant bows of the islands, arrows tipped with poisons we've only just begun to understand. There's another roar, a rushing, and I turn even as I draw my sword, the metal singing as it is freed from the scabbard, and find the very waves rising up, taller than nature deemed possible, filling my vision until it threatens to blot out the dawn's light.

There's barely time to gasp before the water crashes down, instantly dampening the screams, filling my head with the echoing promise that this is really it, this will finally be the end—

"Raylen."

A hand on my shoulder, jostling me through the waves, bringing me back to the weak light dancing above my head. Panic grips, hard and unrelenting, because to break the water's surface is to condemn myself to a painful death from the waiting bowmen. I need to swim, gain what little bearings I can, put some distance between myself and the lurking enemy.

"Raylen!"

A harder shake, and now light bursts through my eyelids, only it's not the sun breaking over the water but a candle, flickering on my bedside table, next to the abandoned journal still lying open.

Liseah leans back as I sit up, rubbing sleep from my eyes and trying to disperse the remnants of the dream. I should have learned long ago not to read Eirah's journal before bed, but these written words are the only thing left of my uncle. Sometimes I can pretend it's his voice and not my own reading to me, the soft timbre as easily remembered as the way he laughed, drew me into his lap to whisper stories of the Knight's Temple, made promises of the adventures we would go on when we were both sworn in.

I draw myself together enough to focus on Liseah. She sits on the edge of the bed, chewing on her thumbnail. Worry creases her face, draws fair brows low over dark eyes that don't flinch away from my own stare.

"What did you do?"

She has the audacity to look affronted. "Why do you assume it's *my* fault?"

"Liseah, I've known you since birth. We've been friends for two decades. When is it *not* your fault?"

She grins as she replies, "When it's yours."

I throw back my blankets, forcing Liseah off the bed as I rise. She's already dressed in a sensible split skirt and plain blouse, golden-brown hair braided past her waist. A knapsack, sturdy but old, waits at her feet. Packed.

My heart skips a beat, and I look at her again, eyebrows raised now. "That better not be what I think it is." I draw my nightgown over my head, exchanging it for breeches and a tunic, drab but comfortable. "Talk."

Liseah has the grace to look apologetic. "I might have spent the night with someone."

It's all I can do not to snort. Spending the night with someone is a simple truth intrinsic to Liseah's being. Unfortunately, in a village our size, suitable partners are limited and often delegated to a few fun nights and nothing more. On the chance some would have liked to stick around because of her beauty and wit, Liseah's boredom usually got the best of them. Staying with one person for the foreseeable future is not her idea of a pleasant life. It's one of the many reasons we're leaving at the end of the week.

I glance again at the knapsack. Or, apparently, sooner.

"Unless you slept with the village elder, I don't think you can do anything to surprise anyone anymore." I swivel to look at Liseah again. "You didn't sleep with him, did you?"

She scoffs. "I don't dally in marriages, much less with someone like *that*." Liseah shudders. "Hameth has been the bane of my existence since I turned sixteen."

"And slept with his daughter."

She waves her hand through the air. "That's neither here nor there. Marieta and I have been friends for years."

I run a brush through my short, dark hair, wetting down wayward strands and watch Liseah as she picks at the skin around her nails. "Out with it." I set the brush down, leaning a hip against the dresser and crossing my arms. Even not

WAR OF MONSTERS   5

standing straight I tower over Liseah, but that's never intimi-
dated her or kept her from speaking her mind. Now, though,
she looks almost... cowed.

"They're sending me away."

Her voice is almost too quiet to pick out the words. I shift
forward, heart picking up its tempo. "What?"

She finally looks back up, eyes dark with anger and unshed
tears. "My parents are sending me away. I heard them talking
when I snuck back in last night. It was late, but they must have
had guests and stayed to clean up."

Liseah's parents run the only inn in Heron Hill, a modest but
bustling affair. Since the village is on the road to Kestral, a
major trading point in the country, we see our fair share of
travelers.

"They didn't know I was there. Father said he's finally heard
from Aunt Tremalle."

We shudder in unison. Liseah's aunt was unequivocally the
worst part of our childhoods, and there might have been a cele-
bration when she finally married and left.

"What does he want from that cow?"

"She agreed to take me in and straighten me out, find a
match that would have me." Every word is a whip, sharp
against my skin, burning with the realization of her situation.

I crumple on the bed. "They can't be serious."

Liseah laughs ruthlessly. "Of course they are. It's a small
miracle it's taken this long, let's be honest. They always warned
my actions would catch up to me." She snorts. "I guess I lied to
myself for long enough. I thought it would matter, being their
daughter."

"They still love you." The words are weak.

She shrugs. "I'm sure they think this is the best... for
everyone else." She's quiet for a minute. When she speaks
again, her voice warbles, torn between anger and grief. "I would

think, after twenty-one years, they would know me better than this."

I think they do but simply don't care. Just as my father knows my own heart and how it longs for the Knight's Temple, but he would do anything in his power to keep me from it. The difference in our parents, however, is that ultimately mine wish to protect me, while Liseah's are too concerned with holding up the proper images, as if they are Nobles in Calire and not simple innkeepers. As if appearance matters more than their daughter.

"If they only would wait till the end of the week, I'd be gone anyway." Liseah wraps her arms around herself. She looks small. "I was never going to come back, but now I really have no choice."

"Do you think you could tell them? That Corran was going to take us to Kestral?" The idea is like ash on my tongue. The whole point of this was to sneak out, spare Father another endless argument that only upset us both. But I have to offer it anyway.

Liseah shakes her head, and I'm ashamed at the flood of relief that follows the gesture. "Tremalle will be here tomorrow. They would never let me leave with Corran now."

It took me three years to convince her she should come with me when I left for knight training. Back then, when the world felt large beyond measure and such talk was really only a daydream, she would wave me off and claim she could find a happy place for herself here, just as everyone else did. Leaving without Liseah scared me to my bones; she's been just as much of a constant in my life as my own flesh and blood. But not leaving at all — that scared me more.

The reality of her situation became clear the older we got. Liseah was someone you had fun with, flirted with, made friends with. But never someone to bring home as a wife. She was too bold, too rebellious, too confident in herself and her own power. After a disastrous engagement ended in a heated fist fight on the town green and Liseah was banned from the only cobbler in town, she admitted perhaps she had grown too big for the confines of Heron Hill.

We left that month, when we were eighteen, with only the roughest of plans. The Knight's Temple for me, some sort of serving maid job for her while she figured out apprenticeships and found connections. We made it as far as a mile outside the village before my brother, Korbal, brought us back. My father would rather see me disowned than leave to follow "a path only ending in death" and didn't speak to me for nearly six months.

When we were nineteen, we made it to Kestral in the back of Corran's wagon before a plague of the wasting sickness returned us to Heron Hill. It was the worst Serabith had seen of the disease in over twenty years, and we spent the days huddled in our houses, alone, praying we wouldn't be taken next.

We weren't, and life returned to normal. Long days in the orchard, evenings gathered around the small fire while one of us read aloud from whatever storybook had been picked, daybreak mornings sparring with anyone willing to go against me, no matter that I beat them silly more than half the time.

As Liseah and I began to talk about our journey again, Heron Hill was hit with a truly frightening season of hard winds, egg-sized hail, and dirt storms that darkened the horizon for days. It was a dismal year for our orchard, and Father needed all hands helping to scrape together enough mealy apples to take to market in Kestral.

Beatriel, two years my junior, apprenticed herself to our aunt, and it's mostly thanks to their bakery that we pulled through the winter as well as we did. With Father and Korbal working sun up to sun down in the orchards, it fell to me — the middle child, the forgotten daughter — to keep the house together, repair the roof when it fell in, take care of the goat and chickens, make sure we had food and water and wood.

Perhaps, too, it was guilt that kept me in Heron Hill. My family had already lost so much. Our grandparents to the wasting sickness when Korbal was a baby. Our mother when Beatriel was born. Eirah in the Zuneshan War.

The choice has dogged my steps for the last three years, since I reached the age of initiation to the Temple: do I sacrifice my dream and join my family in the orchard, ready myself for a boring marriage I have no interest in, and bear children to continue this cycle?

Or follow Eirah's path, and perhaps find my own kind of happiness?

It wasn't as hard a choice as it should have been.

I open the drawer in the dresser I share with Beatriel, already gone to begin the day's baking. I begin dumping clothes into my own patched knapsack, leaving only the two nicer dresses for Beatriel — where I'm going, there won't be a reason for impractical clothes.

"What are you doing?" Liseah hovers over me, eyes darting between my half-filled knapsack and my quick hands.

Clothes finished, I rise and shove my feet into my boots. Comfortable but almost too worn. Hopefully they'll give me a new pair at the Temple.

"Packing," I answer.

Liseah flutters like some kind of trapped moth, useless wings beating against shadowed glass. "We can't go without Corran." Her voice is a muted wail.

I stop for long enough to raise my eyebrows at her. "Why the hell not?"

She begins to pace, short heeled boots clicking against the worn wooden floor. It feels abnormally loud in the small room, floorboards groaning when she forgets to skip over the creaky ones.

"Can you not? You're going to wake my father."

She ignores me. "It's a two day ride to Kestral, double that walking, and another two weeks to Calire. Everyone passing through the inn lately says bandit activity is on the rise." Her hands twist over themselves, quickening with the urgency in her words.

I step forward and place my hands on hers, stilling the movement. "We're going to be fine. I can protect us from bandits until Kestral. Then we'll find a mercenary caravan for Calire, just as we planned. Corran hasn't beaten me in a match in years. We only needed him so we didn't get ourselves hope-lessly lost or outmatched, but as long as we stick to the main road, we'll be safe enough."

She stares at me with wide, round eyes. Frightened. "Two women alone on the road doesn't sound good, and you know it."

Her words, an echo we've heard all our lives, sets my blood on fire. "I should hope the world has come far enough to accept two women as worthy opponents rather than mere fair game. And if it hasn't, I'll show them how wrong they are."

The tears finally spill over onto Liseah's cheeks. "It's not fair," she whispers. "I can't ask you to risk everything for me."

I brush the tears away gently, rough callouses over smooth cheeks. "I would risk everything for you a thousand times over. What's not fair is your parents abandoning you. What's not fair is them never listening to us, to our desires and wants. Never considering, for a moment, that we might know ourselves well enough to decide the course of our own lives."

I step back, turning back to the space next to my bed. I lift the sword gently down from the brackets on the wall, the weight steady and reassuring. Familiar. Like so many of my possessions, it belonged to Eirah before the war claimed him. There wasn't enough of him to send back to us, much less the resources needed to transport the hundreds of dead. The bodies were burned, without ceremony or words from family to carry them to the afterlife. But because Eirah was a knight of some esteem, his sword was recovered, as well as his journal and a meager handful of possessions. His armor was given to another knight. I hope it served him better than it did Eirah.

The blade and scabbard go into the loops on my belt, the journal into my knapsack.

Liseah begins pacing again, scrubbing the tears away with the back of her hand. "But what if we come across something worse?"

She doesn't say the word, but it echoes through the room nonetheless. *Aberration.*

"We won't," I say with a confidence I hope grants us luck.

I take out a sheaf of paper and sit at the small desk in the corner of the room, once used for schoolwork, now intended to write letters to suitors. Beatriel uses it for drawing mostly. "There's no use arguing any more, Liseah. I refuse to let you be thrust into some horrible marriage and live your life in unhappiness." I look up, calm and assured, hoping to give her some of my own serenity in the matter. "I'll get us safely to Kestral. Of that, I'm sure."

Like a sail losing its wind, she sinks into herself, nodding miserably.

I uncap the inkwell and dip the pen inside, keeping the letter succinct. *I'm sorry I couldn't tell you before. I'm sorry to leave you. I love you.* Addressed to Beatriel, although Korbal will probably find it first.

He's the only one who knows my plan. The dutiful eldest child, hardworking and diligent and with a true love of the earth, he couldn't understand why I would throw away everything for a fool's dream, but nonetheless agreed to keep my secret until I was far enough away Father wouldn't attempt to bring me back himself.

It is my sister I'm truly sad to leave behind. Beatriel has been my shadow since she could walk, no matter we're as different as night and day. She used to watch me spar in the early morning hours, sleep still clinging to her small frame, eyes wide and admiring as she tracked each movement patiently learned from the old soldiers. I miss those days.

But the idea of what waits for me out there, that I only have to take a few more steps to grab hold of what's truly mine — that is far more intoxicating.

I heft my knapsack, the straps settling comfortably onto my shoulders, and take one last look around the room. It looks smaller than it did last night, everything just slightly worn. Familiar, but already distant.

"I have food for us for the trip," Liseah whispers as we start down the rickety ladder that leads up to the loft bedroom.

I grin at her as I step down into the kitchen, still warm from the fire Beatriel lit before she left. "And here I thought you weren't prepared to go."

She gives me a dirty look and doesn't bother replying.

I grab apple muffins, a day old from the bakery, from under the checkered cloth on the rough wood kitchen table and offer one to Liseah as we cross silently to the door.

It feels momentous to cross the threshold, knowing this time is really it, and I wait to feel different as we stride through the village, faster now, slinking from building to building as the sun slowly crests the tops of the trees.

But I'm still me as we reach the edges of the village. Too tall, all muscle, hot tempered, too *much* for this place. Nothing truly changes between one footfall and the next, nor the one after that. One foot in front of the other, the new spring day pleas-antly warm, Liseah quiet at my side.

Perhaps this is the only truth: that I've waited my whole life to be altered by leaving, only to find it was not I who should be changed.

We reach the top of a hill. Liseah places a hand on my arm and we stop, wordlessly facing Heron Hill. It looks unbearably small, nestled on all sides by apple trees and hay fields. Quiet. Unassuming.

Liseah spits on the ground. "Good riddance."

I turn my back to the village, looking at the road to Kestral spiraling out before us. I can't help the grin that blossoms over my face, heart seizing with the utter joy of what awaits.

"Let's go."

Liseah takes my hand, and together we begin our journey down.

TWO

For the next several hours, Liseah alternates between lamenting the loss of the few good things from Heron Hill and spewing vitriol against the many faults of the villagers, the council, the elder, and, ultimately, her parents. I keep silent mostly, letting her grief run its course, murmuring confirmations when appropriate, and keep an eye on the world opening around us.

We've traveled to Kestral many times, usually in the back of my family's wagon, fighting for space among the bushels of apples. Kestral is the main trading point for the western central area of Serabith, far enough from Calire to assure merchants still found it viable. Being on the main road from the coast to the capital meant travelers almost always stopped for a night, leading to bustling trade in foods, clothes, and supplies, and dirty business in illegal drugs from the islands. The city guards turned a blind eye to what was brought in as long as some of it made it to their pockets as well, but such trade has dwindled dramatically since the Zuneshan War. Coastal Watchers are harsher now, the queen's verdicts more ironclad than her father's before her to make for a safer city, although the roads to and from are often not patrolled and wild.

Today, however, the air is warm and beautiful, the hills are dotted with nodding white flower heads, and my entire being practically floats with joy.

I could have walked straight through the day and into nightfall, but by midday Liseah tugs at my sleeve. "I'm starving."

It's on the tip of my tongue to offer to eat while we continue, but I look at her face — dark smudges under her eyes, a slump in her shoulders — and agree. She's used to hard work, just like anyone in Heron Hill, but this constant exertion is different from cleaning dishes and making sure the day's food is ready for that night's guests. She doesn't spend every waking hour obsessed with sword forms.

We veer off the road and settle into the shadow of a hill, grass soft and spongy, long enough to tickle our arms as we lean back. Liseah digs in her pack and offers me sausage and soft white cheese.

"Think they're looking for us yet?" Liseah picks at her cheese.

I wash my own food down with a long pull from my water skin. "No. Korbal won't tell anyone till tonight, if he's wandered back in from the trees at all, which he probably hasn't. And your family will think you're with someone else. Me, probably." I grin at her. "Only we're not hiding in Bransen's hayloft today."

She doesn't look comforted. "You're not worried they'll come after us?"

"I think we have the advantage. We'll hear any horses or carts long before they see us. We're on foot and can hide among the hills easily enough." I finish my sausage, wiping greasy hands on the smooth grass. "Not to mention we've got a lead on them, and we won't be in Kestral long enough for anyone to find us."

I stand, pulling Liseah up with me. "Come on, let's make a bet."

She raises her eyebrows, but a smile dances along the corners of her mouth, the morning's sorrow slowly fading. "A bet on what?"

"If your wily charms only get us a free room in Kestral, or if food is included too."

I cackle as she throws her cheese rind at me, then take off running for the main road, her curses leading the way as she has no choice but to follow.

The afternoon is spent in lazy conjecture of what Calire will be like. We spin tales full of shops and markets, flower-covered houses, the streets clogged with initiates from the Knight's Temple, the merchant row, the mercenary guild. Noble girls and boys, heads held high and pompous, walking in a row to the gleaming marble palace. And, of course, the sordid bits too, ruthless dark alleyways and dirty, packed sex houses, unmade beds filling common living spaces while their owners work too hard for too little.

Dusk falls before we reach the wayhouse, but we would have avoided it nonetheless. I lead Liseah off the road, to a small divot in the ground behind a large hill. Not immediately visible from the road, with just enough cover we aren't completely exposed.

Liseah barely has the energy to eat and wrap herself in her blanket before she falls asleep, small form curled around my hip. It's warm enough we don't need a fire, although we'll probably wish for one in the morning.

I watch our surroundings as night falls, darkness blanketing us like a familiar friend. There should be fear, certainly, but when I finally fall asleep, nothing haunts my dreams.

"If there's one thing the storybooks have gotten wrong, it's how completely unromantic traveling actually is. There is *nothing* comfortable about sleeping on the ground, no matter how soft the grass initially seems. It will inevitably be filled with rocks, which try to make their way into your joints so the entire next day as you walk, because you're journeying, you'll be repeatedly reminded of each and every stone."

I raise my eyebrows at Liseah. "Oh do go on."

She takes my quip seriously, unfortunately.

Despite her rambling, there is truth to her words. The second day of travel is undoubtedly harder, and by midday we gratefully accept a passing wagon's offer to carry us to the next crossroads. Keemah, a quiet man with the deep brown skin and dark eyes of a coast dweller, trades the trip for the last of Beatriel's baked apples. We make ourselves comfortable among open barrels of delicate shells and driftwood, still smelling faintly of the salt and sand.

"One day I'll go there," I whisper, running a finger along the soft pink inside of a curled shell. It's easy to picture; Eirah wrote countless descriptions in his journal. I close my eyes and think of myself standing where Eirah did, the bodies now long gone, able at last to give a final goodbye.

Liseah scrunches her nose as a small crab, nearly translucent, scuttles around the rim of a barrel. "I'll leave you to it and keep to the cities, thanks."

"Everyone should see the sea once in their life." Keemah's voice is soft and lilting, the cadence slower, more rolling than ours. It's the voice of a storyteller.

Never shy, Liseah leans forward on the barrel closest to him, head resting on her forearms. "Where are you from?"

"Aziz. Where every breath you take is tinged with salt. There is always a breeze blowing, the waves lapping at the edges of your consciousness as you dream." Longing permeates every word.

"Do you have to leave often?" Liseah asks quietly.

He gives a small, uneasy shrug. "More often than before the war. The islands traded better back then. Now I have to trek to Kestral a few times a year, hoping some art merchant or mage interested in raw materials will appreciate what the sea gives us."

I'm about to join the conversation, to ask about the war and life near the islands, but the world explodes before I can.

The sharp *zzzzp* of bowstrings releasing is the only warning I have. A neat line of arrows bury themselves into the road before us, close enough to startle the horse. She rears back, eyes rolling wildly, her sharp whinny drowned out in the cacophony of hooves suddenly descending all around us. Men and women in drab leathers and piecemeal armor flow from the surrounding hills, half mounted on stocky mountain ponies, the rest on foot. There is no banner, no legion to proclaim their loyalty to a Noble or city, but they move cohesively, quick and sure.

Bandits.

Fuck. I was so involved with our conversation that I failed in my most basic duty: watching our surroundings for potential threats. A stupid, novice move. Hot shame coupled with fear courses through me. Their arrows were seamlessly timed and shot; this group is experienced. Dangerous. I look them over quickly, noting the multitude of eyes that focus on Liseah, by far the prettier of us. There are five bandits here, and I wouldn't be surprised if another two or three were hidden in the hills with bows.

Five against one. Maybe two, if Keemah has a weapon. Surely he must, being a lone traveler without a caravan.

Keemah rises, one hand held back at us to tell us to keep down, keep quiet. Liseah's eyes flicker between the bandits, Keemah, and myself. I will her not to look at the sword strapped to my hip. The bandits may not have noticed it yet, and outnumbered as we are, surprise is our best ally. My blood heats, the fear vanishing as I realize this is it. This is what I've waited for. A chance to prove myself, yes, and confirmation that I know myself better than anyone else could.

"I'm not looking for trouble today." Keemah addresses the bandit closest to him, a burly man with braids in his dark red hair and beard.

The bandit cocks his head to one side and sounds almost civilized as he replies, "Neither are we." Then he grins, revealing a gold tooth, and the wickedness in that smile curls my stomach into itself. There will be no peace reached today.

Keemah holds up his hands, as if he can still salvage the situation. "I know times are rough. But you have stopped a wagon filled only with simple goods from the sea. Shells, wood. I take them to market in Tretali, to be made into beautiful things. In their raw form like this, they are not valuable."

Red looks to the man next to him, nodding towards the barrels. He strides forward, dipping a grimy hand into the shells, leering at Liseah as he does. She shrinks back, but her eyes remain flat, mouth a firm line. The bandit laughs at her bravado, tossing a sizable shell at the leader, who catches it with barely a look. I swallow, watching the swiftness of his hands, the two short swords at his waist.

"As you say. Pretty, but useless." Red admires the shell in his hands, then tosses it back to the barrels. It lands on the wagon floor, chipping into several pieces. Keemah doesn't even flinch, eyes still trained on the bandit.

"Now, them on the other hand..."

Red grins at us, and the other bandits let out a rumble of appreciation. "That one, especially." Red gestures to Liseah. "She'll make a pretty penny in the whorehouses."

Rage curdles any remaining fear. Like hell they'll lay a hand on either one of us.

"They are not for sale," Keemah says flatly. "Just like you and I, they are simply travelers heading to their next destination. Let's not add violence to this day."

"Pretty words, like your shells. Easily broken." Red paces lazily towards us, eyes on Liseah. There is movement behind me, but I resist looking over my shoulder. Not yet.

When Keemah speaks, his voice is sharp, all civility gone. "This is your last warning. Leave us now."

Red looks at him, successfully distracted, and I shift so I'm on my heels, weight balanced to launch myself to the two creeping up behind us. "Get ready to duck." The whisper is so low Liseah barely hears it, but her flickering glance towards me assures she understands.

"I have no intention of letting such a prize walk away from under my nose," Red snarls.

I strike.

The dagger, hidden up my sleeve, falls hilt first into my hand and I send it whipping out as I rise. I don't wait to see if it finds its mark, although there is a satisfying yelp of pain that tells me my aim is true. I stand and spin, sword hissing as it leaves the sheath, knocking away the short sword of the female bandit poised behind Liseah. She has the time to look startled before I spin my weapon, slamming the hilt into her temple. She drops immediately.

I move again before her body hits the ground, catching the strike from the second bandit. He wields wickedly hooked daggers, giving him the advantage of speed, but I claim both strength and the high ground. The wagon creaks as I step to the edge, forcing him back, picking off every blow he tries to land. He's decent, but I'm better. My body knows what to do, senses the next strike almost before he knows it himself, and it's a matter of seconds before he, too, drops, daggers flung away.

Two down, although neither dead.

Liseah lets out a muffled yell. I spin back to her, sword already raised once more, but she's staring not at a bandit, but at Keemah.

The wagoner stands calmly, hands outstretched before him. The remaining three bandits, including Red, hover in the air, legs kicking wildly, hands scrabbling at the invisible bands around their throats. I watch, mouth agape, sword forgotten, as their faces slowly mottle into purples and reds, mouths moving as they attempt to scream. Then, almost simultaneously, their hands drop and they slump in their bonds, heads lolling to the sides.

Shock keeps me frozen as Keemah lowers his arms, bringing the bandits back down to earth. They crumple into a dusty heap on the ground, unconscious or dead I cannot tell.

Keemah wipes his hands on his dark tunic, facing us with a small, slightly pinched smile. "I am sorry about that. I do hope neither of you are injured." He looks over my shoulder at the two bandits I incapacitated and gives an approving smile. "Well done. We need to be on our way, should any of them awake."

And then, as if it was nothing out of the ordinary, Keemah sits back on the bench and clucks to his mare, urging her forward once more.

We wait until the bandits are well out of sight before speaking.

"Thank you," Liseah says, still breathless, eyes wide and tinged with nervousness. I can't blame her. Fighting is one thing, but magic is something else entirely. "We didn't realize..." Her voice trails off.

Keemah chuckles, glancing between the two of us. "That I was a mage? I'm grateful for that, since that's the point."

I look at the barrels surrounding us. "Are you really a merchant?"

"Oh yes, yes. I do take these to Kestral and bring the money back to my village. And when I'm there, I use my other abilities to manipulate the air for the boats, making sure we bring in good hauls of fish." His eyes crinkle in the corners. "Why is it so strange to be both? Mage and merchant? Mage and simple villager?"

I shake my head. "Aren't mages required to work for the crown?"

Keemah waves his hand. "It depends on your magical focus and strength. Many spend their entire lives in servitude to the crown, yes. Just as knights do." He glances at my sword, eyebrows raised, eyes knowing. "But others advocate for simpler lives, away from the hustle of court and politics. We do not seek power, but stillness. Quietness."

"We haven't had a mage from Heron Hill in quite some time," Liseah says.

"Magic is a fickle creature. There is no telling how many will receive the gift when they visit the Crystals."

Just as everyone in Serabith does, Liseah and I traveled the three day's journey at midsummer in our eighteenth year to be judged by the nearest Crystal, the fonts of all magic. It found us unworthy, without the inner will needed to overcome the constant battle magic presented. Magic always demands more, always seeks to be channeled, but if your control slips, if you let the magic win... *boom*.

I have never found the idea appealing, although there is a certain strength in Keemah I can admire.

"Can't the queen call you back into her service at any time, though?" Liseah asks.

"She certainly could. But I did my time, in the war. I am not needed now, do not wish to be a mere instrument again. Unlike her father before her, our queen respects our wishes. There are plenty other glory seekers for her to command."

Keemah does not look at us as he speaks, the heaviness of the war echoing in all our bones.

"Thank you," I whisper. "For your service then, and now."

He nods, and the wagon trundles on in silence.

We reach the waystation as night falls. It is bustling and loud, full of travelers going to market in Kestral or Calire. The innkeeper greets Keemah like an old friend, slapping him on the shoulder and offering us all free drinks with our room. We thank Keemah again, bidding him goodbye as his road ends here, and ours continues east.

Although we keep an eye on the door, no one from Heron Hill barges in to drag us away, and we sleep heavily, the adrenaline from our adventure leaving exhaustion and the knowledge that I did exactly what I hoped I would be able to.

The satisfaction and surety keep my spirits light the next two days of travel. We make certain to avoid a second surprise attack, and take turns keeping watch throughout the night.

When Kestral finally comes into view, it is as if hope itself explodes in my chest.

Easily five times the size of Heron Hill, the city perches on a plateau like some kind of magpie nest, haphazardly strung together and glittering in the dying sunlight. Within a valley would have been a more strategic spot, but Kestral is not a city for war. Unlike Calire, which caters to a bit of everything between the Noble's court, districts dedicated to art, music, theatre, and literature, and the Knight's Temple, Kestral is devoted to one thing only: trade. Merchants from around Serabith come to barter for the best spider-spun silk cloth, pungent spices, and, of course, the widest array of foods. Many of these goods are then taken to the islands or Balure down south.

Liseah grips my arm as we approach the gate. She almost vibrates in excitement, the hours of toil erased from her face. "Light, it's been years since I've been here."

I grin at her as we join the queue. "We actually did it." Triumphs shoots through me.

"Of course we did." She gives me a cocky grin, as if she hadn't had a single doubt these last four days. "I knew we would."

Watchers do a quick search of packs and wagons before beckoning travelers in. They look tired and bored, eyes not quite glazed as they glance over the stragglers entering the city. It takes them but a second to search our things and then we're in, the sounds of the city swelling loudly as if we've breached some invisible barrier.

Even though it is evening, the city is still alive with a cacophony of sights and sounds. Men and women scurry down the streets, some carrying wares back to their houses, others ambling to find nightly entertainment. While most everyone in Heron Hill, myself included, is made from the same rough mold of olive, tanned skin, muscled bodies built for work, sensible clothes and shoes, here there are farmers, softer merchants with silk clothes, frowning Watchers, dark skinned dancers and light eyed musicians, and everything in between.

I tear my eyes away from a group of women packing up

their stall, stowing colorful silks into large trunks emblazoned with swirling designs that remind me of far flung tales told before the fire. "Do you remember how to get to the inns?"

Liseah scoffs. "You might have the advantage in the wild, dear, but leave me to it here."

She sets off, winding her way through the market stalls like she was born here, and within a handful of minutes, Liseah halts before a semicircle of inns. She doffs an imaginary hat as she bows to me. "Your pick, m'lady."

The inns are mostly identical visually, but two have their doors flung open, cheerful music pouring into the streets. I watch as several workers wander into a third, no doubt looking for their nightly drink. My decision is made, however, when I spy a group of men standing around a bullseye target that has been painted on the side of a wall, taking turns throwing their knives at it. Most of them hit the target, but several are embedded in the wall around it. They all wear similar clothes: plain dark tunics and leggings, road-worn boots. Around each of their left arms, though, is a wide band emblazoned with a red hawk gripping a spear in its talons.

I nod to them. "Caravan guards. Probably departing in the morning, hopefully for Calire."

Liseah raises her eyebrows. "Think we've gotten that lucky?"

"We can always hope."

Although the inn is called The Quiet Wellspring, it is anything but. The floors are sticky with old, spilled ale, and mugs already dot the tables around the common room, half filled with an assortment of off-duty workers, travelers, and merchants. The innkeeper, a friendly woman with dark curls and a big smile, gives us a room without question. No wondering who we are, where we're going, who we're leaving behind. Just two more travelers to house for a night.

"Those mercenaries out there," I say as she hands us the key to our room. "Are they with a caravan?"

She chuckles a bit, catching the arm of a passing barmaid and nodding to a table gesturing for more drinks. "Tole's men? Oh sure, they travel between Calire and the coast pretty steadily. They'll be leaving for Calire tomorrow I imagine." She winks when we brighten. "Just your luck it seems."

Our room is small but tidy with two beds against opposite walls and a small table with a wash basin in between. "There's a bathhouse down the street," Liseah says, nearly throwing her pack into one of the beds. "I'm dying, and I smell." She shudders theatrically. "I demand we go immediately."

I laugh but can't disagree. "Excellent plan."

We each grab a fresh change of clothes and make our way back downstairs. The noise has increased in the short time we've been gone, but it's full of laughter and jokes, people toasting each other and the minstrel and the good cooking. It reminds me of a village dance, friends pressing up shoulder to shoulder to tell of the day and share hot food, everyone comfortable in each others' presence.

Liseah leads the way out of The Quiet Wellspring. Night has almost fallen, but the courtyard is well lit with street lamps and lanterns hanging on the posts next to each door. The group of mercenaries is still throwing knives at their target, but they acquired ale at some point, and their shots are getting sloppy as drink sloshes over the cups' brims.

I stop to watch as a particularly inebriated man steps up to throw. He takes a stumbling step forward, releasing the dagger far too late. It clatters against the wall hilt-first, falling into the dirt.

I can't help it. I laugh.

It's a small sound, quickly muffled, but one of the mercenaries looks to me anyway. It's immediately apparent he is very,

very drunk, and when he pushes off the wagon he's leaning against, it is with a visible wobble.

"Now, I must surely be mistaken," he says, voice too loud, words tripping over each other, "but it sounded to me like you just here laughed at us. You," and he looks me up and down, lip curling, "a little girl. Well, maybe not little." He laughs loudly at his joke, his comrades quickly joining in.

I don't bother to hide rolling my eyes. "Oh yes, very clever, making fun of a tall girl. Brilliant. I applaud your intelligence."

"Really?" Liseah hisses between her teeth, giving me a clearly annoyed look. I ignore it, keeping my attention on the mercenaries.

The laughter dies, and the one I'm assuming is the leader looks at me with a sharper gaze than before. "Insulting my intelligence too, now, are you?"

I shrug. "I would be, if there was anything there to insult in the first place." Fire sings in my veins, sending shivers down to my toes and fingers. The rush of power is exhilarating.

A hush quickly falls over the group. The leader straightens, brows lowering as he steps forward. His gaze is nearly level with mine as he steps too close, warm breath misting over my face. My nose wrinkles at the stench of alcohol, but I don't move.

"Think you can do better?" The threat is low and vicious.

I grin. "Better than a group of drunks in half-darkness? There's no doubt."

"Oh, not against us." The man steps back and gestures to another of the mercenaries. "Against him." He raises his voice. "Oy, Vaen, feel like playing with a mouse?"

Vaen pushes himself off the building he's been leaning against, and the movement is confident and sure. There are no empty tankards around him.

"Fuck," Liseah whispers behind me.

I don't dare voice agreement. Instead I hand her my cloak and unsheathe the two knives I used to keep in my bedside table and now wear at my belt. I realize, with some regret, that my third is on the road between here and Kestral.

I look to Vaen, now standing before the target but watching me. He's less than half a hand taller than me, broad shouldered but slim, dark hair tied away from his face in a short braid. Gray-green eyes watch me, bright and curious. He's older than me by several years, olive skin darkened by long days on the road. He is undoubtedly handsome, but I'm more concerned with the knives that have appeared in his hands.

He holds my gaze for a long moment, eyebrows raised, as if questioning whether I am really stupid enough to do this. I scowl at his question and raise my own brows back in challenge.

He throws three knives in rapid succession, and my heart sinks when they all find their target, embedded into the red inner ring.

"Fuck," Liseah says again.

Vaen looks at me calmly, still not saying anything. The leader gives a loud guffaw, slapping another mercenary on the shoulder. "Ready to apologize, sweetheart?"

Anger sizzles in my blood. Before I can think about it, I stride forward, standing uncomfortably close to Vaen until he moves. I don't look at him as I center myself, breathing deeply and feeling the firm earth beneath me.

I knocked two bandits out cold mere days ago. This is nothing.

I look up, inhaling deeply, raising my arm and leaning my weight back. On the exhale I shift forward, snapping my wrist, and the knife flies into the target. It hits the center with the familiar thunk of metal slicing into wood.

The mercenaries, who had been loudly jeering, fall silent.

I loose my second knife, not giving myself time to think or reconsider how to throw this one. It slides into place next to its brethren.

The courtyard is deadly silent as I turn to the watching men and mildly ask, "Anyone have a knife to borrow?"

Vaen silently draws a knife from his boot, offering it to me hilt first. I'm surprised by the smile tilting one side of his face up.

"Thanks."

I heft the knife, getting a feel for the slight difference in weight, tossing it once to test the balance. Then I throw it, stronger than before, eyes locked onto the target, as if it is their jeering and laughter that is really pinned to the wall.

The knife knocks one of Vaen's completely out. It hits the dusty ground, the sound immeasurably loud in the stillness around us.

I turn to the mercenaries with a pleasant smile. "Next time, remember it's never smart to insult a woman with a weapon. She might surprise you and actually be able to use it."

I walk to the wall and pull out my knives. Someone chuckles, and I think it might be Vaen, but I don't look. My heart hammers in my ears, adrenaline finally catching up to my actions.

Pretending I'm calmer than I am, I sheathe my weapons and rejoin Liseah. She pats my shoulder and gives a jaunty wave to the mercenaries as we head for the bathhouse once again.

"That's my girl," she whispers.

I grin into the night.

CHAPTER

THREE

"What if he refuses us?"

"He won't. It's part of a business. He won't turn down good coin."

"But he's also a man, and they've done far stupider things in the name of pride."

I wince at that truth. "If he refuses to take us, I'll find us another caravan."

Liseah raises her eyebrows. "By when? After our coin is spent before we've even reached Calire?"

I don't have an answer to satisfy Liseah, so instead I turn to the mercenaries milling around the caravan wagons that were waiting when we exited The Quiet Wellspring this morning. The wagons, some covered with oiled cloth arched above the wooden beds, already boast an assortment of people and goods. In one, an elderly man and what looks to be his grandson load barrels of wine; in another, a family with three small children sit close together, small packs at their feet, talking quietly. Visiting family, perhaps, or simply going to experience Calire.

There are others, of course, but my attention is stolen as the mercenary leader finishes his conversation with the caravan owner and turns to survey his men — and immediately spies us.

"Ready?" I ask in a whisper as he strides towards us.

"Only if you play nice," Liseah shoots back.

The mercenary shows none of the previous night's intoxication, now standing tall and confident. He's handsome without the flush of too much bad ale, his light hair kept neatly combed back, a scattering of blonde scruff covering his chin. He's younger than I initially assumed, in his early thirties if I had to guess. His skill has to be good if he's their leader at this age.

"Look who it is." He stops before us, an easy grin on his face, no sign of irritation or rebuke in the relaxed lines of his shoulders and arms. "The not-so-little knife girl."

I feel more than hear Liseah groan next to me, but it's just too *easy*. "Look who it is," I mimic, my own smile not quite as nice. "The drunk guard who couldn't beat a knife girl."

We wait for a heartbeat, all three of us frozen, but then the mercenary throws back his head and laughs, the sound long and loud. Liseah lets out a nervous giggle, and I find myself relaxing.

"My name is Tole." The mercenary sticks out a hand, which I take, his grip firm and calloused. "I have to hand it to you, you don't back down from a challenge. That's a good quality to have."

I don't even get the chance to say my name before Liseah says, "Or a stupid one."

Tole grins broadly, dropping my hand to turn his attention to Liseah. "Looks like we have to watch out for more than just sharp blades around the two of you, eh?"

Liseah gives him a wolf's smirk, and now it's my turn to groan. "There are many things you have to watch out for with us."

A light sparks in Tole's eyes and he takes his time looking

Liseah over, earning an ever-broadening grin from her. "Shame-less," I mouth at her from over Tole's shoulder. She doesn't even blink. When Liseah sets her sights on someone... well, she usually gets what she wants.

"Where's your friend?" Liseah asks, propping her hands on her hips. "The one who wasn't skunk drunk like you were last night."

I admit, I had also already glanced at the milling merce-naries to see if I could spot my opponent.

"Vaen?" Tole rocks back on his heels. "He's not coming to Calire. He rides solely with us between the coast and Kestral. Won't step foot in the capital."

That catches my attention. "Why not?"

Tole shrugs. "None of my business. I may run the caravan from coast to Calire, but he told me before signing on that he would do odd jobs in Kestral until I passed through again. I know he's dependable and a good swordsman, so I welcome his presence when traveling, but we have plenty of other men to fill his gap."

There's a shout near the front of the caravan, and someone beckons to Tole. He waves a hand in acknowledgment. "Time to move out. You can tell me why two unwed ladies are headed to Calire later tonight." He sends a glance at my sword, clearly wanting to ask, but turns instead to Liseah and gives her a saucy wink.

We don't speak as we watch him jog away, taking the offered reins of a chestnut horse and smoothly pulling himself into the saddle. "I like him," Liseah says at last. Her face is downright feral in its amusement. "He'll be fun."

"Don't torment him too much," I say, biting back a grin. "He still has to get us to Calire in one piece." I don't bother adding that he'll be gone once we've reached our destination. Liseah never has cared about longevity in her relationships before.

We pay the caravan leader, a friendly woman with a jagged scar across her temple, and find room in an uncovered wagon with the wine makers.

"It's really too bad," Liseah muses as she stares at the city around us, already full into the swing of the new day.

"What is?"

The wagon driver clicks his tongue and the horse starts forward, the wheels groaning as they catch on the uneven paving stones beneath us.

"Vaen," Liseah answers, her sidelong look at me downright sly. "He was nice to look at too. And the way he threw those knives..." She exhales loudly. "I bet his fingers were *very* clever."

I gape at her. "Shameless. You're absolutely shameless, you know that?"

She cackles. "It's time to live a little, Raylen! The whole world is before you."

She stretches her arms out wide, face upturned to the spring sun, and it's impossible not to believe it.

Traveling with a caravan proves to be immensely better than traveling alone. Not only are the wagons far more comfortable to sleep in, but the added security and company make the long days pass quickly. My favorite thing, however, is the sparring.

Every morning I rise with the mercenaries and, while the caravan works on getting breakfast made and the wagons ready to move out, we practice. It is not anything too complicated — simple forms, quick bouts not meant to hurt. But, for the first time in years, I have new partners to work with, and most of them are good enough to actually push me.

It's easy to find our rhythm, our place of being. Here, no one cares we are unwed. The mercenaries think it's a fine idea to try for the Knight's Temple, and many have already mentioned I could always join the guild if the Temple fails. On the road, no one cares who Liseah sleeps with, or what will happen afterwards.

Out here, we help with the food, clean dishes, walk with the horses, converse with those who were once strangers, say what we think, fuck who we want — and it's glorious.

I drop onto one of the old, warped logs that ring one of the fires we've lit for the night. The caravans generally travel the same route, and there are often old campsites like this one with fire pits and rudimentary seating, posts to tie the horses to. The mood is always a bit more festive on these nights. Someone has brought out a lute and plays a cheerful tune, travelers clapping in rhythm while two girls rise to dance a jig.

Liseah hands me a bowl of stew, wrinkling her nose. "You stink."

I huff at the offense and rap her knuckles with my spoon before she can pull her hand away. "I was *working*. Of course I'm sweaty."

"I prefer working up sweat other ways," Liseah says, lazy eyes flickering over to Tole. He stands with a small circle of mercenaries, laughing at something one of them says, but glances over to us as if feeling Liseah watching him. He grins widely at her.

I roll my eyes.

"I know. The whole caravan knows at this point."

Liseah clicks her tongue. "Jealousy isn't becoming, Raylen."

She only grins sweetly when I glare at her. "I'm perfectly fine, thank you very much."

And I am. I *am*. It's not like I'll have time for any fooling around at the Temple.

Tole slings a leg over the log next to Liseah, leaning in to capture her lips before her greeting is even finished. I wait, scrapping the dregs of my stew, until they finally part, shiny-eyed and looking like they'd rather be anywhere else.

A mercenary clears her throat, fighting a smile as she offers Tole a bowl of stew on the way to her own seat. Tole whispers something into Liseah's ear that causes a devious grin to blossom on her face before he eats a few heaping spoonfuls of stew, oblivious to the steam that rises from the contents.

Tole finally takes note of me and gestures to me with his spoon. "Halfway there! Are you ready?"

"I've been ready my whole life." The rush of adrenaline at the mere thought is dizzying.

For the briefest minute, his lips twist, his face falling into something else, something dark with memory, but it vanishes a heartbeat later. I can't help but stare, waiting for it to come back, suddenly desperate to know *why*.

"I was too," he says to my unsaid question.

I glance at Liseah, but she's watching Tole with the same curious look. She doesn't know anything about what he's talking about either.

"You were what?" I finally ask when the silence stretches on too long.

His grin is easy, unassuming. "Excited for the Knight's Temple."

Electricity shoots through me, hot and unnervingly alive, filling my head with a pounding that echoes my heart. "You were an initiate?" The words are breathless, unbelieving.

Tole's amusement doesn't waver. "Sure was."

He doesn't offer anything else, instead slurping at his

dinner once more. Waiting for me to ask, as if I don't already know the conclusion. Bastard.

"What happened?"

When he looks up this time, his eyes are sharp, almost damning in their intensity. "I failed."

All my breath vanishes, no matter I was expecting it. The mere idea of failure makes my stomach churn, the food inside suddenly rotting.

Failure means I threw away this chance. Failure means slinking back to Heron Hill, once more at the mercy of my father. Failure means facing him — facing everyone — and admitting I *wasn't good enough*.

Failure is not an option.

Whether my emotions are plain on my face or Tole merely takes pity on me, he continues, "It's not really fair, what they do at the Temple. They let anyone in, let anyone with enough gumption pledge their next six months to train. But there are plenty of young men and women who have been training their entire lives to be knights, who have been squires and worked under the best swordsmen that money can buy. And then there are us."

"What do you mean, us?" For the first time in a week, Liseah's voice is sharp and loud. Angry.

Tole immediately turns to her with a raised hand, sweet and gentle as he cups her cheek. "No disrespect to either of you. I simply meant, those of us less fortunate. Who come from small villages without the right masters to train under, but who truly believe we're something special." He shrugs, as if it is simply a fact of life. "They give you six months to work at the Temple, and at the autumn equinox, you are tested. It's an unfair advantage to the Nobles, but that's to be expected in Calire."

His words burn, anger sizzling, rising up to overtake the sick feeling, changing me into a creature of righteous indignation.

"My uncle, from a small village without the right masters to train under, became a celebrated knight." Each parroted word, a whip into the night. Tole doesn't flinch, but he doesn't attempt to fight back either. "I may not have the same advantages as the others, but that won't matter in the ring. Because I *will* succeed in the end."

The words are part truth, part bravado, but Tole puts his hands up in surrender. "No disrespect meant, Raylen. I simply was imparting my own experience." He rubs a hand up and down Liseah's arm until she slowly relaxes, but her eyes are firm when they find mine.

"Raylen will be a knight," she says, the words utterly certain. "There isn't anyone better to defend our kingdom."

Warmth infuses me, mollifying the anger until it is nothing but a simmer, nearly forgotten.

"Did you tell her yet?" Tole sets his empty bowl on the ground, looping an arm around Liseah to bring her to his chest. She settles in comfortably but her gaze remains on mine, bright eyed and excited.

Before I can ask, Liseah blurts out, "Tole thinks he can get me a job. His sister works for a Noble family with eight daughters — can you believe that? They've been looking for a handmaiden for some of them, still too young to be courted but starting to need, shall we say, feminine touches." She glows with excitement.

The utter relief that rushes through me is enough to forgive Tole for his earlier words. The idea of Liseah wandering around Calire attempting to find work, alone and beautiful as she is, was not a pleasant prospect. I had started to pin my hopes on a barmaid job at whatever inn we happened to find, but a handmaiden for a Noble family is far beyond what we could have hoped for.

"Thank the light," I breathe, and then to Tole, "I suppose,

thank you that is. This is.... Well, this could change everything."
I mean it, too.

Tole relaxes into a small smile, opening his mouth to say
something, but a sudden shout from the perimeter stills him.
He is up within a moment, Liseah forgotten on the log, as one of
his men jogs up to him. They lean their heads together,
speaking in a whisper, but I don't miss the bared short sword
the mercenary holds.

"Go quickly."

The mercenary immediately turns and takes off, half
running through the camp as others join him. The energy
changes instantly, the peaceful evening cracking like fire-spent
logs, sparks shooting into the night sky only to fall into ash. My
mouth is dry but I stand, hand on my own weapon, and face
Tole.

"What's out there?"

Tole hesitates, glancing briefly at Liseah who watches us
with a face drawn and pale. When he finally speaks, it is quiet,
for our ears only, but the singular word holds power.

"Aberration."

I suck in a sharp breath as surprise, fear, and adrenaline
fight for supremacy. It was always a possibility to come across
one, of course, and the likelihood only increased the closer we
came to Calire and Haven, city of mages. But the reality is nonetheless a hit to the gut.

"How many?" I ask. I'm pleased my voice doesn't waver.

"Just one as far as we can tell. A perimeter guard spotted it."
He points firmly at Liseah, then me. "Stay here. Stay calm. We
don't need the entire caravan falling into chaos. We've handled
Aberrations before."

Liseah nods weakly, apparently glad to be given an order,
but I bristle. "I can help."

"Absolutely not." His tone is sharp, brooking no argument,

although I stubbornly open my mouth again anyway. "We are the caravan guards, not you. No matter how good you might be with that sword, you are inexperienced and young. You've never even seen one, right?"

I don't want to, but I have to nod, the admittance sour.

"Even the best knights have trouble with Aberrations. Especially for the first time. I am not risking my men's lives to fulfill your own pride."

There's another shout, not panicked, but Tole's name is clear. He points a finger at me briefly, face hard as granite. "Do not leave this campfire. Understand?"

It makes me ache to agree, but finally, reluctantly, I nod.

As soon as I do, Tole turns and vanishes into the dark.

The fight is too far away to hear from our position, but I can't bring myself to sit, nervous energy flooding my limbs, leaving me to shift from foot to foot.

"What do you think it looks like?" Liseah asks, arms wrapped around her knees. Her gaze is trained on the spot Tole disappeared.

I shake my head. "I've heard the same stories you have." Monstrous creatures, skin melted like wax, bone shards protruding from every sharp angle. They care only about their prey, their next meal, and lack the proper awareness to hunt in packs, which is really only a small consolation. With strength beyond a mere man's, more animal than human, they would be devastating if working together.

Magic-wrought creatures, twisted beyond any natural form, meant to frighten small children into obedience.

It seems that the old tales have some truth to them after all.

The fire has nearly burnt out by the time Tole returns. He must have cleaned himself off so not to scare the caravan travelers, but the weariness is evident as he slides into Liseah's bedroll next to her, kissing the soft skin of her forehead.

"Is it gone?" I ask, feeling suddenly immeasurably lonely as I hug my knees to my chest.

He nods. "And everyone lives to sleep another night." There is quiet satisfaction in his words, and Liseah lets out a long breath, turning to bury her head in his shoulder.

Even though I should relax, I don't. I find myself scanning the darkness, searching for monstrous shapes, long after the rest of the camp has fallen asleep.

Calire is everything I expect and nothing I envision.

It is loud, to the point where I feel like my ears themselves can barely differentiate between the various noises: merchants hawking wares, workers repairing streets and buildings, prostitutes hanging from windows and calling to the people below, children dodging between legs and horses and wagons, screaming for no reason but the joyful feeling of not being told to shush.

I immediately feel like the noise will swallow me whole and have to adamantly resist the urge to put my hands over my ears. Liseah, on the other hand, seems to revel in it, and rotates in a spot slowly, eyes flickering from place to place, mouth open in amazement.

Tole laughs at her and gently places a finger on her chin, lifting it back into place. She grins at him, bright and full of a vivacity that takes my breath away.

"This is amazing," she breathes.

"It's something," I mutter.

Then we round a corner, and every overstimulated nerve

melts away as I catch sight of the tall white buildings rising in the distance.

The three Temples stand close together, undeniably part of the same whole. White walls with round columns and towers at every corner loom above their surroundings, beautifully woven banners with a sky blue background hanging on the walls. On one, a mounted knight cuts down a faceless enemy. Another shows a knight shooting a flaming arrow into the sky, while a third depicts a knight kneeling before a king. A knight giving medicine to a wounded soldier. A knight, decorated in flowers and laurels, parading down a street during some kind of festival.

Although the depictions are separate scenes, they flow together naturally, one to another, a river winding its quiet way home. The images border on ridiculous and farcical, an over glorified view of what knighthood actually is, but my heart still clenches to see them.

I'm here. I'm actually, finally, here.

After years of longing, of dreaming, of sparring every free minute I had, callouses marking my palms, bruises decorating my sides — I'm actually here.

It feels like a dream, but the best dream I ever could possibly have.

Tears prick my eyes, and the emotion is so unexpected, I let a few fall before catching myself. I wipe my eyes on my shoulder quickly, scolding myself for feeling too deeply. This is not the type of behavior a real knight would allow. And now that I'm here, now that I can practically taste knighthood, I need to start acting like one.

So I straighten my shoulders and put my chin up and grin into the midday sun as my soul sings to the Temple.

I'm here. I'm here. I'm here.

The caravan takes us to a well populated area seemingly

built for new arrivals. There are several different shops, mostly for clothes and jewelry, although I hear from some of the well traveled that there are food and spice districts, weapon and armor districts, and other, more sultry places, not far from here. There are several inns, as well as a horse stable, and a friendly man sits in the center green under a small canopy, children playing with balls and sticks nearby.

"He's the information dealer for travelers," Tole tells us when Liseah asks. "He's happy to give out any public knowledge information, and for a small fee, he'll have one of his urchins take you where you need to go. It's an efficient way to get to places when you don't know the way."

"Smart," I agree. I smile at a girl who watches us, and she gives an impish grin and a wave.

The caravans take their wagons to an area near the stables, and the people we traveled with begin to disperse. Some go to the nearby inns, others start off to find their friends or family they came to see. And just like that, it's over, whatever camaraderie we had dissipating in the warm city air.

"Do you want to go meet my sister now?" Tole asks Liseah. He nuzzles into her hair. "Or should it wait till morning?"

"Morning," she says, a little too quickly. "Definitely morning."

They don't talk about how Tole will leave two days after that, back to Kestral with the caravan and a new group to protect. They don't talk about whether they'll see each other again, which is likely if Liseah gets a job with his sister, or if they even want to see each other after this.

They don't talk about the future, at least in front of me, and I respect Liseah enough to let her business be her own.

"What do you think, Raylen?" My attention returns to Liseah. She grins, practically bouncing on her feet. "Want to explore?"

I do. Calire is a whole different experience than anything we're used to. But I find my eyes returning to those white towers, and I shake my head.

"No. I think I want to go to the Temple."

Tole snorts and shakes his head. "You'll live behind those walls for the next four years. Don't you want to enjoy your last day of freedom?"

Spring equinox is tomorrow. There will be a festival, with flowers and jaunty tunes played by minstrels, young couples dancing around tall poles with colorful ribbons. It is a day of frivolity, drinking, and sex.

It is also the day you pledge yourself to train at the Knight's Temple. If you miss it, you have to wait an entire year before beginning training.

Even though tomorrow is the day I will accept my vows of training, hopefuls would have been arriving for the last several days, filling the inns and nearby lodgings while they try to get a glimpse into the life of an initiate.

Now that I am so close, I find it impossible to stay away for even a second more.

The yearning must be apparent on my face, because Liseah lays her hand gently on my arm. She smiles, and it is both the warmest and most heartbreaking smile I have seen.

"Go on then," she says. "You're here. You made it." Although she smiles, tears swim in her eyes. "You get an afternoon off every tenday, right?"

I nod, my own tears welling.

"Then I'll see you then. Okay? We'll meet there." She points to one of the inns. A wooden sign hanging over the door proclaims it The Slumbering Queen.

She grips my hands, her own palms familiar. "We did it, Raylen. We made it out. We made it here. We really can do anything now, huh?"

I laugh and fling my arms around her. "We sure can." I draw away. "Ten days. I'll see you then."

I'm not afraid for her. Liseah has a good head on her shoulders. She'll make it through whatever this city has to throw at her. Besides, she has Tole to help her settle in.

I'm afraid of being without her. I don't remember a time before Liseah. We've always been one, part of the same great being. Early morning breakfasts while we manned the market stalls, evenings at each others' houses. Long nights spent in the meadows, looking up at a thousand stars as we relay our day, our dreams.

But we knew this was coming, this severing. For all our love of one another, we are two distinctly different halves of one whole.

So, although it feels like breaking off a piece of me, I turn and set my eyes on the Temple. I take a step that shakes. Then another. And another.

By the tenth, I'm not shaking anymore.

By the twentieth, that song is back.

I'm here. I'm here. I'm here.

CHAPTER
FOUR

The wooden blade smacks into my ribs for the fourth time, and I can't hold back the small grunt of pain that escapes.

"Sorry." Krisia winces as she falls back into position.

I shake my head and summon what I hope is a reassuring smile. She is doing exactly what she's supposed to by kicking my ass.

I take in a deep breath and center myself. There is still time to turn the match around. Perthran hasn't ended the round yet.

Krisia steps forward, aiming high, but I recognize the feint and am ready to ward off the strike at my elbow. I push her practice blade away, following the movement by stepping forward and forcing her to retreat a few hasty paces. For the first time since this match started I'm on the offense and eagerly lunge forward again. My blade cracks into Krisia's left knee, earning a yelp from her and a hot flash of pleasure in my victory.

Undaunted by the injury, Krisia lunges forward with a dizzying array of attacks. She is smaller and faster than me and lands two blows in rapid succession, one to my shoulder, another to my hip. The sizzle of pleasure fades quickly, replaced by annoyance. I steal a glance at Perthran, but he's watching another match. Good. It isn't often I lose matches, and I don't particularly want him to see this.

Think. How to turn this around?

Krisia has speed on her side. What do I have? Strength. I can hold my own against most of the men in our year and am undoubtedly stronger than Krisia. My height is often an advantage as well, but not against this opponent. She's told me before how she's had to fight tooth and nail to figure out how to beat first the boys in her family, then her fellows during her squire years. She knows how to fight against an opponent like me.

So, the question remains: how do I fight an opponent like her?

We circle each other warily, weapons held in front of us, neither willing to make the next move.

A dozen scenarios flash through my mind, most of them ending with me losing the match. It would have been one thing to have gained the upper hand immediately. But in this kind of stalemate, Krisia is the likely victor. There's a reason she's in the top of our initiate class — no one ever expects the small ones.

I'm in the top of the class too, though. I may not have the formal training or squiring so desired by initiates, but it turns out there is something on my side: natural talent.

And boy, does it ever piss off all those high born city dwellers.

Not that it helps me now. I have the sinking feeling I am bound to lose this one. I understand no one can win every match, but the autumnal equinox is tomorrow. Our exams are less than twenty-four hours away, and there is no way I am going into them with a loss hanging over my head.

A moment from battle training earlier this week echoes

through my head. *Anticipating the opposing force's movements is half the battle.*

Okay then. If I can't beat her on speed, I have to make sure I am where Krisia is going to be.

"Krisia, Raylen, stop circling each other like damn vultures and get to it!"

We jump at Perthran's all-too familiar voice. He watches us from the side, arms crossed and frowning deeply. He doesn't take kindly to initiates who ignore his orders, either.

"Did you forget this was swords practice and not some damn country dance?" There is no leniency in his tone.

"No, sir," we say in unison.

Before I can act, Krisia moves, slamming her sword hard enough into my knee that the joint threatens to give out.

Hissing against the pain, I block her next strike and parry with two of my own. She's so damn fast, though, her sword is a blur as she goes for my shoulder, then my side. I barely manage to pick off her blows.

Where next? Where will she strike next?

There.

Seeing my chance, I block her strike to the same knee she just injured and step forward, using my momentum and all the strength in my arms to fling her sword wide. It catches Krisia off guard, the sword leaving her hand entirely to clatter loudly to the ground several feet away.

The point of my wooden blade touches her throat.

We stand still for a moment, chests rising heavily, our panting breath the only sound in my ears. Then Krisia grins at me and claps me on the arm. "Well done! I didn't think you'd get that one, Raylen. That's what I get for being cocky I suppose."

I grin at her, using a sleeve to wipe at the sweat crawling down my face. "You almost had me. I—"

"—would likely be dead, having lost from the extent of your injuries," Perthran says wryly.

My smile slips, but only a little. "Are you saying I won on a technicality?"

He definitely is, but all the knight does is shrug.

He doesn't offer any praise for our bout. At this point, I know better than to expect him to. Perthran is not cruel, but he *is* demanding, and getting a kernel of praise from him is worth a king's ransom.

He moves off to observe the pair next to us. Well. No major deconstruction of our match means we passed his rather considerable standard.

Krisia and I share a secretive smile and meander over to the weapon's rack. Second year initiates will be here for their training session soon.

"Are you ready for tomorrow?" Krisia rubs an oiled cloth over the blade of the wooden sword, although most of the weapons are so covered with nicks and scratches it hardly seems necessary.

I think about my answer instead of blurting out the immediate "No" that rises to my lips. My bones ache now that we're finally still. I'm going to be stiff and sore tomorrow, with new bruises to add to the layers of color already on my skin, a visual testament to the strength needed to survive this training.

"I think so," I answer at long last. "I'm nervous. Well, scared might be more truthful."

Krisia looks honestly puzzled. "Why? You're consistently in the top of our classes for all weapon training."

"Not for battle tactics or history," I point out.

She shrugs a little, like that doesn't really matter. "Yeah, well, everyone knows that's not as important."

I'm not sure she's right, but I don't argue it. "I think," I say slowly, tasting each word as it leaves my mouth, "that I've

wanted this for so long, I'm worried I'll have it snatched away."
The truth of the statement leaves me empty.

I don't know what I expect, but it's not Krisia snorting and
waving off the concern like it's nothing more than an annoying
fly. "That's not how it works. You're either good enough to pass,
or you're not. There's nothing mystical going on. No dire
mechanics of fate waiting to tear apart your dreams." She
laughs like the idea is ludicrous to even say aloud.

I give her a smile, but the disingenuousness makes my teeth
ache. "I guess you're right." There's no point in arguing when
she has that tone in her voice. Although Krisia is unfailingly
cheerful most days, she's also painfully stubborn.

Our weapons cared for, we put up the cloths and oil and
head for the gate. The sparring field lies between two of the
Temple buildings and is large enough for several dozen initiates
to practice at once. Grass has been cleared and replaced by well-
packed dirt. The weapons are stored in a small building off to
the side, where they are protected from the harsher elements.
Initiates are not as lucky. Practice goes on whether it rains,
snows, or hails, as a knight has to be prepared for anything.

A second field, the sister to this one, lies between the middle
Temple and the far left one, which contains our rooms and a
large dining hall. That field is reserved for archery and other
projectile weapons, with targets hung in various places to make
a more challenging battle ground. Although I am arguably the
best in my year with throwing knives, I am far weaker at
archery.

For those who pass the exams and survive to second year,
weapons training will escalate to include more varied weapons.
Third year introduces fighting while mounted on horseback.
That takes place behind the Temple, in a large pasture that no
one would guess was actually part of the city. It reminds me of

the orchards in Heron Hill, somehow secluded and quiet, a welcome break from the business of the world.

The Knight's Temple rests at the far side of Calire, sectioned off from most of the general population. The palace, a massive structure of white stone gilt with gold, stands to our right, always visible, looming over the Temple so we can never forget our actual purpose here.

Early on in the start of our training, we were taken to the receiving court in the palace, where Queen Amanali and her consort, King Tridion, meet with petitioners and members of her court. One by one, we introduced ourselves to her and stated our intention of preserving her honor in the Knight's Temple. It would have been an impactful ceremony had the queen's eyes not glazed over well before half of our class had gone up. I suppose she must get tired of it year after year, hearing countless names only to not even care about us until we make knighthood. *If* we make knighthood. Nonetheless, it irritated me that this woman we swore fealty to saw us as nothing more than a crowd of bodies, blending together into one faceless entity.

Krisia and I reach the entrance to the Temple. The sweat from our bout has cooled; with the sun starting to dip in the sky, the air is pleasantly chilly. Wind rolls through the courtyard, nipping at our heels, tugging the edges of our cream tunics like an impish child while it reminds us autumn is around the corner.

"I'm going to find Jairthe," Krisia announces, rolling her shoulders until they give a satisfying pop. She gives me a knowing look. "You should too. Take the edge of your nerves."

I laugh and playfully shove her away. "Get on with you. I'll see you later."

She doesn't push the issue, which I'm grateful for.

Dalliances with other initiates aren't particularly frowned upon, and I admit to thinking about it on more than one occasion. But with the testing tomorrow, there is no way I would be able to concentrate on anything else, no matter how pleasurable. A partner doesn't deserve that either.

Maybe after tomorrow.

I walk back to my room slowly, savoring the familiar calls between initiates, the running footsteps through the corridors of the Temple, the way everything smells faintly of grass and steel and wood oil.

It smells like I always imagined home should.

I wake with the dawn, as tendrils of pink and orange crawl across the lightening violet sky. I sit on my bed, listening to the rise and fall of my own breath, the steady thumping in my ears, as my eyes stay trained on the sliver of sky exposed in the narrow window. No clouds, no rain. Good weather for the autumn equinox.

I can't help but marvel at my own steady breathing, the stillness of my fingers. There is no shaking, no belly clenched tight with fear, no feeling of despair scratching between my shoulder blades. Confidence settles in my bones, the truth etched into them: I was born for this. I have spent my life working towards this.

I am not afraid of this.

I find Krisia sitting outside my door, her head between her knees. "I'm going to throw up," she says, voice muffled by the fabric of her pants.

I pat her back, then gently pull her to her feet. "Let's get some breakfast. You'll need your strength for today."

Looking slightly green, she nods and follows me down to the dining hall.

Most of the first years look the same as Krisia: pale, drawn faces, shaky hands, breakfast plates nearly untouched. We take a seat at our usual table with a few others in our year, none of us looking at one another, much less talking. I know their faces, probably most of their names, but I wouldn't call any of them friends. Perhaps after the testing culls our group, I'll be willing to actually attempt something more.

"You could at least try to look as miserable as the rest of us," Krisia mumbles. She pushes some eggs around her plate, then takes a reluctant bite when I nudge her pointedly.

"I'm nervous too," I say, not mentioning eclipses any fear. "But we've worked hard for this. We know what we need to do."

"Easy for you to say." The comment comes from another first year initiate who seems to have exchanged his nerves for anger. "You're one of the best in sword practice. You don't have anything to worry about."

A small, selfish part of me preens at the praise, but I hide it as best I can. "Anyone can fail." Knight Perthran has told us so again and again.

No one really answers that, and we finish our breakfast in uneasy silence.

When the bell tolls the hour's change, Perthran stands from his seat at the knight's table at the front of the room. What little conversation there is dies in an instant. Even the older initiatives give us the courtesy of quiet.

Perthran looks out over us for a long moment, eyes slowly sweeping the room, seeming to land on each and every first year initiate. It feels like my very blood freezes when he looks at me.

"First years," he says, and his voice isn't loud, isn't even the usual demanding tone he uses in sword practice. "Please make your way to battle tactics for your first examination."

A low rumble fills the room as benches and chairs are pushed back and we head for the archway that leads to the Temple building where our classes convene. We were given no details on how the day would proceed beyond that we would be told what to do when we needed to do it. Blind obedience may rankle, but the ability to follow orders is just as important as any other part of our training.

The classroom looks like it does every day, except for the addition of a piece of parchment and quill at every spot. We file in, almost entirely silent, and take our seats. My hands shake as I rest them on the desk.

Perthran follows us and closes the door behind him. He is not our normal tactician instructor, but it seems that he is in charge of our exams today. "When I say so, you may turn over your exam and write out your responses to the best of your ability. Cheating will result in an immediate expulsion from the Temple. You have one hour. Begin."

Parchment rustles as forty-odd papers are turned over. I scan the first question.

What errors were made in the Battle of Sunrise Hill and how could they have been avoided?

My brain stills for a painfully long second. Then, exhaling slowly to calm my racing heart, I put quill to paper and begin to write.

By midday, it feels like my brain has been burned to ash. I'm fairly confident I at least passed battle tactics, but both history and politics had more blank answers than I would have liked. Hopefully Krisia was right and more weight will be put on the physical tests.

After a brief lunch of cold ham and buttered bread, we assemble at the archery fields. The knowledge that our successes and failures are now on full display for the entire year to see sends shivers racing up my arms. It is a lot easier to be confident when unobserved.

Perthran walks slowly before the line of initiates, hands clasped behind his back. "You will have one minute to strike as many targets as possible." He doesn't raise his voice, but his words are completely audible in the stillness of the courtyard. "We will be judging both precision and speed."

Of course they would be. My mouth twists a bit. Archery is not my strongest suit, but surely I can still manage to outshoot half of the class.

I watch as initiate after initiate is called up, given the same bow but a fresh string so no one can be accused of unfair advantages and a quiver of arrows. I listen as Perthran shouts "Begin!" and the *twang* of the bowstring fills the air, followed by the *thunk* as the arrow finds its target. After the first few trainees go, whispers begin to run through our crowd.

"Ooh, I thought he had that one."

"He needs to start going faster, he's going to miss half the targets by omission alone."

"Nice shot!"

Then, finally, comes: "Initiate Raylen."

I'm vaguely aware of Krisia giving me a quick pat on the back as I make my way forward. My hands blessedly do not shake as I take the proffered bow and arrows. I test the string, nocking an arrow as I plant my feet firmly. I keep my gaze lowered until Perthran's familiar command.

"Begin!"

In a single, smooth motion I raise the bow, immediately sighting the first target. I don't hesitate and let the arrow fly. It strikes somewhere close to the middle, although no bullseye, but I barely let myself see the outcome before I move on to the next. Then the next. And the next.

By the time Perthran shouts the end time, I'm panting, a fine sheen of sweat on my brow, more from nerves than actual exertion. My arms burn from the tension of keeping the bow upright and firing. I finally let myself look at the targets and am pleasantly surprised to find the arrows more or less where they should be. If the targets had been actual enemies, they would be down and bleeding out, if not outright dead.

I hand the bow back to Perthran. A flutter of hope beats in my chest. I might truly have a chance at this.

When I rejoin Krisia, she nudges my shoulder with hers and gives me a grin. "Told you there was nothing to be worried about."

Knife throwing goes even better than archery. My confidence soars, and it helps spur me onto a victory against my opponent in hand to hand combat. By the time we gather for the last test, my heart has yet to slow down, but now it's from excitement. I can do this. I actually can do this.

I knew, in my very soul, that I was knit together to be a knight. The certainty sinks into the fabric of my being, singing an anthem of joy. The song buzzes against my heart and lungs, filling them with tiny sparks that make me feel like I'm actually glowing.

"For your final test," Perthran says as we gather by the gate that will lead us to the weapons training ring, "you will be called one by one into the dining hall."

We exchange looks, a rumble of curiosity and confusion rising from us. "Our last test is sword fighting," I whisper to

Krisia, brows pinched. The sparks lose some of their luster. "Aren't we supposed to spar each other, like we do every day?"

She doesn't have time to answer.

"In the dining hall, you will find a scenario set before you." Perthran ignores our murmurs without batting an eye. "Mages from the queen's court have gathered to mete out this final test. You will be given further instructions when it is your turn." His face is made of ice itself, uncompromising in its sincerity and judgement. "What you see inside may be an illusion, but that does not change its importance." There is something in his words, something ominous, some secret we have yet to discover.

Krisia finds my hand and gives it a quick squeeze. I'm not sure if it's more for her or me, but I wind my fingers with her own and take what comfort I can. The suddenness of it all has me reeling.

Perthran levels a hard, unblinking gaze over us, letting our silence billow in the still air, before calling, "Jairthe. You will begin."

I watch as Jairthe, normally suave and unflappable, approaches the knight with a slight tremor to his step. It disappears by the time he passes through the double doors, and he holds his head high. I'm glad for that. No one wants to go out looking like a coward.

If the wait before our other exams was difficult, this is downright excruciating. The mages must have cast wards around the dining hall, leaving us unable to hear even a footstep after the door closes. Once an initiate goes through those doors, they do not come back out. I expect no less, but it doesn't help my nerves any. A few of my fellow initiates talk to one another in low voices, speculating what awaits us, but I am unable to stand still and spend the time pacing in slow circles, worrying small rocks loose from their dirt homes.

"Initiate Raylen."

My name is flat, almost callous. Not a person, not an individual — just another name on the long list. It rings hollowly in my ears as I step forward.

Perthran waits at the threshold, giving me an impatient gesture when I hesitate. I step over the divide.

It takes my eyes a few seconds to adjust to the dimness inside. The dining hall has been transformed into a cavernous space, tables and benches stacked on top of one another and pushed against the walls. A few chairs have been pulled out and are occupied by a group I can only assume are the mages. One of them sits panting, wiping sweat from under a mop of unruly russet curls while he accepts a plate of food from one of our commanding knights. Another mage steps forward and shakes her loose sleeves back from her hands. She is immediately striking, with vibrant red hair pulled back from a high brow, and she looks at me with clear eyes that betray nothing.

What is this about? Do I have to fight a mage?

I can't imagine that's the test; why would they want us to injure each other, when mages are so precious to begin with?

Perthran's boots echo loudly on the floor as he comes to stand in front of me. He gestures, and the red-head mage joins him.

"You are about to be put into an illusion." The words are calm, little inflection to them, as if they're an everyday occurrence. "Your job is to protect the crown prince of Serabith while guiding him through the market square as it is being attacked."

Clever. I glance again at the mage, and she smiles and gives me a cheeky little wave.

"Mage Sheveil will... muddle your memories a bit." Perthran nods to the woman next to him.

Alarm immediately rips through me. "What do you mean by that?" I've never interacted with magic to this level before, and the prospect is faintly terrifying. Far more so than the task set me. Swords I understand. Magic is far more dubious.

"It doesn't hurt," Sheveil says. Her voice is chipper, like this is the highlight of her day. "I'm just going to... tweak things a little, so you remember what you're supposed to be doing, but not that it's an illusion. It's temporary. As soon as the illusion fades, you'll remember everything."

None of this is particularly reassuring, but there doesn't appear to be a choice in the matter.

"Get on with it, girl!" one of the mages calls out from the side.

Sheveil flips him off without looking over her shoulder, gives me another bright smile, and puts her fingers lightly on my temple before I can say another word.

There is a moment of brightness, of *something* washing over me, somehow both devastating and the single greatest thing I've ever felt before. Fear flares, hot and heady, but it fades as the room begins to melt, and I melt with it. Thoughts slide away, nothing more than rivulets of water that I can no longer hold on to. Everything becomes muddied and thick, details blurring into one another.

Wherever I was before is gone, and in its place is a blazingly hot day, the sun beating down on me with force. Sounds crash into me, loud and overbearing, and I instinctively take a step back from the cacophony. I blink and the images slide into place. A market square, full of brightly colored cloth tents and stalls, where merchants and buyers should be haggling over prices. Instead they run screaming, hands rising instinctually to cover their heads. Bandits are everywhere, running through the narrow pathways, swords and daggers raised, yelling in wordless rage.

Reality snaps back, and I turn quickly, breathing out in relief when I see crown prince Nyer is still beside me. He holds his own sword tightly, watching the bandits with calculating eyes, looking like he wouldn't care if he took them all on himself. Reckless, stupid boy, thinking he holds the world in his hands.

"Come on," I whisper, grabbing his shirtsleeve and pulling him back. "This isn't the time for heroics. We need to get you out of here before they realize who you are, and how much your mother will pay for your safe return."

He scowls but falls back with a short nod. Good. I don't have it in me to argue with a headstrong prince *and* keep him alive.

"Where are we going?" Nyer asks once we retreat enough to be out of any bandits' immediate eyesight.

"We need to get out of the market square." I glance to where the golden domes of the palace are faintly visible, but I know immediately that route is too risky.

"We'll go to the Watcher's tower," I say instead. "It's closer, and a safe place to hole up until I can get you to the palace."

Nyer nods and falls behind me as I start in that direction.

There is no warning, no preamble in the bandit that suddenly *appears* before us, mouth stretched in a wordless snarl, but it is the work of a moment to slide past his defenses and skewer him with my sword. He falls as blood fills his mouth, choking on whatever his last cry might have been.

A few more steps and another bandit attacks, this one to the left and slightly behind, ignoring me in favor of Nyer. I sidestep in front of the prince and parry the bandit's blows. He's fast, but I'm faster, and he soon meets the same fate as his companion.

We are attacked three more times on our journey to the Watcher's tower, but each time I manage to engage the bandits before they can lay a hand on Nyer. Adrenaline roars through me, a waterfall that fills my ears and makes every breath too fast.

But it's good. I feel alive.

The Watcher's tower is before us almost before I realize it. There's an open expanse between us and the gates, but it's a quick run. I look at Nyer, who only has eyes for the tower — and then beyond him, to where a young woman crouches before a girl I can only assume is her sister. The sister can't be older than six or seven and is screaming hysterically. The girl, little more than fifteen or sixteen herself, holds a broken wooden plank in her hands as she faces down the three bandits that converge on them.

My eyes snap back to the tower. It's still clear. I can't see any lurking threats from the shadows.

"Go!" I shout to Nyer, and give him a push to the tower. "Run as fast as you can and get behind the door! I will be right behind you."

Then, not waiting to see if Nyer obeys, I run to the girls.

The first two bandits die before they realize I'm there. Rivulets of blood run down my sword, but I shake it off into the glittering sun as I face down the third man. He grins, teeth blackened and missing, and points behind me.

When he talks, it is with a voice of vipers. "Looks like you lost, little girl."

"Not likely."

A clean sidestep and strike, and he drops, blood pooling from the slash in his throat. I turn, dagger already in hand, and let the weapon fly straight into the chest of the bandit engaged in combat with Nyer. He falls into the dust, and I can't help but grin.

I'm still grinning as the scene fades, colors and sounds melting down the walls until they are no more.

I stand in the middle of the dining hall of the Knight's Temple, gasping for breath, every nerve alive with fire. Awareness comes snapping back, and I turn to Perthran, pride blooming in my chest.

I did it. I defeated the enemies, I even saved the two girls—

Perthran watches me with unconcealed disappointment across his face. I stagger to a halt, words forgotten, and stare at him as the world comes crashing down once more.

"Raylen Nightlark of Heron Hill. You have failed the first year initiate exam. You are no longer welcome here in the Knight's Temple."

FIVE

The movements are mechanical, unthinking. Grab clothes, stuff them into the pack. It takes only a few moments before the room is stripped bare, returned to its original state from so many months ago. I leave the initiate tunics folded at the foot of the bed. There's no point in taking them. When I step back and look at the space, the shaking in my hands worsens. I turn before the gaping hole in my chest rips me clean apart.

The hallway is quiet. The initiates who passed are currently celebrating in the dining hall. The ones who didn't are either hiding in their room till morning or have made a swift exit, like I'm doing. Part of me wishes I could stay to say goodbye to Krisia, but mostly I'm glad no one is here to witness my shame.

Failure.

I ignore the main staircase and take the servant's stairs, traipsing down as quickly as I can while remaining quiet. The idea of someone stumbling upon me, *running away*, is almost more than I can bear. When I reach the ground floor, I pull up the hood of my cloak, put my head down, and walk. I hear the distant voices of my fellow — no, of *the* initiates, but no one is in the main foyer. I don't breathe until I'm outside, in the cool night air of the courtyard.

There are no guards at the main gate tonight. Perhaps to preserve what little remains of our dignity — the ones who leave. Are told to leave. The failures.

I hunch my shoulders against the hateful power of the word. What happened at the final examination is still too raw, too new, for me to unpack and examine it. All I let myself focus on is getting to the house. If I think about what I'm walking away from, I'll fall apart so completely there will be no pieces to pick back up.

Calire buzzes with the beginning of nightlife, but it's easy enough to slip through the city unbothered. One of the many things I've learned about the capital during my ventures outside the Temple is no one really cares who you are and where you're going. If you walk confidently, looking like you have somewhere to be, few people will actually stop you. The market is an exception to that rule of course, but the stalls have mostly closed down for the evening. The night belongs to the merrymaking, the eating establishments, to bards and thieves and prostitutes, to those looking to lose some coin, or looking for something else in the bottom of an ale.

I reach the house after night has fallen. The noise from the inns and taverns has dissipated the further I wind down residential streets. I bypass the main door and seek instead the servant's door, half hidden behind an immaculate, elaborate rose bush. The wait after my knock seems inordinately long, but it is in truth only a few moments. The maid who opens the door peers curiously at me, then smiles and steps aside.

"You're Liseah's friend, right? The one at the Knight's Temple?"

A knot immediately forms in my throat, and it's all I can do to nod. "Can you fetch her?" I manage to ask. The words are thick and stick to my ash-dry throat.

If she notices something is amiss, the maid does not say anything. She gives a nod and gestures to the kitchen, telling me to make myself at home. I wait until she disappears down the narrow servant's corridor before I allow myself to drop my pack and turn to the cold fireplace. It's too warm for a fire, even at night, but I can't stop myself from shaking. I note, in the absent way of someone looking at something they are not a part of, that the cook has left a covered earthen pot in the coals. Bread rising for tomorrow. The act is so utterly mundane, so commonplace, it seems absurd after the day's events.

"Raylen? What are you doing here?"

The familiar voice finds all the cracks in me, spreading them wide open until I'm splintering in a thousand different ways. I turn to Liseah, tears hot on my face, the shaking traveling up my limbs, into hunched shoulders and shallow breaths. Liseah draws back in surprise for the briefest moment before rushing forward and wrapping me in her arms. "Oh, my love, it's okay, whatever it is, it's okay," she whispers into my hair.

I put my head down on her shoulder and weep. "It's n-not ok-okay." Each word is a mountain lodged into my chest, my throat, suffocating me. "I f-failed. I f-f-failed. I'm not go-going to be a, a knight. E-ever." The sobs overtake me, and I can't say anything else.

Liseah doesn't either. She wraps her arms around me tightly, and we sink to the floor as I weep into her lap like a newborn babe.

When the tears finally stop after what feels like hours, I lie still, spent and exhausted, body still quaking. Liseah strokes my hair, humming a wordless tune from our childhood.

"What happened?" Her voice is quiet, soothing.

I do not sit up, but enjoy the comfort of my best friend.

When I speak, my words crack, but I manage not to start crying again.

"During the final exam, they put you in a room with some mages, who create this illusion. You have to protect the crown prince. A version of him, older than the boy he is now. Someone capable of wielding a weapon. I thought all that mattered were my sword skills, you know? My physical ability to protect him." I have to take a minute to swallow and process what to say next. "But I guess that's not the real reason behind the test. I left him. The crown prince. I saw a woman and her sister in trouble, and I left him to fend for himself. I figured, he had a sword, he's had probably the best teachers in the world. He could hold off the attackers while I helped the defenseless."

I sit up finally, wiping away tear tracks. I look at Liseah, at the sadness and fear and unbelief scrawled across her face. "I left him, and Knight Perthran said that as a knight, my only duty was to the crown. All else be damned."

The words he spoke to me — not cruel, no, but heavy with disappointment, with the echo of all that *could have been* lost to one stupid choice — those words are etched into my bones now.

"You should have been the best. But now I am reminded yet again that the best swordsman does not equal the best knight. If you are willing to throw away our crown prince's life, you do not deserve the title of knighthood."

I tried, foolishly, to explain. To tell him, as knights, we have a duty to protect *everyone* around us. It took the guffaws of a mage, of Perthran refusing to even look in my direction, for me to finally gather what little dignity remained and leave the hall.

"But," I look back to Liseah, who has tears crawling down her own cheeks now, "the thing is, I think he's right." My voice cracks, and I can't hold back the second round of crippling sadness. Or the anger that licks at the edges, bright and furious.

"I don't deserve the title of knighthood." The words make me want to vomit. "Because, if I had the chance to do it again, I would do the same thing. I thought being a knight was about protecting those who can't help themselves. Not only caring for the crown."

I close my eyes against the burn, utterly spent and exhausted.

"Stay here for tonight," Liseah says. She tugs me up gently, and I stumble to my feet. "You can sleep with me. We'll figure out what to do next in the morning."

My words have vanished. I hope she understands my gratitude in the grip of our hands intertwined.

I follow her to her room, a small but neat affair with a bed, a trunk, a small table, and a flickering lamp. She helps me change, small hands tugging off my boots, running her own brush through my hair. After we've crawled into bed, Liseah molds herself to me, belly pressed into my back, breath comforting in my ear. Her warmth is an extension of myself, something as familiar as my own body. So I close my eyes, imagining myself home, and let her rhythmic breathing lull me to sleep.

It's a small hand shaking my shoulder that wakes me. I try to burrow into the warm bed, realization and remembrance crashing painfully into me with the return to consciousness.

"Leave me alone to rot."

Even my voice sounds soulless.

"Sorry, can't do that."

The blankets are torn off, the morning chill worming its way under my night clothes. I think about crying, decide I am too tired for even that, and settle for glaring through slitted eyes at Liseah.

"You'll feel better after breakfast." Liseah tosses me a green tunic, too dull, too worn after the white-bright initiate garb. She hesitates, then amends, "Maybe not better. But more human, at least."

Being human sounds like the worst thing I could want at this moment, but I know Liseah's tenacity. She won't let me refuse, and a fight sounds like more emotional damage than I can take. I shrug into the clothes silently. Sit still, like a doll, as she runs a brush through my hair, slips my boots over my feet. I think about protesting, should dislike this childlike treatment, but I can't. It feels good to be looked after.

"There's my girl."

Liseah ushers me through the door and down the hallway. I see, out of the corner of my eye, her hand start to rise, as if to touch me, comfort me, before it falls to her side once more.

The halls are alive with servants walking this way and that, some carrying fresh linens, others soiled ones. One holds a gilt-edged tray level with her chest, the most enticing aroma curling in the tendrils of steam that rise from under the covered plates.

"Some of the ladies take their breakfast in bed," Liseah says, nudging me down the stairs towards the kitchens. "Some will eat in the dining hall. And others, like Lady Citria, are not even up yet."

She casts a wicked grin my way. "Which is lovely for me, since I can have breakfast at my leisure most mornings."

We enter the kitchens, overly warm from the raging ovens and the multitude of bodies bustling inside. The cook and her helpers are a mass of flailing arms and moving legs. Sharp knives slice through baked ham, cinnamon is dusted on top of cream filled pastries, summer-red strawberries are parted from their stems and set neatly on the rims of plates. Servants wait for plates or take their own, more meager offerings, sitting at the pitted wooden tables shoved against one wall.

"How old is Lady Citria again?" My voice is dry, unused, cracking at the words. I don't even remember thinking them, too caught up in the whirlwind churning inside myself. The constant whispering voice wonders if the others have noticed, if the servants here can feel the failure seeping from my pores.

Easier to think of unimportant things.

"Twelve."

Liseah hands me a bowl of oatmeal topped with sparkling sugar and fat blueberries. My traitorous mouth waters at the mere sight. The Knight's Temple believed food was meant to sustain and nourish, not delight.

But this... this is delightful.

"She's a brat most days," Liseah continues as we take seats on the crowded benches. "She's impatient to be married and away from the house, impatient to grow up and go to balls and look like her elder sisters. She has a good enough head, should she deign to use it, but she's too young to be invited to listen in on her father's trades."

A vague memory sparks. The Lankashir family deals in weapons. They came to power during the war by striking up several important trading contracts with the countries to the south of us, the same continent that gave us King Tridion and a strong enough treaty to help turn the tide of the war.

I would hate to profit from the brutality of war, which is probably why I would make a terrible merchant.

A terrible knight, too, apparently.

The thought burns, acid eating away at my stomach, so I quiet it by eating spoonfuls of oatmeal. It's even more delicious than I expected, and the bowl is scraped clean all too soon.

Liseah has the decency to wait until our meal is over before asking the question I've been bracing for.

"Are you going to go home?" Her tone is careful, calculated, almost nonchalant. Like it doesn't matter to her either way, like she's just checking on a trivial matter.

"*No.*" The force of my own dissent surprises me. It also earns a few raised eyebrows from the other maids. I lower my voice before continuing. "I can't go back. What's left there for me? Marriage?" I snort in disgust.

"Your father loves you. He would understand."

It doesn't matter that she's right. I know he would accept me back, and I also know he would spend the rest of his days making sure I knew it had all been a mistake. I shake my head vehemently. "No. That's not an option."

Liseah sighs but doesn't force the issue. "You can probably stay here a few days, but the lady will notice eventually and start asking questions."

"Oh no, I wouldn't dream of putting you out. I'll go to The Slumbering Queen." The inn we meet at every tenday to discuss our lives over cheap ale and stew. "There are plenty of caravans that come through there. I'm sure I can figure something out."

Liseah raises her eyebrows. "Are you going to join the mercenary guild?"

The idea makes my stomach churn. "Not if I can avoid it," I admit. "But I need money while I figure out what my next step is. I'm sure Tole will let me tag along for a few trips, right?"

He still sees Liseah when he comes to Calire, no matter how many weeks have passed. I can't speak for their faithfulness in those days not together, but they seem happy, and I suppose that's really all that matters.

"Sure he would," Liseah agrees, but there's a troubling note in her voice I can't quite identify. "He's said several times that you're a bloody brilliant swordsman. I'm sure he'd be thrilled to have you, even if just for a few trips."

I lean forward on my arms and capture her eyes with my own. "But what?"

She sighs and looks away, not answering.

"Look, I can take it." I'm not really sure I can, but the need to know presses insistently. I can't handle half-truths being taunted before me. "I'm not fragile."

Liseah reluctantly meets my gaze again. Her eyes are so sad it takes my breath away, and I'm afraid I'm going to burst into tears here at the breakfast table. "It's not easy to let go of dreams, Raylen. And you've had this one for... well, for as long as I've known you, which is our whole lives. Beyond that, you're one of the most stubborn people I know. How are you going to handle this? Just getting up and moving on?"

I scowl at the tabletop, unable to take the reality reflected in her face. "Do I have a choice?"

"Not really. But that doesn't mean you won't try to find a way."

I sit back, surprise and a little bit hurt. "Find a way? Liseah, I'm stubborn, not stupid. Once you fail, there's no second chances in the Knight's Temple." Saying the words out loud brings a foul taste to my mouth, makes my stomach clench until I worry about the breakfast I just ate. "I don't know what I'm going to do. I don't know how I'm going to make my life work now." Now that the thing I dreamed about every single night is ripped to shreds. "But I'm also not going to just shrivel up and waste away."

Although, to be honest, it sounds a lot more peaceful than struggling through the tightness in my chest.

Apparently satisfied, Liseah nods. "Okay. I believe you." She rises, taking our plates to the wide sink and dropping them in. "I have to get my day started now. Will you be okay?"

"Of course." I try on a smile, but it feels fake. "I think I'll walk through town a bit, see what opportunities might be around."

Liseah pulls me in for a strong, quick hug. "Okay. I'll see you soon?"

I nod. Then, pretending to be braver than I feel, I retrace our steps to her room, pick up my pack, and leave once again.

I intend to follow through on my words. I really do. But barely an hour goes by and I can't rip my gaze from the white steeples of the Temple. Imagined celebrations over the initiates' successful exams rings in my ears, the backdrop to whispered conversations.

Where did Raylen go? Surely she didn't—

Or, perhaps even worse, the reality that no one even notices my absence at all.

I was supposed to be the golden one. Successful. Strong. Following through in my dreams, in Eirah's footsteps. Instead I waver in the market square, unable to bring myself to take a step in any direction. Alone and adrift in a sea of relentless noise.

It's too damn much.

Somehow I make my way to The Slumbering Queen. The inn is quiet, the common room empty. The innkeeper eyes me oddly but takes my coin anyway and trades me for a room key. The metal is cold and foreign in my hand as I shakily climb the stairs, room numbers blending into plain wooden walls as my vision tunnels and blurs.

It's a miracle I manage to open the door, stumble through, and lock it behind me, the key clattering loudly in the lock from how violently my hands tremble.

I collapse onto the bed, falling in on myself, and allow the despair to once again consume me.

The man shakes his head, a vaguely disappointed look on his face. "I don't think I'm willing to take on a guard without the backing of the mercenary guild. I'm sure you understand."

My smile is frozen in place even as disappointment hollows out my stomach. "Of course. Thank you for considering me anyway."

The words are automatic, meaningless, only there to conceal the bubbling anger.

I walk away before I say something I'll regret.

It's been three weeks since the autumn equinox — three painful weeks of depression, too much coffee, too much wine. Five days ago I gave in and took up a barmaid job at The Slumbering Queen to pay for my meals and bed. It's not a bad place, and the travelers who frequent it tell good stories, but every time the door swings open, I'm petrified the person on the other side is a former classmate, an instructor.

The days are spent combing the streets, ears alert for any whisper of a guard job, but every interaction is the same. Interested Nobles, merchants, travelers looking for a guard, excited to hear my feats and qualifications, only to close off immediately when they realize I'm not part of the mercenary's guild.

I understand it, no matter how much it also frustrates me. Since the mercenary guild was established, it offers a guarantee of excellence, as well as the reassurance that the guard won't try to steal all your valuables behind your back. Even if I were to join the guild today, though, I wouldn't be likely to get a good position immediately. I would have to prove myself with caravan jobs, to show I am trustworthy and good with a blade, before being able to strike out on my own.

Liseah is convinced I should do it. And although the logical part of my brain agrees with her, I can't convince myself to take the blow to my pride. Anyone can become a mercenary. And it's a good, respectable job, just like being a part of the soldier's battalion or the Watchers. I respect every single person that takes on those mantles.

But I can't disregard the small, quiet voice begging me for more. To do more, be more, than another faceless body joining the army. Neither can I ignore the unease that rises every time I think about the exam and what it would mean to leave those children undefended, ready for the slaughter. Was it merely an example, designed to test our loyalty?

Perhaps. But I know, in that dark part of myself, that the queen would call for that same loyalty without question. Perthran and all those others would let those innocents die if it meant preserving queen and crown.

And I simply couldn't live with myself if I made that choice.

"—another Aberration spotted up north—"

I look at the man speaking, but he's already passed by. This is the third time I've heard about increased numbers of Aberrations up north. Last night during dinner, the traveling party at the table next to mine held the audience rapt as they described how the Aberrations prowled through the northern hills at night, flitting between trees like shadows. Most of the inn seemed to think it was a sham, that Aberrations didn't act like that. Except for the arbitrariness of their presence, Aberrations have always obeyed a set of rules, standards. How they look, how they behave, how they are slain.

But everything changes at some point, doesn't it? Who is to say it couldn't happen to monsters as well?

The more I hear about it, the more intrigued I am by the notion. Perhaps it is self-serving; the more monsters there are in the world, the more people will need to be protected.

"Are you investigating the north too?"'

The question is entirely unexpected, especially coming from someone standing suddenly, surprisingly close. I can't help but jump a little. I turn, hackles raised, ready to snap, but the man facing me smiles so disarmingly that the words die in my mouth.

He's a few years older than me, perhaps twenty-five or twenty-six, with shaggy russet curls cut short in the back. His lighter skin says he's city born, likely from Calire or somewhere close by. He wears simple clothes of good weave, without any identifying markings from a guild. He has some money, then, and doesn't want anyone to pay attention to him.

Something about him is hauntingly familiar, like a remembered word dancing on the tip of my tongue. Just out of reach.

When I don't say anything, he continues in the same guileless tone. "I am too. I think there has to be some stock to the rumors, even if *everything* they're saying can't be true. Rumors have to start somewhere. So, I figure, either the Aberrations really are acting up and will eventually take down this monarchy—" he smiles, but I can't tell if it's supposed to be a joke or not "—or someone started these rumors for a very specific purpose."

I raise an eyebrow and cross my arms, intrigued despite myself. "And what purpose would that be?"

The man's grin broadens. "Well, I can't say that, since I wasn't the one to start them, mmm?"

"You're offering more questions than answers." I shake my head, tempted to walk away, but something weighs down my legs, keeping me rooted to the spot.

The man raises a finger as if I've landed on the heart of the issue. "You're not wrong. The difference between myself and all of these other rumor mongers, however, is that I actually plan to do something about it."

I raise my eyebrows. "What would that be?"

"Go north of course."

Despite myself, I can't help but grin. The stranger is enigmatic and boyishly charming in such a way that defies people not to like him. I'm about to say something, perhaps to ask him who else is crazy enough to investigate Aberrations of all things, when the man is suddenly and violently lifted off his feet. His head jerks back, mouth open in surprise. The man holding him is easily a foot taller and bulging with muscle. Showy, but effective.

"Gotcha, ya rat," he growls. "You filthy, lying cheat! You will pay us what we're owed."

Holding the stranger in one hand, he reaches for a knife with the other.

I don't think. I lunge forward, delivering a rapid series of strikes to the attacker, focusing on the weak points of knees, sides, and throat. He stumbles back, spluttering and gagging, and his grip loosens on the man's tunic.

"Run!" I tell the stranger. I pinch the attacker's hand ruthlessly, and his fingers spasm, releasing the last bit of cloth. Still moving fast, I deliver one last, quick jab to the man's nose, earning a howl of pain, before I grab the stranger's hand and follow my own advice.

We run.

CHAPTER
SIX

Prowling this area of Calire for the last few days finally comes in handy as I expertly weave amongst the stalls and city folk. I keep a tight grip on the stranger, who manages to clumsily keep pace with me. Running is clearly not high on his list of activities. I jump over a crate next to a stall selling cinnamon sugar sticks, and he immediately bumbles into it, sending the goods skittering across the cobblestone street.

"Sorry!" he calls over his shoulder, face flush. "Sorry, I'll come back and pay for that!"

I dare a glance behind me and find not just the original hired hand following us, but three others as well. We're drawing a good amount of attention; the city Watchers will be on us soon. I doubt they'll deal judgement in our favor, especially considering the mess we're creating in our wake.

My companion must have come to the same conclusion. "We need to find a place to lay low." His words are whispered between gasps for air.

"No shit." I take a hard left, my companion nearly losing his footing as I drag him behind me. The alleyway is mostly clear of rubble, giving us a moment to put on some speed.

Or we would, if it was two trained, athletic people in this chase.

"Run faster!"

We burst out of the alley and immediately dive behind a long row of stalls selling various fruit. I pull him down into a crouch, and we run awkwardly, half on our hands and knees.

"I'm doing my best," the man says, indignation clear in his voice.

"Well, it's not good enough."

We find a shadowed alcove. The noise of our pursuers is fainter. I figure we have a minute to gather our breath before needing to find another route. I scan the marketplace, eyes darting from one spot to another. There's plenty of stalls out today, which is both good and bad. Stalls mean people, both buyers and sellers. We can possibly hide in their midst, but they also might give us away. The fruit merchants haven't noticed us yet.

"You any good with that thing?"

I look at my companion, distracted from my objective, and find him staring pointedly at my sword.

I hesitate for half a heartbeat, thinking of those times in the Temple when I was beaten fair and square, ass in the ground, aching from half a dozen bruises.

You are no longer welcome in the Knight's Temple.

"Yes," I say, forcing confidence in my voice. Because it's true. I may make a terrible knight, but I know my own skill.

"Good. Now, listen very carefully." He leans close, speaking fast. "You're going to go out there, sword drawn, and offer a challenge."

I draw back immediately, mouth opening in protest, but he

puts a finger to my lips and presses on, ignoring my indignation. "I just need you to hold them for a few minutes. I'll handle the rest." His eyes are wide and honest and also ruthless in their intensity. "I will not leave you alone in this. But you have to trust me."

He obviously expects his words to mean something, but I scoff. "I met you ten minutes ago. I don't even know your name, much less trust you." But then I shrug, a bit helplessly. "But that doesn't mean I won't help you anyway."

I look back to the alleyway mouth where our pursuers have stumbled out, splitting up to tackle the market square. A few of the merchants give them dirty looks, but no one moves to stop them.

Worry gnaws my innards like a wolf at a carcass, but I step out of our cover and stride to the center of the square with as much authority as I can manage. Chin up, head high.

I will not be a coward. Even if this all implodes in my face. Even if I make the wrong choice.

Again.

So many things I've fucked up.

But that will not be my story today.

I unsheathe my sword, the satisfying *shhhk* of blade against leather sending delighted shivers down my skin. It has been too long since I held my sword. Since I settled into myself, feet firm and flat, reaching down through myself and into the earth to ground me. Since I've felt powerful.

"This is a foolish choice." The man I assume is the leader steps in front of me, freeing his own weapon. His nose has stopped bleeding but the front of his shirt is streaked with red. Out of the corner of my eye, I see two of the others flank me. There's a third somewhere, but I don't know where yet. That will probably come back to hurt me later.

I give a wolfish grin. "I beg to differ. They sent four of you after one man. Your skills must not equate to much."

Fury blossoms red across his cheeks. "You don't know what you're getting yourself into, filthy bitch." There's the echoing sound of more weapons being drawn, but I don't bother to grace the henchmen with a look.

"Come on then." I hold up a hand, curling my fingers to beckon him. "Because I don't think you have the balls to back up those threats."

There's a faint tittering of laughter from the merchants and their buyers who have stopped to watch. The hired hand's face darkens, and, with an animalistic roar, he charges. I step forward to meet him, but even prepared as I am, the force of his blow against my blade sends me back a step. He's *strong*. There's a flash of worry, but I push it aside. Too late now. Either my mysterious companion will come through... or he won't, and I'll end up a pretty splatter on the ground.

There's movement just out of the corner of my eye. I move, but not quite fast enough. The tip of the blade digs into the tender flesh of my upper arm, gouging a short but deep line. I hiss at the unexpected pain and dance backwards, more mad at myself than the man who harmed me. I let him get close, too focused on the main target. That won't happen again.

The leader strikes, and I parry the blow, followed by several others from his hired men. It's a dizzying blur of speed and strength, my feet sliding from one movement to the next, arms moving, body twisting. Through the movements, something in me breaks. But whereas in the last few days it has felt like pieces of myself have been chipped away, this is different. I feel exposed, raw. Parts of me somehow had been covered with armor, to protect whatever remained after the Temple destroyed me. But now there are cracks, sunlight leaking in, and my chest swells with a feeling I can only describe as joy.

As stupid as that is, with blood trailing down one arm, muscles shaking from exertion, protecting a stranger I have no reason to help.

A stranger who promised not to leave me alone, and I am starting to think he lied, and now I am about to be in very, very deep trouble.

But then there's a creaking, like wood straining in a storm, and before I can blink or say anything or even turn to look, there's a dull roaring that fills my ears and *something* sweeps past me, enveloping me in semi-opaque darkness.

The fight stops abruptly as shouts of surprise rise from the crowd. I am covered in shadows that writhe and flow like a living being. They twine around my legs, my arms, my back, stretching behind me to flare outward. I glance over my shoulder and see the shadows rising above me, like wings made of smoke. When I raise an arm, the shadows follow, clinging as a second skin.

I should be afraid, but I feel nothing except a small bubble of excitement.

Magic. It has to be magic. There's no other explanation.

He's a *mage*.

Embolden, I point an imperious finger at the hired men. "I suggest you take your leave." Low and cold, authoritative, and the man pales. "This fight is over. Leave my companion alone, and I'll leave you alive."

Bravado in its finest form.

My opponent hesitates, glancing at his men, hand convulsing around the hilt of his sword.

I need to end this now, while I still have the momentum.

Light, I hope the mage is paying attention.

I tut and step forward, bringing my arm back then forward, palm outstretched, like I'm throwing an object. The gamble pays off as more shadows spring from my palm, racing through the air towards our attackers.

The men turn and run without another word.

Whatever bubble enveloped us pops. Shouts of panic rise from the marketplace as viewers stumble backwards, fear and morbid interest mixing amongst them. There's a crash as a someone knocks over a stand of crates filled with various cooking tools, more yells following as the noise heightens the panic.

I drop my hands, the exhilaration of winning the fight rapidly receding as I realize we now have to contend with the backlash of our actions. Uneasiness stirs through me. Getting involved with a mage could spell far more trouble than I'm prepared for. Mages are set apart, in a way even knights aren't, an invaluable weapon to the crown and a dangerous unknown. They work for the crown, for their own society of mages, but mostly for themselves.

Even as I think this might become an even worse mistake than the Knight's Temple, the shadows vanish. There is no receding, no pause — one minute they're there, I blink, and they're gone.

"It was merely an illusion!"

I turn to the mage, who has emerged from his hiding place, hands up and outstretched. He addresses the whole courtyard but keeps one eye on me. I realize, belatedly, that I still grip my weapon, body now turned to face the mage. The fight boils in me, adrenaline a thick and heady concoction.

The hysteria does not vanish, but I see a few heads turn towards him.

"There was a misunderstanding between myself and those lovely gentlemen," he continues. His voice is loud, bordering on jovial, as if the misunderstanding is nothing more than heated words over afternoon tea. "They would not listen to reason, so, sadly, I had to resort to more dramatic gestures."

He stops next to me. I see the sweat shining on his forehead, the slightest way his hands tremble. The illusion took more out of him than he's willing to show, and it gives me a strange reassurance. If it comes to a fight between us, I might have the upper hand, even injured.

"Now, if you'll excuse us."

He gives a flourishing bow, which earns raised eyebrows and looks of disbelief. Then he gestures to me, and, not knowing what else to do, I follow the mage.

He sets a quick pace, not fast enough to draw even more attention — I can already hear Watchers calling to each other as they close in on the market square. Too little, too late. Like usual. I can't help but wonder if they let this stuff happen sometimes, just to see who wins.

"I told you I wouldn't leave you to face them alone."

I look at the mage, who focuses more on where he's going as he weaves a dizzying path through the less prosperous areas of Calire.

"You could have mentioned who you are."

He glances at me from the corner of his eye, a grin twitching the corner of his mouth up.

"Where's the fun in that? And my name is Lyr."

After wandering through a good portion of Calire, Lyr finally brings us to a collection of inns and taverns near the north gate, leading me into a tavern already crowded with travelers. A quick look around shows no Watchers, and the general atmosphere is easy and relaxed. When we enter, no one gives us a second glance. Maybe they'll have the Watchers track us down, but since no one was killed or even seriously injured, and no property was destroyed, it seems more probable this whole thing will just be forgotten. There is more crime in Calire than the Watchers can deal with; they won't spend valuable resources on an errant mage and a swordswoman with no title.

Lyr nudges me to a small table. I obediently sit, taking the spot where I can keep my back to the wall and eyes on the door. Just in case.

"I'll get us something to eat and drink," he says before disappearing back into the crowd.

He returns a few moments later bearing two plates of food and two tankards of golden mead. It might not be the wisest thing to accept food and drink from someone with obvious secrets, but he could have left me in the fight at any time. What would be the point of helping me then, only to hurt me now? I drain half of my mead in a few swallows, relishing the way it warms my belly.

It doesn't take long before Lyr puts down his fork and leans forwards. "Thank you," he says, the words sincere and soft. "For helping me."

I stuff a bit more buttered roll into my mouth. It's good — I'll have to tell Liseah about the quality of food here sometime. "I'm sure it's what anyone would have done."

Lyr chokes on his food. I lean over, slapping him on the back as he gasps for air. "Not likely," he says when he can comfortably breathe again, wiping streaming eyes on his sleeve. He laughs like *I'm* the crazy one. "What kind of gold touched village are you from if you actually think people want to help strangers?"

I frown at my plate. *The kind of place that raised someone to think being a knight was about protecting people.* I don't say my thoughts aloud.

"Well, wherever you're from, thank the light you were there to save my sorry ass."

"You're welcome," I say, even though it isn't exactly a true thank you. I watch as he rips off a chunk of meat from his skewer.

Another mage. First Keemah, now Lyr. Both hid their true selves — not that mages have ever been forced to reveal themselves. They do not wear armbands like Watchers, crown colors like knights.

It doesn't matter that I've been here for months now; the idea of magic remains nerve wracking. Mages are an entirely different breed. I may be strong physically, but a mage is different. In order to tame the magic bestowed upon them by the Crystals, their mental will must be unwavering. Even then, more than half of their novices die within the first year of training, burnt out on the power surging through their veins.

No, a mage is a far more terrifying opponent than a swordsman ever could be.

I lace my fingers together and lean forward a bit. "So, what did you do?"

Lyr grins. "I was wondering when you'd ask. Would you believe me if I said it was all a misunderstanding?"

I take him in for a minute — tilted smile, head to one side ever so slightly, brown eyes bright with amusement. "I wouldn't believe it for a second."

Lyr throws back his head and roars with laughter. It's an infectious sound and, despite everything, I find myself grinning too. The thrill of the chase, the fight, even the magic... I haven't felt this alive since I left the Temple.

When his laughter finally calms down, Lyr looks back at me, wipes a tear from his eye, and says, "I like you. You should come with me."

I openly laugh at the suggestion, but he doesn't look away, eyes utterly serious. My grin slowly fades.

"Come with you? Where?"

"Why, to the north of course. Where else?"

My heart pounds erratically at his words. The north. Wild territory, with people too stubborn to leave the land they were born to, insisting on trying to grow things in the hard, unyielding ground. The north, where there has only been talk of Aberrations, strange happenings, and overruling fear for the last several weeks.

I shake a finger at Lyr. "You're trying to distract me. Tell me why I just saved your sorry ass, and then we'll discuss the north."

He raises his eyebrows. "Not many people talk to a mage like that."

"Yeah, well." I down the rest of my mead, slamming the tankard back down with more force than necessary. "Not many people would help you either. Like you so eloquently said earlier. Stop shoveling shit at me and give me a straight answer. You asked for my help, and I gave it. You asked me to trust you, and I stayed. The least you owe me is an explanation."

Lyr leans back, hands linked behind his head, and watches me inscrutably for several breathless moments. Just when I decide there's no point in staying here, he says, "I tried to steal a necklace."

I frown, open my mouth, close it again. "A necklace? But why? You're a mage. Surely you aren't desperate enough to need the money."

Lyr laughs again, and I have to fight down the urge to scowl. I'm tired of feeling left out, privy to only part of the conversation.

"No, not just a regular necklace. What do you know about magic... why, I don't think you've mentioned your name to me."

I'm in it now. There's no point in lying. "Raylen. I've never had to give magic much of a thought."

He gives me another long look, something new in his eyes

now, some... remembrance. It's on the tip of my tongue as well, but I can't manage to articulate this almost-memory.

"Well, let me give you a bit of a history lesson then. You know how mages are given magic, right?"

I roll my eyes at this. "I might be from a backwater village, but we had to go through the Summoning too, thank you very much."

The Summoning happens once a year at the height of summer, when every eighteen year old journeys to the closest Crystal to be tested. No one knows when they first appeared or how they came about, but as long as we humans have been here, so have the Crystals. Although the Crystals have been studied exhaustively, they remain a mystery — are they sentient in the same way magic is? They must be to some extent in order to tell who is strong enough to bear it.

The judging of the Crystals is painless, the verdict less so if you had other plans for your life. If the Crystals find you worthy, it's off to Haven to train as a mage, for better or worse.

"Magic is wild," Lyr says, ignoring my sharp words. "It is difficult to control, and every time you wish to use it, you have to fight for dominance. If you don't have a strong enough will, you're consumed by it."

I nod. All common knowledge.

"Well, all mages tend to be stronger in some magic more than others. For instance, if you haven't guessed, I'm exceptionally strong at illusions. I can cast fire or wield water, sure, but it wouldn't last very long or be particularly powerful. Mages tend to have their specialities, and we don't like to stray from them.

"That said, mages can grow their power by using a magically imbued object."

My eyebrows rise. Ah. So there's where the necklace comes in.

Lyr nods, acknowledging my understanding. "As you might

imagine, these objects aren't very common. They can only be created during the death of a mage. When the mage dies, the magic has to go *somewhere*." His hands wave in the air, gesturing at nothing. "Most of it usually dissipates into the world, although if the mage is unusually strong, this dissipating can create reactions like a natural disaster. An earthquake, a fire, a flood... you really don't want to be around when a mage is violently killed."

I know all this from Eirah's journals, although he never went into detail about the intricacies of magic. Just the aftermath of their deaths, of the tidal waves that rose to wipe out allies and enemies alike, the sudden quicksand that swallowed horses and battalions whole. The constant need to protect their mages first and foremost.

Lyr continues, "If a mage is wearing some kind of natural precious stone, however... well, I guess magic is drawn to what resembles a Crystal. The magic becomes trapped in the gem and is able to be used by another mage from that point on. Sometimes the jewels are very powerful, sometimes they aren't. But even a small boost of magic can make the difference between a weak mage and a powerful one."

I tap my lip. "So, to put it simply, you're not a very strong mage and want to acquire an imbued object so you can gain more power."

A look of hurt flashes over Lyr's face. "You don't have to put it so bluntly."

"But is that it?"

"Well, yes, I suppose you could say it like that."

I nod. Wanting power is something I understand. "Is that the only way to get an imbued object? Stealing one?"

"Or killing a mage, pretty much." Lyr stabs the last of his potato. "Or inheriting one. But most of them are stolen goods, yes. It's quite common, really. More so than you would think."

"That doesn't make it right."

Lyr groans. "Oh light, did I misjudge you? Are you one of those insufferable followers who only do what the crown sanctions as 'right'?"

I think about that for a moment. The proper knight response would be of course I err on the side of justice. But I'm *not* a knight. Why should I force myself to constantly act like one?

"Someone only concerned with what's right wouldn't have saved you without hearing the whole story first," I finally say. I look at my arm with a grimace, the clothing bloody and stuck to my skin. Cleaning that would be fun. "Or get hurt for them, either."

Lyr has the grace to look abashed. "Sorry about that. Although, I must say," and he leans forward, a grin taking over his face, that irresistible charm returning, "I haven't seen such elegant fighting in a long time. Brutal. But beautiful."

I surprise myself by blushing. It feels good, to have an outsider praise my skills.

"So, why are you going north?" I ask. Something unfurls in my stomach, hot and insistent. I know, without a doubt, that even thinking of going north with a virtual stranger is a terrible idea. And yet...

"Two reasons." Lyr holds up two fingers. "One is the reason I told you already. I believe the rumors of the Aberrations are true. But I also think something has to be at the core of it. They aren't increasing in activity on their own. That means magic of some kind." He puts down one finger. "And two, I've finally managed to track down the honorable Mage Sunillen. He is rumored to have the largest collection of imbued objects."

I raise my eyebrows. "And you want to steal one from him?"

"Not necessarily. I'm happy to apprentice myself to him, see if I can gain his good graces. Find a way to serve him and, perhaps, gain an award for myself."

It sounds sly and underhanded, but what do I know of the world of mages?

"And if that doesn't work?"

"Oh, then I'll try to steal one," Lyr answers without hesitation.

I shouldn't, but I chuckle at his honesty. "And you're going by yourself? It's a long journey."

"Well, it wouldn't be if I had you there to help guard me." He gives that disarming grin. "I can pay you. Not handsomely, but anything is better than nothing, right? And you seem like the type of person eager for new challenges, new experiences. Am I wrong?"

Is he?

Before, I would have agreed with him. Before the Temple. Before I lost myself.

And the longing to reclaim that woman, to be *myself* again, is so strong I can taste it.

"Tell you what, give it the night to think about it." Lyr stands, wiping his mouth and throwing a few coins on the table. "If you want to join us, meet us at the north gate at dawn. We'll figure out mounts when you come."

When, not if. Presumptuous of him. But my attention catches on a different part of his invitation. "Wait, us? Are you going with a caravan?"

He laughs. "No, no, there aren't really any caravans that go that far up north. As you noticed, I'm not exactly a good thief. So I hired someone for that job, should it come up. He's a fair swordsman, although I must say, I think you have him beat. And beside, the more the merrier, am I right?"

The idea of an unknown person puts a damper on the idea, but not enough to smother the truth.

For better or worse, I'll be at the north gate in the morning.

"You've lost your fucking mind."

I watch as Liseah paces back and forth in the small confines of my rented room. My bag already lies packed, waiting for me next to the door. We met for dinner, but I had to shoo her up to my room once she began to yell at me in front of the rest of the inn.

"So you've said. Multiple times." It's only by the grace of the light I keep my voice level, but something must give me away, because Liseah shoots me a knowing look anyway.

"What do you want me to say, Raylen?" She throws her arms out, frustration radiating through every line of her body. "Do you want me to say okay, see you later, love you, hope you survive and these random strangers you've met don't kill you? A stranger who already got you injured, I might add!"

I glance at the bandage around my arm. "What do you want me to do instead, Liseah?" For the first time tonight, irritation laces my tone. "Sit around and twiddle my thumbs?"

"Find a respectable job that's actually safe!" She stops pacing, standing in front of me with balled fists and flushed cheeks.

"What, like Tole? Traveling the same path eternally? No thanks."

"There's no shame in what he does!"

"I didn't say there was shame. I just want *more*." I'm on my feet now too, my own anger rising up to meet hers. "Don't you get it? I've lost the only dream I ever had. I don't know who I am anymore—"

"You're my friend!"

Her voice cracks like a whip through the room, stunning me into silence. I stare at Liseah, eyes shining bright with unshed tears.

"You lost your dream," she whispers, anger still dancing around the sadness, "but why does that mean I have to lose my best friend? We were supposed to be here *together*."

Shame courses through me, leaving me hollow in its wake. "Then come with me." I grip her hands tightly. "We can still go on adventures. We can be together."

She smiles, but it is bitter and sad and makes me want to weep. "Raylen, that's not what I want. I wanted out of Heron Hill, but not so I could spend my days on the road hopping from village to village, town to town. Never settling down. I like it here. I like the people I work with, and even the ones I work for. I'm... I'm happy." She falls silent, staring at me like she's begging for reassurance.

"Of course you are." I brush a tendril of hair out of her face, tucking it behind her ear. "Of course you love it here — you should. It's perfect for you. And I really, really wish it was perfect for me too."

I hug her then, too tight, but she returns the embrace just as fiercely, tears now soaking into my shoulder.

"I don't want to leave you," I whisper into her hair. "But I need to know who I am. What I consist of, besides a shattered dream. And this journey is the only thing that has made my soul sing since I left the Temple. Maybe I'm idiotic for it. I probably am. But what if I can do something, up there? What if the Aberrations really are attacking, and someone needs me to protect them?"

Liseah draws back and stares while tears trail down her cheeks. "But I need you too. What about me?"

Light, I'm being ripped apart. How am I supposed to choose

between myself and someone who has been a part of me almost since birth?

Before I have make that choice, Liseah takes a step back, scrubs her sleeve across her face, and nods. "You have six months," she says, tone permitting no argument. "If you haven't come back here in six months, I'm coming to find you. And you don't want that, because I'll be pissed as hell at you for making me sleep on the road again."

I laugh even as I hug her once more. "What did I ever do to deserve you?"

"Fuck if I know. I'm a damn saint for putting up with your crazy ass."

We laugh at that, which then turns into more crying. She sleeps with me that night, bodies curled around each other, hands clasped on the pillow. And when the time comes, I wake her, and she walks with me halfway to the north gate. We say goodbye as the predawn light casts violet shadows around us.

I reach the north gate just as dawn grips the horizon. Lyr is already waiting, holding the reins of two horses, one who snorts and pulls angrily at the bit. He grins broadly when he sees me, waving his free hand in greeting.

"I knew you would come," he says when I join him. He offers me the reins of the cantankerous horse. I eye him like he's gone out of his mind.

"Your first payment." He gestures with the reins again, and I finally reluctantly take them. "Can't get to the north on foot, after all."

I look around. There are several people moving towards the gate, ready to get their journey underway. "So, where is he? The thief you found?"

"Here."

The voice comes from behind me and is deep as the night,

rough at the edges. It reminds me of a wolf's growl, full of power and the promise of danger.

I turn, the hair on the back of my neck rising, and find myself looking into clear eyes that dance on the border between gray and green. Eyes that regard me with thinly veiled annoyance. Eyes that, to my utmost surprise, I recognize.

The mercenary I beat in the knife throwing contest so many months ago.

Vaen.

SEVEN

"Wait a minute. A thief? You were a mercenary six months ago."

The words slip out before I can stop them. The annoyance in Vaen's eyes grows as he looks to Lyr.

"What the hell is this about? I thought we agreed no strays."

I bristle. *Stray?* Like a fucking cat?

Lyr shrugs as if it's inconsequential. "She's good with a sword. Better than you I bet, although I'd have to see you two spar to really give you an answer."

Vaen grits his teeth. "I'm not asking who's the better swordsman, I'm asking why the fuck you thought it was a good idea to bring someone else along when we clearly said the less people involved, the better."

"Oh, yes, that." Lyr checks the bridle on his horse, no matter that it sits exactly where it needs to. "She helped me yesterday, you see, and I figured we might want a bit more muscle in the north, if it's as bad as everyone says." Vaen clearly does not look swayed by his words, but Lyr grins brightly and gestures between the two of us. "So you guys know each other? What a coincidence!"

I look at Vaen, who continues to glare, narrow-eyed, at Lyr. "Yeah, I don't think he's as thrilled as you are."

I'm feeling decidedly less warm and fuzzy about the excitement of this adventure now. I thought Vaen had been respectful of me if nothing else when we went toe to toe. But now the irritation coming off him in droves is enough to make me question the entire thing. "Why should I bother coming when the opposition is so strong?"

Lyr glances between the two of us again and offers, "The excitement of an adventure? The mystery of what awaits us? The knowledge you could help someone? Also, the money. Don't forget the money."

You have nowhere else to go, whispers the insidious voice inside my head. *Do you want to stay here, in the city you failed? Serve food to the knights you can never join? Look at the Temple and be reminded every day of what you could have had?*

There's nothing for me here, or at least nothing I'm willing to take. Whether or not Vaen likes the idea of my presence, he is not the one holding the purse strings. At the end of the day, Lyr hired both of us, and he's the only one who can force us to leave.

"Let's go with the mystery," I say. I offer Lyr a small smile, which he returns with exuberance. Out of the corner of my eye, I see the scowl deepen on Vaen's face.

"Excellent!" Lyr claps his hands together, choosing to ignore Vaen as well. "Let's get on the road then. It's a two week journey to Ulingard if we keep up a good pace. I assume you've ridden before?"

I busy myself securing my pack to the back of the saddle. "A little. I wouldn't say I'm proficient at it." The horse twists its head back, trying to nip at me, and I sidestep in just enough time.

"Even better. An inexperienced stray."

The words are quiet, spat at Lyr as Vaen smoothly mounts his own horse, a massive thing with a beautiful russet coat and white mane. I bite back any heated response. I've only ridden a handful of times, bareback and clumsy, on the plow horses at our neighbor's. We did not own horses ourselves, and riding never appealed enough for me to work at it. As much as the remark stings, it's also the truth.

"What's the horse's name?" I ask. I edge towards the stirrup, keeping a close eye on the flickering ears and stamping front hooves. Lyr's horse, a pale golden, calmly pulls at a few weeds peeking from between the cobblestones. My mount has none of their elegance and looks like a patchwork quilt, with splotches of brown and white haphazardly splashed.

"Mudslide."

I can't help a groan escaping. "That's not reassuring."

"I had limited options on such short notice," Lyr grumbles. "It's hard to find a good horse for a cheap price when the rider is half-behemoth."

The words don't hurt — I've heard them my whole life. When I continued to grow, surpassing all the girls my age and more than half the boys, I was elated. I would never be a delicate maiden, and there are certainly times I find myself dreaming of another form, a soft body that twines gracefully around a partner's, small and contained and cared for. But *this* body is strong and good and has gotten me through a lot. I could never hate it.

"True, it must be much easier to find mounts suitable for overgrown children." I'm at least four or five inches taller than Lyr, although I'd wager Vaen is almost eye to eye with me.

My words earn a snort from Vaen, which I decide to ignore, and a chortle from Lyr. "You're definitely going to make this journey fun." His grin is broad and only slightly mischievous. "I can't imagine how bored I would be on the road with no one else to talk to."

"Enough," Vaen says. He turns his mount towards the gate. "We're wasting daylight."

Lyr raises his eyebrows, muttering under his breath about who the real leader is, but follows nonetheless.

I put my foot in the stirrup and swing myself up into the saddle. The movement is stilted and awkward, but I manage it in one try, which is victory enough.

We join the small river of people winding their way out of the city. Most of those leaving look to be farmers or workers heading to the nearby cotton fields. There are a handful of mercenaries who meander down the road slowly, talking quietly and seriously. I wonder for a moment if Vaen will draw their attention, but we pass them without being noticed.

"Were you ever really a mercenary at all?" I can't help the question. Every time I glance his way, I see the way his eyes danced when he handed me his knife. The respect he had when I beat him. And now — this. The shift in attitude is dizzying.

"I don't see why it matters to you." The words are distracted, almost flippant, and that bothers me more than outright anger.

Irritation sizzles under my skin, heating my cheeks. "If we're going to be traveling companions, I thought it would be nice to actually talk to one another."

Mudslide dances beneath me, tossing his head and pulling at the bit, wanting to go faster than the steady walk we hold them to. I pat his neck, but he rolls his eyes back and flicks his ears at me. I have to clench my thighs tight around the saddle to keep from sliding off. Vaen watches, lips twitching in amusement at my struggles, and I'm half a moment away from saying or doing something I'll probably truly regret when Lyr pipes up.

"Talking is not Vaen's forte." He sounds like he's holding back outright laughter. "Neither are feelings."

"I did not know that was something any man was well versed in."

Lyr puts a hand over his heart, feigning hurt. "Ah, my lady, you wound me. I am exceptionally in touch with my feelings. Comes with having four sisters."

"I'm not a lady." It was never a title I was comfortable claiming. The rest of his words process, and I add, "*Four* sisters?"

Lyr nods sagely. "And one of them is my twin. Awful things. Always chattering around the house, always upset with a friend or each other or me. Usually me. It was a bit of relief to receive the call and be able to escape them for a bit."

"Fighting for your life every day against magic in your very blood is preferred to living with your kin?"

Lyr thinks about that for a minute, then gives a decisive nod. "Undoubtedly. At least the magic is thrilling."

Mudslide has maneuvered his way up to walk next to Lyr's mare. Vaen rides behind us, close enough to hear what we say, but I feel better to put his prying eyes behind me. It's easier to ignore him when he's out of my sight line. I realize belatedly that Lyr has fully managed to distract me from questioning Vaen further, and I can't help but wonder *why*.

"I'm not sure if you're intriguing or just plain insane," I tell Lyr.

He shrugs like it's not the first time someone has said that to him. "I think that's mostly true for every mage I've met."

"You trained in Haven. Doesn't that mean—"

"That I know all of them? Pretty much, yes." His grin is quick and easy. "The thing anyone who isn't a mage can really understand is that we'll choose it every single time. The magic. It doesn't matter how close to death we walk every single day.

We'll choose it, and keep choosing it, every dawn and dusk. It consumes us, holds us in thrall, the moment we're asked to carry it." He closes his eyes, a minute shiver making its way across his face. His rapture is bewitching.

"What's it like?"

The glory fades a little, returning Lyr to a semblance of normalcy. "What?"

"Knowing you might die any day."

He doesn't bat an eye at the harshness of the words. His gaze is unfocused as it sweeps our surroundings. "It was terrifying in the beginning. There's no way to prepare for it, that power flooding you, being told by some disembodied voice in a Crystal that now it's time to fight. But you're only fighting yourself, and the pull of the magic. The desire to use it more and more, to let it fully encompass you, until you *become* the magic..." He shivers. "But it gets easier every day, until you wake up one morning and it just *is*. There is no more fear because now you know how to walk that line, how to keep yourself from falling off into oblivion. You know how far you can push yourself, how much you can use. And you always want to do more, sure, but by then you've found your common sense, your boundaries, and you know how to say no more for today."

He looks at me once again. "Or you die. It's as simple as that."

The picture he paints is deceptively beautiful, and, truly, not that different from swordsmanship. Of knowing myself, how hard I can push my body until it gives in.

"Do any of your sisters have magic?" I ask.

Lyr inhales sharply. "Thank the light, no. I could barely tolerate them at home. Having to train with them? That sounds like a true nightmare." He dips his head a margin. "It might have been nice for the family, though. We don't live in a very prosperous area of Calire. The money I bring in as a mage helps, but a second mage might be transformative. A bigger house that doesn't half-slide into mud pits during heavy rains, a front yard for my mother to garden in, enough wood to heat all the rooms for the entire winter."

My tongue feels heavy and ungainly as understanding settles into the tight band around my chest. I try to think of something to say — I'm sorry seems so insignificant, so paltry when faced with this tendril of information — but the words jostle against one another, syllables tangling together so I can't even begin to speak them.

Lyr's eyes slide to mine, undoubtedly reading the shame, the discomfort. He nods at me. "What about you? Enough of my own blathering. You're not from Calire." It's a statement, not a question.

With the attention focused on me, my skin prickles with discomfort. It was easy at the Temple. We were all there for the same purpose, and backgrounds only mattered when it came to how much training you came with. What do I even tell him of? The apple orchards with their endless trees, rows bleeding into more rows, every breath tasting and smelling of them until it became sickly sweet? Of Liseah and I lying in the fields in the dead of night, whispering our secret wishes to one another, laying down plans of when we would leave and how we would tell our families? Of the endless sparring bouts, of my uncle, of all the yearning and effort I poured into my work?

I know what he really would want to know. What brought me to Calire... and what made it so I could leave so easily.

Panic grows, threatening to wash me under, sinking me slowly into a mire of my own dread with every breath I take. I've managed to avoid speaking the words aloud to everyone but Liseah. It was a fool's hope I could agree to this journey and never be forced to confront the truth.

Vaen abruptly pulls his mount up beside our own, giving

Lyr a wide eyed look of disbelief. "Do you mean to tell me you invited a stranger along without knowing *anything* about her?"

Lyr gives a sheepish grin, and if I wasn't the subject, I would admit Vaen has a point. As it is, it's all I can do not to shrink in on myself when both men turn their gazes to me, clearly waiting for an answer.

I could lie. It would be child's play to come up with some sort of story, whip together the barest details. But, inexplicably, I know that if I lie now, there will be a foundation of mistrust laid. I'm not willing to spend the next three months, or however long we're together, struggling to keep up with a mountain of lies, knowing what will happen should they find out the truth.

"I left Heron Hill to join the Knight's Temple." The words stumble over each other, but at least they're out. "I did not pass the midyear exams."

Lyr gives a sudden gasp, so loud that my first reaction is to grab for a weapon. It takes me entirely too long to realize his attention is not on our surroundings, but on me.

"I remember you." His voice is faintly shocked. "You saved those girls instead of helping the crown prince."

My mouth goes dry. It all clicks into place, *finally* — he was there. Of course he was there. His magic deals with illusions. He had asked for water, barely even glanced at me as I received my instructions. I don't remember looking at any of the mages when I left in disgrace. But of course he had watched me.

My stomach bottoms out. Saying it is one thing, but knowing he was *there*...

"You were the only one to save them." There is no condemnation in Lyr's voice. "Everyone else who failed, simply wasn't good enough. But you — you made a choice, and the crown prince lived, and so did the citizens."

"But that's not what a knight is supposed to do." The words ache.

Vaen's *tttch* is loud and abrasive, erasing the self-pity trying to swallow me and leaving only anger in its place. "Knighthood is a fool's dream." The words are harsh, bordering on cruel, and the look he gives me is so flat it steals my breath.

"Don't be a dick," Lyr says, soft but firm.

Vaen shakes his head like he can't comprehend us. "The crown will always use people for its own gain, and *only* for itself."

Lyr clears his throat. "You know, I still serve the queen and crown."

Vaen presses his lips together tightly, turning them thin and white. Without another word, he nudges his horse into a trot and quickly outpaces us.

"I guess he wants to scout ahead." Lyr sighs, like Vaen is an overgrown child having a tantrum. "Sorry about that. I didn't realize he would have such an adverse reaction to you. He doesn't trust a lot of people. Or like them, either."

"How did you meet him?" It's easier to keep my eyes on the countryside than to look at Lyr. The rolling hills are dotted with spots of brown, dry grass, and the small copses of trees have fully transformed into their autumnal counterparts, showering the ground with bursts of red, orange, and yellow color. Summer has fled, leaving a wind that weaves its way through our limbs, edged with cold. I realize, with a sinking stomach, that we'll likely be in the north for the winter. Heron Hill always got snow, like most of mainland Serabith, but nothing like the north.

"I heard of a situation he had gotten himself into and decided to help out, with the agreement he would lend me aid when I needed it. His varied skills are valuable to have." Although his tone is light, it sounds forced. Before I can comment on the ambiguity, Lyr adds, "That's his story to tell."

I shut my mouth and nod. I don't blame him; if our situations were reversed, I would not appreciate Lyr telling everyone my business.

The day passes slowly. We ride at a steady walk, trotting and cantering only occasionally to ensure our horses last the long journey. Mudslide does not appreciate being forced to walk and repeatedly tosses his head, yanking on the reins, so I have to always make sure they stay tight in my fists. I don't trust myself to keep my seat should he bolt.

Vaen keeps away for the most part, riding ahead or behind, and he finds our camp site for the first night. There are several small towns and waystations between here and Ulingard, but not enough to avoid sleeping on the road for the majority of our journey. I volunteer to gather firewood while Vaen brushes down the horses and Lyr sets up our bedrolls and readies the food.

I find enough broken branches from the scrubby grassland bushes that litter the area to build a small but adequate fire. When the fire is going, I help Lyr finish our food, warming up some cold sausage to eat on bread with melted cheese. It's simple but filling.

"Do you know how to set traps to catch rabbits?"

Vaen's voice startles me out of the stillness we'd fallen into, and I look to him blankly. Apparently taking that as my answer, he sighs heavily and rises. I'm quick to follow, brushing crumbs onto the ground.

"I've never had to before." I dust off my hands and force myself to meet his eyes. His disapproval sets fire to my bones, makes me want to spit and demand a fight right then and there. I swallow my instinct, and it burns bitter down my throat, settling into my stomach like a coal. I need to try to play nice. It's only the first damn day. "But I would like to learn how." It's true, too.

He hesitates, watching me for a long moment before

deciding I'm being honest, and nods once. He walks into the underbrush without looking back. I glance down at Lyr. "Will you be okay by yourself?"

He snorts and waves me off. "I set a perimeter charm around here before you got back with the wood. I'll be peachy."

A reminder that he is in no way defenseless.

I trot to catch up to Vaen, falling into step with him, our long strides nearly perfectly matched. He doesn't look at me, doesn't say anything, and I take a moment to watch him out of the corner of my eye. His jaw is set firmly, lips pressed in a thin line, annoyance coming off him in waves. Even through it all, he is breathtakingly handsome.

Not that it matters. He wouldn't touch me with a ten foot pole, and frankly, I'd sooner stab him to teach him a lesson in manners.

We don't go far from the camp. I can still see the flickers of our fire through the bushes, rivulets of smoke that float slowly skyward. Vaen crouches in the dirt, setting out rope. He gestures to the ground beneath him, and I bend down next to him.

"See how the grass is worn through here?" He points to a path I hadn't noticed before, but sure enough, the grass is bent away, like something has gone through this area countless times.

"This is one of their paths. One end of it connects to their burrow, the other probably to a water source." He grabs the rope and holds it up, then ties a knot around it, so it creates a loop that tightens when one end is pulled. I've made the knot countless times at home. "The rabbit will run through the loop, get caught, and choke itself trying to get free."

He ties the end of the rope around a strong stick, then drives it into the ground with a small grunt. It sinks several inches. Seeing his intention, I draw one of my daggers and turn it, using the pommel to hammer the stick further into the ground, until it cannot be pulled out easily. We do the same for a second stick across the path, and leave the loop hanging at rabbit height, stretched over their route.

This is repeated four more times in different areas, and by the time we finish, I'm confident in my ability to both spot rabbit trails and craft a snare for them. Vaen doesn't praise me, but he nods when we're done, tucking the last of the rope in a loop around one hand.

I ache with curiosity. Why was he a mercenary six months ago and now a thief? Rabbit snares mean he was in the country-side, at least for a bit. Why? How exactly did Lyr get him out of a situation?

As if sensing the burning need to question, Vaen halts and turns to me. It's nearly entirely dark now, twilight lying thick around us. For the first time since setting out this morning, a flash of fear runs through me. I'm strong, and confident in my ability to hold my own, but Vaen is obviously a competent warrior. Who knows what he's capable of? The fact is, I jumped into this with both feet, refusing to think about the conse-quences if I chose wrong.

I shift one foot back, finding better purchase, and leave my sword hand open and ready. Vaen notices and snorts loudly. "I'm not going to fucking attack you." His words are smoke and danger, and I don't relax.

"All I was going to say, is you should take the first watch tonight. I would rather be up early. And tomorrow is your turn for patrol duty."

He turns and walks back to camp, leaving me blinking in confusion. I have the feeling that planning guard duty is the closest thing to agreeing to my company I'll get from him.

Guard duty is an excellent time for thinking and not for much else. When I finally rouse Lyr for his shift, I'm bone tired and aching from the long day in the saddle, thighs rubbed raw and chafed. I drop into my bedroll gratefully and watch the fire sputter, almost out, until my eyes drift closed.

The next thing I know, someone grips my shoulder and shakes it violently, ripping me from sleep with a gasp of fear and pain as the gash on my arm screams its protest. I sit up, cursing, trying to rub the sleep out of my eyes, but the hand is still on my arm, fingers too tight, drawing a whimper from me despite myself.

"Get on your feet!"

Vaen's voice pierces the fog surrounding me, and I stumble, finally getting my feet under me.

"What—"

He presses my unsheathed sword into my hand and panic flits through me, banishing the last of sleep.

"Aberrations are coming."

EIGHT

The night crystallizes in startling clarity. The horses whinny and snort in panic, stamping their feet, pulling at the reins tied into the wooden stake driven deep into the ground. The fire had gone out sometime in the night, but a strange, dimly glowing ball now hovers over the cold ashes, casting just enough light to illuminate the scene unfolding before us.

The first thing I see is Vaen, his own sword drawn, striding away from me now that he's assured I'm fully awake. Second is Lyr, standing near the ball of light, hands out and facing the bushes around us. His face is pale and streaked with sweat, curls damp on his forehead. My gaze slides from him to, finally, the creature shambling towards us.

To say Aberrations are the figments of nightmares would be putting a lot of faith in someone's ability to imagine such a creature. The *thing* that approaches is easily over six feet tall, vaguely humanoid with spindly legs and arms that drag down far past its knees. There is a head atop its rough torso, but the face lacks any humanity. There are only holes where eyes should be, darker than night and ringed with red, as if the eyeballs had been plucked out and the blood left to dry. The jaw is longer than any normal creature's, leaving a great, gaping maw like a chasm, dark and unending. Its skin is a mottled conglomeration of yellows, grays, and greens, reminiscent of food that has been left out to rot. As if nothing more than candle wax, skin sloughs off the body in pinprick spots as well as great awning holes, exposing speckled white bone and dark red ligaments.

My body freezes, hand gripping my sword but unable to raise it. I tell my feet to move, to get in front of Lyr because that's my purpose, my reason, all I am right now is something made to protect him, but the soles of my boots are welded to the ground. Muscles lock and shake, bones pressing so hard against each other I swear I can hear them creaking.

"Fucking hell, girl, get your ass over there and do something!"

Vaen's shout breaks the spell enough for me to turn my head and look at him. He stands in front of Lyr, my supposed position, crouched and ready. Waiting for me to join him.

I look back to the Aberration in time to see it move. Whereas before, when it stumbled into the campsite, it moved slowly, almost painfully, something about Vaen's shout drew its attention. Before I can collect myself, the creature surges forward, breathtakingly fast. One of those unnaturally long arms swings up and out, and I see the wicked claws a second before they sweep away Vaen's weapon. The other arm grips him around the torso, fingers and claws long enough to wrap partway around his chest, before it flings him through the air, like he weighs nothing, simply an empty pile of clothing. I hear his body hit the ground several feet away, a shocked grunt forced out, then... nothing.

I don't dare take my eyes off the Aberration to see if Vaen is alive. The creature stands in front of Lyr now, twitching violently. Its claws click against one another, the sound like a blade being sharpened against stone. It will pounce at any minute. How can I manage to beat it? There's no way I'll be at Lyr's side before it strikes. Fear grips my insides, turning them to liquid. My breath is harsh and jagged, forced out from constricting lungs that can barely expand from the tightening band of iron around my chest.

I have never been so afraid in my entire life.

My eyes are drawn to a small movement — Lyr's hand at his side, the fingers stretching and rubbing lightly against one another, as if gesturing. I raise my gaze to his face and find his eyes darting between me and the Aberration. Once he knows he has my attention, he says clearly but softly, "Just like in Calire, okay?"

I'm confused — just like what? Before I can fully process his statement, the world explodes in color. All around us comes a symphony of popping and cracking as dozens of tiny, brilliantly bright lights spring into being before exploding in a shower of sparks.

Fireworks.

Or, that is, the illusion of them.

A guttural sound, something between a wail and a screech, erupts from the Aberration. It spins, head violently flinging side to side to try and focus on multiple lights at once.

Finally, like ice cracking, I force my body into movement. The first step is slow, almost ending with my face in the dirt, but the second is more sure, and by the third I'm sprinting. I reach the Aberration while it still spins in an aimless circle, arms arching out to swipe through the fireworks. They pop and disappear when touched, but there are always more to appear a heartbeat later.

The upward swing of my sword catches the Aberration off guard, sending it skittering back several paces and almost pushing it to one knee. Its left arm now dangles uselessly, sinew and bone barely attaching it to the body. The creature's head turns unnervingly fast, cracking with the movement, and those soulless eyes pin me to the spot. Whatever intelligence it has is enough to label me as the dominant threat.

It moves with that same breathtaking speed, but I'm ready for it. I duck under its swing, side stepping to get behind it, and fully cleave the left arm from its shoulder. The Aberration lets out another of those strange, undulating screams, half-lurching, half-falling forward, but I back away and slam my sword into that gaping maw. I realize half a second later it was a mistake as the creature's head rears back, yanking my sword from my grip. It clatters to the ground several paces away, streaked with red gore and yellow pus.

Daggers now, then. That makes things trickier. The Aberration has a far longer reach than I do; I will put myself in striking distance when I go in. But there's not another choice, and I don't give myself time to think about the consequences. I dive in, twin daggers clutched tightly. The first quickly finds its mark in the taut muscles behind the knee, and the Aberration falls forward onto its hands. The more wounded it is, the more animalistic it becomes, and it wildly tosses its entire body at me. One dagger slides down into the thing's gut, but I'm not fast enough to roll away. The creature's weight falls into me, overwhelming every sense even as the stench of rotting meat invades my nose. I hit the ground heavily, knocking the wind out of myself, and it's pure instinct that makes me fling up my arms over my head, my one remaining dagger a meager protection.

The Aberration catches the dagger on the side of its face, slicing into the stretching skin of its wide jaw. Gnashing teeth as long my finger and black as night catch my forearm in a blaze of pain. The dagger and our awkward angle keeps the creature

from being able to close down in a true bite. Rolling my hips
beneath me, I bring my knees up and push with as much
strength as I have, somehow managing to wedge a boot into the
Aberration's body with just enough leverage to roll out from
under it.

Luck is on my side, or Lyr managed to get my sword to me.
Whatever the reason, I find my weapon within reach. I snatch it
up, turning with it raised just in time to catch the Aberration as
it comes in for another strike. The blade slides through its
throat, immediately ending the guttural cries spewing from it.
There is no glory, no slow realization of its death. The life extin-
guishes, quick as a candle's flame, and the Aberration slides to
the ground, where black-red blood rapidly spreads beneath it. I
stab the sword straight into its skull for good measure, arms
aching with the strength it takes.

I stand over the body for several agonizing seconds, not
daring to blink in case it, inexplicably, moves. Lyr lightly
touching my arm is the only thing that finally draws my attention away.

"It's dead." He stares down at the Aberration as well, face
twisted with disgust. Sweat shines on his face, barely illumi-
nated now as the glowing orb dims and flickers.

I nod and lick my dry lips. I feel sticky with ichor, and my
arm burns from the thing's teeth. "What about Vaen?"

Lyr doesn't wait for me to finish my question before he's at
Vaen's side. He checks his pulse, shoulders dipping in relief as
he finds it. I let loose a breath I hadn't realized I was holding.

"Has a nice knot on his head, but otherwise okay, as far as I
can tell." Lyr fetches a water skin from our supplies and lets it
drip into Vaen's face. I follow suit, but take small, careful sips
from mine. My stomach roils, threatening to bring up dinner.
All I can see, smell, and feel is this malaise blood.

While Lyr works on waking Vaen, I busy myself cleaning my

weapons and saddling the horses. It isn't quite dawn yet, but there's no doubt about staying here.

"Do you think there will be more?" Tasks done, I approach the two men crouching on the ground. Vaen sits, head bent towards his knees, as Lyr passes a softly glowing hand over his bloody hair.

"Probably. They don't always travel in packs, but we're close to Haven, which is why this one was out wandering in the first place. There's always a plethora of magical energy, misused and sent into the universe, as the kids try to figure out their power." He snorts in disgust. "There's supposed to be Watchers and soldiers around the city, but they don't try too hard to actually kill the things if they wander off."

Lyr sits back, looking vaguely pleased and very tired. "There. Feel better?"

Vaen looks up, hand touching the back of his head tenderly. He nods. He does not even glance at me, and shame floods my veins. He's only hurt because of me. Because I froze up. Because I was too scared to move, like some kind of pathetic child.

"I didn't know you could heal." I focus on Lyr so I don't have to think about my damning hesitance.

Lyr stands wearily but almost loses his balance as he straightens. I grab his elbow, glad I used my uninjured arm when he grips my forearm tightly for a moment.

"Theoretically speaking, a mage can use their magic for anything." He walks slowly to his horse and leans on my shoulder as he mounts. "But some things take a lot more energy than others. Illusions, lights, that sort of thing are easy for me. Healing is not. But it can still be done."

He looks steadier on his horse, and I back up, hesitantly looking to Vaen to see if he needs my help as well. He's kicking dirt over the remains of our fire, looking as fit as ever, and I relax a hair.

I finish tying on our packs to the back of the saddles as Vaen approaches. I offer him the reins of his horse. The look he levels me puts ice to shame in its coldness. I open my mouth, useless words bubbling in my throat, but he speaks first.

"Never let that happen again." There is no grace in the lines of his face, in the eyes that pin me to the ground and make me feel so very small. Something in me wilts, threatening to dissolve altogether.

"Hey, relax." Lyr's voice cuts through the ice. "She killed the thing, didn't she?"

Vaen doesn't look away. I'm captured by his peculiar gray-green eyes and the reckoning in them. I know the truth. It doesn't matter that I rallied and killed the Aberration. All Vaen cares about is, when the moment came to strike, I hesitated.

Failure, that voices hisses in my head. *Another failure.*

I want to dissolve into the ground but— no. This isn't right.

I force myself to straighten rather than cower. I raise my chin, and I look in Vaen's eyes, and I counter his ice with my own fire.

"I apologize for my inactions leading to your injury." My voice wavers, so I stop, taking a fortifying breath. "But you aren't being fair." Surprise flares in his eyes, which quickly narrow. *Danger.* I ignore the warning and gesture to the Aberration. "I have no doubt that when faced with a creature of nightmares, most would pause."

There is no sympathy in his face as he leans in close. Warm breath mists over my face. A shiver rolls down my spine, another warning going off in my head. He is all power, anger in every line of his body, and I should be afraid, I know that. But I refuse to back down now.

"Then be better than most."

He turns without waiting for a response. It isn't a concession. We both know he's right. But I'm still proud of myself for standing my ground, however tenuous.

"Go check the traps," he orders, like I am nothing more than a servant, "then catch up. Or not. I don't care."

He turns his horse and starts off back down the road. Lyr looks from Vaen to myself, mouth agape. "Well, I care. Catch up quick, Raylen, okay?" He gestures, and a small orb appears over my shoulder, casting just enough light to illuminate my surroundings for a few feet.

Then Lyr turns too and follows the road to the north.

I stand alone in the campsite except for a very irritated horse and the stinking corpse of a monster made from terror. After a moment considering my options, I turn and do as I'm told. We need to eat, after all.

Only one hare has been caught. It looks big enough to give the three of us a good meal that night at least. I disassemble the other traps and roll up the rope. No sense in letting it go to waste. The hare I strap to the back of the saddle and hope it doesn't stink too bad before we can skin and cook it.

As I ride back through the campsite, I take one long moment to stare at the Aberration. Every instinct tells me to hurry past it, to avert my gaze from its wrongness. But I make myself look. When we come upon another one, I refuse to let the same mistake happen again.

When I finally move on, it's not because the Aberration has become any less strange or horrifying. Looking at it still fills me with unease. But if I stay any longer, I'm afraid I'll have too much trouble catching up to Vaen and Lyr, and I won't be left behind.

I will do better. I have to. There's no other option.

I make it a dozen paces before I remember the wound the Aberration caused. I pull Mudslide to a halt, awkwardly holding up my arm closer to the light Lyr left. My sleeve is still wet with blood, but it doesn't drip, giving me hope the worst is passed. Now that I've paused to assess it, it starts throbbing with a sharp ache I've somehow ignored till now. I know I should ask Lyr for healing, but it feels wrong, after he already used his energy to heal Vaen from my mistake. I can last a few hours, surely.

I use a spare bit of cloth to bind the wound, then steer Mudslide to the north road and urge him into a steady trot.

The day passes excruciatingly slowly. Except for the measly hour when we skin, cook, and eat the hare, I spend the day cantering ahead, scanning the road, waiting for Lyr and Vaen to catch up, then repeating the process. It's lonely, although I doubt Vaen's company would be preferable. He ignores me every time we cross paths, and I end up reporting my nonexistent findings to Lyr. He gives me sympathic glances but doesn't get involved.

I fill the long hours thinking of questions for Lyr. I know so little of the intricacies of magic and its history, of the dangers, of the Aberrations themselves — it's time to educate myself.

I refuse to be a liability in any form.

By the time dusk has settled on the edges of the world, I spy the best thing I've seen all day: a waystation. The idea of a bed, hot food, and protection from natural and unnatural elements is almost overwhelming.

Lyr agrees, road weariness vanishing as we come into the small stable yard.

"Thank the light for a bath," he half-moans, handing his mount over to the waiting stable boy. He doesn't have much room to talk, as I'm the one still half-covered in Aberration blood, but I keep that thought to myself.

I dismount, hitting the ground heavily, surprised when my knees threaten to buckle. I hadn't realized how tired I was in the saddle, but the weariness settles into my bones now. Everything aches even worse than yesterday, and I can barely lift my injured arm.

It takes more effort than I want to admit to walk over to the stable hand and give over my reins, and several long moments to unbuckle my pack. My left hand doesn't want to work, the fingers slow to respond, so I do everything one handed.

By the time I finally sling the pack over my shoulder, Lyr and Vaen are already inside. The two steps leading up to the front door seem impossibly high; I almost lose my balance on the second one and have to put a steadying hand on the doorframe. My hand hits the wood harder than expected, and the stab of pain that shoots through my entire left arm is breathtaking. I gasp aloud, snatching my hand back, looking at the door to see if there was a nail I might have caught myself on. There is no mark on my palm, nor on the wood, but it continues to throb.

The inn is only half full, but those inside are already rowdy, road-weary lines slowly erased drink by drink. Lyr and Vaen have claimed a small table, drink and food in front of them. Did I really take that long? The idea of food makes my stomach churn, although not two hours ago I would eaten practically anything.

I stop by their table, gripping the back of the free chair with my right hand. Sweat crawls down my back. Everything in the inn is too loud, hammering on my head until it pounds the rhythm back.

"Raylen?"

I focus on Lyr. He's staring at me with worry, and I have the feeling that was not the first time he said my name.

"Is there a bathhouse attached?" The words are mine, but the voice is distant, abnormal.

"I think there's a tub and pitcher in the room. Just cold I'm afraid." He frowns, eyes flickering over me. "Are you okay?"

"Cold is good." Now that I have a moment to be still, I realize I'm shaking, heat pressing from inside. My skin is hot and too tight, I want to peel it off, to let the cold night air inside and ease the buzzing, I want—

"Raylen."

My eyes snap back to Lyr. He's out of his seat now, hovering next to me, face too close to mine. I blink, slow, wanting to back away from the uncomfortable proximity, but I can't convince my body to listen. Out of the corner of my eye, Vaen puts down his drink. It's the first time since we left the campsite he's looked at me.

"Something's wrong," I say. The words slur and meld together, barely coherent.

"Did something happen?" He reaches for me, hand brushing my arm, and it's everything I can do not to scream. A thousand needles push against my skin, lighting me on fire.

The pain pushes me back into coherence.

"The Aberration bit me." I try to roll up my sleeve, but even touching the fabric is too much. "It was fine before, I bound it as best I could on the road."

"Fuck." Lyr gestures to Vaen, who rises immediately. "Some of them carry poison in their blood and bite. Why didn't you say something immediately?" Then, anger still lacing his words, he says to Vaen, "Help her up the stairs. We need to get her to the room. I can't heal it, but I can draw the poison out."

"Can you walk?" Vaen's tone is brusque, but there is no heat to his words.

"Well I fucking better. I'm not letting you carry me." Just the idea makes me burn with shame.

I think I see the smallest upturn of his lips, but it vanishes before I can be sure.

He loops his arm around me, under my shoulders to take the majority of my weight. I don't want to, but I lean into him, realizing after the first step there is no way I can manage alone. The room spins with each movement, the light from the torches throwing flames onto the walls that dance and shimmer into a dizzying haze.

The staircase to the upstairs rooms is just barely wide enough for us to walk up together. I'm thankful for that, as well as Vaen's surprising patience as it takes an excruciatingly long time to haul myself to our room. He never questions if I can do it, just keeps me moving even when my feet threaten to stop.

By the time we get to the room, I'm shaking worse than ever, breathing fast and shallow. Vaen sits me on one of the two beds, where I focus on not passing out while Lyr closes and locks the door quickly behind us. He stoops before me, saying something to Vaen that I don't catch, before working on the ties at the front of my tunic.

"You have something on underneath?" I'm grateful for the surprising thoughtfulness. He barely waits for my nod before finishing the ties, sliding the tunic over my head and unceremoniously stuffing my good arm through. He pauses when the only part that remains is the left sleeve, then crouches down so he's between my knees, face almost level with mine.

"Can you listen to me?" I nod again, because though the world spinning, his words are the only thing tying me to reality. "Okay good. Once we get your shirt off, we're going to move fast, because this is going to hurt like hell." His eyes are serious, and although the words should scare me, I find a strange calm-

ness settle over me, reassured by the lack of panic in Lyr's open
face.

"Vaen is going to hold you down and make sure you don't
bring the whole inn down with noise." I feel the thief move
behind me, his warm body pressed suddenly against my back. I
want to arch away, but I can't bring myself to move. Lyr's gaze
forces me into stillness. "I am going to take off the cloth and do
my best to draw the poison out. It isn't going to be pretty. I
don't have the strength to heal the wound, but I think you'll be
fine once we handle the poison. Don't force yourself to stay
awake. Okay? Do you understand me?"

I do, but questions burn at my mouth. What if he doesn't
get all the poison? Is he strong enough for this, or will it hurt
him too? How can I trust that everything is going to be okay?

There are no answers. So instead, I gather a fistful of blankets with my good hand. An arm snakes around my shoulders,
pressing me tight to Vaen's chest. I can feel his heart against my
back, steady and calm, unlike the wild, thrashing beast in my
own chest.

"Go," I whisper.

Lyr doesn't wait for another word. He takes a knife and
cleanly cuts away my sleeve, but the fabric is sticky with old
blood and clings to my skin. It hurts as he pulls it away, but the
pain is manageable. I focus on my breathing rather than the
rushing in my head as I watch him cut through the hasty
bandages I wrapped around the wound this morning. That
hurts more, and my head swims. Copper explodes in my mouth
as I bite the inside of my cheek.

My arm is a ragged mess of blood and black ichor that
weeps from the deep gash. It should have congealed by now,
but black-red sickness oozes from the open laceration. My
breathing rattles in my chest as panic spirals. Lyr places a hand

over the wound, careful not to touch it, and his skin seems to take on a faint blue-white aura as simultaneously the most immense pain I have ever felt in my life slams into me. Knives drag from inside, cutting their way through muscles and ligaments and organs, leaving a thousand burning fires in their wake.

I scream, a primal sound of fear and pain, but Vaen's hand covers my mouth before the sound is fully realized. He cups some kind of fabric over me, and I scream into it, uncaring how loud it still is, how the blanket smells of hard soap and now my sweat and blood.

I keep screaming as the black ichor is pulled from the wound, pulled from every piece of me, as every organ and blood vessel is stripped and pulled apart, as *I'm* pulled apart. I'm vaguely aware of Vaen's arms tightening, holding me in place, while every muscle tenses and tries to *get away* from the pain.

I scream as the colors bleed together, vision melting like the candle wax skin of the Aberration, until finally the welcome darkness steals over me.

Awareness returns slowly. The first thing that comes back is the pain, but it's lesser now, a sharp throbbing that is manageable. I'm lying in bed, naked from the waist up except for my broad breast band, but soft blankets have been pulled over me. My left arm lies out of the covers, hotter than it should be, and I lie utterly still as I feel my heartbeat in those veins, the fever in my skin. Still, despite everything, the wound lacks the sinister intensity from earlier.

Someone is snoring loudly in the other bed. I roll to my side, the movement slow but manageable, to see Lyr sprawled with arms above his head, mouth open in the deepest type of sleep.

Next to him, sitting against the wall, is Vaen, reading a small leather bound book by the wavering light of a single, dim candle. He looks up at my movement, eyes immediately finding mine. The anger from the day is gone, and although I wouldn't call it concern in his face, he certainly doesn't look ready to bite my head off again.

"Is Lyr okay?" My voice is soft and cracks on the words. My throat hurts from screaming.

"He's fine." Vaen glances down at the sleeping mage, who hasn't so much as twitched at our voices. "Exhausted, but fine. Mages recover quickly."

I can't keep the relief out of my voice. "Thank the light."

He continues to look at me, as if searching for something. "Why didn't you say something?"

I start to shrug, but that hurts my arm, so I stop. I debate about lying for a moment, but I'm too tired. And after the day we've had, I owe Vaen the truth.

"I was too ashamed to, after you were hurt because of my hesitance." *Cowardice.* The word sears through me as much as the poison did. "I wasn't sure Lyr would be up for another healing, and I didn't want to call attention to another one of my mistakes." It's an ugly, vain, stupid reason, but Vaen doesn't say anything. "As the day went on, it became less and less important." I crack a smile. "I'm really good at lying to myself."

That might be one of the truest things I've admitted aloud to anyone, much less a stranger.

Vaen huffs and turns back to his book. "It was fucking stupid. Don't be a martyr again." His words lack any real heat, and I can almost hear the thing unsaid: allies don't keep secrets from each other.

My eyes are already starting to slide closed again. As I drift off to sleep, this time peacefully, the last thing I see is Vaen's angular face over his book, and I can't help but miss the heat of his body pressed against mine.

CHAPTER
NINE

Our days fall into a steady rhythm that, although boring, is at least comforting in its regularity. Vaen and I trade off scouting days, which are by far the more mind-numbing hours. I prefer the days I spend with Lyr, listening to him complain about Calire and Haven and the intricate politics of mages. For the most part, I nod along politely and try to slip in questions when I can about the explosive side effects of magic, or where it comes from in the first place — which is inconclusive at best, as no one has made much headway into studying the Crystals. Most of it goes over my head, but it's still better than the oppressive silence of the forests and hills as we scout.

As we travel further north, the landscape transforms from rolling hills spotted with low brush to sparse clumps of trees that steadily thicken as the days go by. Between the thickets are flat stretches of grassy plains, dotted here and there with rocky hillsides, small caves we don't venture into.

Autumn grips the land firmly, giving us pleasant days with plenty of sun, brisk breezes that promise more is soon to come, and increasingly chilly nights. We sleep close to the fire on days without an inn, making sure to gather enough wood throughout the day that it doesn't burn out completely. Lyr is reluctant to use magic to keep the fire going, claiming the wards he sets around us are more important.

I don't disagree. Despite the rumors of Aberrations, we do not run across another one the further north we go. Lyr is disappointed, but I'm secretly glad. The wound on my arm takes days to heal even part way, and I'm not eager to repeat the experience. I want to say that of course I won't freeze again, now knowing what they are like, that they *can* be killed, that *I* can kill them, but insidious doubts try to worm their way into my thinking.

What if I'm not as strong I thought I was?

Vaen isn't exactly pleasant company, but we spend so little time together it doesn't really mean much. The outright hatred is gone, replaced by a simmering hostility targeted mostly at me and sometimes at Lyr. Any resolve to keep my mouth shut vanishes at the first snarky comment, and we end up spitting at each other like angry cats most of the time. It's always over something ridiculous, meaningless, and Lyr has taken to providing commentary as we bicker until, inevitably, one of us grows annoyed and rides off to scout.

Three times in the fourteen day journey scouting proves invaluable when we find signs of bandits. They don't scare me, not like the Aberrations — these are just men, after all, and I know my strength compared to theirs. But Lyr insists we give them a wide berth, cloaking us in a simple illusion to avoid a scuffle. Part of me aches for the chance to prove myself, to show that I'm *not* a coward, but I cannot deny the logic of avoiding fights when we can. I run through my sparring forms for twice as long on those nights, though.

And then, without preamble, we arrive at Ulingard.

We had seen the smoke from homes curling into the sky for

quite some time, but it's still somewhat of a shock to finally reach our destination. Ulingard lies nestled just beyond the thickest forest we've traversed so far. A last barrier between central Serabith and the true north. Although unable to compete in size to Calire or even Kestral, Ulingard is nonetheless larger than the villages we passed on our way here, and certainly bigger than Heron Hill, with multiple storied buildings clustered around the town green. My father always said you could tell the size and prosperity of a town based on the height of its buildings. With that measure, Ulingard seems to be doing well for itself.

A simple wall of stone and dark hewn wood surrounds the town, a narrow parapet devoid of any guards winding at the top of it. The gate stands open, a bored looking Watcher positioned in front of it.

Beyond Ulingard stretches a wide swath of land, similar to what we've seen on the journey. Copses of trees, grassy plains, small outcroppings of rock. The grass is dotted plentifully with sheep and small, hardy mountain ponies. The forest thickens after that, a wide, seemingly impenetrable barrier of dark trees, their dull trunks close together, evergreen branches twining together. The longer I stare at the forest, the tighter the tension in my shoulders grows. Nothing seems to move within, but I can't shake the feeling that if I look long enough, the very trees themselves will meld and bend into some horrifying creature.

Lyr gives a loud sigh, one hand slapping his thigh, the sound enough to draw my attention away from the trees. "I thought we'd never get here."

I echo the sentiment. All I want is a hot bath, a hot meal not cooked over a campfire, and a bed free of rocks digging into my spine.

By the time we reach the gate, the Watcher has straightened, eyes bright with interest as she surveys us. She's young, probably close to Lyr's age or even my own, and short, with long strawberry blonde hair tied into a complicated series of braids. Despite the innocence of her stature, she holds her spear tightly, and the slightest shifting of her feet tells she's ready to defend her post.

"Hello," Lyr calls out, gallant and charming as ever.

That first glimpse he shows strangers is little more than guile aimed to elicit sympathy and ease. The more days we are together, the more I come to wonder just how much is the truth, and how much is merely a front. The Lyr I've come to know is hungry — for knowledge, for power, for magic.

I wonder if that hunger will turn to devour him in the end.

The Watcher does not soften, wariness remaining in every line. "What brings you to Ulingard? We do not get many visitors, especially this close to the change of the season."

It is indeed brisk. I hope Lyr has enough coin to buy us all winter clothes, because what I own will not be sufficient as the days grow shorter.

Lyr puts on a faintly outraged face. "Why, that's shocking! I've heard the beauty of the north is incomparable. I would have thought people would be knocking down your door to come and marvel."

The Watcher doesn't even crack a grin. I can't help but laugh, but turn the sound into a cough when Lyr shoots me a dirty look. I catch Vaen hiding his own grin behind his hand, and we share a conspiratorial look. The lack of animosity makes hope flare hot in my chest. Maybe we can become... what? Allies? Friends? Something more than our current argumentative selves.

Lyr clears his throat, gesturing vaguely in our direction. "My allies and I have heard many rumors surrounding the city. We wished to investigate and separate truth from lies. Perhaps we can even lend aid and get to the bottom of the mystery."

The Watcher immediately pales at his words. Her eyes skitter to the side, as if begging her to turn and look at the forest at the city's back, but she stays rooted to the spot, almost quivering with the restraint. "Well, you're more foolish than you look then." The harshness in her voice makes Lyr take a step back. "If you think you'll gain glory, then you'll be dead as well as foolish."

Vaen and I exchange looks again. The stories Lyr heard were strange and disturbing, but I admit, I did not actually believe most of them. It seems I may have been wrong.

"I mean no offense." Lyr holds his hands up as if attempting to placate a wild animal. "Please. We're simple travelers, looking to do a few good deeds and help out our fellow men. I have connections here as well, to the Mage Sunillen." Not exactly the truth, but Lyr could claim any mage has a connection to their brethren through the bond of magic.

If anything, the Watcher's face darkens. "The mage? He stays holed up in his house, refusing to admit his magic is the cause of the Aberrations."

Lyr raises both eyebrows. "Is that a fact?"

She spits on the ground, and Lyr steps back hastily. "There's no other possible answer beyond magic."

I step forward before Lyr or Vaen can stop me. "So what exactly is happening?"

The Watcher focuses on me, her eyes as light and blue as a summer sky. The naivety of her appearance is at odds with the deep smudges under her eyes, the darkening of her gaze as it holds mine.

Run, those eyes say. *Run as fast as you can, and don't look back.*

But of course I don't, and she breaks eye contact first, looking away and into the city.

"There are a few inns in town, to host the merchants we get in the summer months for the wood trade, but your best bet is

The Night's End. That's where the locals gather. The Watchers, too, when they want to. I'm sure you can get first hand accounts there."

Lyr gives her a dazzling smile and a sweeping, ridiculous bow, drawing her attention back to him. "Thank you, my dear. We appreciate it. Do you happen to know where Mage Sunillen's house is, while we're at it?"

She gestures vaguely towards the far side of the village. "He doesn't reside in the town walls. He's made his home just past us. It's impossible to miss."

Now that she's drawn attention to it, I see the peaked rooftops of a house, larger than anything the town boasts, nestled next to a rocky outcropping where the edge of the forest dips towards the plains.

Lyr gives his thanks and begins to step into the village, but he stops when the Watcher adds, "Tread carefully. Tensions are high right now, especially concerning magic."

Lyr holds up a hand, acknowledging her words as both a warning and a promise, then mutters as soon as we're out of earshot, "Fucking hell, she needs to lighten up with the end of the world warnings."

"Better to prepare us than throw us to the wolves."

He shrugs like it's the least of his concerns and doesn't bother to argue.

We come into the town green, where the majority of businesses are arranged in a semi-circle around a large square of grass. Unlike Heron Hill, where the businesses were little more than stalls set up near their owner's house, Ulingard is large enough to boast actual shop fronts. Most of them are simple, essential businesses: a seamstress, a blacksmith, a leather worker, a baker. Shops selling a variety of food and home items. Many of them are closed for the day, windows shuttered and dark. The few people still weaving through the streets give us long, lingering looks, but don't try to speak. I watch a woman, heavy with child, slowly make her way home with a basket of bread discards and bruised fruit. She meets my eyes for the briefest second before looking away quickly, back bowed, pace quickening.

There is a building dedicated to the wood the town claims its prosperity from: stacks of cut wood are layered by the door, brought in only recently, and a man sits just by it, carving an intricate bird out a small discarded piece. I stop to watch a moment, fascinated by its beauty. The carver's hands move quickly and confidently, whittling knife sending smooth curls of wood to rest on the floor in a growing pile.

I can't help but look at my own hands, large and long fingered and covered with callouses. Would they be clever enough to make something of such beauty? All my life, the beauty I sought lay in the sword and its delicate dance. The search for knighthood and the fight with the Aberration showed me an uglier truth in what I practiced. This bird, though — there is nothing ugly or bloody or deceptive in this small carving.

"Is there any particular reason you're staring at a wooden bird like you're about to cry?"

I jump and turn to Lyr, immediately flushing. My eyes sting but I blame the intensity of my gaze and not the strange, melancholy ache in my chest.

"It's beautiful. I admire craftsmen who can create beauty where there was none before."

Lyr smiles and holds out a hand, letting a tendril of pinkish light appear. It twists and turns, sinuous in its movements, minuscule golden sparks hovering in the air around it.

Vaen snorts and slaps his hand, dispelling the light and earning a yelp for his trouble. "Show off. Do you think it's a wise idea to let your true nature show the minute we step into the village?"

I look around, but the only one watching is the carver, who has stopped his work to stare narrow-eyed at Lyr — not with fear, like I foolishly expected, but with distrust.

Lyr doesn't notice the carver. He gives a carefree shrug. "Why should I hide who I am? That's like asking Raylen to disguise her sword. Mages are not outlawed in Serabith, or even particularly disliked."

"I disagree," I mutter at the same time as Vaen says, "Don't be a fucking idiot, these people think they're being harried by magical beasts. Throwing around your magic is only adding fuel to the fire."

I don't miss the insinuation that this is all in their heads, that a simple explanation is waiting at the shadow's edge. I have a feeling, deep in my twisting gut, that whatever is happening in Ulingard is far more complicated and dangerous than Vaen expects.

"He's right." I put a hand on Lyr's shoulder and push him towards The Night's End. "Come on. We can figure out our next steps once we get settled."

The inn is nothing special, landing somewhere between the nice ones of Calire and the better-than-the-hard-ground ones of the road. There are a handful of villagers scattered around, nursing their drinks and talking in low voices. As soon as the door swings shut behind us, I feel their eyes on me, assessing, observing, judging. Some are quick to look away when I meet their gazes, but others lock eyes, brows lowered, the challenge clear. They don't trust us, but it's more than that. There is a darkness to their faces, a worry that goes deeper than rural villagers wary of outsiders.

My heart sinks a little when Lyr asks for a single room and pays for a tenday up front. I miss having my own room. I miss

Liseah. Hell, at this point, I just miss other women in general. I never was one to shy away from male friendships. They go hand in hand with being a knight, with choosing a male dominated profession. But there's something special about the bond between women, born of blood and pain and the soul crushing weight of expectations. Of trying to straddle two realities: to be proper enough to satisfy the world, and to be yourself enough to make the little girl you once were proud.

I'm also really, really tired of listening to them snore.

"Raylen, do you want to go up for a bath first?"

I perk up instantly at that and practically bound forward to snatch the key from Lyr. He laughs. "I'll take that as a yes."

"I stink." It's the truth, but I'm feeling petty, so I add, "But I'm sure you can't tell under your own stench."

I take the stairs two at a time. Vaguely I hear someone laughing, but when I glance back, Lyr and Vaen are settling at a table, drinks already in hand. Good. That will give me a decent amount of time then.

Unlike some of the other inns we stopped at, where the "bath" was a basin of ice cold water and a wash rag, The Night's End has a proper tub, squeezed into the corner of the room next to the dresser. There's a pipe over one end of it; when I twist the knob on it, a rush of water starts filling the tub. The water here isn't exactly hot, but lukewarm is better than nothing and feels like bliss itself when I lower myself into the tub.

I take my time, going over every inch of skin with a soft cloth filled with sweet smelling soap. It feels like an avalanche of dirt is dislodged from my hair alone. I haven't washed it but once since Calire, and it shows. It's grown in the flurry of change since the Temple, long enough to tuck behind my ears now. I should probably cut it again, but I have to admit, I like the feeling of the dark strands against my cheeks.

A heavy knock at the door draws me from my vain thoughts, and I realize the water has grown cold.

"Are you ever coming down to dinner? Lyr's worried you've drowned."

The door creaks open, Vaen unabashedly entering. There's a moment of frozen surprise as our eyes meet, and I don't even have the chance to sink below the lip of the tub — not that it would make a difference with his vantage point. Flames erupt across my face, lending their heat to my words.

"Decent people would wait for a response before opening the door."

I don't know what I expect, but it's certainly not an insufferable smirk and raised eyebrows, as if he's the innocent one.

He doesn't withdraw, and has the audacity to lean against the doorway, arms crossed but muscles loose. *Relaxed.*

Fucking bastard.

When Vaen speaks, it's in a slow drawl, amusement dripping from each syllable. "Since when have you thought me to be a decent man?"

The word "never" is on my tongue, but the moment vanishes as Vaen slips from the doorway, letting the door fall shut behind him without another word.

I'm still fuming when I make my way downstairs, wearing my only pair of clean clothes — soft brown breeches and a yellow tunic. I hate yellow, but my sister spent hours sewing small blue flowers around the hem and the sleeves. I rarely wear it, for fear of dirtying the delicate material so impractical to spar outdoors in. The outfit makes me feel strangely girlish, like I might actually exist as a person outside of the sword and my skills.

The inn is busier than it was when I left, the noise a dull roar that ebbs and flows like storm tossed water. I ask a barmaid to send a plate of food and a drink to Lyr's table before edging around a group of boisterous villagers, tankards over spilling with ale, to sit across from my companions.

Lyr rises almost as soon as I'm settled. He's flushed, mugs scattered in front of him. The excess surprises me, but I keep my mouth shut. It's none of my business. Everyone has their own ways to settle down.

"I am going to bathe, and then I'm going to come back down to find someone to fuck," he announces. His words slur and trip over themselves, too loud even in this din.

Vaen and I exchange looks. The only time we're ever on the same page is when it comes to our benefactor. "Be back in a bit," he mutters to me, then rises and claps Lyr on the shoulder. It almost sends him stumbling to the floor, and I hide my grin behind my hand. "Come on, I'll help you up the stairs."

"I don't need help." But Lyr allows Vaen to usher him to the stairs anyway.

And he was worried about *me* drowning. I accept my plate of food from the barmaid, who wrinkles her nose at the mess on our table and begins to load her platter with empty mugs and plates.

"Well now, who might you be? I've never seen such a pretty face in Ulingard."

It takes an embarrassingly long minute to realize the words are spoken to me. I turn in my chair, looking up... and up. The man looks to be around my age, with a mane of golden hair falling to his shoulders and a carefully trimmed beard that does nothing to hide his strong jaw. His eyes are blue, bright and pinned directly on me. But more than his features, I notice just how big he is. Even standing at my full height, he would tower over me by half a foot, making him one of the tallest men I've seen in my life. He is clearly muscled, arms bulging against the sleeves of his simple, sturdy working clothes.

While I try to formulate a reply, the innkeeper passes by

with an armful of drinks and a cheery laugh, eyes almost wicked as he watches us. "Leave the girl alone, Haith, she just got in this afternoon."

Haith grins, his eyes never leaving me. I feel pinned to the spot, unable to move from the magnetic tension of his gaze. Maybe it's because of already being seen naked once today, but my skin feels warm and tight, and I am acutely aware of every ounce of clothing touching me. It's all I can do to shove the carnal yearning away. This man is a stranger. I can admire his beauty, but I'm certainly not going to pant after him like some animal or heartsick idiot.

"As Dorrn so kindly introduced me, my name is Haith." He pauses, clearly waiting.

"Raylen." There is none of the weak-kneed wilting I feel present in my voice, thank the light.

"Well, Raylen." My name sounds like a forbidden delicacy on his tongue. I feel myself flushing again. Haith clearly notices it as well, because his smile grows till it threatens to swallow me whole. I don't know if I would try to stop it, even if I could. "What are you doing in Ulingard?"

He gestures to the table, silently asking, and I nod. Haith settles in Vaen's abandoned seat. I risk a glance at the stairwell, but the thief has not yet reappeared. I don't know why I care. I'm allowed to talk to people. Fuck, I'm allowed to flirt if I want, and more.

"My companion has business here," I answer. I wonder how much to reveal, only now realizing Lyr never set clear boundaries on what is to be public knowledge. Erring on the side of caution, I add, "He has business with Mage Sunillen."

Haith nods, some of the joviality slipping away. "Lots of people have business with Sunillen these days."

I frown. "What does that mean?"

"He has come under a lot of scrutiny since the creatures

started appearing." Haith shrugs, as if the matter isn't serious, but the darkening of his eyes and the air of forced casualness reveal otherwise.

My breath catches, and I lean forward, almost too close, but I don't draw back. "So they're real? We've heard rumors... we came to see the truth of that matter as well." My hand finds my sword hilt absentmindedly. "See if we can help."

Haith nods again. His gaze dips to my lips, then back to my eyes but not nearly quickly enough to be anything but deliberate. My heart stutters. *Don't be silly. He's just looking for a fresh fuck.*

Maybe that's true. But would that be such a bad thing?

Somehow I manage to force my eyes away from his own lips, full and firm, and stop thinking about what they would feel like long enough to ask, "Can you tell me anything about what's been happening?"

Before Haith can answer, a hand falls on his shoulder. The peaceful bubble that surrounded us pops, returning the inn's noise full force. "Come on, you bastard, you promised to buy us another round!" The man, clearly in the joyful stage of inebriation, slaps Haith on the back.

Haith gives me an apologetic look as he rises. "I hate to cut this short, but these idiots are the reason I'm here in the first place. I have a small shop by the smithy where I sell my jewelry, and tomorrow I'll be in the forge to work on some pieces. Your presence would be a happy interruption."

I watch as he rejoins his companions, so I see him glance back over his shoulder at me. He grins when he catches me staring, and I can't help it.

I smile back.

CHAPTER
TEN

Although the beds are the most comfortable we've slept in since Calire, my sleep is restless. I dream of warm limbs twisted around each other, teasing tongues that know exactly where to dip and stroke, panting breaths that end in shuddering moans.

I wake drenched in sweat and aching with need. But it's still dark, and Lyr's snores have turned to deep seated rumbles. I can't bring myself to even think about touching myself with Lyr and Vaen within arm's reach. So I press my legs together tightly and turn away from them, urging the dream to vanish, wishing my skin didn't shiver with want.

The need eventually morphs back into drowsiness, but now I dream I'm in a forest, speckled with sunlight that filters through leaves bigger than my hand. There is no path to be seen. The ground beneath me is soft, carpeted with a bed of moss and loose dirt, clusters of cherry red mushrooms dotted throughout like wildflowers. It feels serene. Peaceful. I walk slowly, letting a hand drag across the rough bark of a tree. The branches sway above me, whispering their secret for happiness in a language I cannot fathom.

The further I walk, the dimmer the forest becomes. Soon the branches grow too close together, leaves overlapping one another, blocking out the bright sunlight. The moss turns dark, crinkling brown around the edges, and the mushrooms rot before my eyes, becoming flaccid and sickly white, caps curling in on themselves. I stumble to a stop, trying to look back, to see if I can still see the beautiful place, but my body is slow, each movement excruciating. I feel heavy, weighted down, everything begging for sleep. If I just lay down and sleep, I'll forget the wrongness, the ever deepening darkness. Perhaps I'll even forget myself.

Something tells me to stop, to fight the drag of sleep. I try to turn again, this time succeeding. But there is no sun behind me, no warm dappled clearing. Instead, a face leers at me, mouth open wide, the dark cavernous chasm framed by knife sharp, black teeth. Teeth that gnash, thirsting for blood, knowing I'm right there, easy prey.

Can't run, a voice, not my own, whispers. It twines through me, caressing exposed skin like a lover's touch.

I try to stumble back, *get away away away*, but the creature moves forward, jaws opening impossibly wide, darkness rushing out to sweep over me, through me, devouring me in a single terrible moment. The panic and fear slam into me, obliterating all other thoughts, a wave that drags me under until I drown.

This time I wake with a scream, sitting straight up in bed, once again sweat-soaked but now shaking not from longing but from that all-consuming fear.

"What's wrong?"

I turn. It's still dark, Lyr now lulled into complete silence in the deepest part of sleep. Vaen props himself up on one elbow, looking at me over Lyr's unconscious form. The only light comes from the dim glow of the moon peering through the wood-slat windows, not quite enough to illuminate his face beyond the vaguest impressions of features.

Embarrassment immediately courses through me. I shake my head, dragging a hand through sweat-soaked locks. "Nightmare. It's fine. Sorry for waking you."

Vaen waits a moment, as if inviting me to say more, to tell him the awfulness of the Aberration and how I can't shake the terror that grips me every time I think of one.

But I don't, and eventually he just nods and lays back down.

I stay awake until dawn, staring at the ceiling and imagining all the ways those creatures can be killed.

Compared to the frivolity of last night, breakfast is a dreary affair. Usually the most talkative of us, Lyr spends most of it huddled in his cloak, shoulders hunched, wincing whenever someone walks by too loudly. Another time I might have teased him about it or offered some of the remedies the drunkards in Heron Hill liked the best. Today, however, I feel irritable from the restless night, the dreams that refuse to leave my thoughts even now, and sit silently, staring into my mug of dark coffee.

"Well then." Vaen clears his throat, glancing from me to Lyr and back again. He seems vaguely irritated by our silence, at being forced to start the conversation. "Lyr, what's your plan for today?"

"Die." The mage takes a tentative sip from his own cup of coffee, steam curling around his scruffy cheeks.

"Can we not be so dramatic?"

"Can we not be an insufferable asshole incapable of human feeling?"

Rather than take offense, Vaen leans back in his chair with crossed arms, a grin stealing across his face. For a moment, looking at him, I'm reminded not of the grumpy thief that has been a constant thorn in my side, but the mercenary I met so many months ago, laughing when I beat him soundly and rubbed it in their faces. The words teeter on my tongue, begging to be allowed out.

What monsters reappeared in your life?

But they slip back down my throat, oily and thick, when Vaen says, "You've called me a lot worse over the years. Now, what are we doing today?"

Lyr sighs, takes another fortifying sip of coffee, and puts his mug down at last. "I would like to approach Mage Sunillen and see what I can find out from him." Then, to my surprise, he tilts his chin to me. "Raylen can go with me. I want you to see what you can find out about the town and the area around it. Talk to some of the wood workers if you want, the ones that go out of Ulingard. See what they have to say about these Aberration rumors. Or not, and just observe and skulk around and leave the talking to us. I don't really care, as long as you can manage to handle it *gracefully* and with some sort of decorum."

"Doubtful," I mutter, too quietly for them to hear, although Vaen shoots me a look that clearly says he knows I said *something*. Then, louder, "Why me?"

"You're less likely to piss me off and make me say something I regret in front of Sunillen." Breakfast arrives, and Lyr spears a fat sausage, grease slicking the side of the meat. "Plus, people like you."

I laugh aloud at that. "Me? You have to be joking."

He looks genuinely puzzled at my reaction. "Why wouldn't people like you?"

A thousand reasons jump to my lips. "I'm too much. Too brash, too quick to anger, too—"

"Never," Lyr interrupts, suddenly fierce, leaning forward so I can't look anywhere else, "say that you're too much ever again. If someone says you are too much, it is merely because they are too small. Do you understand?"

I search his face for a hint of mockery, but there is none. He believes what he says. He wants *me* to believe it too. Like it's actually truth.

My chest is tight, heart clenched, and I'm afraid if I speak, I'll say something truly embarrassing or, light forbid, cry. So I just nod, lips pressed together so they don't quiver. Apparently satisfied, Lyr returns to his breakfast.

We finish our food companionably, perhaps the most amicable we've been this entire journey. I stay quiet, letting Vaen and Lyr discuss things they noticed last night. It's not much. People are on edge, tense, jumpy. Quick to drink, as if trying to avoid whatever reality awaits them outside these doors. Quick to fight, too; a scuffle broke out after we retired, which the serving maid said was pretty rare for this inn.

The people here know something is wrong.

It's comfortably chilly outside. I'm wearing the same clothes as last night, the rest soaking in the tub upstairs for the chamber maid to clean for an extra fee, but my cloak is warm enough and blocks the wind that dances lithely around our limbs, whispering promises of frost covered fields soon to come.

"Remember," Lyr says to Vaen before we part, "decorum. Quiet. Observant."

Vaen visibly rolls his eyes. "Take your own advice, Lyr. You're more likely to explode than I am."

Lyr looks like he's about to start arguing, so I step in front of him. "Be safe."

Vaen looks at me, surprise darting across his features, as if he never would have expected me to say such a thing to him. I shrug, uncomfortable under his scrutiny. "It doesn't matter if we're friends or not," I say. "We're still allies, and allies need each other to stay in one piece."

Yet again I see a reminder of the mercenary — the slight respect as he tilts his head in agreement before motioning to Lyr. "Try to keep him from doing anything truly stupid."

Lyr has already started walking off, apparently unconcerned whether I'll follow or not. I have the sudden feeling that I got the harder job.

"No promises."

Ulingard is fully awake as we head towards Sunillen's residence. The tension from the previous night has dulled, replaced by the weariness of daily work, and curious eyes follow our progress across the town's central green. Our presence is either not threatening to them now, or gossiping whispers have already made the rounds on our intentions in being here. I would bet on the latter.

I can't help but find myself staring at the blacksmith forge as we pass it. Smoke curls above the building, suggesting Haith is already at work, but I can't see him without going inside. My whole body warms at the simple thought of him, of the teasing, flirtatious words he offered me.

If I was Liseah, I would have already been on top of him. She takes what she wants, without fear of consequences or others' opinions.

Perhaps it's finally time to try her way of looking at things.

We reach the north side of the village, the peaked tops of Sunillen's house just past the wall now. There's a small gate here, much like the one we came through, but—

"Four Watchers?" Lyr stops, open mouthed in amazement. "Why do they need four Watchers at one entrance?"

I look past the Watchers, to the field and forest beyond. Sheep mill about, apparently unconcerned. It's bright and sunny today, even with the wind's chill, and nothing about the sight rings any alarms.

"Well, let's ask them. Aren't we supposed to be gathering information?"

Lyr looks faintly pained, eyes focused on the house just out of reach. "I'd really rather just talk to Sunillen."

"There's plenty of time for both."

Knowing the possibility of a magically imbued item is within reach is almost too much for Lyr, the longing painfully obvious. But he gestures for me to go first, never looking away from the house.

I swallow back my hesitance. This is all part of the job. So, throwing my shoulders back, I walk forward with far more confidence than I feel.

"Morning." Four pairs of eyes swivel towards me, two of which quickly dismiss me as unimportant and return to watching the land behind Ulingard.

"What business do you have?"

The Watcher sounds bored and vaguely annoyed as if I'm bothering them. None of them are the same one we met at the gate yesterday, not that I particularly think she would be of any help. They all look like they've been born and bred here — pale skin, pale hair, bright eyes. I wonder if it gets boring, seeing yourself reflected in one another without the myriad of skin tones down south.

I do my best to channel Liseah and the open charm she exudes when talking to strangers. The smile feels foreign, stretched thin.

"We're new in town." I gesture to Lyr, who gives a grumpy nod of acknowledgement. "We came to inquire at the Mage Sunillen's residence, but we have heard countless rumors on the journey here." I nod to the field stretching beyond and the forest that seems to guard it.

Immediately the Watcher who first addressed me scowls. He exchanges looks with his partner, a woman with steel gray hair and lines around her eyes and mouth. She wears an additional starred band around her left arm, indicating a Watch commander.

Her face is hard when she speaks. "Are you another group here to try and disprove us, mocking Ulingard?"

I draw back at the venom in her words. "No, not at all."

She doesn't relent, so I continue, "I have seen nothing to either confirm or deny any of the rumors, and the world of magic is still new to me. But I've seen an Aberration, and I know what it's like to be under attack from one. I don't know what to believe, but I want to help, if I can."

Vaen certainly would not be happy to hear me pledge my help so readily. But it feels like the right thing to do.

The Watcher still doesn't relax, but her quiet anger seems to dim.

"Have there been many to come here?" Lyr asks.

Her attention flicks to him. "A few. They come, ask questions, wander the fields, and leave a few days later, saying that a few noises on the wind are no proof."

The male Watchers adds, vitriol in his tone, "They claim we are doing it to lure travelers here to rob them or use them."

Now fully involved with the conversation, Lyr asks, "Do the... instances not occur every night?"

There is a long moment of hesitance where the captain's eyes skip from me to Lyr and back again. Weighing us, seeing if we're just another group here to mock and demean. After a long moment, she shakes her head. "No. Sometimes we go several nights with nothing unusual. Other times there are voices in the wind and shadows skulking through the forest for nights on end." Her eyes settle on Lyr's, sharp and interested. "Are you a mage, then?"

He bows at the waist, one hand flipping his cloak so it flares out behind him. I barely manage to choke back a snort.

"I am indeed, Watcher...?"

"Olivie," she answers. She stands straighter, shoulders squared, taking on the responsibility of all of Ulingard with its uncertainty and fear as if not utterly exhausted.

Olivie's eyes bore into Lyr. He doesn't look away. "Well then, if you are indeed a mage, perhaps you can try and convince Sunillen to get off his damn ass and help us find the source of the creatures."

"Wait." Lyr holds up a hand, brow furrowed in puzzlement. "Has Sunillen done nothing to investigate?"

Olivie shakes her head, her own expression darkening once more. "Sunillen is our only mage in Ulingard. When these appearances first started, we of course approached him, asking if he was experimenting or using magic in some way that has backfired. He denied it, and has denied it every time we've tried to approach him since. I'm no mage, nor a scholar, but I know Aberrations come from magical energy."

"But are these creatures actually Aberrations? What you describe is not what a typical Aberration is like."

Olivie hesitates. "I can't answer that. They are like nothing I've seen before, and I have lived many years here. I can tell you, with certainty, that they are not natural."

Lyr crosses his arms over his chest, fingers tapping against his elbows. He doesn't look frustrated by the puzzle before us. On the contrary, his eyes gleam with anticipation. With excitement.

"There is undoubtedly something magical going on. And Sunillen denies any connection to it, and refuses to help find the source... very interesting." His voice trails off, eyes once again wandering to fixate on Sunillen's house.

"How can we help?" I ask, taking a step forward. Olivie

doesn't soften, exactly, but it seems she believes we mean no harm at least.

"The first thing is for you to see the happenings for yourself." She nods to the field, and I look at the picturesque sight. It's hard to believe anything sinister happens here. "The creatures only ever come at night. You can tell they're near by the animals. Wildlife grows still and quiet, as if afraid to be noticed. The sheep will become restless in their pens, seeking a way out, to run as far as they can if given the chance."

"What about the forest?" Just the question makes my heart heavy, my lungs constrict. Dread slowly seeps through my limbs.

Olivie shakes her head. "We don't go into the forest at night."

Chills race up my arms, drawing all the hairs to standing. I barely dare to breathe my next question. "Why not?"

"It feels... wrong. Worse than the fields. I am no coward, nor are my men. But the forest is dangerous after dark. The loggers go in only because it's our livelihood, and they never dare walk alone. They finish their work earlier and earlier every day, just to make sure they are well out before night falls."

I shiver, pulling my gaze away from the dark trees. "Okay. No forest, for now. We'll come back after dark and investigate the field tonight." I look at Lyr for confirmation, and he nods.

"I'll open the gate for you." Olivie's unsaid words hang on the air: *but I won't come with you.* A flash of anger follows the realization. If these creatures are as bad as she says, she should do everything in her power to destroy them, not rely on strangers to do it in her stead.

But no. That's not fair. Surely she's done what can. The creatures, Aberrations, whatever they may be, seem to be ethereal at best, immaterial at worst. How do you fight something you can't even hold?

"Thank you for the information," Lyr says, tone absent, the Watchers already half-forgotten.

Olivie nods, gesturing for her Watchers to step aside. I thank her as we pass. She doesn't respond, but in her silence there is uneasiness. *There are things to fear out there.*

Before I can address the unspoken warnings hanging like glistening spiderwebs around us, we pass the Watchers and are, finally, in the fields around Ulingard.

I can't help but tense, waiting for something to happen. For a creature to rise from the gently swaying grass, maw gaping wide, ready to rend and tear until blood turns the dirt into mud.

Of course, nothing happens. I shake off the thoughts, quickening my pace to catch up to Lyr.

"What do you think?" I ask.

"About what?"

"Do you think it could be Sunillen creating the Aberrations?"

Lyr hesitates before he answers. "I think it's the most likely possibility."

"But you don't like that."

"No."

We reach the edge of Sunillen's house, a veritable mansion compared to the buildings in Ulingard. Although large and imposing, it lacks overt signs of wealth a Noble's dwelling would have in Calire or even Kestral. There are no stone statues or gargoyles leering down at us from turrets, no precious gems ringing the towers. The stone is old, decorated with patchy moss and clinging ivy. Despite its age, the house looks to be well cared for, with neatly trimmed bushes and the remains of summer flowers, now wilted and brown.

I put a hand on Lyr's arm, keeping him from knocking on the door. "Why not?"

He faces me, jaw set, eyes hard and flinty. "Because if he's doing this purposefully, he's not likely to be someone on our side. It means there is little chance of attaining an imbued object for me. And if he's actually that powerful, to wield magic the rest of us can't even dream about? I don't know how I'm supposed to stop him."

I start to say something, perhaps to reassure him we're in this together, that he doesn't have to fight him alone. He doesn't give me the chance, raising a curled fist to bang loudly on the door.

It opens quickly. A small man, immaculately put together, keeps one hand on the door, as if ready to slam it in our faces should we say what he doesn't want to hear. His neat but unadorned clothes suggest a servant. He raises one gray eyebrow, focusing on Lyr as the important one in this conversation, although I don't miss the glance he throws my sword.

"May I help you?"

Lyr immediately smiles, once again becoming the most charming version of himself. Gone is the festering impatience when talking to the Watchers, the gathering storm of uncertainty and doubt that assailed him on our walk.

"Good morning! We were hoping for an audience with Mage Sunillen. My name is Mage Lyr, and this is my companion, Raylen."

My heart gives an uncomfortable squeeze at the lack of a title. No knight, not even Watcher. Just Raylen.

"I have heard of Mage Sunillen in my travels and studies, and would love nothing more to have a discourse with him. His knowledge on imbued objects is well known." Obsession would be closer to the mark, but Lyr knows how to spin his tale.

The servant stares for a moment longer, then nods and steps back, gesturing for us to enter. "Mage Sunillen is never one to turn down a fellow mage. I will show you to the sitting room and have tea brought."

He leads us through the main foyer, where a grand staircase adorned in deep blue carpet takes up the majority of the space. The room is well lit with large windows that stretch towards the high ceiling, giving life to an otherwise plain hall. The walls are a deep, rich wood that speaks of class and money, but they remain bare, without the opulent tapestries most Nobles houses have.

Our guide takes us to a small door set to the right of the stairs. I assume the second floor is reserved for personal and guest quarters. Up there, somewhere, is a room full of imbued objects that could entirely change the course of Lyr's life. Out of the corner of my eye, I catch him staring wistfully upwards, as if he is thinking the same thing.

Like the servant, the sitting room is immaculate, with rich brocade fabrics on the sofas and heavy crimson drapes framing the large windows. Statues large and small litter the corners, and an impressive oil portrait stares down at us from the fireplace mantle. The woman in it is clearly a northerner, with pale skin, high cheekbones, and fair hair. She looks at the artist wistfully, her smile small and sad.

"I will return shortly," the servant says, giving us a small bow on his way out.

Lyr settles onto the couches, idly flipping through a leather bound book left on the table. I catch a glimpse of line drawings of flowers amid the fine printed text, but my eyes repeatedly return to the oil painting. I find myself standing before it, entranced by the woman's own strange melancholy.

"It's like she knows something we don't," I murmur. "Something terribly sad."

"My late wife," says a voice from the doorway, nearly startling me out of my own skin. "She was from here, and why we chose to settle in this light forsaken place."

We turn, Lyr gracefully rising from the couch. Mage

Sunillen reminds me more of a Noble than a mage. He stands tall and proud, shoulders back, head lifted high, almost haughty. He looks nothing like his pale wife, with tawny skin several shades darker than mine and dark hair starting to gray, but the same faint sadness permeates the air around him. He's not an overly muscled or tall man, but his demeanor crackles with restrained power.

I am not afraid of many men, but unease settles into my bones as I look at him.

"I'm so sorry for your loss."

Sunillen waves off Lyr's words, gesturing for us to sit. Lyr does, but I stand behind the couch, hands clasped at my back in a show of both peace and readiness. A soldier's position.

"It was several years ago," Sunillen says. He pours himself and Lyr a cup of tea from the tray the servant brought in but does not offer me any, clearly accepting my role as insignificant. Good. Nobles never pay enough attention to the help.

"My doorman says you are here to discuss magic. That you are also a mage."

Lyr sits forward in his seat, taking a long sip of his tea. "That I am. Graduated from Haven only a handful of years ago."

"What is your speciality, Mage...?"

"Lyr. And illusions. Tricks of the mind, sleight of hand, falsifying appearances. Things like that."

I glance down at him but am unable to see his face. Sunillen, sitting across from Lyr, has one leg crossed over the other and looks mildly bored. Not a good first impression so far.

"You, of course, are well known throughout Serabith," Lyr adds.

I wince a little when Sunillen raises one perfectly manicured eyebrow. "Am I now? Tell me, what exactly am I known for?"

The tension thickens in the room. This is nothing more than a complicated game, and Lyr might have already misstepped. I know nothing of courtiers and politics, have never been interested in such things much less had an opportunity to learn the intricate dance. Now I feel woefully out of my depth, nothing more than a child listening to their parents talk.

Lyr doesn't seem the slightest bit ruffled by these complicated steps, words smooth and slow like honey.

"You are an incredibly talented mage. You deal primarily with fire magic, which put you at the front lines of the Zuneshan War. Because you were intimate with so much fighting, you saw a plethora of other mages die, and became the possessor of an inordinately large amount of imbued objects. After the war, you became one of the queen's roving mages, meant to scout out insurrection and displeasure, to quiet murmurings made against the crown, and of course to protect the people of Serabith." Lyr spreads his arms and settles back, apparently satisfied with himself. "Then you came up here, settled down and had a family, and have been keeping our northern borders safe from Aberrations for several years now."

Sunillen claps, but the sound rings hollow, mocking, in the quiet room. "Well done, Mage Lyr. You do know my history. I'm impressed."

My hackles rise. I don't trust this man, not one bit, and I understand now why the villagers are upset with him.

"So, please enlighten me." If Lyr notices the tension, he ignores it supremely well. "Your villagers are frightened half to death. Rumors of the Aberrations' rising numbers have reached as far as Calire. Do you have an inkling why this is happening?"

Sunillen's face hardens, eyes darkening. The threat of danger, dark and electric as a storm, fills the air. I find my hand falling to my sword.

"If you have come here to mock me, you are a fool."

I swear, for the briefest moment, that I see fire flitting around Sunillen's fingers. An ember of a flame, a whisper of red-orange light that weaves cleverly between tapping digits. For the first time, a sliver of fear works at me. I can't fight fire with steel. My only hope is that I am faster than Sunillen.

I don't risk a glance at Lyr, unwilling to look away from Sunillen for even a moment, so I'm surprised when his tone is light and jovial. "On the contrary, Mage Sunillen, I've come to offer my help."

Sunillen doesn't relax, but he doesn't attack either. I feel as taut as a bowstring, shaking with pent up energy.

"I don't think you're behind the recent sightings. From what the villagers have said, the creatures behave differently than traditional Aberrations, meaning they aren't created the same way." Out of the corner of my eye, I see Lyr hold up a finger. "So how are they created? By magic, surely, but is it yours? From your collection of imbued objects? Or is there someone else here, using magic secretively?"

"There is no other mage in Ulingard." It is said with absolute certainty, and Lyr puts up a reassuring hand.

"Of course not. You, of all people, would know. Which then begs the question, once again: what is happening? And how can we stop it?"

He falls silent, and Sunillen doesn't say anything for a long moment, eyes locked onto Lyr. I find myself holding my breath.

"There is nothing to stop you from investigating," Sunillen finally says. I hear the unspoken words: that *he* won't stop us. I relax a hairsbreadth. "Perhaps, if you can actually find one of the creatures, we can work to uncover what it is."

"No one can manage contact with them?" I ask, surprised. It's the first words I've spoken since he entered the room, and the mage glances up at me, unimpressed and perhaps even annoyed.

"No. They terrorize and flee before they can be hurt or captured."

"Has there been physical contact at all?"

He gives a slight, irritated shrug. "Cuts and bruises that could easily be explained away by tripping in a dark field at night."

"Well," Lyr interrupts before I can speak again, "we plan to be back tonight, to hopefully see these creatures for ourselves."

"You can tell me your findings in the morning, and whether you also think I am behind this, as every villager has so eloquently decided."

Sunillen rises, clearly dismissing us. If he's irritated, Lyr does a magnificent job of hiding it. He gives a small bow, which is returned with the barest nod of acknowledgement.

I don't speak again until we've left the house and are on our way back to the city.

"That was useless." I kick at a rock, watching it skip down the autumn-dried grass.

I expect Lyr to be irritated, especially after his earlier mood, but he surprises me by smiling.

"You have to play the long game sometimes, Raylen. Maybe not much happened today. Or, maybe, Sunillen knows my name, knows I believe his side of the story, and knows I am willing to risk my neck by investigating. I'd say that's far from useless."

And, humming a little ditty, he picks up his pace.

Fucking mages.

B y the time we reach Ulingard's center green, I'm buzzing with leftover adrenaline. My nerves are alight, my hand continually drifting towards my sword. All we have done the last several days is walk and talk, ride and talk, then talk some more. My bones ache for the energy of a fight, my ears empty without the ringing of steel on steel.

"Since we're going to hunt some monsters tonight, I think I'll take a nap," Lyr says, breaking me from my thoughts. "You should rest too."

Like that's possible. I shake my head. "I'm going to the Watcher tower to see when they spar. It's been too long since I've regularly trained." I can't help but cast a covert look at the smithy, which is conveniently close to the tower. Running into Haith wouldn't be the worst thing either.

Lyr follows my gaze, raising his eyebrows. He wasn't in the common room when Haith approached me, meaning somehow word got to him and probably Vaen anyway, or his intuition is better than mine. "Don't get yourself into trouble."

I give him a mischievous grin. "No promises."

He waves me off, already turning to the inn. "If you run

across Vaen, let him know what the plan is. Otherwise, I'm sure he'll come back here before long."

I doubt he'll be pleased to know we've made plans without his agreement, or Lyr's lackadaisical dismissal of his own findings, but there's no way in hell I'm going to be the one to find and tell him.

I turn to the smithy once again, suddenly nervous. I haven't initiated willful flirting in so very long, I have a moment of blind panic, thinking that perhaps it is a skill that can be lost.

Idiot, I scold myself. He called me beautiful last night. Just the memory makes my cheeks flush. Surely that means something, however small it might be. It at least means I won't look like an utter fool for going in and striking up a conversation, even if it doesn't turn into anything.

The most surprising thing of all, is how much I want it to turn into something.

Now or never. I force my feet to move and it's easier this time, although my stomach clenches tight with nerves and anticipation. I knock at the door, entering at the faint holler of "come in" from somewhere beyond.

The smithy is blisteringly hot, which must be excruciating during the summer and is already more than uncomfortable now. I pause for a moment inside, adjusting to the heat and taking in my surroundings. The building is one large room divided into several sections. The roaring kiln is at the far back, a haze of heat shimmering around the grated door. Near the entrance are hung racks of weapons, gardening and farming tools, and hunting supplies. I pause for a moment to admire the swords, picking one up to find it perfectly balanced, if a bit too light for my taste. A second, broader sword feels better, and I give it a few practice swings. It doesn't hold a candle to Eirah's sword, but is far better than most of the half-rusted weapons we trained with in Heron Hill.

"You know your way around swords."

I almost drop the blade but manage to catch my balance at the last second. Flushing, I put the sword back, turning like a naughty child caught stealing pie. Haith stands near the anvils in the center of the room, soot-blackened sleeves rolled up, a heavy leather apron covering him. In one hand he holds a set of tongs that grip a small iron circle. The metal glows white-red hot, and a gush of steam hisses into the air as he plunges it into a nearby water barrel. He inspects the circle, turning it carefully in the air, before nodding in apparent satisfaction. He looks back to me, eyebrow raised, clearly waiting for an explanation.

"I'm sorry. It's a lovely weapon, and I just wanted to see if it felt as good as it looked. It does, by the way. Feel good. When I wield it." I press my lips together before more mortifying words can come tumbling out.

Haith puts down the tongs and tugs off the heavy gloves, leaving them carefully on the anvil. I find myself holding my breath as he approaches, not for fear of chastisement, but because he hasn't looked away from me once, and his eyes are full of the same fire as the kiln behind him. The flames jump from him to me, lighting molten liquid through my core that leaves me breathless and aching.

I know now what Liseah means when she says she just can't help herself sometimes. Any previous entanglements, while pleasant, have been planned and thought out. This all consuming desire is something I have never experienced before. It scares me, the fierceness of this want, of how much I yearn to *beg* for Haith to touch me, to feel his skin press against mine.

He stops a foot or so away, closer than perhaps necessary but still not near enough to satisfy the need thrumming across my body.

"No need for an apology, Raylen." He draws my name out, rolling the letters in the inflection of the north, the two syllables

distinct, slow like the drip of molasses. "Where did you learn to
wield a weapon so well?"

The echo of my own word makes my ears burn. Never has
wield sounded so charged before.

"I trained for years to become a knight." I offer a small smile
that, somehow, isn't as sad as it once was. Something prompts
me to add, "And I'm good at it, too."

"I would wager you're good at many things."

My breath hitches, but before I can ask what he means or do
something even more foolish like kiss him, Haith continues,
"What happened? To being a knight, that is."

"I was told to leave the Temple. My ideologies did not
match theirs."

There it is, the succinct truth in all its ragged, wild glory. I
keep my head raised, even with the echoes of Vaen's cutting
remarks. *Knighthood is a fool's dream.* Maybe once I was a fool.
Maybe I even still am. But today I feel strong and powerful and
beautiful.

Haith makes a humming sound in the back of his throat. I
wonder how nice it would be to have that hum against my
throat, the crook of my elbow, the back of my knees. Against
parted lips, soft with desire.

"I have not had the pleasure of visiting Calire, but I can
only imagine what their idea of right is." He leans against a
wooden pillar, arms crossed over his muscular chest. "I am
glad for the diversion, but I'm afraid I haven't let you say
why you're here in the first place. Can I help you with
anything?"

A dozen inappropriate images flood my mind. I bite my lip
to keep them contained, but Haith notices, eyes dipping to my
mouth. It takes considerable effort to stay on task.

"Two things, actually. Is there a courier in town?"

Haith looks momentarily puzzled, clearly surprised at the

direction of my question, but says, "We can send a letter out without a problem. Writing to a forlorn lover?"

It fills me with glee to have him ask as if I'm desirable enough to be wanted so ardently, and that it concerns him it might be true. I grin from ear to ear. "Not in the slightest. But I do have a friend in Calire who will want to know I'm alive and well. I promised her I would keep in contact."

Haith leans closer. "I would be lying if I said I wasn't relieved at that." His gaze is full of the promise of fire, but he still says, "And the second thing?"

It takes an effort to stop thinking about what that fire means and to formulate letters, string them together into coherent words. "We're going to the fields by the forest tonight, to try and find the Aberrations. Any suggestions?"

The light, playful aura is tempered immediately, like we too are hot metal suddenly doused in a bucket of ice water. Haith straightens, serious, and it's on the tip of my tongue to try and pull the words back, to say nevermind, let's get back to talking of lovers, but it's too late.

"I went one night." Not what I expect, and I raise my eyebrows, gaze fixated on him and the careful way he speaks. "It's been, oh, five or six days since then. I think we were the last group to try and do reconnaissance." His voice is quiet and deep, all frivolity far flung away. "We stayed out half the night. Near midnight, perhaps a little after it, we started to hear the voices."

Shivers prickle across my skin. "What kind of voices?"

"Whispers, always floating just out of reach. First there was just a wordless sound, like leaves rustling, but there was no wind to move the branches. Then words, just audible. We could just pick out one or two, nothing concrete."

My lungs ache, and I draw in a quick breath, not even realizing I had been holding it. "What were the words?"

His eyes, so expressive before, are now flat and dark.

"They said to run. They said to die."

We fall silent after that, the weight of the words hanging over our heads. The hammer about to strike.

"But..." I shake my head, unable to get past one thing. "Aberrations don't talk, do they?"

"None that I've heard of before."

"Could it have been human?"

"Absolutely not." The words crack, a whip that shreds the air with its ferocity. Haith grimaces and softens his tone. "Whatever they are, they aren't human. So as for tonight, I can't offer much advice. Whatever is out there is something none of us have faced before. Be prepared for anything. And don't let your guard down, no matter what."

Now, more than ever, all I want is the comforting weight of my sword, the movement of my body, the power of each swing. Things I know. Things I can control.

"Thank you," I say sincerely. I shift my weight back, preparing to go. "I need to handle a few more things before tonight. But I appreciate the advice."

Haith's eyes are unreadable, but he nods. I have my hand on the door when he calls out, "I apprenticed here, when I was younger, and the blacksmith lives with his family deeper in the village. He rents the room here to me, and I use the forge for some of my jewelry pieces in exchange for helping with the bellows from time to time."

I look at him, confused, and he adds, "Perhaps, tomorrow evening, you can come tell me what happens."

There is a clear promise hanging in the air between us, lightning charged and ready to strike. But he's also giving me a way out, another moment to think about it.

I push open the door, rusted hinges almost overlapping my response.

"See you tomorrow then."

I find Vaen sitting on a tree stump outside The Night's End, a whetstone in one hand and a dagger in the other. He has his considerable arsenal of weapons neatly laid out next to him on an old horse blanket, the bright steel a sharp contrast to the dulled oranges and reds of the wool. I think briefly about ignoring him, but we're in this together, for better or worse. There's no point in being standoffish and rude, even when he is. I don't *want* to be his enemy.

I drop down next to him and hold out a hand. "Have an extra?"

He looks at me out of the corner of his eye for a moment before procuring a second whetstone and handing it over. I draw out my sword and begin to sharpen it, the comforting *shttttk* of stone against metal filling the courtyard. The sweat I worked up during my practice starts to dry, aided by the chill breeze that winds around us.

The Watchers don't hold formal practice sessions, but they have a small ring they use for sparring and were happy to let me borrow it. Once they saw I actually knew what I was doing, they asked to join me, and I ended up in several bouts. The first few were rocky as I regained the momentum of actually sparring against a human and not simply running forms by an early morning campfire, but that hesitance didn't last long, and I ended up trumping most of my adversaries soundly. I feel more like myself than I have in days.

The silence between Vaen and I is heavy but not exactly

uncomfortable. Still, I find myself unable to stay silent. "Did you find out anything interesting?"

Vaen puts down one dagger and takes up another. "Not particularly. There was a lot of talk, but nothing corporeal. More stories along the lines of what Lyr, and I assume you, have already heard."

He doesn't sound overly annoyed, so I take that as a sign to continue. "Do you still think they're lying?"

I risk a glance up to see Vaen frown, but it lacks any real heat. "I tend not to believe anything unless I see it with my own eyes," he says. It's one of the most personal statements I've ever gotten out of him.

"Why?"

He doesn't watch me but keeps his eyes on his whetstone. His movements, slow and careful and precise, mirror the tenor of his words. "The world is full of empty promises. Just look at your own life and the Knight's Temple." He does glance at me now, but it lacks any animosity. "If you hadn't gone, you would have kept believing a falsehood. That it was a place of justice and honor."

I don't know why, but the words sting. Like I'm some child, willing to accept the things before me based on what I've been told and not what I've actually seen.

Maybe because it's the truth, a traitorous voice whispers.

I put down my sword and face the thief. He meets my eyes, but looks back down a heartbeat later, apparently disinterested.

"What the hell happened to you, to make you lose faith in the world?"

Instead of lashing out like I expect, Vaen sighs. The sound is heavy and broken, leeching the ire right out of me. His shoulders bow forward under the weight of whatever secrets he holds, and

I think for a wild moment that this is it, this will be the answer to his mystery, this will breech the barrier between us and we can finally move past this awkward, reluctant allies storyline.

But then he meets my eyes, shoulders square once more, whatever secrets he keeps now again buried.

"That has nothing to do with our current situation. The better question is, what is your job for tonight?"

I don't have time for disappointment, too thrown off by his change of subject. "My... job?"

The door to the inn slams shut, startling me. Vaen doesn't even blink. Lyr squats down next to us a moment later, frowning at the array of weapons. "Well, I had a fabulous nap. I can't say the same for either of you. You're going to regret that later. Come on, let's eat something before we head back out." He slaps us on the shoulders, jovial, like we aren't talking about monsters made of mist.

Vaen doesn't look at Lyr, but he begins to sheath his daggers once more. And I get it suddenly. My job. In the turmoil of today, in the excitement of sparring and the heat in the forge and the knowledge that tonight could actually show us why we came up to this village in the first place, I let myself forget.

"I won't let him get hurt," I say, quiet but fierce. "My job is to protect Lyr. No matter what happens."

Vaen looks at me, the weight of the world in his eyes, and nods a single time before he rises and joins Lyr inside.

I follow, but my stomach clenches against the maelstrom of uneasiness.

It won't be like last time. I won't freeze again.

I won't.

Night has fully fallen by the time we reach the northern gate. This far north, the stars are scattered thickly across the dark sky, shining like a thousand glittering promises. There is no cloud cover tonight, but the moon is just a pale sliver, almost completely dark. There is still enough light between the stars and the flickering torches, wavering wildly in the chill breeze that slides against my skin, whispering of a cold night.

As promised, Olivie waits for us, one hand on the gate, the other gripping her spear.

"No one else has been out tonight," she says, nodding to the field. "There was a group two days ago, and they came back telling of invisible creatures that did little more than breathe down their necks. The next morning, we killed two Aberrations before they could reach our walls."

That would have been the day we arrived.

Lyr rubs his face, scowling as he thinks. "Could your sightings somehow be the start of an Aberration, before it's fully formed?"

Although the words are quietly murmured, apparently aimed for none but himself, Olivie still shrugs. "That's what you're here for." She turns her attention to Vaen but must find him unimportant, because she directs her words to me. "Stay aware. No one has been able to hurt these creatures yet. I can't speak for the mage, but my gut says they're getting stronger."

An unspoken connection fizzles between us. "A fighter's gut is never wrong," I say.

She nods grimly.

Taking a fortifying breath, I turn to the fields. The grass waves in the wind, beckoning us forward. Unwillingly, my eyes travel up, to the forest beyond. The trees huddle close together, dark and quiet. I know, deep in my soul, that we will eventually have to breach that barrier.

But not tonight.

Lyr starts forward, but I grab his sleeve and pull him behind me. For a brief second, fear threatens to wash over me, drag me beneath its churning waves, but I take that first step anyway, beyond the reassurance of the wall and into the field.

I left my town. I faced down bandits. I killed an Aberration. I stood toe to toe with the greatest warriors of my age, and I shouldered the burden of everything crumbling down upon me.

Stepping into a field is nothing.

We walk until the light of the torches fade to dim pinpricks in the distance. The fields around us are dark and quiet, all revelry from the city gone. This is a place of solitude, of sacredness. Of secrets.

We don't speak as we stop, instinctively turning our backs to one another so we face outwards, towards whatever might await us. I dare to close my eyes, focusing on breathing deeply, feeling the firm ground beneath my boots, the slight resistance of grass against my shins as it undulates in the breeze. My hair tickles my neck and cheeks, but any time I try to push it behind my ears, the wind invariably loosens it once more.

Distractions. Those are just distractions.

I breathe out, counting to seven, turning my focus away from my own body and to what lies around me. The wind, the grass, the whisper of movement from my companions. Lyr talks quietly to Vaen, saying something about magic, but that's not important right now.

An owl hoots from somewhere above, wings silent in the sky, and I relax. Olivie said to watch the animals. They would be the first warning.

I open my eyes, awareness dwindling, in time to hear Vaen say, "Does Aberration activity increase near Crystals?"

Lyr shakes his head, arms crossed over his chest, fingers tapping against his elbows. He paces slowly, a lazy circle around us, head bowed in thought. "Yes, but the closest Crystal is several days journey to the southeast, closer to Feir than here."

My eyes are drawn again to the shifting limbs now so much closer, unknowable dread settling into my chest like an old companion. "What about beyond the forest?"

"Nothing is beyond the northern forest except plains of empty ice. Nothing lives up there." Lyr kicks at a rock, irritated. "Didn't you learn anything from school?"

I don't mention I wasn't exactly the best student, sneaking off to work with knives and fist fighting. Education beyond agriculture and trading wasn't highly valued in Heron Hill anyway.

I take Lyr's irritation as a cue that he is done conversing. He mutters to himself as he paces, hands moving in the air around him. I don't catch much of his theories, beyond a vague word tossed here and there.

What started as agonizingly tense turns dull very quickly as the hour stretches on, then turns into another, then a third. It is well past midnight now, the world dark and quiet around us, the peace drastically at odds to what I envisioned happening.

I yawn. I gave up standing a while ago, sitting in cool, moist dirt that does little to help protect from the wind's chill. It's been picking up the longer we're out, until my very bones ache from the constant pressure of it. Vaen and Lyr sit nearby, Lyr perched on a small collection of broken down boulders and rocks that might once have been a well. I can't hear what they're saying; the only thing that reaches me is the mumble of voices, almost indiscernible from the wind.

Is that what this whole thing boils down to? Groups that come out here and are terrorized by perfectly ordinary happenings?

I groan as I stand, leaning to the side so my back lets out a satisfying pop. Anytime the tiredness gets too much, I take a few minutes to patrol around this spot we've claimed. It's time to ask Lyr how long he intends to keep us out here anyway.

I go to move forward, but a hand catches my elbow, yanking me unexpectedly back. I stumble, angry at Vaen for pulling a stupid test now, angry at myself for not hearing him approach. I turn to look, but something catches my attention from the corner of my eye.

Vaen stands with Lyr, shaking his head at something the mage is saying.

Ice travels down my limbs, raising every hair on my body. There is no doubt *something* touched me. Hardly daring to breathe, dagger slippery in my suddenly sweaty palm, I pivot on my heels slowly.

The fields sway before me, grasses gently rubbing against one another. There is not another being, human or animal, in sight.

Something cold brushes against the nape of my neck, soft like silk, the touch so light it could be a lover's caress. I reach back without looking, hand shaking, but there is nothing to grasp.

Panic slams into me full force, blinding in its ferocity. I turn, fast now, not careful, but nothing is there. For a moment doubt seizes me. It's late, I'm tired, the wind is so very strong, it could have—

I realize, with startling clarity, that the wind has died down. The grass lies still and silent, as if holding its breath.

Waiting.

It doesn't matter that this is what we've been warned about since we arrived. Logic has fled, replaced by a deep rooted terror I never would have thought possible before.

Every inch of my skin is tight, coiled and ready to spring apart. Knowing my knees are shaking and not caring, I turn with mouth open to warn the other two.

Only to find Lyr standing a few paces from me, frowning as though irritated, shaking his head as he says something about not seeing anything tonight.

I can't reply, because just past his shoulder is a form of fog and mist, so fine to nearly be invisible. But I see it, nearly identical to Lyr's height. I see the twin dark swirls where eyes should be. The hand that rises, mist fingers abnormally long, to hover around Lyr's throat. And I see the gaping chasm that appears in its face as the creature grins, cocks its head to one side, and closes those fingers in a vice grip as tight as death itself.

TWELVE

There is a moment where Lyr stops, eyes wide, mouth open and gaping like a fish thrown onto jagged, dry rocks. I see his chest heave, searching for air that is not there, his arms tense, hands start to rise to his throat. Panic blooms in his eyes, bright and so utterly scared it sends shivers down my spine. His fingers try to find purchase in the shadows but they slide off like water against glass, smooth and unerring. There is no gap for him to wedge even a nail under, because fog does nothing better than slither its way under cracks, through the slivers in your shelter until all light is blocked.

What is your job?

The dagger leaps into my hand and I throw quickly, before the shot is lined up. It's too far left and the dagger grazes Lyr's cheek as it parts the coalesced mist. I hear Lyr suddenly yelp in pain, instantaneous relief flooding me because it means he has breath to make a sound.

There's a roaring in my ears, overwhelming and consuming, and the mist around Lyr swirls, parting around him. It reforms as soon as it's past him, apparently unhurt by the dagger, and part of me is screaming because I knew this wouldn't work, I knew I wouldn't be able to hurt something like this, but the rest of me knows my sole purpose and I draw my sword anyway.

The creature is taller now, wider, and I watch as wisps of fog glide from the ground to join it, multiple pieces becoming whole. The more pieces that are added, the more substantial it becomes, the dark chasm of its mouth widening and growing until I feel like it could swallow me whole. The eyes that were dark holes have become fire, glowing a deep red that I know, without doubt, are sentient and knowledgable and malevolent.

The thing looks at me, undeniably stares *at me* then turns, faster than lightning, to reach out with multiple tendrils of fog to try and entangle Lyr. The mage has his hands out, concentrating on something I can't see, and the steps he takes backwards are too slow, too late. A tentacle whips out to slide around his waist, yanking him forward, and Lyr yells, the sound a mix of pain and utter terror.

But if the creature is corporeal enough to grab Lyr, then surely—

I leap forward, sword slicing down to cut into the tentacle, and suddenly Vaen is there as well, reaching out to grab Lyr by the back of the tunic. Vaen pulls him back as the fog retreats. A horrible hissing fills the air, high pitched and whining like steam from a kettle. And somewhere in that sound, buried beneath the noise, comes a string of words, barely above a whisper, more felt than actually heard.

Hunt kill destroy maim rip limb from limb blood ruby blood kill decapitate eviscerate pluck eyeballs sever tongue

Then, with crystal clarity, a roar that fills my head:

I will rend your limbs one by one from your body and feast on the pulsing organs within, ripping you apart piece by piece until all you can do is scream.

There's more fog now, swirling around my feet and ankles,

inexorably drawn to the creature who becomes more substantial, more solid, more *real*.

This is nothing like bandits or even the real Aberration, so far beyond the scope of my imagination it's almost laughable. I'm a piece of broken wood on the sea, tossed high by the waves, and any second I'll come crashing down to shatter into splinters. But through the hurricane, one thought holds firm.

Real things can break.

Only a few seconds have passed since Vaen grabbed Lyr, but it feels like an eternity. I stumble more than run forward, swinging wildly without any of my usual finesse. The attack is powerful, though, which is all that's needed as the blade's edge bites into the creature's side. It roars, fury and pain rolled into a wordless scream, immediately turning to focus on me once more.

I step back, readying my blade to parry, but something slides up my ankles, bone chillingly cold, locking my feet in place. I glance down to find more tendrils of mist leeching out of the ground itself, holding me captive.

"Fuck!"

I try to move my foot, but it is as if I have stepped into a swamp; my boot only lifts an infinitesimal amount. "Lyr, do something!" I shout, looking up just in time to see the creature split straight down the middle. From between the two halves stands Vaen, his own sword pointed to the ground as he gasps for breath. I can see the beads of sweat shining on his face.

For a breathless moment I think Vaen has done it, that he's found its weakness and has ended it, but within a second I realize the truth. The two halves shiver, fog reforming, and now *two* of the creatures are before me, one of them grinning at me with its soul empty eyes while the other turns to confront Lyr and Vaen.

My whole body shakes, but my mind is clear and empty. For

the first time, I clearly see how I'm going to die, and the thought fills me not with peace, but a staggering emptiness.

There was supposed to be more.

More moments, more friends and lovers and partners. Meals spent together, good food paired with good conversation. Early morning sparring matches, long nights on the road and traveling from city to city just for the joy of seeing what else lies out there. More time with Liseah and my family and maybe even Lyr and Vaen. More time to find myself, figure out what I am beneath the hard edged steel.

More, so easily wiped away.

I think, in this moment, to just lay my sword down and accept fate. Accept my own weakness, my own foolhardy bravado that led me here.

Don't you even dare think about it.

The voice might be mine, it might be Liseah's, might be my aunt's or sister's. Voice layered on voice, coalescing into one to tell me absolutely not, this is not how I will die today.

I will not lie down and accept death.

So even though my feet cannot move, I adjust my balance and bear down, blade diagonal before me, daring this thing of nightmares to devour me.

The creature takes a step forward, dark mist flickering like it contains a thousand miniature bolts of lightning.

That's not right.

The thought crosses my mind a millisecond before I realize the lightning is not coming from within the creature but behind it. Even as I watch, the lightning expands rapidly, joining together into one ball of pure white energy that explodes outwards. Heat burns my face, the brightness forcing me to look down.

When my vision clears, I find an empty field once more, all traces of fog banished.

We stand in stunned silence for a moment, the only sounds our gasping breath.

"Well." Lyr steps forward, brushing shaking hands on his robes. Blood drips from the cut on his cheek. "I think it goes without saying, but we're well and truly fucked this time."

I stare first at the mage, then down at the ground, then back to Lyr once more. "That actually happened, didn't it?" My voice doesn't shake, but my hand does as I slide my sword back into its scabbard. "That, that thing... that was real, right? Not just one of your stupid illusions?"

It's an idiotic thing to say, and Lyr doesn't even grace the comment with a reply as he uses his sleeve to wipe the blood from his face. "I think this is a lot worse than even I expected," he admits. He pitches his voice low, as if afraid someone might be nearby, listening to our conversation.

Let them hear.

The anger boiling under my skin surprises me, but a distant part of me knows it's born of my own overwhelming fear. I turn in a slow circle, eyes roving over the field, searching for any sign, any hint of fog curling around the blades of grass. All is still, like the nightmare that gripped us never even happened.

"Do you still think the villagers are lying?" The words spat at Vaen are venomous, no matter that he's as much a victim as the rest of us. His earlier disbelief simply makes him an easy target.

Vaen's shoulders are a harsh line as he stalks near me. For a wild second I think he's going to physically return my attack, but he stoops to grab a dagger uncomfortably close to my feet. I don't even remember him throwing any.

When he straightens, he doesn't immediately move back. We're nearly chest to chest, breath mingling in the cool air between us, and I can clearly see the rage reflected in his own face.

"You need to learn to hold your tongue when your opinion isn't asked for or warranted," he growls. "Try acting like you are capable of an actual productive conversation instead of throwing insults like a fucking child."

The words are harsher than an actual slap to the face, instantly silencing me.

He steps back and turns to Lyr just as the mage says, "I need to talk to Sunillen." He rubs a hand over his face, exhaustion settling into the circles under his eyes. "Maybe if he hears it coming from another mage—" He trails off, shaking his head ever so slightly.

"Not tonight you don't." Vaen starts back towards Ulingard, Lyr a half step behind. He doesn't look to see if I follow.

It takes me a moment, but I do. It's easy to blame my words on the encounter, on my own heightened fear, but that would be a lie. Anger is easier than fear, easier than these mysteries I cannot begin to unravel. If I was a better person, I would apologize. Instead, silently, I bring up the rear, unable to let go of my sword hilt. Every nerve is on fire, muscles tense and aching as I fight the urge to run. I look back once, to the dark swaying trees, but nothing stirs. I don't know what I would do if something did.

We're almost back to the gate before I work up the courage to speak again. "The monster targeted Lyr. Even when I was the easier target, it chose to go after him."

We stop, the lights from Ulingard a welcome relief from the darkness. Vaen watches me, sharp eyed, but my focus remains on Lyr.

"It was hunting for magic," Lyr agrees grimly. "By all accounts, this was the most active the monsters have ever been."

"Because there was a mage out here."

He nods before turning to look at Sunillen's house, two

pinpricks of lights burning in the windows on the upper floor. Did he see us? Does he know what happened? The idea chills me more than the growing cold.

"The question now," Lyr says, "is how I convince Sunillen to get off his ass and help."

Or expose him as the person behind all of this.

That thought I keep to myself.

After a tense, quiet walk back to the inn, we sleep four or five hours before rousing once more. It looks to be mid morning, perhaps closer to noonday. I'm the last to rise, and find Lyr and Vaen have coaxed a late breakfast from the cook. Food isn't appealing, despite the excitement of the night — or perhaps because of it. The few bites I manage turn to ashes in my mouth. I can't banish the monster from my mind. Every time my eyes close, even just to blink, all I see is that malevolent grin, the way it grew and expanded to take over the very sky. The way it looked at us like it was merely waiting to turn the world red.

"Raylen, I want you to come with me again."

I push my plate away, glad to be moving again. "Sounds good. Vaen?"

"I'm going to the Watchers," he says, apparently already decided. If there is the memory of our harsh words, he doesn't show it. "Give Olivie an update and see what their thoughts are."

I frown. "I was sparring with them yesterday, and I've been the one to talk to them. Shouldn't I go?" Their company sounds far preferable to Sunillen's.

Vaen raises an eyebrow. "You were hired to protect Lyr. So isn't that what you should do?"

Vaen rises and leaves the inn before I can gather the words to protest.

Lyr clucks his tongue and slaps my shoulder. "He's an ass. Let's go."

I fume silently all the way to Mage Sunillen's house, until we reach the fields beyond the city. Anger vanishes, replaced with wariness, and I step in front of Lyr. A sheep contently munching the grass nearby raises its head and bleats at me, assuring me I'm the closest thing to an enemy here.

I wonder if it can smell the residue of darkness clinging to my skin.

We're almost at the door when Lyr stops short, pulling me back with him. Immediately I reach for a weapon, eyes flicking from spot to spot, trying to see what I possibly could have missed.

"I'm talking to Sunillen alone today."

My focus snaps back to Lyr. "Excuse me?"

"I'm talking to Sunillen alone today. You can find somewhere useful to be, like the kitchen."

My astonishment must be apparent because he holds up a hand, panic immediately pinching his face. "Wait, that came out wrong. What I meant to say, is you'll do better in some highly populated area, like the kitchen. I want you to see what the servants are saying about Sunillen."

I don't disagree with the logic of splitting up, but... "I'm supposed to be your guard. That's going to be a little tricky if we're not in the same room."

"I'll be fine." He waves off my concern without batting an eye. "Sunillen will talk to me more without you hovering."

I'm still not entirely convinced. "Maybe, but Vaen will have my hide if something happens to you when I'm not around, whether it's by your orders or not."

"Do you work for me or for Vaen? Besides, I didn't think you were afraid of him."

I scoff. "Afraid is not the right word. Annoyed by. And you know, when you say things like that, you sound like just as much of an ass as him."

His only answer is to knock on the door, a telltale grin lifting his lips.

The door is answered by the same servant as the day before. He doesn't seem surprised to see us, but definitely resigned.

The man takes me to the kitchens at Lyr's request, a sprawling room easily three times the size of any kitchen I've seen before. A fire roars in the corner, heating the room almost past the point of comfort. A stout man in a stained apron slathers a dark, sticky honey glaze onto a loin of meat that turns slowly over a low fire, while another in the awkward years between boy and man rolls out a thick dough. My mouth waters at the smells that fill every inch of the room, and I'm debating whether it's rude to ask for something to eat when the cook looks at me, grunts, grabs a plate of rolls, and passes it to me.

"Eat," he says, voice thick with an accent I don't recognize. "If you're still hungry before your master is done, ask for more." His words are broken but clear, and the plate in my hands is deliciously hot. Fat pats of butter ooze on the tops of the rolls.

"Thank you," I reply. I take a seat at the large wooden table that occupies the center of the room. The table is heavily notched, and a knife lays abandoned halfway down it.

The man rolling out dough looks at me from the corner of his eye but doesn't try to say anything, and the kitchen is comfortably silent as I polish off the first roll. It melts in my mouth, salty butter mixing with pillowy soft dough to form a beautiful cacophony of flavors and textures.

I'm halfway through the second roll when the door opens from where I assume the gardens are, and a young woman with two children enter.

Interesting. I hadn't expected any children to be on the estate, but Sunillen is not particularly old. The question of whether they are his is incontestable — they look like a painter painstakingly transformed his features onto a smaller form.

The older of the two, a girl, looks to be around eight or nine and notices me first. She pauses, brows rising, and asks without a hint of trepidation, "Who are *you*?"

The woman with them gives a barely audible gasp and lightly taps her on the top of her head. "Amilla, manners!"

She gives me an apologetic smile. Her face is smooth and unlined, but there is a clear tiredness pinching around her eyes, dragging at her shoulders. I can't imagine being the governess for two motherless children is a particularly easy task, especially with the current atmosphere around Ulingard.

"My apologies. I have been trying to teach these miscreants manners, but it seems the lessons have not yet stuck," she says with another pointed look at the girl.

Amilla grimaces, staring down at her muddy boots, clearly unimpressed by the chastisement. Her brother, a wild looking creature with a head full of curls, gives her a curious look, as if wondering if the pronouncement is directed at him too, before shrugging it off and reaching for a roll.

In a single quick, smooth movement, the governess grabs his wrist before he can reach the food. "Ah, Thomalen, what have we talked about?"

"C'mon, that's not fair!" He looks plaintively at my own roll. "How come she has one?"

"Because she's a guest," the governess smoothly replies. She withdraws her hand, folding them neatly over her stomach, and waits.

Thomalen sighs, eyes locked onto his prize. "Cook, may I have one please?"

The cook, who has been merrily chopping vegetables this entire time, chuckles a little at the forlorn request. "Of course. Wash up first, the both of you."

The children scramble out, and I can hear them squabbling about who goes first before the kitchen door swings shut behind them.

The governess drops into the chair next to mine, a deep sigh escaping. She rubs her temples with small, dainty fingers. She's a tiny thing, all wisps and bird bones, probably just four or five years older than me. I wonder what lot in life cast her as a governess so young when such a job is usually reserved for matrons with grandchildren of their own.

Find out what the servants are saying. Lyr's words ring in my head.

"You look absolutely exhausted." I immediately want to kick myself. No preamble, no introductions... just a disparaging remark.

And this is why Liseah did all the talking.

But to my surprise, the governess just gives me a faint smile, apparently unperturbed. "I am," she admits. The cook brings her a cup of steaming tea, which she receives with a wide smile. "Thank you."

She breathes in the steam, eyes closing for a brief moment before raising the cup to her lips and drinking deeply. I think, for a wild moment, she won't even continue this conversation with me, but finally she puts her teacup down.

"You always think children will be easy, but I have not found it so." She says it with amusement, not annoyance, and her small smile is open, waiting for me to respond.

There's a fine line to walk between trying to draw out information while appearing merely friendly.

I focus on the friendly portion. That, at least, is easier.

"I can only imagine. I barely remember my sister as a child, and I never bothered to learn to care for any of them." I smile a bit and admit, "I've always liked them though."

The children in question return, falling over each other in their eagerness for the treat. The cook sits them at a smaller table with cups of bright juice and their buttered bread.

The governess's easy smile, the fondness in which she watches her charges, makes me miss Liseah, her absence a sharp ache in the pit of my being, as if a vital organ has been removed and I'm only now realizing its importance.

"I love children." An almost bashful smiling turns her lips up as if it's a guilty secret. "I always have."

I nod to Amilla and Thomalen. "Have you been with them long?"

Careful, careful.

"Coming on to about a year," she answers. "They've run off their last few governesses. Of course, Ulingard itself isn't for the faint of heart. You practically have to be born and bred here to withstand the winters." Her own dark curls clearly label her as an outsider too.

She eyes me curiously, and I meet her gaze with a relaxed, open smile even as my hands tremble in my lap. This deceitfulness is far more nerve wracking than a sparring match could ever be.

"We just came to Ulingard a few days ago," I offer. "My name is Raylen. My traveling companion is a mage." I gesture a bit in the general direction I imagine the mages are.

"Nalista." Her hazel eyes glimmer with amusement. "Be glad you're down here with me. I'm much better company than them. You'd be bored stiff up there between their posturing and nonsensical conversations about traits of magic."

We share a conspiratorial look and, almost simultaneously,

burst into laughter. My heart swells. Not because I have done my job and wormed my way into their home, but because, for the first time since leaving Calire, I don't feel quite as alone. I enjoy spending time with Lyr, but there's something vastly different being in the company of another woman who seems to think and act like you do.

Maybe I'll actually have to thank Vaen for making me stay with Lyr today.

Not aloud of course.

Now is the time for more important questions. "Is it hard?" I ask. "To work for a mage like Sunillen?" *Careful.*

Nalista's smile doesn't fade, but she cocks her head curiously to one side. "What do you mean?"

I wave my hand, like it's a minor thing even as everything in me is stretched taut as a wire. "Just the general mage attitude. High and mighty, like they're better than everyone else." I feel a little guilty, talking about Lyr like that, even if it's true.

"I don't talk to Mage Sunillen much," Nalista admits, her voice carefully neutral.

"But you're his children's caretaker. He doesn't want to check on them?"

"He does of course. But I think they make him sad more than anything else." She glances at the children before lowering her voice, leaning in over the table towards me. "He spends a lot of time alone, reading from his library or walking the gardens. I don't think he's completely recovered from his wife's death. But as for knowing him? I don't think anyone here truly knows him."

I frown, a thousand more questions at my lips, but Nalista rises, dusting crumbs off her dress, and my heart plummets. "I need to take the children for their afternoon studies. It was lovely to meet you, Raylen. I hope you come again."

The bench squeaks unbearably against the stone floor as I

rise as well, earning a wince from the kitchen boy and a whine from Thomalen. My smile feels shaky, and I'm worried she can read my disappointment in myself, for pushing too hard. Wishing I had pushed harder.

Still, it is completely truthful when I say, "Me too."

"So you learned nothing?"

I scowl at Lyr's incredulous tone. "That's a bit harsh. Nalista said Sunillen is odd and—"

"—keeps to himself," Lyr finishes. "Yes, you mentioned that. But that's nothing to go on. It's certainly nothing suspicious, for light's sake."

I know he's right, but it irks me nonetheless. "I don't think we should dismiss it that quickly. But even if you think that's a dead end, at least I have an acquaintance there now and can start asking deeper questions. Tell me again what *you* discovered?"

Lyr mirrors my frown. "We talked about the war, about schooling. About magic in general. Just like you laid the groundwork, so did I."

"Did he ask about our foray last night? Did you mention our theory?"

Lyr rolls his shoulders in an uneasy shrug. "We talked of it, but he did not want to dwell on it. He isn't convinced it's anything out of the ordinary."

Surprise followed by incredulousness and finally anger roll through me, one after another. "That's ridiculous!" When Lyr gives me a look, I lower my voice, but the heat doesn't leave my words. "He's a mage. He should be out there with us, trying to put a stop to it instead of staying holed up so he can ignore the whole damn thing!"

"I know."

It isn't much of a consolation.

Pebbles skitter under our feet. I kick a few of them, feeling petty and small. "When are we going out again?" Not if. But when. We all know there isn't another solution.

"Tonight," Lyr says with a grimace. "We need to run some experiments." He takes a deep breath and faces me, pulling us to a halt.

"That's why you and Vaen are going out alone."

THIRTEEN

There's a moment of silence as I merely stare at Lyr, processing what he said and what it actually means.

Then I flatly say, "You're sending us off to die."

Lyr has the decency to look horrified. "I am not! If our supposition is correct, an Aberration won't show up at all without magic present. Last night was the most concrete appearance we've witnessed, if the rumors are to be believed."

"Most concrete appearance? Is that what we're calling that fucking nightmare?"

He doesn't even pause to address my justified concern. "—but in every other instance, without the presence of magic, the sightings were nothing more than whispers and smoke."

"Plus more Aberrations during the day," I snap. It's all I can do to keep my voice down from a full out yell. "You can't say that last night wasn't the catalyst of something more. We would have died without your magic."

Lyr worries his bottom lip between his teeth, eyes unfocused as he thinks. His tone is flippant, almost uncaring, as he says, "I'm sure you would have found a way."

"Damn it, that's not good enough and you know it. If that creature comes back, we're going to *die*."

He shakes his head, irritated now, as if my words are nothing but a fly buzzing around his head, imparting only useless sounds. "You're clever, Raylen, and so is Vaen. You wouldn't have died."

"Give me an idea on how to fight this thing, and I will. But just throwing out placating words doesn't help anything. That doesn't tell me how to survive."

"Does that mean you won't do it?"

He pins me with an unwavering gaze, devoid of his usual wry humor. The utter coldness of the situation leaves me breathless. My skin goes numb with horror before flushing hot with rage. It sweeps through me, blazing an incandescent trail that lights every nerve along its path. I want to scream at the betrayal, at the realization that Lyr doesn't care about us as friends, that this is just another job to him, another chance to get an imbued object, to show his worth as a mage.

It was all just another illusion.

It takes everything in me to not punch him straight in the face. I force myself to straighten, to put back my shoulders and face him down with the same coldness he showed me.

"I do not go back on my word," I say, and the tone is not my own, it is so full of anger. No hurt, even though it tears my heart apart. Just anger.

Something flashes in Lyr's eyes. Realization over what he's said, perhaps. I'm not in the mood to listen to any attempts at explanations. What was said was said. His intentions are clear enough.

I need to go, need to move my body, forget myself in motion and work and sweat. I look towards the Watcher's tower but stop.

I remember the promise of fire, of what could happen if I strayed past the threshold.

Maybe it's time to burn.

"I'll see you tonight." I turn towards the forge. "Don't bother waiting. I'll meet Vaen at the gate."

I walk off and don't stop when Lyr calls my name.

My heart pounds in time with every step as I draw closer to the forge. Every beat is another surge in the tidal wave sweeping through me. I am made of molten fire, to the point it obliterates everything else.

How dare he.

The words are a mantra, growing louder and louder the further away I get from Lyr.

How dare he throw away our friendship like that? How dare he pretend to care at all?

No, I need to not think anymore. Thinking hurts. Thinking makes me ache, and I don't want — can't — deal with another heartbreak. With losing something else that has grown to importance.

I reach the forge and only give a single, quick knock before entering.

The ring of metal against metal fills the forge, once again blistering hot. I welcome the heat, letting it add fuel to the fire already burning within. Haith stands at an anvil, legs braced wide, one arm raised as he brings down the hammer once again. The clang reverberates through my bones.

As if sensing my gaze, Haith pauses and looks up. Strands of hair fall loose from his braid, sticking to the sweat that dusts his brow. He wipes his face on his shirtsleeve, eyes never leaving mine, then slowly puts down his hammer. Then, even more slowly, he reaches behind him to untie the apron, sliding the heavy leather over his head. Gloves next, one at a time. He doesn't speak, doesn't ask why I'm here. Just watches me, looking for any hesitance, as he approaches.

My hands are shaking as I undo the buckle on my belt and scabbard, propping my sword up against the wall. Whether it's from nerves or anticipation I can't tell, but it sure as hell doesn't stop me.

Haith stops a few feet from me, those beautiful eyes unwavering as he searches for an answer to the unspoken question. "Are you here for something?" he asks. His voice is husky and low, telling me exactly what he hopes I'm here for.

I reach behind me and find the lock on the door, sliding the bolt without looking away. "I am."

Still he doesn't move, and I realize this has to be my choice. Whether he's been burned before by initiating or he just doesn't believe my willingness, Haith waits, hands held loosely at his side.

Fuck that.

I stride forward, two quick steps that bring me chest to chest with him. He's taller than me, probably the only man I've known to tower above me by half a foot or more, but I rise on my toes and grab his face, pulling it down to me. Our mouths meet in a clash of open lips. There is no soft parting, no gentle asking. I swirl my tongue around his, fighting for dominance, and can't quite hold back my gasp when he kisses back fiercely, broad hands finding my hips and bringing my body close to his. His tongue dips and darts with eloquence, stealing all rational thought, eradicating any lingering hesitation immediately. Heat radiates from our points of contact, and all I want is to erase the rest of the distance between us.

My hands tangle in his hair as I lean forward, hips moving to press into his, shivering as his fingers tighten, pressing into skin alight with desire. He slides those fingers under my shirt, finding the smooth expanse of bare skin at my stomach. One thumb traces lightly over it, the touch so delicate it makes me want to beg for more. I probably would if my mouth was not otherwise preoccupied.

We finally break our kiss, gasps taking over where words fail. We stare at each other, chests heaving, and he looks absolutely intoxicated, drunk on our kiss. My head whirls with the intensity of my desire, but all I can think is that I *need* more.

Haith must feel the same because he dips his head down for another consuming kiss. That clever tongue slides against my own willing one, his teeth nipping unexpectedly at my lower lip. When he draws away I start to say *not yet* but the words are swallowed in a gasp as he peppers feather-light kisses along my jaw, drawing up to my ear, where his teeth graze at that tender space behind the lobe. I positively melt with delight, fingers tightening where they grip his shoulders, nails digging into skin. He chuckles, the sound reverberating from where his mouth is pressed against me. I don't remember if I've heard him laugh like this before, pleased and promising more of the same. I know I could quickly become addicted to the sound.

Even as he continues his ministrations, kissing now lower, towards my collarbone, his hand rises, thumb continuing its slow sweep against my skin. He grazes the underside of my breast, touch still so damnable light I would demand more if I had the breath for words.

I don't want hesitance or sweetness. I crave that fire, no matter how fiercely it might burn.

I break away, taking a step back. My body immediately misses his. I can feel my nipples harden to points, and the ache between my thighs is positively mind-numbing. Haith draws back, confusion and maybe even a hint of hurt ghosting over his face. It disappears quickly as I waste no time in shrugging out of my tunic and undershirt, bared now to the waist. Gooseflesh dances over me despite the heat of the forge, drawing the skin

around my breasts even tighter. There's a flash of embarrassment, of an instinctual need to cover up and turn away. It
quickly melts away when Haith draws in a short, appreciative
breath, eyes drinking in my body. The shame turns to pride and
I can't quite banish the grin that steals over my face.

He takes my face in his hands. For the first time in my entire
life, I feel dwarfed by him, like I'm finally one of those girls that
seem to surround me: delicate, ethereal, dainty. Something I
always said I never wanted to be, but secretively wished I could
call myself.

"You," Haith says, his voice low, husky, and rough, "are
breathtaking."

Not beautiful. Breathtaking.

He kisses me again, and I want to burst with all of the
emotions swirling in me. Wanted, desired, worshipped. Important. Needed.

He grips me around the waist and lifts me with apparent
ease, earning a decidedly undignified squeak. He places me on
an empty table and wastes no time in dipping his head, mouth
latching around one breast even as his hand grips the other. His
thumb rubs over the sensitive skin, but his mouth is what
captures my attention. He sucks, hard then soft, testing me as
his teeth graze my nipple. I can't help but release a shaking
moan. I lean back, bracing myself on my elbows, eyes sliding
closed as the pleasure continues to grow.

"Light above, you taste so good." Haith switches breasts,
but now his hands drop lower, tugging at my pants.

I lift my hips, *yes yes yes*, and he fumbles with the buttons
only for a moment before sliding the obstructing material
down. When my boots stop his progress, he gives a growl of
annoyance and works quickly, tossing the offending items over
his shoulder. My undergarments, already wet with longing, are
discarded quickly next. I'm bared completely before him, and

there is not an ounce of shame as I spread my legs, breath uneven.

"Please," I beg. I can't remember the last time lust gripped me so fiercely. Perhaps never. Sex has already been enjoyable, but never longed for with this ferocity. I feel like I'll go mad if he doesn't do something more.

Haith chuckles, the sound dark, curling around my stomach and making it squeeze. He finally raises his head, dragging his tongue across his bottom lip like I'm the best fucking thing he's ever tasted. His eyes pin me more effectively than any physical restraint. Desire swirls in his gaze, which darkens as he drags a finger down my opening. I don't even try to hold back my gasp.

Up and down his finger travels, the tip just barely grazing past the entrance, until I want to writhe and whine with the maddening need.

"Stop teasing," I demand, but the words are breathy and broken.

He laughs again, still not looking away. "Why should I? This is entirely too much fun."

I open my mouth to say something most likely entirely degrading to my willpower, but without preamble Haith suddenly slips a finger inside me. My protests end in a sharp groan, which only grows louder as he adds a second finger. My eyes flutter closed, all focus zeroing in on those strong fingers sliding in and out of me.

"Yes," I whisper, sliding down a few inches, trying to open myself wider for him. "Light, that feels so damn *good*."

He bends down, nuzzling my neck even as his fingers continue their perfect rhythm. He bends them, tips grazing against my inner wall, and I almost lose it then and there. "You have no idea what I can do," he whispers as he grips my earlobe in his teeth. His tongue traces the shell of my ear, and I clench tight around his hand.

"Ah ah ah." He draws his hand away, and I whimper at the loss of contact, the heat that was spiraling in my core flattening out. The glimmer in Haith's eyes is downright wicked as he says, "Not yet."

He steps back, shedding his shirt and revealing a truly impressive display of muscles. I've barely started admiring them when he steps out of his pants, and only now I belatedly realize his impressive size wouldn't be contained to just his height.

I never thought my previous lovers were lacking, but now it's apparent I have been shorted this entire time.

Haith grips his cock in one hand, rubbing his own length as a bead of moisture glistens on the tip. He never looks away from me as he steps forward. I don't either, even when he grips my hips and pulls me to the edge of the table, throwing me onto my back. I can't think beyond the thrum of unfettered desire pulsing fiercely throughout every inch of my being. Haith takes his cock and rubs the head against me, parting the wet skin but not daring to enter yet. His free hand rests on my pelvis, and all thoughts spiral up and away as he finds the bundle of nerves there and presses his thumb against it.

His touch is just right, not too light and not too hard, as he circles my clit, still teasing me with what's about to come. Within moments I'm a writhing, panting mess, back arching as pleasure rolls through every muscle, every nerve.

As if from far away, I hear Haith ask, "Ready?"

All I can do is nod. Words have become impossible.

He doesn't ask again. There is no hesitance as he surges forward, thrusting himself in to the hilt in one smooth movement.

I cry out, mostly in the fierce pleasure of *finally* being filled, but there's pain too as I'm stretched more than I expect.

Haith leans forward, capturing my mouth in a kiss, even as

his hips begin a slow, steady rhythm. "There you go," he whispers as the pain fizzles into molten fire.

He doesn't stay gentle long. Needing this as much as I do, Haith quickly picks up speed, one hand gripping my hip while the other continues to press against my clit. With every thrust, every bit of me filled, I clench tighter and tighter, the fire building to an unstoppable force. As if sensing me teetering on the edge, Haith presses down more firmly, the tiniest bite of his nail digging into the delicate skin.

It's all I need, and I fall over the edge, a galaxy of light bursting behind my eyelids as everything collides. The fire consumes me completely, eating away at every minuscule part of myself, until all I can do is gasp and shake and try to breathe.

It doesn't take long for Haith to join me, his rhythm becoming disjointed and harsh, the slap of skin against skin rising in tandem to our gasping pants. When he comes, his hands dig into me almost painfully, but I grin up at the ceiling, feeling almost unbearably *alive* and wonderful and whole.

Haith pulls out, his pants turning into chuckles as he wraps his arms around me and lifts me with effortless ease. My body melts into his, head falling against his chest, every limb loose and relaxed.

He takes us into a small room off to the side of the forge. Inside is a modest kitchen with a large bed against one wall, the blankets haphazardly piled on top. He slides me onto the mattress, climbing in after, pulling the blankets over us both. I sink into the warm comfort, head pillowed on his shoulder.

We don't speak for several long moments, drinking in each others's warmth, the gentle rise and fall of chests. He plays with a strand of my sweat-soaked hair, fingertips brushing my temple, and the moment is everything I ever wished for in a lover.

"Well," Haith says at last, "I'm glad to see you survived last night." His chest rumbles with every word, lifting my head as he breathes.

I groan at the memory, and the realization that I don't have much longer until I have to face tonight's own *unique* challenges. I'm calm enough now to admit I probably overreacted with Lyr, but still not in a particularly forgiving mood. I embrace the moment of vulnerability, burying my head into his skin and reveling in the smell of iron and cedar that envelopes me.

"Don't remind me." The words are muffled, but I know Haith hears because he lets out a low chuckle that makes my core shiver.

"That bad?" He draws lazy circles on the naked skin of my back, making me both relax and clench tighter.

"We were attacked by a creature." I tell him the bare minimum, skipping over the details we're still not sure of — if it was targeting Lyr, if it could willfully change its corporeal form or if it was drawing magic from the land itself, from our fear, from Lyr even.

When I finish, Haith lets out a long breath. His fingertips never stop moving across my skin. "That's a shit night," he agrees. He turns his head, pressing a kiss into my hair. "I'm glad it made you decide to come back, though."

"I am, too." I think about acting on the sizzling feeling deep in my gut once again, but decide to instead say, "Enough of that. Have you always lived in Ulingard?" When he stares at me, clearly confused by the abrupt change, I add, "If I'm going to fuck someone, I should at least get to know them a little."

His laugh is loud and deep and I absolutely love it. "Oh yes, my parents and their parents and their parents all grew up here. We're northern stock. Dad used to joke about our ancestors coming from across the ice plains, but, well." He trails off with a shrug.

"No one comes from the other side of the ice plains."

"Exactly."

"It sounds a lot like where I'm from," I admit. "Small village you can never escape from."

I realize my words may be too harsh when Haith takes a moment to reply. "I don't mind it,'" he finally says. "It's rather nice, being able to expect the same thing every day."

"And what is that? What you do every day."

"Well, you already know I'm a jeweler. I make pieces with iron, precious metals, even bits of discarded wood the cutters bring back. None are quite what you might think of when you see a ring. But they sell for a pretty penny when merchants come in the summer months to trade for wood, and I've made nearly every villager's engagement ring by this point."

He speaks with pride in his work, and I think about asking to see some pieces, but the bed is too warm, his arms too strong.

"Some days I plan new designs or make wax molds. Berilt has been absent lately, a newborn babe at home, so I've helped out more in the forge. Some days I run the shop and set gems or carve wood." His words rumble against me, painting a picturesque image of the slow, unassuming beauty of his work.

"That sounds nice," I admit. And it does. It sounds perfectly nice. A good trade, a *smart* trade, something to invest in and pass on to your children.

A life akin to what I could have lived in Heron Hill. A life I so desperately sought to avoid.

Then Haith chuckles, loud enough for me to jump. "I do wish we had more visitors up here. Seeing the same old faces gets to be a bit boring after a while."

I feel mischievous and not even close to tired, so I sit up and swing a leg over to straddle Haith. He gives an appreciative hum, hands reflectively fitting around my thighs.

"Well, it's a good thing I'm not an old face yet," I tease as he grows hard against me.

And I show him exactly how far from boring I am.

It's well past nightfall, probably well past when I said I would be at the northern gate, and Vaen is obviously pissed.

We're alone except for the Watchers on duty, Lyr nowhere to be seen. I can't decide if that's a good thing or not. My good mood is far from gone, the earlier anger a distant if still clear memory, but I'm thankful it isn't put to the test by the mage's presence. A flicker of uncertainty roils through me, chasing the tail end of my euphoria, as I remember that I might very well die tonight.

"Sorry," I say to Vaen as I stop next to him, breathing only slightly heavily from my jog here. "I didn't realize how late it had gotten."

It's clearly the wrong thing to say, and Vaen's expression remains stony. "What the hell is more important than the whole reason you're here in the first place?" The words are practically spat out.

I debate giving a half-truth answer or even an all out lie, as the real truth would undoubtedly send him over the edge. Instead I cross my arms over my chest and raise my eyebrows. "You have your secrets, as you have been very clear about this entire time. I'm allowed to have mine."

This is clearly not the expected answer, and surprise followed by... amusement, perhaps? — flickers across his face. "My secrets aren't likely to harm us."

I snort at that and stride out into the field. Every bone in my body protests, as if the memory of last night has been engrained into my very being. But I do not let my feet stop walking. Vaen joins me half a step later, keeping up easily.

"Mine aren't either," I tell him, trying to keep my tone light and open. If we're going to survive the night, we need to work as a team. Pissing him off even further won't help either of us in the long run, no matter how fun it might be.

I can feel him looking at me, but I don't take my eyes off our surroundings. Already the tension seeps into me, dread curling in my stomach where lust was only a few hours ago. There's nothing to see, and the only thing I hear is the distant bleating of sheep, reassuring in their normality.

Vaen grunts, apparently taking me at my word.

We walk in silence for several minutes until we come to a rocky outcropping that rises a bit over the rest of the fields. It's closer to the forest than I'd like, certainly closer than last night, but there's no room to let fear drive our actions. We're here to find a source of the Aberrations and end them, not twiddle our thumbs in safety. I forgot that, earlier. I don't plan to again.

I hoist myself onto a wide, flat portion of the rock and unwrap half a loaf of bread and some hard cheese Haith gave me before I left. I tear the bread in half and offer one to Vaen. He hesitates, but eventually takes the food and sits next to me. I feel hyper-aware of his proximity, of how close his leg is to brushing mine, and I can't help but remember that night so long ago now, when he held my screaming body against his.

Those thoughts quickly switch to how *else* I was touched today, and it's everything I can do to not flush. Sex is the last thing I should be thinking about right now.

"Lyr was in a right state after coming back from Sunillen's." Vaen looks at me and raises one eyebrow. "He said there were words exchanged. Care to elaborate?"

I scowl at my bread, good mood threatening to evaporate

like mist in the morning dawn. A part of me is pleased that our conversation bothered him.

"I was upset he was sending us out here to die."

"What do you mean?"

I gesture to the fields around us, still mercifully empty. "Do you not remember what happened last night? We would have died without Lyr's magic. I didn't fancy going for round two and coming up short."

Vaen's sharp eyes flit from fields to me to forest to me again. "He isn't trying to sabotage us, if that's what you're thinking. How else are we supposed to test his theory? Send out a defenseless villager? At least we can hold our own."

I know he's right, but it's a hard thing to admit. "Maybe we'll be fine, that's true. But he didn't have to brush aside my concerns so, so... callously. Like he couldn't care less if we actually did die."

I expect Vaen to laugh at my silly dramatics. To sigh and say all women are ridiculous, they think too much into things. I don't even know if I would disagree with him. But, to my surprise, Vaen seems to consider my words, the thought behind them.

"There are times Lyr falls into the typical mage imagery."

"Stubborn, narcissistic, insufferably proud?" I interrupt.

Vaen acknowledges it with a chuckle. I can count the times he's laughed at me with true amusement, no malice hidden, on one hand.

I like the sound.

"Mages tend to turn their survival of their own magic into a strange, bitter pride. Lyr is no exception. But he's also not a particularly strong mage, so he must face his own insecurities as well. I'm sure you know how that goes."

I bristle at the implication. "Excuse me?"

There is no sympathy when he says, "Losing knighthood

and the Temple broke you, in a way you probably have never dealt with before. It changed you. Introduced an element of failure."

The words hit me like a wave of cold water, leaving me spluttering in their wake. The worst part is, I know he's right. Ever since leaving the Temple, I've been quicker to anger, more defensive, and worst of all... more afraid.

"This isn't about me," I say through gritted teeth.

Another eyebrow arch, and there is *definitely* amusement glittering in his eyes now. "Oh, did I strike a nerve?"

It's a struggle to keep my anger from surging and sweeping us both under. "Tell me a defining moment of your life that I can twist and throw in your face, and we'll see how calm and collected *you* are."

I'm staring straight at him, so I don't miss the shadow that passes over his features. It's quick, gone before it can settle, the familiar smugness falling back into place. But it was there. I saw it, no doubt about it. I wonder, yet again, what Lyr could have possibly saved him from.

Feeling strangely emboldened, I lean forward, forearms braced on my knees. "Tell me something about yourself."

Vaen snorts and looks at the fields. "Why?"

"Well, it's not fair, really. You know so much about me. About Lyr, too. But all I know about you is you're a thief who poses as a mercenary." I throw the heel of my bread into the field for the sheep tomorrow. "Give me something else. Tell me who Vaen actually is."

Vaen is quiet for so long I think he's going to ignore me and we'll spend the rest of the night in awkward silence until the mist swallows us whole. But then, to my surprise, he says quietly, "I wasn't posing as a mercenary. I did join the mercenary guild, and worked for them for a long time. Thieving is something I did many, many years ago, and has only recently become part of my life again."

He copies me, throwing the last of his bread out. It arcs out over the grass, and I follow it before the morsel disappears into the waving strands.

I swallow, throat strangely dry, and work up the courage to ask another question.

"What happened in those months between our first meeting?"

He shakes his head, not looking at me. "A mistake in my past caught up to me. A dangerous mistake. Lyr offered me a way out. For now, at least."

"That's not a fair answer." I want to push, want to ask what exactly happened, what mistake could be bad enough to tear him away from his way of living, but the words that come out are entirely unexpected. "Why were you so livid about me joining you and Lyr?"

I'm mortified as soon as the words are said, but there's no taking them back now. I grip my hands together tightly while I wait for his answer.

"You were a liability," he says with a slight shrug, as if it should be obvious. "It's safer to work alone."

"Yeah, well, you're not a delight either," I mutter.

He cracks another grin at that, an honest one, but the smile flickers as something just past my shoulder catches his eye.

I turn, all frivolity immediately wilting as dread claws its way up my throat.

The mist seeps across the field, slow and steady in its inevitability, sending long fingers to rake across the swaying grass as it searches for its prey.

For us.

CHAPTER

FOURTEEN

We're about to die.

But there's no figure in the mist, not yet, and I scold myself for my own panic. I need to be *better*.

I rise into a crouch, feeling pinned by a thousand watchful eyes, and turn in a slow circle.

Nothing.

I don't know if that's a good sign or not. I carefully climb a level higher, booted feet slipping on the smooth rock. I find my balance again and start to take another look from this new vantage point.

"What are you doing?" Vaen hisses, voice low and almost angry.

He's hiding something. He has no right to question a simple movement, no reason to... unless it brings me out of his easy reach.

The thought surprises me, and the surprise is enough to shake off the queasy anger that had started to churn in my stomach. How utterly ridiculous to even entertain such a notion. Vaen and I are allies. We're on the same damn side. He might not like me, but he wouldn't try to kill me.

Not like whatever waits for me out there.

In the dark are creatures of shadows and night, barely formed wisps of smoke that curl and undulate as they slide through the grass. Eyes nothing more than pits of darkness that somehow see everything, see straight to my soul, making me nothing more than a meal served before even worse monsters.

They're here before I know it, tendrils that reach up, whisper thin yet somehow steel strong, to glide against my ankles, my calves, up to my thighs, burning where they touch, bringing the agony of fire with every inch they gain. Tendrils that anchor me to the spot, wrapping around me like a lover, holding me down even as they crawl higher and higher, over my chest and my shoulders and spilling down my back, a river of a starless night.

Smoke fills my open mouth, my eyes, my ears, flooding through every orifice to eat me from the inside out, replacing working lungs with fragile butterfly wings that hysterically beat together, begging for air, begging for relief, knowing that none is coming.

Die. About to die.

I shiver, hopelessness rushing in to replace the fear, a great well of overwhelming despair that chokes the air that remains, stealing all breath, all *will* to breathe—

"Fuck!"

I slide my sword a few inches free of its scabbard and press my thumb against the blade, hard enough to draw a line of blood. The pain does exactly what I want, clearing my mind and banishing the veil that had fallen over me.

I stare down at myself, hands shaking as I run them over my legs, but the shadows are gone.

They were never here to begin with.

The world remains the same, with the hint of fog creeping across the fields, but that inner voice is gone, and I realize finally it was never my own at all. None of it was.

"Be careful," I warn Vaen. My voice shakes even after I try to clear it, the memory of blackness unable to be banished. "Their mind tricks have already started."

He grunts an acknowledgement, shooting me only the briefest glance before resuming his endless stare at our surroundings.

I join him, watching the fog with trepidation, every muscle tense. Something is out there. It whispered to me. Cloaked my mind with lies. It won't be long now before it makes itself known.

Long minutes pass, made longer by the amount of times I have to remind myself to breathe. I try to keep my eyes focused on the fog, which ebbs and twists around our rock outcropping now, a never ending sea just waiting for us to drown in it.

"Do you see anything?" I finally dare to whisper to Vaen.

"No."

His answer is terse and short, something hidden behind that single word. For the first time since I shook off the voice, I take the time to really look at my companion. A layer of sweat shines on his taut, almost unrecognizable, face.

"What's wrong?" I don't dare step closer to him, as if the movement will provoke the voice again. Will beg me to raise my sword against him, poison my mind into thinking he's the villain here.

Vaen is my ally, I tell myself again, each word unbroken and unyielding.

There is no surge of that feral hatred, no whispers to beckon at the edge of sanity. I look at Vaen again, the moonlight just bright enough to show the wild glint in his eyes, and I finally put two and two together.

"What is it trying to tell you?"

Vaen shakes his head, strands of dark hair coming loose from his horsetail, sticking to the sweat glazed across his skin.

"It's clever," he admits. His voice is tight, as if trying to hold something at bay. "It keeps begging me to kill you."

I almost laugh, but the dryness in my throat swallows the sound before it can emerge.

"It did the same to me," I say.

"What kind of Aberration could do this?" He slams his hand into the rock face, hard enough for me to jump. The physicality is enough to ease some of the tension in his shoulders, the pain slacking the creature's hold on us. "Aberrations aren't intelligent enough to play mind games and turn people against each other."

"The Aberration last night wasn't like what we've seen before." I stare hard at Vaen, muscles ready to move should he give in and attack. "Think about it. It went for Lyr. It split itself in two when I proved to be a veritable threat as well. It was *thinking*. It has been playing mind tricks this entire time. Haith says it talks to the men who come out here, whispers things to them."

"Who the hell is Haith?"

My answer hovers on my tongue, but I swallow it back. I don't know why I'm hesitant to admit the truth, but something keeps me from saying it aloud. As if it's too new, too precious, to risk. Would Vaen even care? There's no reason for him to.

I have to offer something. "One of the villagers, a jeweler. He described some encounters, and they all seemed more like... this." This is worse than he said, though. Is it growing in power? Does it remember us from yesterday? That idea is the most terrifying so far.

Vaen accepts my answer and closes his eyes, breathing deeply. I wonder if the creature is still there, looking for a way back in. I touch my sword again, the cool pommel steadying amidst the fear.

"I didn't hear any voices last night," Vaen says.

"I did, but it was different." I can't help but shiver as I recall that roiling, monstrous voice that described my death, that ached with such intensity for our destruction. "This one doesn't sound the same at all. Last night was raw power and hunger. This one is more cunning. More insidious."

He shoots me an incredulous look. "Do you think they come from two different creatures?"

The idea makes me want to throw down my sword and flee, but I nod all the same. "Yes. I do." I hadn't really considered the possibility until he voiced it aloud, but I know with utter certainty that it's the truth.

Vaen swears, loud and angry. "What does that even mean?" He has always been unflappable before, scolding me for my own emotion, but now there is a raw wildness to him that both unnerves me and reminds me that, despite his callous words, Vaen is human as well. "How many are there out here?"

I shake my head, unable to give him an answer.

"Shit." He runs a hand over his head, dislodging more hair.

"See," I mutter, unable to help myself. "Now you know why I was so pissed at Lyr for sending us into this mess."

For a moment, there is nothing. Then a laugh bursts from Vaen, startlingly loud, and I nearly lose my footing. "It wasn't that funny."

"I think this proves his theory, though," Vaen says once his mirth dies down. He gestures to the empty field around us. "See anything?"

I don't. Nothing but whispers and fog, the same as every other non-magical villager. What's even more, the fog looks to be lessening, thinning out to expose autumn-dry patches of earth.

I sigh. "I hate when he's right."

"That we can agree on."

And despite everything, despite the fear still working along my veins, the memory of thoughts that hover just out of consciousness, the images of dark creatures and a spiraling sense of unknown... despite all of it, I grin at Vaen.

And, miracle of miracles, he returns the grin for the briefest moment before looking away once more.

"So, what happens now?" I gesture to the dissipating fog. "We proved Lyr's theory as far as we can tell. The creatures seek magic. Do we drag him back out here, see if he can find the source of them?"

Vaen's face has returned to its usual grimness as he nods. "But not yet. We need more power if we're going to face off against those shadow Aberrations. Our swords only do so much. It looks like it's finally time for me to join you at Sunillen's."

It takes my tired brain an inordinately long time to realize what he's implying.

Vaen is going to steal an imbued object from under the nose of the very man we might be fighting against.

"Come on, Raylen. Please."

I stare at my porridge, dusted heavily with cinnamon and honey. Steam curls in the air above the bowl, bringing the heady scent to my nose. It's easier to focus on the food rather than the man sitting across from me looking decidedly well rested. Vaen is the late riser in our group this morning and has not come down from our room yet.

Or maybe that was on purpose, so he wouldn't have to listen to this excruciating conversation.

"I'm not interested in apologies, Lyr."

Last night I would have been, maybe. But he was fucking *asleep* when we returned, and we were too weary to wake him. Now with the heavy knowledge that whatever we might have found out about the Aberrations is nowhere near enough, my anger returns with a vengeance.

I dare a glance up at the mage but look down again before he can catch my eyes. He seems properly pathetic and apologetic, but I don't believe a moment of it.

"You used us," I say, the words slick with poison. I throw down my spoon, not caring that porridge splatters across the table. Lyr flinches back from the verbal and physical assault.

"You agreed to this," he whispers, the words lacking any heat. I finally raise my head for more than a second. He looks drawn and pale now, but meets my eyes regardless. "When I offered the opportunity, you took it. You knew the risk."

I snort as I cross my arms and lean back in my chair. "Bullshit. Don't try and pull that on me. I knew the risks, sure. I knew I might die. But that's not what I'm talking about."

For the first time, Lyr looks confused.

"When you told us to go out there without magic, I panicked." It's not easy to admit, but it *is* true. Not that I owe him any more truth. "I was scared, and rightly so. I turned to my ally, my companion... my friend. And you told me it didn't matter if I died. It didn't matter to you if we sacrificed ourselves, as long as you got what you wanted in the end."

Understanding flashes across his face, followed quickly by guilt. "Raylen, no, that isn't—"

It takes everything in me not to slam my fists into the table. "Do not," I say, low and absolutely unyielding, "even try to tell me it wasn't what you meant. Don't lie to me like that. Don't lie to yourself."

Lyr sits unmoving, breath shallow, not even daring to blink. Then, abruptly, he nods. "You're right. That was wrong of me, to try to convince us both of something that didn't happen. I'm sorry."

I keep still and silent. Waiting.

"When I first attended Haven," Lyr starts, "I was ecstatic to make friends. I didn't have many before then, mostly because all I did was work to help feed my family."

He waves off any sympathy, but I have none to offer. This isn't what I want to discuss, but for whatever reason, I decide to keep my mouth closed and give him the benefit of the doubt. In my heart of hearts, I can't shake off the idea of him as my friend.

"One of them was a girl, Atteva. She was smart and pretty and popular, but poor like me. We grew close. As we went to classes and learned about magic together, I was so excited to finally have someone to join me on this journey."

Still I don't speak. I have a suspicion I know where this story is heading.

"Anyway, one day, we were outside practicing our magic. I wasn't very good back then. Still aren't, really, in the grand scheme of magic. But Atteva, she was powerful. She was an elemental, so breathtakingly good at manipulating ice. The professors all said she would be the best in our year. And I was so *proud* of her. So proud that my friend was going to become this amazing mage, worthy of glory and honor.

"It was summer. Hot. Muggy, with the promise of rain. No one really wanted to be outside, but there we were, sweating our assess off, most of us probably just waiting for lessons to be over so we could return inside.

"I remember looking down, working on my illusion, when everyone started gasping. I remember them yelling to back away, watch out. I looked up, at Atteva across from me, to see the cracks form on her face. She only had a moment, baffled and confused, looking at *me* for help, and then the pain overtook her. After that she just screamed. She screamed as the magic ate away at her from the inside out, as she lost that delicate balance of control and let too much out at once. I watched as those cracks chipped away at skin and muscle and bone and she shattered into a thousand pieces."

His gaze is faraway, seeing another time, another person.

"Her blood was cold when it landed on me. And that night was the first time I ever saw an Aberration. It was outside the walls, born of her explosion of magic, and the Watchers and mages took care of it before it even had an inkling to harm anyone. But the teachers, they brought us first years outside to see it. To show us what happens if we lose the battle, as if cleaning your friend's blood and marrow off your face wasn't enough."

I shudder at the imagery. Lyr just stares down at his clasped hands, shaking his head.

"Atteva was the first of my friends to die, but she wasn't the last. And each time it happened, I told myself I wasn't going to have friends anymore, because losing them was just too damn painful." The look in his eyes is haunting, gutting me and erasing the anger like a balm to a wound.

"And each time, I failed. I found someone else. I made friends with them. And, inevitably, I lost them one way or another. They died, or they became powerful and too high and mighty for poor little Lyr." His lips twist in a sneer, and I see the mage again, the one yearning for power, always at odds with a boy just looking to belong. "So I told myself to stop. To let it stay at the surface. Stay friendly, enjoy conversations and companionship and sex, but never, under any circumstances, was I to let them in deeper.

"When you challenged me yesterday, I realized I'd done it again. Let myself open up. Let another person worm their way under my skin, into my heart. I realized I cared about you, and I *didn't* want you to die. Don't want you to die. But when I thought that, my old defenses came up. And I told myself, told you, that it didn't matter if you died. That I would be okay no matter what.

"But that's just not true. I can't keep lying to myself. If you or Vaen died because of my thirst for power..." He hangs his head low, shaking it slowly. "I'm not sure I could ever forgive myself for that."

I sit there for a long moment, letting his story sink in. A part of me cruelly questions if this is just another of his illusions, meant to trick and cajole into getting what he wants.

But looking at Lyr, at the rounded, hunched shoulders, the slight tremble to his tightly held hands... I can't help but believe him.

"You're my friend, too." The heat is finally gone from my words, and Lyr looks up, the first glimmer of hope entering his eyes. "Became one that first day, when I saved your sorry ass." I sigh and lean back. "And I guess me saving you is just going to be a theme of our friendship until we can figure out how to stop these Aberrations for good."

He gives me a small, hesitant smile. "Thank you. For forgiving me, and trusting me."

"Thank you for opening up to me."

I gesture to our breakfast and take a bite of the now-cool porridge. "Come on, you better eat up. You're going to need your wits so you can distract Sunillen long enough for Vaen to steal an imbued object."

Lyr fumbles, nearly dropping his mug as he chokes on his sip of coffee.

"Wait, *what*?"

FIFTEEN

"Let's alert the whole city to our plans, shall we?"

Vaen slides into the bench next to me and is brought coffee and breakfast within a few moments. He smiles up at the serving maid, who seems startled for a minute before returning the gesture.

"Thank you," I murmur as she refills my coffee. Her hand shakes as the dark liquid streams into my cup, almost sloshing over the side. I look up, about to ask if she's all right, but the words die in my throat. The serving maid watches me with lips thin and tightly pressed together, a look close to fear in her eyes. Fear of... me?

It doesn't make sense. I start to ask, but Vaen suddenly slips a coin out and pushes it across the table towards her. Her attention switches to him, the fear vanishing, taking with it my certainty that I saw it at all.

"Keep the coffee coming," Vaen says, quiet but not unkind.

The serving maid whispers her agreement, pocketing the coin as she slips back into the kitchens.

"Wow," I say. "Look at you, being downright pleasant to other people. Did someone drug you?"

Lyr snorts into his breakfast while Vaen very casually flicks his dining knife, sending it deep into the wooden table inches from my hand.

I scowl and pull it from the table. "Message received. Jackass."

Vaen retrieves his knife, fingers brushing mine for a moment, and I swear I can see an insufferable smirk on his face as he cuts into his piece of caramelized ham. "I didn't realize we were using terms of endearment. Sweetheart."

Lyr chokes on his coffee, and I'm torn between stabbing Vaen with my own knife and laughing out of sheer amazement. I settle for a slow shake of my head. "Damn. I can't decide if this is better or worse than your outright dismissal of me."

The corners of his eyes crinkle in amusement. "I'm sure my senses will return and we can go back to insufferable silence."

Lyr looks between us with wide eyes. A slow smile curls his lips. "I knew you two would eventually get over the bullshit." Before we can protest, he says, "Tell me about last night." Lyr spears a bite of egg on his fork and waits for one of us to start.

I glance at Vaen, but he only dips his head in my direction. "It was unnerving," I say, "but not like when you were with us. Based on the villagers' descriptions, what we came across last night is what they've seen before. Mists, voices, an overall feeling of despair."

"There wasn't any physical manifestation." Vaen nods to me. "But the voices were destructive."

"They tried to turn us against each other." I still can hear the echo of those words, begging me to kill Vaen.

I wonder if he does too.

"Raylen thinks there are different types of Aberrations."

Lyr raises his eyebrows. "I hadn't considered that. But how would that be possible?"

"You're the mage. You tell us."

Lyr's eyes grow faraway as he works through this new puzzle. "Aberrations have always been somewhat of a mystery, but we do know several concrete facts." He holds up a hand, fingers curled to his palm, then raises one digit. "Aberrations are created from an outpouring of magic, usually when someone loses control. Two: they can vary somewhat in appearance, but ultimately take a human form, albeit a twisted version of it. Three: their intelligence is more in line with an animal's than ours, and they do not distinguish between their enemies. They will attack anyone and anything. Four: they are strong and fast, but have no control over the magic that made them."

"Nothing earth shattering," Vaen says. "Have they ever been captured alive, studied? Brought about purposefully?"

Lyr snorts in derision. "You're asking the wrong person. Those are questions for people in power. I may be a mage, but most of us just totter around following the queen and conclave's orders. If experiments have been done on Aberrations, the public is certainly not privy to them."

"The idea of someone *building* an Aberration... potentially burning out a mage purposefully..." I shudder.

Vaen sucks on his teeth while his hands make idle motions, turning the dinner knife over and over between lithe fingers. The movement is slow and hypnotizing, a welcome distraction from the rapidly darkening conversation. "It just doesn't make sense. Excessive magical energy creates an Aberration... but from what?"

Lyr stills.

"What do you mean?"

Vaen points the knife at me, but not threateningly. "Think about it. Does the magic just create them out of thin air? I have never cared to delve into magic, but even to my own knowledge, a mage can't, say, create a wave without the water already being there. So how does the Aberration actually form? Surely it can't be created from nothing."

We both look to Lyr, but he doesn't meet our eyes. He rubs a hand over his face, lips pressed into a thin whiteless line, before sitting back with a quiet exhalation and muttered curse. He glances around, but we are alone in the common room, the only guests in the inn.

I'm surprised, then, when he waves his hand in a circle around us. I can't see the magic, but I've travelled with Lyr long enough to recognize a circle of protection. "No one can hear us now," he explains when Vaen raises his eyebrows pointedly.

"That's not a good sign."

"Look." Lyr leans forward, eyes pinning me in place. What little joviality he still had is gone now. "This doesn't leave this room. You absolutely *cannot* tell anyone this. Not even another mage, because they'll realize I broke the order."

I glance at Vaen, but he seems just as puzzled as I am.

Lyr shifts in his chair, hands twisting around themselves. "Listen. If we weren't up here, fighting something wholly new, I wouldn't break order to tell you. Even as friends," he adds with a look at me. "This has been protected by our conclave for hundreds of years, only told to mages because, well, we have to know. To watch for the signs." He wets his lips.

"Light above, spit it out," Vaen growls.

Lyr takes a fortifying breath. "Vaen is right. You can't create something out of nothing — that's a basic rule of life. A tenant of magic. Yes, Aberrations are made from an expulsion of energy, but that energy can't do anything by itself. It simply lingers, where it was displaced. Until..." He gestures vaguely.

Vaen inhales sharply before cursing. I glance between the two, thoroughly confused. "I don't understand."

"Until someone walks into the magic," Vaen clarifies. His eyes don't leave Lyr.

My brain whirls, trying to finish putting the pieces into place. "So you're saying, Aberrations are formed when *someone* walks into the magic..." I trail off.

"It corrupts them," Lyr confirms. His face is so unbearably grave, features carved from stone itself, that my stomach hollows out from the horror of it all. "Magic is naturally drawn to life. But when it's contained in the Crystals, it can't be unleashed on just anyone. That's why the Crystals choose who is strong enough to control it — because when they can't, they are eaten away by it. Sometimes it's quick, destroying them immediately. But sometimes it... twists. Holds the life force together even while nothing of the original creature remains."

"Humans," I snap. "Not a creature."

He holds up a hand to my anger. "Yes, I'm sorry. The conclave uses specific wording, probably to undermine their humanity. Make it easier for us to deal with the Aberrations."

"So every Aberration is actually a human who happened to be in the wrong place at the wrong time? Who just walked through the magic, something they can't see or sense, and — that's it? They're just gone?"

"It's why mages patrol so much," Lyr explains, as if that small kernel is enough to offset the awful reality. "We can sense the magic, albeit not until we're within a certain range. But we dispel it if we find it."

"But you're the ones causing it in the first place!"

"Not intentionally. It's not like we're trying to kill innocents." He won't meet my eyes.

I sit forward, head in hands, breakfast forgotten. "But why keep it a secret? Why not tell the people? Aberrations are one of the great mysteries in our world and you mages have always known the actual cause." The betrayal that, yet again, the people who are supposed to be keeping us safe have been hiding information — that they aren't what they say to be — cuts deeply.

"Look, I understand you're upset. I would be too. I *was*, too. But what would happen if everyone did know? Travel would become slower. Fewer people would dare to cross between cities, impacting trade. Mages could become ostracized, forced to travel along preselected routes only. Or, let's go one step further. Magic becomes constrained. Forced to obey certain rules. So bandits and raiding parties start to increase. The Zunesha Islands realize we're hobbled and wage another war against us. Only now we have fewer mages who know what the hell they're doing, and we lose."

The reality he paints is all too easy to imagine. "I don't like it," I stubbornly say, but the fire has gone out of my words.

"So the crown knows?" Vaen asks.

Lyr gives a small shrug. "I believe so. Let's remind ourselves I'm not in a position of power. I don't know the secrets between the conclave and the crown."

"I'm tired of secrets." I push my plate away. "Why hasn't the conclave *sent* a mage up here yet? Or a knight? They're supposed to protect the cities when the Watchers aren't enough."

Lyr spreads his hands. "I suppose the queen didn't take the rumors seriously. Or she did and passed it off to the conclave, for them to deal with magic issues, and they..." He groans. "I don't know. Maybe Sunillen is in talks with them. Maybe they figured he could handle anything up here. Your supposition is as good as mine."

"We're going in circles. We aren't in a position to know those things, so let's get back to what we can actually deal with," Vaen says. "Are we assuming our shadow Aberrations are created the same way?"

"No. Normal Aberrations are tangible. Something that hurts

when you cut it. But the shadows... they're here one minute and gone the next. They don't adhere to any of the rules of a true Aberration. The way they vanish and reappear... I would be surprised if they're made of physical material at all."

"So they're pure magic?"

"I think that's closer to the truth, yes."

"Is someone making them?"

Lyr looks at me grimly. "If they aren't, then the very laws of magic are changing before our eyes. I'm not sure which one scares me more."

"We need to go out again." It isn't a question. "But this time we need to actively search for the mage responsible." Sunillen's name hangs in the air, unsaid but clear.

Lyr nods. "Yes. I agree." He points to Vaen. "Which is why you're stealing me an imbued object today. I'm going to need all the help I can get."

"Do you think you can ask him first?" My words sound feeble and idiotic. "So we don't make an enemy where there might not be one?"

Vaen snorts. "Don't be dim. We all know there isn't another mage up here."

Lyr clears his throat. "Unless someone is hiding their powers."

I gape at him. "But why? What would be the point of that? I've never met a mage who wasn't proud of being one."

"Perhaps they're like me." Lyr's smiles reeks of bitterness and grim acknowledgement. "Maybe they're weak and searching for power any way they can."

"Fuck." Vaen massages his forehead. "If that's true, it could literally be anyone."

Lyr nods grimly.

The reality of our situation — the almost impossible task

we have to find the true perpetrator — grips my heart in an iron fist.

"How do we find the answer before it's too late?" I whisper.

Lyr stands, grabbing his cloak and swinging it around his shoulders.

"Like we do anything. One moment at a time. And the next thing to do is to go to Sunillen's."

Vaen moves to stand, but I shake my head with a grimace. "You may be ready to go off and save the world, but I'd like a bath first please." I look them both up and down. "You probably should take one too."

"Don't want your smell to give you away," Lyr cheerfully adds with a clap on Vaen's shoulder.

Despite the teasing, Vaen is last to bathe, leaving Lyr and I to twiddle our thumbs by the cold fire. I can't help but think of Haith as I stare into the hearth, fresh coal already waiting for a match. Finally unable to take it, I rise and brush out my own cloak.

"I'm going to the forge," I tell Lyr. "I'll meet you two outside in a few minutes."

His eyebrows immediately shoot up. "Why the hell are you going there?"

Suddenly embarrassed, I shrug and don't meet his eyes. "I want to update Haith on what happened last night. We've... been talking since we arrived here."

Lyr snaps his fingers, mouth a perfect O of realization. "That's who was down here last night! I knew I recognized him, but I couldn't remember why. You were talking to him that first night, right?" Without waiting for my reply, he continues, "He was here last night with some friends. I thought he was looking for someone, and he kept looking over at me but I didn't know why. I guess you're the reason, huh?"

I can feel my face flushing even though my logical adult brain tells my traitorous heart that there is nothing to be ashamed about.

Lyr notices and snorts, waving a hand dismissively. "Light, there's no reason to look at me like that. Good for you, I say. I wouldn't say no to someone in my bed either." He pauses, then adds more seriously, "Don't tell him what we're doing today. I'm sure you have excellent judgement about people — you saved *me* after all — but we still need to be careful."

"Of course." My words are steady, but his request shocks me back to reality.

The truth is, I don't know Haith. Not really. I would like to believe he can be trusted, but I don't know that. It doesn't matter there has been no hint of magic. If there really is a hidden mage, they've taken enough precautions to fool an entire village.

It doesn't matter that Haith has given me no reason to doubt his integrity or honesty, no reason to see him as a possible villain beyond sheer paranoia.

Lyr is right. It's safer to keep our plans for today unsaid.

The blast of heat from the forge has become almost welcoming, especially as the days march ceaselessly towards winter. The sky outside is gray today, and although it doesn't yet feel cold enough for snow, the possibility hangs in the air. The idea of combing the forest for a mage while trudging through knee high snow drifts is not something I'm looking forward to.

It is not Haith who looks up at my entrance, however, but an older man, bald headed and with a wiry black beard. He wears smithy leathers, soot across one cheek, and his smile is friendly but tired. I pause, taking a furtive glance around the forge, but there is no one else to be seen.

"What can I do for you today?"

Be someone else isn't a good answer, so I settle for, "I'm so sorry, I'm actually looking for Haith."

His smile turns knowing. "Ah, of course. I was able to sneak away from the wife and baby for a bit today, so I sent him back to his own shop." His eyes crinkle. "He's next door."

I thank Berilt and return to the street, finally noticing a small shop tucked into the corner of the row of buildings next to the forge. It's small, with a single window display showing an arrangement of strange but beautiful jewelry. A series of iron circles, similar to what I saw Haith forging, rest atop one another, each smaller than the previous, with a braided leather strap running through them. Next to it lies a piece of wood cut into a heart, lacquered and oiled so it shines brightly, framed with delicate gold wire. And finally there is a ring, the metal band twining around itself, a triangular blue sapphire glistening in the center.

The wooden sign above the door simply reads *Jewelry*. I hesitate for only a moment before pushing my way inside.

The inside of the shop is softly lit by the light through the window and several shuttered lanterns hanging at intervals across the walls. Simple shelves covered with green velvet line the walls, each holding an assortment of jewelry similar to the window display. A counter runs across the middle of the store, behind which is a large desk covered with a variety of tools. Haith hunches over the desk, brow furrowed as he delicately uses thin pincers to twist a golden chain. His long fingers manipulate the chain precisely, and I can't help but remember what else they are good for.

I take the time to admire him, how focused he is on his task, and wait patiently until he gives a noise of satisfaction and sits back.

"See anything you like?" He glances at me with a smirk.

"Sure do," I reply, not bothering to look away.

A grin unfurls, devious and knowing and amused all in one, and I try not to blush at his clear intentions.

"Would you like some tea?" Haith asks, rising and coming around the counter.

I shake my head regretfully. "I can't stay. We're going to talk to Sunillen again."

His lips twist in disappointment. "How did last night go?"

"It was... eye opening, but far less adventurous than our first outing."

"That's a relief." Haith steps to me, one hand trailing up my collarbone and the side of my neck, fingers whisper soft, sending molten shockwaves through me as they glance over my skin. He lowers his head, mouth hovering over my ear, breath warm and decadent as he whispers, "I would hate for you to be tired out already."

My core turns to jelly and warmth cascades over me as he kisses the shell of my ear.

"You have no idea how much I want to stay." I put a hand on his chest, relieved when his heart pounds as erratically as mine. "But I can't. We have a lot of things to do today."

He doesn't stop kissing, and I don't exactly push him away. "I'm sure you do," he agrees between kisses. Now he's at the hollow of my throat, his murmured words vibrating against my skin. "That is very important business. But so is this."

He trails a hand up my thigh, clever fingers just barely brushing against that tight bundle of nerves not hidden well enough by clothing.

I let out a soft, heady gasp, leaning into him, breathing in the already comforting scent of coal and metal and wood. Then, body aching, I pull away. "I can't, as much as I want to. And I *do* want to." Almost enough to say to hell with everything else.

"I just can't stop yet. There's so much to understand, to try and figure out. I feel like... like we don't have much time left before something happens." Before something snaps, changes, twists, destroys.

There is annoyance on Haith's face now, in the darkening irises of his eyes. "These creatures have been here for weeks now. They can wait another night."

He steps forward again, ignoring my hand on his chest. I think briefly of letting him convince me to stay, but I just *can't*. The pulse of duty, mirrored by my own pumping heart, is too strong.

I put both hands on his chest now, stepping back even as I push against him with just enough force to let him know I'm serious. I don't think I would win in an all out strength contest if it came to that, but it's enough to finally stop Haith.

He sighs, disappointment clear in the sound, but the annoyance I saw earlier has vanished.

"I understand." He takes my hand, turning it over so he can press a kiss against the inside of my wrist. My toes practically curl over themselves in my boots.

"I'll be back tonight," I promise. Lyr said it would be too risky to go into the fields today with our newly acquired object, assuming we actually manage to steal one.

Haith kisses my other wrist, then captures my mouth, immediately claiming the territory as his. When he finishes, I'm shaky and weak-kneed.

"Be safe," he says, finally releasing me and stepping back.

"You are more at danger here, with all those sharp metals and wood carving knives," I tease. "Everything will be fine. I'll see you tonight."

He nods but does not break my gaze as I step back into the dreary, cloud covered streets.

It isn't until the door swings shut that I wonder why, exactly, he had been *annoyed*. Disappointment I can understand. I'm disappointed too. But annoyed? Like I'm messing up some sort of plan...

No. I shake my head and force that thought out. There's no way Haith is involved in any of this. The coincidence would just be too great.

Unless he planned it all. Unless he knew who I was, and willingly jumped into a sexual relationship with me to get close to me. To distract me, or maybe to even—

"Raylen, are you coming?"

My head jerks up, eyes focusing on Lyr and Vaen standing halfway down the street. Vaen shifts from foot to foot, clearly impatient, while Lyr waits with hands on his hips, a cocky, knowing smile curling his lips upwards.

Haith is innocent. I have to believe that, because if I let conspiratorial thoughts consume me, I could very well ruin something that has the potential to be amazing. Until I gather more evidence, until something else becomes very apparent, Haith will remain innocent.

"Have fun?" Lyr asks as I join them.

I elbow him in the gut as I pass, then hook one foot around his ankle and pull, bringing him abruptly to his knees. "Like we had the time for that. Be nice."

Coughing, Lyr hauls himself up, shaking the dust out of his robes. "I thought I *was* being nice," he grumbles, falling into step with Vaen.

As we pass the Watchers tower, I pause at the gates for a moment, staring up at the intimidating gray stone. "I think I'll pay them a visit later, after we finish with Sunillen," I announce. "I need a good training bout anyway." I look at Vaen, cocking an eyebrow. "Want to join? You might hear something I don't."

He hesitates but eventually nods. "Lyr should come too, though. To see if there are any fluctuations of magic."

So many secrets from so many people. I feel like a fishing boat on the sea in a storm, riding the waves higher and higher — waiting for the inevitable drop into the impenetrable black depths of the water.

When will the fall come?

SIXTEEN

I can't help but wonder if the servants are as tired of seeing us as I am of coming to Sunillen's.

"Is Vaen coming with me or you?" I ask Lyr as we wait for the front door to open.

"You," Vaen says immediately. Lyr rolls his eyes, irritated at the interruption, but waves his hand for the thief to continue. "It will be easier to excuse myself from the kitchens than the mage. Less noticeable."

"Your entire presence is noticeable," I say wryly. "Don't you think you'll draw attention suddenly being here for the first time?"

"Well, you may give me particular notice, but I assure you, I am not worried about remaining inconspicuous." He raises one eyebrow at me.

Is that how he wants to play then? Challenge accepted. "I know I'm distracting, but you should really start paying closer attention to your own job than where my eyes are *not* looking."

A slow grin unfurls across his face. Whatever the reason, Vaen seems to enjoy the verbal sparring — and, if I'm being completely honest, I do too.

His reply is cut off as the door opens. And yes, the servant looks a little exasperated to find us here again.

"We'll stop bothering you one of these days," Lyr says cheerfully. "Unfortunately, today is not that day."

I turn my snort into a cough when the manservant looks to me, eyebrows raised and clearly judging.

"Ah, Master Lyr. Back again, are you? I can't say I'm surprised."

I look past the manservant, into the dimmer hallway behind him. Sunillen stands on the grand staircase, a bundle of scrolls in his arms, his descent halted as he watches us file in. I stare unabashedly, desperately hoping to find some change from the previous day, some sign of exhaustion or hopelessness, *anything* that will give us damning clues towards his villainy.

There's nothing, of course; he would have been caught long ago if guilt left such visible marks.

"It is a shame you were not here half an hour ago," Sunillen says. Immaculate scarlet robes swish around his slippered feet, every inch of him manicured and polished as he descends the stairs. His shoulders do not bow with the weight of our quest, but something intangible, something so slight I would not even dare voice aloud, reminds me of my own shadow of worry. The last hint of a nightmare you can't shrug off.

"You could have joined Captain Olivie in interrogating me." Sunillen's words ring with a wryness that lacks any true humor. He watches Lyr closely, although his eyebrows rise a fraction when he notices Vaen.

"The Watchers were here?" Lyr asks. "Surely not to *actually* interrogate you."

"Not in the sense of being at war, no of course not." The idea clearly disgusts him. "The Watchers do not have the disposition for that."

His disdain for them is apparent. I clamp my lips together,

repeating in my head, *It's not worth it. Your ultimate goal is more important. You need him on your side.*

Still, a large part of me hates this man. Hates his immediate dismissal of a group of good, hardworking fighters because they aren't, what, harsh enough? That they haven't turned cold towards the world, as he obviously has?

"What reason did they give for coming?" Lyr's voice remains carefully neutral.

Sunillen gives a short, angry shake of his head. "What else? The fog came again last night, and a shepherd looking for a lost ewe claimed to have heard strange sounds. They wanted to know where I was." There is a darkness to his words, the hint of a promise at something worse.

Vaen and I exchange looks, and I wonder if the same thoughts are running through his head.

We did not see a lost sheep or her herder last night. If he was out there, he wasn't anywhere near us.

Which means either the Aberration could somehow interact with *anyone* in a certain area... or there was more than one Aberration out last night.

Fuck.

Every day these creatures simply grow more powerful, more dangerous. And still we are so far from being able to stop them.

Sunillen holds up his armful of scrolls and nods to the door that leads to the kitchens. "I am tired of looking at dusty tomes in the library. Join me in the garden. Perhaps the fields will give us some inspiration to the nature of these creatures."

Lyr nods in acquiescence and follows Sunillen, completely ignoring the two of us.

I linger for a moment in the kitchens, half-hoping I can simply slide into the seat at the kitchen table and have rolls and pretend the everything isn't as dire as it truly is. Have a cup of tea with Nalista and talk about our lives instead of this unending cascade of abominations.

It hasn't been long enough for my letter to have reached Liseah, much less a reply sent back, and I miss female companionship with an ache that burns fiercer every day.

I look around covertly, searching for any sign of the children or their governess, ignoring Vaen's nudge to keep going.

But Sunillen glances back at us as he exits, holding the door open for a bare second as if waiting for us. Almost involuntarily, my feet shuffle forward and I follow them outside.

Although the nip of winter is clearly in the air, the day is surprisingly nice for autumn this far north. The sun has burst through the layer of gray clouds and shines merrily down, giving the earth a false hope that winter is not as close as it seems.

Sunillen's gardens are the first things I've seen that do not abide by his neat and tidy life. From the kitchens is a plain stone walkway under a wire trellis tunnel, woven through with thick growing ivy to create a forest-like passage. Beyond the tunnel is a low hedge, coming only to my waist, that marks the boundary of the gardens proper. And within the hedge...

Flowers bloom from every available space, a mix of wildly grown and carefully cultivated. Autumnal flowers — mums, hydrangeas, calla lillies, and small shoots of sage — in a cacophony of colors create a maze through round evergreen bushes speckled with red berries. The flowers bend and sway in the breeze, fragile stems tangling together to create a stronger plant, faces eagerly turned upwards to the sun.

"It's beautiful." Lyr gazes at the gardens with true admiration. "Have you done all this?"

Sunillen gestures to a small stone table and set of chairs. "My wife had a gift for plants. Her passion did not rub off on me, although I enjoy coming out here to be reminded of what she loved. My daughter, Amilla, has inherited her love of flowers and keeps this place alive with the help of her governess." He looks at the sea of petals almost wistfully. "I have never seen them last quite this late into the year. Her gift may surpass her mother's."

It's the longest, and most personal, I've ever heard him talk.

Sunillen shuffles the scrolls on the table before peering at Lyr, all former trace of benign friendliness gone. "Mage Lyr, I have been questioned repeatedly over the last few weeks. I admit, I grow weary of it. I believed you were an ally and understood that I am innocent despite the village's multiple claims otherwise."

"I do think you're innocent." Lyr sounds appropriately appalled and worried, but the tension radiating from him is almost palpable.

"Tell me why, then, you have felt the need to bring an additional guard with you today." All our eyes swing to Vaen, who has the grace to look mildly surprised at the claim. I look back to Sunillen just in time to see a mirthless smile curving his lip. "If I am not the villain Ulingard so desperately seeks, why do you insult me so?"

This was a mistake. We never should have brought Vaen here. Of course his mere presence would bring suspicion. We were fools to think otherwise. I put my hand on my sword's pommel, palm already slick with sweat. Sunillen notices the movement, eyes sliding from my fighter's stance to my face, and the humorless smile grows. Fire dances in his eyes.

Vaen coughs lightly, breaking Sunillen's stare even as the tension climbs to unbearable heights. I don't dare to look away from the mage even as Vaen speaks. "You're mistaken, honorable mage. I am no guard, no fighter. I'm a simple scribe, here to record the sightings of these Aberrations."

He says the lie so smoothly, even I believe it for a second. He speaks calmly, blandly even, without any of the snark and disgruntlement I have become used to.

Sunillen's eyebrows shoot up, the disbelief written clearly across his face. "A scribe?" He laughs, deep from his belly, but the sound rings coldly. "You truly take me for a fool then. I know a fighter's build when I see one. You are as likely a scribe as I am a bondsman." Tendrils of fire lace around his fingers, barely visible in the afternoon sun.

I move slowly, inching my way closer to Lyr. There's no way to physically get my body in front of his without drawing a preliminary attack, but I can at least get close enough to throw myself in front of him should Sunillen target him first.

Out of the corner of my eye, I see Vaen inhale deeply. His hands clench at his sides before he forces them to loosen and I swear I see his fingers tremble for the barest second.

"Honorable mage, you are as keenly observant as Mage Lyr has suggested." Vaen spreads his arms wide, shoulders rising in a hapless shrug. "It is true, I once was a fighter. I was one of the queen's own guards, privy to every move she made, my life sworn to keep her safe."

My breath catches. The way he speaks now, an almost... tenderness in his tone, in the dip of cadence as he breathes the word *queen*... This is not a lie. This is a Vaen I do not know, someone who has only been hinted at in between barbed comments and constructed silences.

Sunillen cocks his head, watching the thief curiously. The flames flicker, dying down to the slightest ember-like glow, and I allow myself to breathe again. "Did you really now... interesting. Very interesting. Why in the name of the light would you resign from that job? A queen's guard is set for life."

Vaen doesn't blink. His thin, open smile never wavers as he says, "After time, a conflict of interest developed. I cannot say I would be welcomed back to the garrison happily." Something about his words, the delicate way he pauses before finishing the sentence, makes me think this "conflict" is what caused Lyr to intercede. Beneath his calm demeanor hovers an air of... sadness? Regret? I can't tell for certain.

Vaen continues, "I stay away from Calire now, choosing instead to travel and record what I can about Aberrations. There are too few scribes willing to venture out of their libraries these days, but the best records are those garnered first hand."

Kernels of truth laced in a network of lies.

Sunillen must agree, for the fire finally vanishes from his hands. He doesn't apologize for the near attack but gestures instead to the scrolls. "Well then, scribe, you should be a valuable asset today. Please join us in reading through these texts. Perhaps you can help us decipher the more complicated ones."

My heartbeat picks up again. How can Vaen possibly steal an imbued object if he's stuck here? But he must see there is no logical excuse to give that wouldn't tear his story to shreds within seconds because he nods graciously and settles in next to Lyr. The mage shoots me a quick look over Vaen's head, the slightest widening of his eyes the only acknowledgement of how precarious our position truly is.

I stand there, hesitant, yearning for nothing more than to slip off and find Nalista in the groves of flowers and have a moment to simply *breathe,* but my feet stay firmly planted to the spot. I can't leave now, not when our presence here teeters on a needle-thin weapon's edge.

So I stay, listening to the rustle of parchment as they painstakingly begin searching through them. The garden is almost eerily quiet, devoid of anything beyond the birdsong and whisper of the wind through the foliage around us. Occasionally one of the readers coughs or shifts or makes a remark that doesn't mean much to me. At some point, long after I've

grown glassy-eyed, a servant brings a stack of bound leather
books.

"These are newer," Sunillen says, the words almost jarring
in the silence that has encompassed us. "I figured to start with
the oldest and proceed out, but perhaps we will find more
information here."

Lyr says something but the words fade into a lulling drone
as my gaze slides away from the table, towards the woods
swaying in the distance. The same feeling of uneasiness permeates me as I watch the branches ebb and flow. They are evergreen trees, untouched by autumn, their dark green bristles
thick and adept at hiding the secrets that live there.

We need to go there. The thought is insistent and undeniable,
no matter the uneasiness that accompanies it, sliding oil-slick
through my gut.

Whether it is tonight or in another week's time, we will find
our way to those woods.

There is no doubt that Lyr needs to have an imbued object
before then. I glance to the mage, but he's dutifully reading still,
lips moving silently.

I can only see Vaen's profile from my position, but he seems
wholly focused on his work, for all intents and purposes the perfect
scribe. In another life, perhaps I could see him as one, despite his
muscular, tall build. He looks to be at peace. I envy that in him.

There is a sudden, joyful screeching as the nearby kitchen
door bangs open. I jump, immediately embarrassed to be
caught off guard, and turn to see Amilla and Thomalen
bounding down the covered path towards the gardens.

Sunillen rises, his face dark as thunderclouds, and the children stumble to a halt, eyes flickering to the ground. Amilla
presses her lips together tightly. Not in fear, but in resentment.

"Children, what's—" Nalista comes around the corner,

grinning and out of breath, but the grin slides from her face as soon as she sees the mage. "Sir, my apologies." She folds her hands in front of her, eyes focused somewhere on Sunillen's chest. "I did not realize you were taking your studies outside today. I would have instructed the children to be more aware of their surroundings and quiet accordingly."

Children shouldn't have to be quiet outside. The words are on the tip of my tongue, barely bitten back.

Sunillen considers them for a moment, and while his eyes do not soften exactly, he nods and gestures for the children to come forward. "Tell me about your day, Amilla."

It's more of an order than a request, and Amilla obeys slowly, reluctance clear in her steps. As she comes to the table, Vaen rises, murmuring, "If you'll excuse me, I need to find the privy."

Sunillen clearly hears him, waving a hand in acknowledgement, but his focus is on his daughter. It's a struggle not to beam with outright excitement at the thief's seamless exit.

Watching him feels like drawing unnecessary attention, so I turn to Nalista, who has stopped at my side, Thomalen dawdling just behind her.

"It's good to see you again," Nalista says, tone warm and welcoming. Her hand touches my elbow, and joy bursts into my chest like a sunflower opening.

I smile broadly back. "I'm glad as well." I gesture to the garden. "It's beautiful here. I never expected to see such lush greenery in the winter."

There is obvious pride in Nalista's features as she also examines the gardens. "The flowers have lasted extraordinarily well this year. Usually we have to replant our favorites in the hothouse much earlier than this." She points to a small glass building at the edge of the property. "It's already full of tomatoes, peas, potatoes — plenty of food to get us through winter and beyond."

"Mage Sunillen says you and Amilla tend to it?"

Her smile is kind as she looks once more to her young charge. "Amilla takes on most of the physical labor. She loves being out here, dirt to her elbows, figuring out everything these plants need to survive." She gives a wry laugh. "I mostly just talk to the flowers and try to give them encouraging words."

It should sound ridiculous but somehow is not.

I nod to Amilla and her father. "Do they get along well?"

Nalista watches the pair, her smile wavering slightly. "That's hard to say. Their relationship is complicated. There is no outright hatred I suppose. I think they both crave things from the other that they may not be able to give."

"It's hard to picture Mage Sunillen as a doting father." I make sure my voice is cast low, for her ears only.

"Losing his wife was hard." Nalista eyes flicker from the mage to the children. "For everyone. They haven't been able to bridge the gaps her presence left."

Her voice is tight. I glance at the governess, whose eyes remain fixed on Amilla. Thomalen has wandered off, digging at something interesting in the ground, but Nalista doesn't seem to have noticed. Her face is carefully controlled, but there's a tension around her mouth and eyes that speak to something deeper.

I want to ask more about Sunillen's oddities, but I'm afraid it will draw too much attention. We have tried so very hard to craft the illusion that we are completely on his side, I'm afraid of dispelling it. Instead I say, "You care very deeply about them."

The sadness that sweeps over her is instantaneous. Her shoulders droop with the weight of some unnamed grief, the lines around her eyes deepening. Then, almost before I can process what I see, she straightens again, one hand wiping at the skin beneath her eyes.

"I do," she says, voice firm and quiet. "I love them as I would my own."

Something lingers there, in the unsaid words, but before I can give in to my questions, Sunillen's voice rings out.

"Where did that scribe go? We need return to these texts if we hope to make any sort of headway."

My pulse ricochets, but Lyr answers calmly, "Your house is a maze to those of us without Noble blood. I'm sure he's merely lost and will be back any moment."

Sunillen appears to accept this reasoning, returning to his reading. Seeing the dismissal, Amilla makes her break, quickly walking into the gardens with barely a nod in our direction. Nalista gestures to Thomalen, offers me a small wave, and follows her charges.

I barely breathe the next few minutes while I wait for Vaen to return. When he finally does, offering apologies to the mages, I catch his eye as best I can.

The look in them is a wave of ice water cascading down me, erasing any relief his return offered.

Something went wrong.

CHAPTER
SEVENTEEN

Waiting for the mages and Vaen to finish reading for the day is absolute agony.

Could he not find where the items are kept? Was there a spell to keep him out? Was he caught by the staff? The questions are useless, but it doesn't stop anxiety from turning my stomach into a pit of knots.

"We will not be going out to the fields tonight," Lyr says, breaking me out of my fear-filled stupor. The mage nods at us. "We all need a rest."

It's true enough. The weariness, worse now after this excruciating wait, eats at my bones. We had decided earlier today that stealing an imbued object then using it immediately would be far too obvious. Now it seems we'll be spending the night trying to make up for whatever happened with Vaen.

"Every day my hope for an answer grows a little dimmer." Sunillen stares at the gardens, face turned from us. "I wonder if we can ever hope to defeat these creatures if we cannot even find their source."

It's the first time I can remember him speaking of this with more than broad indifference or anger at his own personal attacks. It makes him seem unnervingly innocent.

"It does seem like we are caught in never ending loop devoid of answers." Lyr opens his hand, and a small volley of sparks materialize, forming the pattern of a flower in the air before us. "But I believe we are on the right path and will see a change soon."

Sunillen watches the sparks fade. "The real question remains: is the change for better?"

He gathers his scrolls and returns to the house silently, leaving us standing alone in the gardens.

I look at Vaen, desperately searching yet again for a clue, but his features are a mask as he rises and follows Lyr towards the house.

Sunillen does not bid us goodbye, the manor cold and quiet as we pass through.

We make the short trek back to town, but Lyr does not head back to The Night's End. Instead he takes an abrupt turn down a side street, not even bothering to check if we follow.

We do, of course.

The mage leads us to a small, cramped back alleyway, long forgotten by most of Ulingard. Crumpled bits of trash litter the ground, and it smells unpleasantly like mice, mildew, and old urine. I haven't explored the totality of the city, but this section seems akin to any other city's poorer districts, a place I wouldn't be keen to explore at night. The houses are small and squashed together, walls abut to their neighbors as if the shared space will help them stay upright. A few taller buildings hint at the type of businesses you frequent under a false name. For now it's quiet, the occupants distracted still with the day's work or drink.

I look around, unable to hide my displeasure. "What—?" I start to ask, but Lyr puts up a hand to silence me.

He spends the next few moments tracing elaborate patterns in the air, walking around us in a slow, deliberate circle.

"Shielding wards," he says when he finishes. A light sheen of sweat glimmers on his forehead. "It protects us not only from being heard, but seen as well."

"Handy," I comment.

"Difficult," he responds, a wry smile twisting his lips. "It requires constant concentration. Many of my year mates have excelled at creating wards and keeping them intact in the back of their mind, like an afterthought. I never quite learned to do it that well."

Lyr focuses his attention on Vaen, crossing his arms over his chest. "Now, what the hell happened back there?"

Vaen copies his stance, whether innocently or purposefully I can't say. "I covered extremely well and played the part of a scribe beautifully."

It's the sort of comment Lyr himself would make. I can't hide my chuckle, which earns a withering look from Lyr. Vaen doesn't deign me with an acknowledgment beside the slightest lifting of the corner of his mouth. Despite the light hearted response, the skin around his eyes and brows is pinched. He presses his fingers against his arms harder than necessary, as if trying to keep himself together.

"Was what you said true?"

Lyr levels an astonished look at me, but I don't look away from Vaen. I'm tired of the half-truths, the hidden secrets, the feeling of not knowing a damn thing.

"What I said at the manor was the truth." Vaen's voice is low and coldly bitter, each syllable an icicle that pins me to the spot. "And you will *not* ask me anything about it again."

A logical person would nod and change the subject. Instead I say, "That's not fair. You know about my previous life, about my failures."

From over his shoulder, Lyr gives me a look like I've grown a second head. "Dumbass," he mouths.

Vaen never blinks. "Who said it was a failure?" I flinch at the accusation but can't look away from him. "What happened as a result of my choices was an unfortunate consequence. But it was one I knew could eventually come about. I was not disillusioned enough to believe in the purity of people, unlike *you*."

The word is whip-sharp, stealing my breath with its ferocity. I feel, immediately, that whatever ground I might have made with Vaen is gone in this instant.

A thousand questions burn my tongue, all of which I would be a fool to utter.

Vaen turns his back to me, solely addressing Lyr. "There were too many risks to take one today. The room is accessible through a revolving bookcase in the library."

"How did you find it?" Lyr asks.

"I counted the windows on the outside of the house while we were in the gardens. They didn't add up to what was visible inside." He speaks like it's obvious, but I never in my life would have thought to do such a thing.

"Sunillen displays the gems in glass cases, like prizes won at a carnival. Everything was meticulously cleaned; anything missing would have been painfully obvious, and our proximity places us the prime suspects." Vaen hesitates, then adds, "There were a few missing spaces, as if he keeps some of the objects on his person."

Lyr nods. His earlier annoyance is gone, replaced by razor-sharp focus. "What do you suggest we do?"

Vaen raises his eyebrows and nods to the mage. "What you do best."

I look from one to the other, not completely understanding until—

"You want Lyr to make a fake?"

Vaen still doesn't look at me, but the earlier rage seems to have dulled. "Lyr is a mage of illusions. I can't imagine it will be difficult for him."

"Can you describe some of the objects in enough detail for me to accurately replicate them?" the mage asks.

"I imagine so."

Lyr nods, apparently pleased. "We'll make it tonight and plant it tomorrow."

I frown. "Is it okay to waste that much time?"

"I don't think we have a choice." Lyr shrugs. "We can't be too suspicious. If we plant it tonight, I fear it will still be connected to us."

"It probably will no matter what," I point out.

"Perhaps. But it's better to stack the odds in our favor any way we can."

Fair point. "All right then. So you'll work on your magic and we'll just... hang around?"

Lyr snorts, amusement lacing his words. "If you're asking if you can safely visit your jeweler, I think the answer is yes."

I huff and try to own my sexuality instead of being embarrassed by it. "He's not *my* jeweler. It's not that kind of relationship." I don't even know if I would want it to be. Emotional relationships are a lot harder to deal with than purely physical ones. On the other hand, knowing someone is waiting for me, knowing someone wants to see *me*... it's a nice feeling.

Lyr waves his hand in the air impatiently. "Yes, yes, well whatever type of relationship it is, feel free to go enjoy it."

I rub my hands together, fingers having gone cold in the autumn air. "I need to work out some aggression first." I ignore Lyr's choked laughter as I finish saying, "That was a long time to stand around and do nothing. I'm going to spar at the Watchers' tower if no one has any objections."

Lyr gives a dramatic shudder. "Better you than me. I'm

going to warm up with a hot drink." He claps Vaen on the shoulder. "You joining me?"

"Might as well."

Vaen doesn't look at me as he walks off, even when I try to catch his eye — to silently apologize, perhaps, or to simply see if whatever trust we've built has crumbled.

I definitely need to work off the stress of today.

By the time I reach the Watchers' tower, I'm buzzing with a titillating mixture of energy and anxiety. All my worries — about my comrades, the gems, the Aberrations, my own standing in relationships and life — vibrate through me at blazing speed, leaving me short breathed and shaky handed.

The tower is a simple enough construct, surrounded by a low wooden fence meant more as a demarcation than any worthwhile protection. Inside the actual tower are the Watchers' rooms, kitchens, dining hall, and the Watch commanders offices. To the west is a small stable with around half a dozen horses; since they are not calvary, there is no need for every Watcher to have a mount. Their armory and storehouse are always there. To the east of the tower, still within the fenced boundary, is a large grassy ring. Half of the area is covered with thin mats to spar on, while the other half is littered with various targets for archery and sword practice.

Watchers are broken into patrol groups that are in charge of a portion of the city. Because of Ulingard's relatively small size, there are not many groups, nor many Watchers. Still, there are morning, evening, and night patrols, leaving those not on shift the opportunity to train. I've come at the right time, the familiar sound of sparring weapons rippling across the area.

A Watcher stands at the fence at all times, more of an early warning or messenger than a true guard. Today it's the same girl who was at the front gate when we arrived. I've seen her a handful of other times, but still have yet to learn her name.

She clearly recognizes me, raising her brows in question. "I see you haven't caught the Aberrations yet."

The challenge startles a laugh out of me. I can't bring myself to take offense. "Not yet," I agree. "But I think we're getting closer."

She nods, accepting my statement. "Are you here to see Captain Olivie?"

"No, I came to spar." As far as I know, updating Olivie is Lyr and Vaen's job.

To my surprise, the girl's face splits into a broad grin. "That's good to hear. They could use a challenge." She nods to the half dozen men and women milling around the practice yard.

A flare of pride blazes through me at the realization that she thinks I'm a worthy enough opponent. It sends a new wave of adrenaline through me, and I walk into the sparring ring.

The Watchers are working on hand to hand combat today. While I will always prefer a sword as my primary weapon, there is something comforting about the baseline necessity of hand to hand — just you and your body, your own strength against another's. No flashy moves. Just strength and speed and cunning.

I strip off my weapons, leaving them in a neat pile by the gate. The Watchers who are sparring have all seen me or sparred with me before, and don't question my presence. Their trainer, a gruff man in his mid-sixties, gray hair shorn short, still muscled and lithe despite his age, gives me a once over and nods. "Ilitha, you're up."

A slim woman, several inches shorter than me but seemingly composed of pure muscle, approaches. We face each other on the mat, the others forming a loose ring around us, panting from their own bouts and sharing water skins as they take this opportunity for a break. I adjust my center of balance, bending my knees slightly, holding my hands loosely in front of me. Eyes on my opponent, who watches me with cockiness.

"Begin!"

She moves like a serpent, darting forward before the word has barely left the Watcher's mouth. Her hands whip out, aiming quick jabs at my head, but I knock one away, skittering out of the way of the other. Her blows are quick but powerful; there is no holding back. I can't help but grin. *Well if that's how you want to play it...*

I let Ilitha continue her onslaught, unworried when I do not get a blow in between. We circle the mat, the onlookers calling out advice.

"Hurry up and actually do something!" one shouts.

"Don't have to ask me twice."

I'm ready for Ilitha's punch, grabbing her fist in one hand while my other pushes back on her shoulder. I slide my heel around her ankle, yanking her off her feet. The move catches her completely by surprise, and she falls flat on her back, barely rolling out of the way when I try to come down with a knee to her chest.

She attempts to surge forward, to grab around my knees and bring me down, but I bear my weight forward instead of backwards, landing on top of her. It's almost too easy to pin her after that.

"Match," the trainer calls out.

Ilitha gives me a dirty look as she rises, dusting herself off, but the remaining Watchers line up to take her place, laughing and betting who will be the first to bring me down.

And they try, they really do. Some of them even land a few punches and kicks. One hits me right in the cheek, splitting my lip and no doubt earning a nasty bruise come morning. It only makes me grin and try harder, the pain a welcome beat alongside my heart, telling me I'm alive, that I can do this, that there is another physical, breathing enemy to defeat. Not some monster made of smoke and mist. Not some creature I have barely begun understanding how to fight.

No, this is brutal and bloody and painful and exactly what I need.

By the time the supper bell rings from inside the tower, half the garrison has turned up to watch the progression of matches. And each time, even as I accept the blows that show I too am merely human, I somehow manage to come up on top.

Either I am very, very lucky tonight, or some god of fortune has smiled on me, knowing how desperately I craved this.

This feeling of life. This feeling of victory, when the rest of my world is so radically out of place.

"Are you quite done showing off then?"

I turn at the familiar voice, still euphoric, and can't help but grin at Lyr, who leans against the fence with raised eyebrows. His lips twitch upwards, perhaps the first honest smile I have seen from him in quite some time. To my surprise, Vaen stands next to him, looking like he always does — vaguely annoyed but generally unruffled. There is none of his earlier iciness from our stilted conversation, my blundering words that did more harm than good.

I match his cockiness. "I don't see you offering to go next."

Lyr outright laughs at that, hands raised in mock surrender. "My dear, I have seen your skill for weeks now. There is no way in light I would ever attempt to cross blades with you, and you know enough of my tricks to likely navigate any magical attacks as well."

"I will then."

I swivel to Vaen, shock skittering through me. He's already pushed off the fence, striding confidently into the practice ring, placing his numerous daggers into a neat pile next to my own things. He shrugs out of his overshirt, leaving only a plain white tunic, the sleeves quickly rolled up to his elbows.

In all our time on the road, never had Vaen offered to spar with me. *Never*. Even when I ran practice drills in the early morning light, Lyr muttering about the hour over a pot of steaming coffee. He never once gave me a second glance as I went over forms, both with swords and without, as I threw countless daggers into the trees we passed while on horseback, as I sharpened my weapons diligently in the dying firelight while they snored in their bedrolls.

When he steps onto the mat, I don't look away from his unflinching gaze. And I see there, half-hidden in the depths of his curious gray-green eyes, a shimmer of the icy rage from earlier.

Perhaps he has not forgiven me as entirely as I thought.

I swallow, hoping to hide my sudden nervousness. But why should I feel nervous? Am I afraid to beat him and make him even angrier at me? Afraid that maybe I won't be *able* to beat him? My muscles ache from the matches I've already been through, the bruises on my face and ribs throbbing now that my attention is on them.

Vaen must sense my hesitance, because he grins at me, all teeth, devoid of humor. "Having second thoughts, Raylen?"

I bristle at the mere suggestion and bare my teeth back at him. "Of course not."

The tension in the ring, between us, is almost palpable. Whereas before the onlookers took bets and called out to one another, now they remain near-silent, the only sound a soft murmur that slips between them.

"Begin!"

I move before Vaen can, jabbing quickly at his ribs before skittering away. The first hand hits, the second is knocked away, but I achieved what I wanted: the first blow. I know I need to end this match quickly. Vaen has reservoirs of energy I do not; pure adrenaline is what keeps my feet swift now. Against another opponent, it may not matter as much. I might be able to wait for my chance. But Vaen clearly needs something from this match, and he has no intention of letting it go.

He follows after me, striking at my face and shoulders. I duck and weave, trying to make the movements as precise and controlled as possible to keep myself a smaller target, to conserve what energy I have left.

Whether he makes an educated guess or sees the beginning of tiredness in my movements, Vaen takes full advantage of the situation and presses forward with a ferocity that leaves me gasping for breath. He is all power and force, moving from one form to another with barely a pause. There is an undeniable beauty in his elegance, even if I'm pushed too hard to truly appreciate it.

His first blow to find its mark is a fist driven high into my ribs, pushing the air from my lungs as I fly backwards. There's an audible intake of breath from the crowd watching, and it is pure pride that keeps me from landing straight on my ass. I take advantage of the momentum, spinning myself around and throwing an elbow into Vaen's face as he tries to follow. It misses his nose but will undoubtedly leave a bruise on his cheek that matches my own.

I'm panting now, sweat dripping from my face and back despite the rapidly cooling temperature as the day saunters closer to evening.

Vaen steps forward, too close, chest pressed against mine, and the move is so startling I momentarily lose focus. He hooks his foot around my ankle before I can sidestep away, viciously yanking me to the ground just as I did my very first opponent.

Not yet.

I follow the movement through, allowing gravity to pull me

down. As I go, I grab his shirtsleeves, using my momentum to yank him down with me. Off balance, he teeters over me for a brief instance — just long enough for me to roll my hips up, plant my feet on his hips, and channel all my strength into throwing him over my head. The surprise on his face is deeply satisfying as he goes sailing over me, unable to stop.

I follow his movement, still holding onto his shirtsleeves, and roll backwards so I'm straddling him. I lean forward with all my strength, pinning his arms to the ground, knees digging into his sides as I squeeze.

Vaen tries for a brief moment to dislodge me, but quickly realizes it won't happen. He stills beneath me, and we stare at each other, both gasping for breath, chests rising and falling rapidly. Leaning over him as I am, our faces are inches from one another, breath mingling together in a way that is almost sensual. I am suddenly acutely aware of every single place our bodies touch, my skin alive and burning. The situation changes then, the fight won and forgotten, and I tell myself to get up, to move, but my body doesn't want to listen.

If he's as uncomfortable as I am, Vaen doesn't show it. That damnable smirk curves up one side of his mouth, and if I wasn't already using both of my hands, I would be tempted to smack it off his face.

"It would seem you are indeed the victor." His words are soft, for me only. I can't read anything in his tone, but it takes the fire out of me, leaving satiated exhaustion in its wake.

"Did it help?"

He blinks at my question. "What?"

I sit up a little, loosening my hold on his wrists, his waist. But I don't look away.

"Did the fight help level things between us. For what I said earlier."

Understanding dawns on his face. Vaen sits up, dumping

me unceremoniously out of his lap. He stands, offering me a hand, which I take. My entire body aches now, the bruises and strained muscles begging for a hot bath and soft bed.

"As much as I am loathe to admit it, you had every right to ask what you did." Vaen sighs heavily, looking away to some unseen sight. "It was uncouth and rude, but within your right, especially should it jeopardize our work here."

"Will it?"

He shakes his head firmly. "No." He looks back at me, inclining his head ever so slightly. In acknowledgement of our disagreement and now, what... an apology? Is that what this is?

Lyr comes and claps both of us on the back, ending whatever moment we might have been having. I wince at the pressure and lock my knees so they don't buckle.

"Well, that was exciting," he announces jovially. He holds up a small purse of coins. "And you won me enough for a couple rounds of drinks."

Vaen gives him a glare devoid of any real heat. "You bet against me?"

The mage nods seriously. "Absolutely. No doubt about it." He starts walking towards the gate, waving merrily to the Watchers as they disperse, offering me congratulations and asking if I'll be back tomorrow. "Now, how about those drinks?"

I meet Vaen's eyes over Lyr's head and give a little shrug. "Sounds good to me. Those are my earnings after all."

I snatch the purse from Lyr, ignoring his affronted shout, and lead the way back to the inn.

Drinking turns out to be an excellent idea, which Lyr says loudly several drinks in. He is always the first to feel the alcohol's effects, although I find myself laughing a little too loud and long at his terrible jokes. Vaen watches us joke with lazy, lidded eyes, leaning back in his chair as if this is the first time he's allowed himself to relax in weeks. Perhaps it is.

The door opens, bringing in a small group of off duty Watchers. They cheer when they see me, raising their hands, and buy me another drink before taking over their own table closer to the fire.

"I should go down there more often," I muse, sipping from my refilled tankard. The pleasant buzz of alcohol washes over me.

"Oh? And where is that?"

I look up, surprised. Haith stands awkwardly by the table, hands tucked into his breeches pockets, still in his soot stained shirt. I grin at him, barely restraining myself from jumping up.

"Oh, it's Raylen's jeweler!" Lyr stands, clapping Haith on the shoulder even though the man towers over the mage.

Haith looks Lyr up and down, eyebrows rising, and glances at me. His face is closed off, emotions hidden behind a smooth mask of perfected indifference. "Raylen's jeweler?" he repeats. I can't read the tone behind the words, which worries me for a reason I can't explain.

I do stand now, tugging Lyr back into his seat with more force than absolutely necessary.

"He's drunk," I say with a shrug. The room spins just enough to tell me I've probably drank too much as well.

Haith does smile then, but it's thin lipped, without any real mirth. My stomach sinks. This thing between us is too new, too tentative, but I don't want to lose it yet, not over something stupid I can't even name.

"Of course," he says smoothly, no hint of irritation in his words. "How about you come by when you're done here?"

It's on the tip of my tongue to ask why, to ask what could possibly be wrong with him staying and socializing with my companions, if the idea of being with me more than just sexually was really that abhorrent of an idea.

But I bite the words back, swallow them down. They burn more than the alcohol does.

"Sounds good." I smile at him, trying to reassure him that everything is just fine. Perhaps that reassurance is just as much for me.

He nods, returning my smile only slightly, before leaving once more. I watch him go, trying to decide if it's worth it. If I care enough to pursue something that all of a sudden seems messy and complicated.

It's only been a handful of days. I'm not sure what I want exactly, but I owe Haith a conversation at least.

I sit back down, ignoring Lyr's chortle, his prattle about Haith and how *very* generous he's sure the jeweler is.

A plate of food is suddenly before me.

"Time to sober up a bit," Vaen says, nodding his thanks to the serving maid.

She murmurs something, too quiet to hear, as she begins to put empty tankards onto her broad serving platter. As she takes my last one, she pauses for a minute, head lowered towards me. I meet her eyes, and the look in them is almost enough to drown out the alcohol's influence. She stares at me darkly, not with anger, but with worry. Fear. A warning I can't place.

"What—"

My words are cut off abruptly as the door to the inn blows open fiercely enough to send it clattering against the wall.

The inn falls into surprised silence, and we swivel almost as one to stare into the growing night.

At the group of strangers who hover at the threshold, armed to the teeth with an array of swords, axes, bows, and the fierce, delighted grins of hunters.

CHAPTER

EIGHTEEN

There is a moment of breathless anticipation as the entirety of the inn stares at the group. The one I assume to be their leader steps forward, a clear swagger in his step despite the days of road dirt and grime caked onto his clothes. He doesn't look wealthy, but he wears a nice fur cloak over cracked leather armor that has undoubtedly seen combat.

"Any guesses?" Lyr whispers, the words so low I can barely hear them.

"Mercenaries," Vaen and I say at the same time.

"Not with the guild," Vaen clarifies, eyes narrowed as he watches their leader.

I try not to shiver. Rogue mercenaries are little better than bandits, operating under their own rule. They aren't hired by anyone doing respectable business.

The innkeeper's mistress steps forward, wiping her hands on her apron. She doesn't smile at them. "How can I help you?" Her voice is mild but devoid of the warm welcome we've come to expect when townsfolk come looking for a night's distraction. She's always been friendly to our little group as well.

The mercenary leader tosses her a gold coin from a fat purse that promises more. "Some hot food to start with," he says, his grin exposing the blackened hole of a missing tooth. "And three rooms for me and my friends here."

The regulars turn back to their food and company once they realize there is no overt threat. Vaen does as well, nudging Lyr when the mage continues to stare. He reluctantly returns to his meal, but his eyes remain observant, tracking the newcomers as they saunter to a table and settle into it. Food and drink are brought, and the noise in the inn returns to its usual rumbling hum.

Always logical, Vaen says, "It was bound to happen eventually. The rumors brought us here; we knew they would lure others as well."

Lyr raises a finger. "Actually I came here first because of Sunillen." When we merely stare at him with raised eyebrows, he shrugs and mutters something about nuances.

I look back at the mercenaries. They are jovial despite the toil of the road, joking and jostling each other. There is no fear, no trepidation leeching from them. Just excitement.

They don't know anything yet.

"I don't think they came just to fulfill their curiosity." I spear a potato but don't bring it to my mouth. My appetite is rapidly dwindling. "Where do you think they got that purse?"

Lyr scowls and shakes his head. "This doesn't change anything."

I give him an incredulous look. "It changes *everything*."

"How?"

"We're doing this for the right reasons." I shoot the mercenaries another look and lower my voice even further. "We want to help save these people. We want to extinguish this threat before it grows. What are their motives?"

Lyr stands, his chair scraping against the floor. I sit back, startled. "Well, let's just go ask them, shall we?"

I gape open mouthed at him and mutely shake my head. "You know I'm not good with that. Conversing. Not being... blunt."

"The word you're looking for is 'rude'." Vaen takes my abandoned potato and eats it while I do nothing but stare.

With another mutter about useless help, Lyr plasters a cheery smile on his face and saunters over to the mercenaries's table.

Vaen and I are too far away to hear their conversation, but Lyr appears to have charmed them as he does nearly everyone, and sits down with them within a few moments.

I shake my head. "How does he do that? Fit in so easily?"

Vaen gives up and slides my plate on top of his own empty one, finishing off the remaining chicken and green beans. "He's a mage," he says around a bite of food. "Charming people is second nature to them."

"Not the ones I've met." I watch as Lyr throws back his head and laughs at something one of them said. "They're just as bad as Nobles. There always seems to be some sort of agenda."

"That's true of everyone. Mages and Nobles just generally have more serious agendas to worry about."

I mull over his words. "Well, I'm just glad I'm not one of them. Either of them. Give me a simple life, with simple intentions." I wave a hand in the air. "All those politics, the court intrigue... I couldn't handle it."

There's a beat of silence, of a restrained breath. I tear my eyes away from Lyr to find Vaen staring down at his plate, brows deeply furrowed, something akin to sorrow on his face. I don't dare speak, my own breath freezing, unable to look away. I have never seen so much emotion on the man's face before; the sadness makes my own soul ache.

"It's not all bad." Vaen's voice is as soft as falling snow, new and glistening. "The courts. Calire. Some of it is redeemable."

And I know, deep in my gut, that it's not a what but a *who*.

My fingers itch to reach out and touch his sleeve, but I keep them pressed together tightly, as if he's a deer poised to bolt. "Who was she?"

I think the question is too much, too vulnerable, too unforgivable, but Vaen shakes his head, the sorrow fading into something much worse.

Hatred.

"A dream," he says. "A mistake."

Before I can ask anything else, he rises, nodding to the door. "Go see your jeweler. I'll keep an eye on Lyr tonight. We all need to take advantage of a night off and get some sleep."

I hesitate, longing to stay, to beg him to sit down and tell me who destroyed him so thoroughly, but Vaen is already leaving, weaving between people as he makes his way to Lyr.

I wait for a minute, but my companions don't look at me again.

So I leave.

The air is bitterly cold outside, by far the coldest it's been this year, heralding the winter's first frost. My tunic and breeches are not made for a northern winter, my cloak left upstairs in the room, and the wind slices through them like they are intangible.

I half run to the forge, grateful it is merely a few hundred feet from The Night's End. The food and the weather have sobered me up enough that my head only spins a little as I hurry.

The forge is dark, but the door is unlocked when I slip inside. "Haith?" I call out, suddenly nervous at the great yawning blackness, the kiln nothing but ashes.

The door to his private quarters swings open just the tiniest bit, emitting enough light to guide me around anvils and neatly lined up tools.

I barely have stepped past the door when a hand grabs my waist, spinning me around. Haith pins me to the door, which clicks shut against my weight. He leans forward, towering over me, one hand easily holding both of mine above my head. For the first time, I'm glad I had so much to drink; it dulls me enough I don't lash out, don't try to hurt him or free myself.

I stare up at the man, breathing too fast, trying to calm my panicked heartbeat. He stares down at me, only the barest hint of a smile curling his lips, eyes dark and sultry and holding something unreadable in their depths.

He kisses me without preamble, no words exchanged. Only heat. Only need. A knee pushes between my legs, his body pressing down on mine, hips grinding into hips. I rise to meet him, mouth opening, the familiar coil of fire bursting into life deep in me.

There is no slow lovemaking, no teasing, no tantalizing whisper of what is to come. Haith releases me only to strip off his clothes, his cock already full and tall. I must be taking too long to rid myself of my own garments, because he helps when he's done, yanking my shirt off impatiently, seams popping as it's flung to the side of the room.

When I'm finally naked, he wastes no time in claiming my mouth once more, hands on my waist as he lifts me up, back pressed against the door for leverage. There is no warning, no gentle preparation, as he rams himself inside me. My gasp is swallowed by his kiss.

His thrusts are hard and brutal, hands helping to support my hips, mouth dancing down my neck to suck at the skin above my collarbone. I have no breath to protest, if I even would, and do my best to match the frantic rhythm as the fire coils tighter and tighter.

He comes with a muffled groan, body tensing against mine, teeth just barely pushing against the kiss-bruised skin. I only have a second to be disappointed, my own release dancing along the edge, when he drops to his knees before me.

My half hearted murmur to wait transforms to a breathy whimper as he latches that clever mouth over my most sensitive spot, fingers finding their way into my aching, slick entrance.

The combination doesn't take long to send me over the edge. I cry out and curl over him, hands gripping his corded shoulders as I shake, completely undone.

When my vision clears and I can straighten, Haith stands, a devilish, pleased grin on his face. He pushes me back to the bed, where I crumple, knees shaking, breath uneven. He slides in next to me, pulling the warm blanket over us both, and I curl against his side, half lulled to sleep by the warm cocoon.

"I'm glad you came to see me tonight." His words rumble through his chest, vibrating against my cheek. "I wasn't sure you would."

"I'm glad too." I hesitate before admitting, "I wasn't sure you wanted me to."

I can almost feel him frown. "Why is that?"

"You seemed upset at the inn." I shrug. "You can't take anything Lyr says too seriously. He doesn't know what he's talking about half the time."

Haith is quiet for a long moment, fingers slowly running through my hair, now sweat-streaked and tangled.

"It caught me off guard," he says at last, fingers never losing their rhythm. "I wasn't sure how to take it. I guess we haven't really discussed what this is." He gestures to our entwined bodies.

I roll onto my side just enough so I can see his face. "So,

what is it? This. Us. What do you want it to be?" My heart beats wildly, but I'm relieved he has to bare his feelings first.

He considers my words carefully. "I think we are two very attractive, energetic people who have very, *very* good sex together, and I would like to keep having sex together."

I prop myself up on his chest and grin at his description. "I agree."

He smiles lazily at me, one arm folded beneath his head so he can meet my eyes. "I also think you are a traveler, not intending to stay in Ulingard long term, and I don't really see the need for a formal relationship if you're just going to leave again in a few weeks."

I let out a breath I hadn't realized I was holding, relief sharp and clear. "I agree again."

"Not to say," he adds, "that I would be against a relationship. I think you are brave, and talented, and very beautiful, and I would dive headfirst into pursuing you if I thought I had a chance of convincing you to stay longer."

My breath catches at the utter sincerity of his statement, stealing any potential words. No one has ever said something even remotely romantic to me before. I was always just that girl who wanted to be a knight. A decent enough person, someone to be friends with, someone to maybe fool around a bit with knowing full well it wouldn't turn into anything.

Never someone to be pursued.

"But," Haith says, eyes laughing at me, "that doesn't matter if you aren't going to stay. So, for now, I suppose we are at an impasse. For now, I will have to be content with a physical relationship, with perhaps a few moments like this, where we can talk and I can convince you bit by bit that maybe you *could* indeed remain in Ulingard after this monster hunt is over."

My words and thoughts swirl around each other. Do I even

want that? A real relationship, with the possibility of it being permanent? Because that's what Haith seems to be suggesting.

The thought sends shards of panic shooting through me.

No. I do not want that.

I am not ready for my life to be bound to someone, to be tied down to a single place — stuck, like my parents. Like all the other people in Heron Hill. All the people here who might wish to leave but can't.

"I'm not ready for commitment," I finally force out. I smile, but it feels broken, off center. "I don't want to be in one place for the rest of my life." I laugh, trying to shake the awkwardness that has settled over us. "Besides, you don't even really know me. You may not *want* to spend your life with me."

He kisses me again, this time slow and sweet. "I like what I see so far." Then he tucks my head back under his chin, arm warm around my shoulders. "But you're right. We don't know each other. So, we'll do it your way. Just physical."

I nod, only somewhat comforted by his words. Something still feels off, a heaviness in my gut that wasn't there before.

Still, when Haith starts talking about his day, casual conversation that feels natural, I relax again, the weight drifting away bit by bit, carried away on the cold northern breeze.

I don't stay, although a very large part of me wants to.

We talk for a while, innocuous things that don't have anything to do with our previous conversation. Talking soon turns to kissing, which turns very quickly into other things. When we lie there, spent and sweating, it takes an enormous amount of will to roll over and start gathering my clothes, but I do it.

Haith props himself up on his pillows, frowning. "You can stay here for the night, you know."

"I know." I didn't, really, and the idea frankly unnerves me. Even if I could convince myself it means nothing, I can't face the idea of leaving Lyr and Vaen in the inn with a new, strange party whose intentions we don't know yet. I can't shake the idea that I need to be there.

Or I'm just a coward and too afraid of what staying would mean.

It's well past the midnight bell when I finally leave the forge. The cold slams into me like a physical weight, now accompanied by an icy rain that stings with each impact, and I sprint to The Night's End, covering my head as best as I can.

The common room is still warm, embers glowing in the fire-place, but I doubt our own room is half this warm. Everything seems normal — there are no bits of furniture thrown around, no splashes of blood on the tables and walls. I take a moment to go through the room, checking around each table, to make sure there is no one waiting in the dark.

I take the stairs quickly despite the weariness dragging me down, shivering violently as the now-wet clothes stick to my skin. Only now, as I start to fully relax do I feel each and every ache and pain from the sparring, muscles strained too far from a day of exertion. My trysts with Haith did nothing to help, and I'm half worried my knees will start shaking before I reach the top of the stairs.

I make it somehow, sliding my key into our locked room. I open the door quietly, but there is still a candle flickering on the small shelf, suggesting my companions have not been long retired, or were kind enough to think about me.

I start to strip off my overclothes but pause halfway through as my eyes land on my bed.

Where Vaen sleeps, one arm tucked beneath his head, back towards Lyr.

I whirl to Lyr's bed and let out a startled yelp, only half muffled, when I find him tangled in another man's limbs. They are both soundly asleep. I do not recognize the man, but it's safe to assume he is one of the mercenaries. He looks to be from a coastal city, skin deep and tan, broad shoulders and sun-streaked hair at odds with the current temperatures. Lyr sleeps deeply, mouth open slightly, but the lines around his eyes are relaxed and easy, the permanent worry eased for the moment.

Well fuck. What am I supposed to do now? I think about returning to Haith's, but the rain pounds relentlessly at the window now. My entire being aches. All I want is to curl up and sleep.

I look back to my bed, grimacing, to find Vaen watching me with one eye open.

"Fuck!" I try, and fail, not to jump. "What are you doing?"

"Waiting for you to blow out the candle and go to sleep," he replies, a scowl on his face. "You should have stayed at your jeweler's."

"Yeah, I see that now." I hesitate, dread curling in my chest. What in the world should I do? Demand him to sleep on the floor? No, that's not fair. I've gotten lucky, having my own bed this entire time. And I certainly don't want to sleep on the floor feeling as I do.

I blow out the candle and finish taking off my rain and sweat-stained overclothes in the dark. Even though I still wear a simple shirt and undergarments, I feel more naked than I ever did with Haith as I hover by the bed.

"I didn't even know Lyr preferred men," I mutter. Anything to delay the awkwardness of sliding into bed with *Vaen.*

"He prefers everyone," Vaen answers drily. "Lyr doesn't have many preferences, as long as they look nice, talk nice, and aren't complete idiots. I'm surprised it took him this long to find someone to play with, honestly."

I snort and almost make a comment about Vaen feeling left out. But then I remember our conversation, about his past in Calire and whoever his mistake was, and I swallow the bitter words down.

"Stop gawking and acting shy and just get into the fucking bed."

I flush, embarrassment and annoyance vying for dominance. Annoyance wins, and, mostly for spite, I do as he says.

The bed is warm from his body heat, something I can't help but appreciate. I always felt like I had more than enough room, but now the space seems unbearably cramped. My leg brushes his without meaning to, one shoulder nudging into his own. I try not to breathe too loudly, try to settle my pounding heartbeat, the beginning of panic that creeps into my chest. How in the world am I ever supposed to relax enough to sleep?

He shifts, hip bumping into my own, and my entire body jolts so badly I nearly end up on the floor.

Vaen's voice is muffled but clearly annoyed. "You need to get a fucking grip on yourself and act your age."

He's right. It shouldn't be a big deal. But every nerve is on fire, every particle of skin taut. All I hear is his breathing, all I'm aware of is how very little space remains between us. How the slightest shift from either of us leads to skin brushing skin. And I remember how he held me, that night so long ago when I was hurt and Lyr healed me. How warm he was then, too.

My whirlwind thoughts coalesce into aggravation, because at least that emotion I understand and accept. "Oh, am I bothering you? Shocking."

There is a moment of stillness, and I wonder if he'll actually ignore this one.

He moves before I can even think to react. One minute he's next to me and the next he hovers over me, legs pinning my own, arms caging in my head. Everything in me freezes as I stare up at him, mouth agape in shock.

My eyes have adjusted enough to the darkness to see the predatory look on his face. Vaen leans down, head next to mine. Silky strands of his undone hair fall around his bare shoulders, the finest hairs tickling my cheek. His lips brush my ear and I practically jump out of my skin, racing thoughts unable to understand what is happening, why he's doing this, what he could possibly intend.

"As a matter of fact, you are bothering me." His words are a whisper, hot against my ear. I can't look away, can't fathom a reply.

"You come into my bed, smelling of sex — you, a beautiful woman, half naked. And you dare provoke me? Of course I'm bothered, Raylen. I would be a fool not to be."

I can't breathe, can't think. The only thing I muster the words to say is, "You think I'm beautiful?"

The idea is so outlandish, I would have laughed in any other situation. But now, Vaen's form suspended above me, I can see the truth in his eyes, the tight lines of his face. My heartbeat is so thunderous, I'm sure he can feel it in the pulse of my neck.

Vaen draws back, a devilish smile curling his lips. "It's a damn good thing the rest of you leaves much to be desired."

Outrage floods me, erasing all speculation, all momentary hesitance, all thoughts of *what if*.

He grins at me — actually *grins* — and rolls off and over, his back once more to me. And he says, as if nothing has happened, "Go to sleep, Raylen."

"Fucking *asshole*."

I roll over as well, my back to his, absolutely fuming. I don't even notice when my body grows heavy with sleep instead of anger and, miraculously, I do exactly as Vaen orders.

When I wake, it takes a few bleary seconds to remember what happened the night before and why the bed is so deliciously warm. Why my back and side still linger with heat, as if a body had been pressed there, an arm thrown over me in the throes of sleep.

I sit up, looking around the now-empty room, at the strewn clothes and weapons. Vaen couldn't have left long ago. I admit to myself that I'm glad he left first, giving me a few minutes to gather myself and my thoughts, to bury the memory of his body above mine, lips against my ear, and how my flesh prickles at the mere thought of it.

I dress in the warmest clothes I have — once outside the blankets, the room is decidedly chilled. My first order of business will be to ask Lyr for an advance of some of my pay and purchase wool-lined clothes for our nightly adventures. He told me, one day on the road here, that the queen and crown give each mage a yearly amount, although they often earn more throughout the year by completing certain duties. Some of those are the primary job of each individual mage, chosen by the conclave, such as helping new mages when they are chosen by the Crystals, while others are special requests.

I'm not quite sure what Lyr's exact purpose is, beyond a general "ensuring the kingdom is safe." I guess this quest falls well within those lines.

The common room is full when I arrive, mostly with the

new travelers, half of whom look fairly miserable and regret being out of bed at all.

Lyr sits at our regular table, head held in his hands, a plate of food barely touched next to his elbow. I fall into the seat across from him, causing the plates and silverware to clatter, and earn a loud groan for my trouble.

"Could you be any louder?" His voice is a miserable whisper.

"Probably," I say, cheerful, spearing a sausage from his plate and helping myself. "Did you have fun last night?"

"Yes, yes I did." He doesn't sound like it and gives me a fairly pathetic look from between his hands, mussed hair falling into his eyes. "Sorry about that, by the way. Making you guys bedmates. I assumed you would stay at the jeweler's."

"It's okay." My face feels like it's on fire. I try not to meet his eyes and quickly say, "So, did you find out anything from your nighttime companion?"

Lyr sits up, reluctantly taking a piece of buttered bread and nibbling on it. "Yes, actually. They're not quiet about why they're here. The rumors have been growing down south; it looks like we left right before some travelers came down, talking of the Aberrations they saw. A tradesman and his family were here, inspecting the lumber, and ran across our spectral friend in the fields. Once word got to the Mage Superior — the head of the conclave— he sent out a message across Serabith, stating that investigating the cause of the Aberrations takes priority over all non-essential duties."

I frown. "So, is one of the mercenaries a mage?"

Lyr swallows his bread, washing it down with water as he nods. "Mercenaries is a bit of a stretch, but yes, one of them is a mage. I don't know her personally; she finished at Haven a few years before I arrived. She specializes in ice magic. Probably a good person to have at this time of year."

"Okay, but why is she with the others, then? Why such a big group?"

Lyr points at me, face grim now. "That's the exact question I asked. It seems the Mage Superior is paying a handsome amount for each Aberration body brought back to Haven."

I suck in a sharp breath. "They want the bodies brought *back*?"

"They have a potion meant to delay the decay of the bodies." Lyr scowls at his plate, dropping his half-eaten bread.

I shake my head at the sheer lunacy of the idea. "So that means—"

"Yes." Lyr looks back up, eyes flat and grim. "They're going out there tonight and will try to draw the damn things out. They have no idea how these creatures actually behave, how different they are from regular Aberrations. When I tried to tell them, they laughed. It's going to be an absolute bloodbath."

"And if they fail," I say as the dread unfurls in my being, "there will be another group waiting to replace them. This place is about to be flooded with mages seeking glory and riches."

Lyr nods, lips pressing into a thin line. "We don't have the luxury of time anymore. We need to find the origin of these Aberrations before this entire town is torn apart. And us with it."

NINETEEN

I t's always hot here.

If there's one thing I've come to know about this place, it is the heat. The relentless sun pounding down on us, day after day, baking us alive in our armor. The only relief we get is the ocean breeze, but even that hasn't been enough lately. Some have taken to slipping out of their breastplates, leaving them in arm's reach. I choose to suffer. There is no time to spare, should an attack come, and armor is the difference between life and death out here on the sand.

More mages have arrived. I'm grateful for their presence, because magic is the only thing saving our asses most days, but I can't say I enjoy their company terribly much. Prideful creatures, even out here where death makes all men equals.

I don't complain to their faces. I thank them for coming, for joining this fight, and they pretend to care what I think. That's the way it's always been, between those of us who wield power so differently.

I don't know how many we have now at our base camp. Fifteen? Twenty? More than the Zuneshans, surely. Some look young and green, but we all were, before this war started. I don't judge them for it.

They—

"What are you reading?"

I respond by dropping Eirah's journal straight into the dirt.

"I'm sorry, I didn't mean to startle you." Nalista bends down, gathering the journal and carefully shaking dirt particles free. "Good thing the ground is half frozen right now."

She offers the journal back to me with a smile, which I return even as I take the book.

"So, what is it?" She nods to the book, now closed and held tightly. A precious artifact, nearly lost.

"My uncle's journal. He was a knight in the Zuneshan War." I scoot over, making room for her on the bench.

With a glorious day free of going to Sunillen's, I decided to preoccupy myself with... trying to find Sunillen. It took me absurdly long to remember Sunillen fought in the war, and while there were hundreds of combatants, dozens of different sites of battle, there was a slim chance of Eirah having come in contact with him.

I'm not quite sure what I want to glean from the journal — glimpses of Sunillen's traitorous heart, perhaps, a clue that tells us he's always been a villain. Two hours in, and I've found nothing beyond cramped shoulders and half-frozen toes, despite the two layers of socks I put on before coming out.

Nalista lowers herself onto the bench, sweeping her sensible skirts out of the way gracefully. Her eyes widen as she catches onto my words, and she asks in a lower voice, "Find anything useful?"

I shake my head. "No. I don't think they ever met."

"Shame. That was a good lead, though." She touches my arm, almost consolingly, a little thrill leaping in me at the contact. At the way she looks at me now, almost knowingly.

"Has anything happened?" I keep the question light, careful.

I fully believe Nalista suspects Sunillen to be the perpetrator, but he's still her employer, and we have to tread carefully.

"No. Last night was quiet."

She doesn't look rested for a quiet night; quite the opposite in fact. The shadows under her eyes have darkened, the lines around her mouth deeper. Her hair is sloppily drawn into its bun, wisps escaping to frame her pretty face.

"Are you sure?" I ask, worry lacing my tone. "You look exhausted."

She laughs a little at that and leans into me so we're thigh to thigh, shoulder to shoulder. As if I can take some of the weight off her. "I had nightmares last night. They happen more often than I'd like to admit."

I can understand that. I haven't dreamed of the war in a long time, dead body beaches replaced by faceless knights telling me I'm no longer welcome. Shadows waiting for my blood.

I want to ask Nalista what she dreams of, but it seems too much, too raw, for this budding friendship. Instead, I say, "Where are the children today?"

"Probably terrorizing the cook after Sunillen got bored spending time with them." She shrugs away the darkness behind the words. "I needed to update their winter wardrobes. Attempting to visit the seamstress is next to impossible with them with me, so I merely bring their measurements."

"That's a nice break for you. I'm sure you don't get many days off." She grins wryly at me, but the smile slips when I plunge ahead and add, "What did you do before you came to Ulingard?"

If I hadn't been watching her, I might have missed it: the tightness around her shoulders, the thinning of lips as they press together. She doesn't say anything at first, eyes watching two farm girls line up jars of preserves and jams at their small market stall. I wonder if I stepped too far out of my line, if perhaps this friendship is more imagined than reality.

"I was away from my home for a few years," Nalista finally says, words not quite as carefree as before. "I lived near my aunt and was tasked with helping her as she recovered from the war — she was involved with the Battle of Trelitt and was badly injured, both mentally and physically."

I freeze, ears ringing with the word over and over. Trelitt. The name is emblazoned on my heart, carved with blood into my being. Outside the city, on a beach that ran red with blood, my uncle took his last stand.

"Are you all right?" Nalista lays her hand on my arm.

I shake my head, swallowing back the bile that always rises when I think about him, dying beneath a dozen muddy boots, face pressing into unforgiving sand as he bled out.

"Fine," I say, banishing the image. It's been so many years, it still surprises me when the gaping hole of loss swallows me whole. "Keep going, I'm sorry to interrupt."

She waves my apology away. "When I returned home, I was ready to find a place in my own self. I *wanted* to stay there." She scowls, eyes darkening. "I was young, younger than you are now. I was stupid, lured into a promise of a lifetime of love. Needless to say, it did not turn out as I wished, but I became pregnant anyway. When it came out what happened and the man refused to marry me — which was impossible since he already had a wife and children of his own — I was given the choice of giving him the child upon its birth, or leaving."

I knew several girls who became pregnant suspiciously quickly after marrying. It was different in the big cities, of course. Unwed women gave birth all the time, although the children usually did not have a good life, either forced into an orphanage or cast into poverty as their mother tried to work and care for them simultaneously. If the girl's family stepped up to care for the child, it was wildly fortunate.

The idea of being faced with that decision while still so young leaves me cold and aching. The injustice of it all, of the most vulnerable people being forced into such dire, often fatal, circumstances, makes me want to scream. To rage against every person, male and female, who thought this was the right thing to do. To raise my sword and summon an army of the oppressed, of the powerless, and give them back their power, so they can obliterate those who stand before them telling them *no*.

"What did you do?" The words are barely a whisper.

Nalista studies the cobblestones under our feet. "I kept him of course. I returned to Calire and to my aunt, and we raised him together. His name was Kallum."

Dread sours my stomach.

His name *was* Kallum. Not is. Was.

She does not look at me as she continues. "He was two when he died. He caught the wasting sickness, and there was nothing I could do." Her voice breaks, but her eyes are dry. She clears her throat. "My apologies. I haven't spoken of him in quite some time."

I don't ask but simply throw my arms around her and embrace her tightly. Nalista stiffens in surprise for a minute before melting into my arms, her small form molding into mine. I do not say anything, ignoring the looks we receive from the housewives on their way to the market, the small army of dirty children who run barefoot, impervious to the wind and cold.

When she finally withdraws, I pretend not to notice the tears on her cheeks, although there is no shame in them. She wipes her eyes and gives me a small, watery smile.

"I came up here after," she continues, the barest hint of a

tremble in her voice. "It was the furthest I could go to get away from his memories."

"I'm sorry." The words are completely inadequate to describe the depths of her loss, but I can't think of any others.

Nalista nods, accepting them for what they are. "I never thought I would become the governess to two other children. I thought it would be too hard for me, bring back too many memories. But it's been healing in a way. I can't care for Kallum anymore, but I can protect those two. I would have done anything for him." There is a fierceness in her voice that only comes from speaking of the deepest love possible. "I still would. I would go to the ends of the world for him."

And again I see that tiredness, both physical and mental. I put my hand on her shoulder. "You need to protect yourself too. You can't give to others if you have nothing left for yourself."

She nods, but in the distant way that says she has no intention of listening to advice. I understand that well enough.

"I need to commission some new shoes for the children," she says, shaking off our conversation like droplets of water. "Would you like to join me?"

There are undoubtedly things I could be doing — checking in on Lyr, practicing with the Watchers, scouting for magic users and rumors and any little thing that could give us a clue in this damnable chase. But instead I smile and nod, and we spend the next hour talking about things that don't matter. Our favorite foods, our childhoods, our families. It is the most relaxed I have been since coming to Ulingard, and when we finally part ways, I feel filled in a way I haven't since bidding goodbye to Liseah.

The Night's End is bustling when I return, the mercenaries out in force, devouring a midday meal and loudly discussing their plans for the night. I spy Vaen sitting alone at our table, his own plate mostly empty, watching the joviality with a look of utter disdain.

I slide into the seat opposite of him despite the sudden tightness in my chest as I remember the night before. He glances at me then away, but there is no turbulence on his features, no indication he's thinking about the matter at all.

And I hate him for that, for how much he affects me only to walk away unscathed time and again.

"Where's Lyr?" I ask, determined to mimic him. If he can pretend it never happened, I surely can too.

"Upstairs."

"And the item?"

"We have the materials needed. He's working on it now. It'll be ready for tonight."

My heart hammers in my chest. "What do we do?"

"Wait until tonight." Vaen's eyes are flinty as they turn back to me but lack the outright disdain from the weeks before. This is not personal. "Then I'll do my job, and you'll keep guard."

I nod, accepting my role. "What about Lyr?"

"I don't want him anywhere near there if we can help it. We need witnesses of his innocence. He'll stay here, in view of everyone."

"But what about us? Do we need alibis too?" I keep my voice low and my face smooth.

Vaen shrugs. "I'm not concerned for that. We'll make sure someone sees us going upstairs, and slip out the window later."

The situation he is implying makes my face flame, and reality slams home again. His body above mine, breath warm on my face, desire in every line of his body.

And maybe in mine, too.

I rise abruptly, not caring my food hasn't even been brought out. "Sounds like you've thought of everything." I need to get out, to clear my head, to stop thinking. "I'm going to spar. I'll see you at dinner."

I don't wait for him to respond.

Sparring doesn't erase my thoughts and fears, but it helps. I work until I'm drenched in sweat but stop before I can use every reserve of energy. The Watchers beg for a few more matches, but I decline and instead sit with them in their small dining hall, sharing coffee and stories with those off duty.

Olivie sits with me. She was the only one to best me in the sparring ring at hand to hand combat, but I'm glad she did. It wouldn't look good for their commander to lose to a guard for hire. And I'm glad for me, too. I need the reminder that there are still things to improve on.

"We spotted several Aberrations late last night," she tells me, voice low enough I know this is just for me. "One was normal. But my guards heard the whispers and felt the presence when they went out to deal with the creature."

I contemplate this information, scowling at the well worn wooden table. Knowing what I know now, I wonder who wandered into the magic and if they've been missed yet. "They're getting closer to the walls of the city," I finally say.

She nods grimly. "I get the feeling the *normal* Aberration was meant as a distraction."

I close my eyes at the horror of the thought. "So the spirits are planning attacks and using them as bait?"

I swallow more coffee to get the rancid taste of that idea out of my mouth, but it doesn't help.

"But what are they trying to distract us from?"

Olivie swallows the dregs of her coffee and rises. "That's what you need to find out, I guess."

"No pressure," I mutter. I follow her, dumping my dishes in the kitchen before leaving.

To my surprise, Vaen waits for me at the gate. I raise my eyebrows at him, and he gestures with his chin. I fall into step with him, our strides nearly perfectly matched.

"Did he finish it?"

Vaen nods as we take the long way back to The Night's End, detouring down a side street cluttered with discarded pieces of lumber. "He did a good job. It should fool Sunillen, at least for a while."

"So you sneak in and I, what, stay on the ground? Make bird noises if anyone comes around?"

A faint smile flickers, easing the hard lines that seem to be permanently engraved in his features. "I'm not sure you could make a passable one, but Lyr has a trick for that, too." He holds out a smooth, simple piece of glass. "He charmed it to allow a single message through. You run your finger around the outside edge three times, then speak your message. I have the glass's twin; when the message is spoken, it will heat to alert me and speak the message only once. After that, the charm will fade. There will not be any second chances."

I examine the glass. It's perfectly smooth, slightly smaller than the palm of my hand, and thick enough I don't immediately worry about it shattering. Lyr told me once that glass is the only material intentional magic can latch on to. It's how the Nobles have mage lights in their homes, why many weapons masters have tried to craft glass weapons. Unlike imbued objects, which never run out of magic as far as we know, charmed glass loses its magic eventually. Mage lights need to be relit, glass swords shatter, and our contact shards will only last for one use apparently.

I pocket the glass, moving on to the next worry. "What if someone comes inside the room?"

Vaen doesn't hesitate. "I'll deal with them one way or another."

I stop, putting a hand on his arm to halt him as well. He looks at me, surprised. My own heart beats erratically, palm practically on fire from the simple touch. I push the thought away as hard as I can. We don't have the luxury of figuring out that moment.

"You can't kill anyone." My tone brooks no argument. "Especially the servants or children. They have no part in this. This subterfuge, this fight, is not theirs. They don't deserve to be dragged into a mages' feud for stepping into the wrong room at the wrong time."

"Feh." Vaen doesn't meet my gaze, but the annoyance is obvious. "I will do what I need to do to succeed in my mission."

I lean up the barest hint so we're at equal height and surprise us both by grabbing his chin non-too-gently and turning his face to mine. Shock followed by outrage rolls across his eyes, but I meet the anger head on. "I am not afraid of you," I whisper. "Swear to me you will do anything in your power to keep from killing tonight."

We stand toe to toe, faces too close, chests nearly pressed together. An intimate scene, if not for the tension roiling from every clenched muscle.

Just when I think he's not going to give in, something changes. The anger dims, not gone entirely, but fading to something akin to respect. "You really want to save everyone, don't you." The words are whispered, his eyes searching my face for the answer he already knows.

I start to step back, denial on my lips — I'm not some savior, not some hero. But now Vaen is the one pressing forward, matching my retreat step for step until my back hits the wall. My hand has long since fallen from his face, palms now pressing against the cold stone. He leans forward, caging me in once again, arms on either side of my head. Just like last night.

Only this time I'm not fresh from sex, and there is not the same desire dancing in his gaze now. He looks curious more than anything.

"Have you always been this way? Or did the Knight's Temple force this change into you?"

I stare up at him, denial forgotten, that day slamming back into me. The stern faces, heavy with judgement. The confidence that slowly turned to dread, the knowledge that I did the *right* thing but it wasn't actually right at all, not to them. That my good actions were somehow, impossibly, wrong.

"I thought knighthood was about saving those who needed it." I shake my head, slow, not breaking our eye contact. "But it turned out it was only about saving the most important ones. I will never believe in that lie."

Vaen studies me in silence, time stretching on endlessly. I want to say something else, to break free of his hold on me, but my limbs are too heavy, my breath too short. I can't think of anything beyond this shared space of ours. What it means to happen yet again. That the sacredness of myself is fair game for this man. On one hand is that familiar anger, coating my throat and mouth with fire, begging to be let out in a stream of heat to incinerate him. And then there is also a peace, somewhere deep inside, because I feel like perhaps this space is still sacred, but it now belongs to him and I, and that sharing it fills a part of myself I never even knew was empty.

Without another word, Vaen pushes away from the wall and turns, walking back to the inn. I sag against the wall, the will gone out of my body, everything suddenly so much louder and brighter, as if I had forgotten a whole world existed.

"I will not kill them," he says, the words snatched away by the sudden wind that howls around us.

I nod dumbly into the empty air before me. Then I follow, skin pebbled with cold, the memory of warmth between us already vanished.

"You know what to do?"

I scowl as I wrap my new fur lined cloak around myself. Our room, with the small corner brazier lit, is almost too hot for these new vestments, but the outside is another story. The locals have said the first serious frost is upon us, and I do not fancy spending the night more miserable than it already will be.

"We know, Lyr." I watch the mage as he paces back and forth, nibbling on the nail of his thumb. He's pale with worry, brows drawn and tight. "We've been over it a thousand times."

Vaen claps the mage on the shoulder, hard enough to stop his endless movement. Lyr looks at him with glassy, wild eyes. "Get a grip," the thief says flatly. "You need to play your part, too. You need to convince everyone down there that we're occupied, you're annoyed at it, and no one need think we're up to anything else."

Lyr nods, but he doesn't look convinced. "I just hate that it has to be this way. It seems like for every dangerous situation, you two have had to face it alone while I putter around here like some useless idiot."

I shoulder Vaen aside and grab Lyr by the hand. He focuses on me immediately, and I can see the exhaustion waging war with his restlessness. "You've done so much," I say as gently as I can. "You've brought us here, played endless rounds of politics with Sunillen, created magical items for us to use, and made the forgery in the first place. And tomorrow, with the imbued gem, you'll go out into the field with us and we'll finally be able to track these damnable creatures to their source. Sometimes the most important thing we can do is wait until our time comes around. That doesn't mean we're useless. It means you know the power in the people with you, and you trust us to do our part in it."

Lyr wets his lips, nodding faintly. A little color returns to his cheeks and he straightens his shoulders a hairsbreadth. "Right. Right. Tomorrow, I'll show them just how powerful I can be."

Tomorrow. This could all be over tomorrow.

The idea doesn't bring as much happiness as it should. *Because once this ends... what happens to me?*

I shake the thought away, trapping it behind a steel door to deal with another time.

Vaen holds out my sword and leathers. I take them, sliding the belt and scabbard around my waist, and give him a slight nod.

"We'll be back soon," I say, giving Lyr's hand one last squeeze.

"Watch out for each other. Be safe. Be quiet. Be fast."

Another nod, then I go to the window and look out. We're on the second floor, the ground a good distance away. Vaen pulls out a rope he procured from the stables, tying it firmly around the bed post before tossing the rest out the window. "Pull it back up and lock the window when we're gone," he orders Lyr. Then, so smoothly it looks surreal, he swings his long body out the window and shimmies down the rope, landing without a sound on the hard earth a moment later.

I know I will not be that graceful. I look out again, my stomach squeezing uncomfortably at the height. My hands tremble embarrassingly as I grab the rope. I remember now why I never climbed the apple trees as high as Liseah.

"Move your ass," Vaen hisses from below. He clings to the shadows of the building, barely visible even when knowing where to look.

"Mind your own fucking business," I mutter back. But he's right. We only have so long to get this done.

Taking a fortifying breath, I swing one leg over the sill and sit precariously there, feeling the empty air beneath me. My dinner threatens to come up as all logical reasoning leaves me. All I can see is myself on the ground, a pile of broken bones, split ends that pierce the skin and gleam whitely in the moonlight.

Lyr's face appears next to mine, questioning.

"Can you, I don't know, create some sort of air bubble around me and lower me to the ground?" I ask through gritted teeth.

Lyr's confusion morphs to sympathy. "No. But I can do this." He leans out, hand outstretched over the earth. I follow his movement and am shocked to see the ground rise up until it's a mere few feet from me. I only have to lower myself down the rope by a body's length or less.

"That better?" Lyr asks.

An illusion. Of course it is. But, even knowing the truth, the sight gives me comfort. I swallow the last of my fear, nodding. "Thanks, Lyr."

Only a few feet.

I can almost believe it, too. I swing my other leg over the sill, gripping the rope in my hands, the bottom wrapped around one foot. I lower myself down, the rope sliding across my foot to help control my speed. The ground stays where it's at — a few feet away. I do it again, and again, and again, until my feet touch the actual ground. I want to cry with relief.

"Fucking finally." Vaen pushes off the wall and gestures for me to follow.

We creep through the city on silent feet, staying to the shadows and taking the long way to the gate through the poorer district.

We can't risk the Watchers seeing us, so Vaen came through earlier and planted another rope a good ways away from the gate. Ulingard is not a town full of riches and treasures; while the gates are guarded, the top of the walls are not patrolled. It is the work of a moment to scale them and drop back on the other side. There is no illusion to trick my mind this time, but I focus on the stones next to my face and the absolute fury of Vaen if I mess this up, and am able to slither down the rope once again.

We run silently through the field, giving the manor a wide berth until we come to the back of it. I can hear the wordless hum of talking and laughing from the central area of the fields and spot a handful of lit torches.

The mercenaries are already out here, looking for their prey.

"They're like a beacon," I say, watching the wavering flames jump and splutter in the wind. "The Aberrations are going to be drawn right to them."

"Just like they hope," Vaen agrees. I can't tell what he thinks of that.

Vaen chooses his place of ascent on the wall of the manor that faces the forest. The stone is pitted in places but I can't imagine a full grown man using those grooves as hand and foot holds.

As if reading my mind, Vaen takes out two small metal picks, holding them lightly in his hands. "Remember what we said." He doesn't look at me as he talks, eyes already trained on his goal: a window more than halfway up the wall. I hope he's certain in his layout and it isn't someone's bedroom.

"I'll use the glass if I need to," I reassure him. "Stay quiet, stay hidden. Don't risk your life for anything."

He gives me a brief grin, all teeth and wolf-like impishness, then takes a step back and *leaps*, all strength and momentum carrying him upwards in a graceful arc. He lands on the stone, picks diving in between invisible cracks, boots braced against whatever rough patches they can find.

His voice floats down, barely a raised whisper. "And no killing anyone."

Then he's gone, pushing upwards with a speed I never could have imagined.

I stare after him, mouth open, waiting with bated breath for him to fall. But he never does. In less time than it would take me to walk through the front door, he reaches the window and unlatches it. It swings smoothly open, telling me he must have unlocked it during his previous search of the house. I watch his dark form slip inside, heart beating loudly in my ears.

This is it. The moment that could truly change the tide for us.

I pick up Lyr's nervous energy and pace at the foot of the wall, one hand on my sword. My shoulder blades itch, the spot right in the middle burning, as if someone is watching me. I look around slowly and carefully, but there is no sign of a hidden watcher, whether it be friend or enemy.

The feeling grows with every moment that passes. I find my eyes drawn continuously back, not to the group of mercenaries making fools of themselves, but to the trees. The forest that lies just beyond reach, although I am closer to it tonight than I have been before.

I stare into the dark trees, darker shadows moving from spot to spot, shifting as the limbs dance in the wind. The longer I stare, the more I feel like someone is in there, staring back at me. That if I just got a little closer, looked a little harder, I could find out who.

I've taken three steps before I even realize it.

With a gasp I skitter backwards, hitting the wall hard. I press myself against it, shaking, still staring into those dark depths. Daring the creature to stare back, to reveal itself, to end this torment of waiting.

Because what is in there is not playing games. It yearns for my blood. Cherry red, splattered across the ground, arc of droplets that glisten in the moonlight.

Just one step closer.

A stick snaps beneath my foot. I draw in a great shuddering breath, my entire body heaving at the motion, and realize *I'm not next to the wall anymore.*

I turn in a frantic circle, breathing loudly, sword half drawn from its scabbard from hands that shake wildly. A little sound, almost a sob, is ripped from me when I see the manor lies dozens of feet behind me.

And the beckoning forest is only a few steps in front of me.

I stumble back, breath now turning to stuttering gasps, my chest hurting with the force of trying to breathe, each inhalation frantic and closer to the last but still not enough air I'm running out of air I can't breathe can't—

I look wildly over my shoulder at the forest.

And, finally, I see something staring back.

I start to scream, mouth opening wide, terror caught in my throat, but the sound is swallowed by another screaming. Then another. And another.

The thing in the forest flickers and vanishes, releasing me from its terrible gaze. I slump forward, barely catching myself before falling to my knees. Then again there is a scream, born of pain and utter terror, that rises unendingly into the sky.

The Aberrations have reached the mercenaries.

TWENTY

Although the thing in the forest is gone, I cannot banish the image of shadows that grew from hunched, deformed shoulders, a head twisted halfway around, skin pulled taut to show the muscles underneath. The bone crown that sprouted like antlers from its skull, as gnarled as a thicket of thorns, twisting and turning around itself in the air above its head. The arms that curled backwards, elbows jointed wrong, everything was *wrong*. And the teeth that gleamed, too big and shining white like shards of broken off bone. The teeth that would tear and rip and rend flesh, scattering parts of me into the field so far it would take days for them to piece me back together.

The eyes that shone, moon white but still seeing, looking at me with more intelligence than any Aberration had the right to have. Eyes that stared into my soul, telling me with utter certainty that one day soon it would kill me.

And I believe it.

I don't forget any of it. It is burned into my mind, emblazoned with fire and pain and fear and death. And nothing will ever take the image from me.

But now I cannot afford to think of it. People are screaming, cries that shatter the night, and I hear weapons and the low creature-like sounds that surely come from the Aberrations. I can't tell by sound alone how many are there, but it's undoubtedly more than one.

I'm closer to the mercenaries than the Watchers at the gate are. And, although the thought of abandoning my post is abhorrent, worse still would be to just let them die. Not when I can do something to help. It doesn't matter they were idiotic to come here in the first place, totally unprepared for this ugly truth, seeking only glory. It doesn't matter, because in the end, they are still human.

They are still worth saving.

I glance at the tower, but there is no sign of Vaen. What if I leave and something happens? He's my companion, my ally. I'm to watch and protect his back.

Another scream, and I know I cannot stay.

I turn and sprint across the field, freeing my sword. I'm there within a heartbeat, but it takes several more moments to process the scene before me.

An Aberration, skin mottled gray and green, swings out with a great clawed hand, connecting with the head of a mercenary. It jerks to the side, too far, bones clearly snapping. The blade-like claws rake down the man's face, leaving bloody furrows within the plains of his skin.

The Aberration staggers back, head swaying, dumbly looking for its next target. It falls to all fours, elongated arms acting as another set of legs, and jerkily gallops to the nearest mercenary, a woman twice my age who wields a battle axe against another of the monsters. A third Aberration is engaged with two more mercenaries a few more paces away. A fourth and fifth, down on all fours like the first, circle the mage, surrounded by pinnacles of ice that erupt from the ground at her feet, spiraling high for a moment before shuddering under the weight of the Aberrations' attack.

Five. Five Aberrations—

No, that's wrong. I watch, mouth dry with terror, as black shadows ripple across the ground. As one shadow grows and grows, looming over an Aberration, tendrils of smoke and darkness forming a bottomless mouth to whisper something, red glowing eyes focused not on the monsters but the mage. The Aberration turns and, lightning fast, snakes toward the girl. Its movements are *wrong*.

The shadows retreat but they do not vanish. Their corporality lessens, and the monster slides once more into the ground, almost inseparable from the dark grass that glistens with blood.

I count four bodies, but that's a hasty guess. There's no time to sit and count and wallow in my fear. I need to tell the mage to find the shadows and figure out a way to destroy them. If she can.

Bracing myself, I dive into the battle.

Everything instantly fades away except for what I can do and the next step I need to take. I move and stab, dance and slice, stumble backwards, push another mercenary out of the way, duck under the swinging arm that tries to cleave his torso into two. The arm is heavy, but the skin and bone are brittle, and a strong upward swing rids the creature of his appendage.

I don't stay to kill it, leaving that work for the mercenary it was fighting. I keep my eyes roving, waiting for the shadows, the fog, the otherworldly masterminds of this, but nothing comes as I forge onwards.

Three Aberrations attack the mage now, but one is distracted by a mercenary at its side. Good. I like these odds. One on one is manageable — maybe. I start for the closest

Aberration, but movement in the corner of my eye stops me cold.

The mercenary trying to reach the mage stills, weapon dropping from suddenly loose hands. His back arches, head thrown back so violently I can see the ropes of muscles as his neck strains. As I watch, horrified, he lifts off the ground, legs kicking wildly, arms spasming and useless. His eyes bulge, mouth open, but the only sound that emerges is a low, insistent whine, as if he can't draw the breath to speak.

And I see it — the tendrils of fog, winding around his body, smoke gray bands that grip his chest, shoulders, neck. I watch as the substance pours in his open mouth, so much fog, a never ending stream that fills him until—

The body bursts, distended skin giving way, pieces of flesh scattering in all directions. Blood rains down, drenching me, still hot, the copper tang immediately filling my mouth. There is a wet smack as sections of stomach and intestines land next to me, the rotting stench immediate and visceral.

I stumble back as acid scorches my throat, body reacting even as my mind struggles to understand.

It's pure intuition that tells me something moves just outside my sight, and I move forward and twist, spying rotten skin and pitted bone. The swipe that would have caught my head grazes my back instead, sending lines of white sharp pain shooting across the back of my shoulders.

Training kicks in, overriding the horror enough for me to turn with a raised sword, catching the next attack. I skip to the side, letting the creature barrel forward, and take a swing at its side. It isn't nearly enough to down the monster, but the howl of pain is satisfying.

"Do something!" I yell to the mage, who stands stock still, hands raised but shaking, glazed eyes staring at her dead companion.

"You need to use magic to banish the shadow Aberration." I point with a shaking hand at the rolling fog, which is rapidly starting to coalesce into a corporeal form once more. "If you can get rid of it, we might have a chance."

Because I truly don't think we will survive the night otherwise.

The mage stares wordlessly at me with wide, terrified eyes. "*Now!*" I roar, channeling every ounce of fear into authority.

It works, and she turns to face the Aberration. Her hands shake as she raises them, but her aim is true. Wickedly sharp icicles larger than my own body erupt from the ground, splitting the earth with the ferocity of their growth. The wind howls, the temperature dropping rapidly, as a rope of ice snaps out, wrapping around the shadow Aberration in its half-formed state. I hold my breath, every inch coiled tight with the hope that it works, it has to work, these things have to be destroyed or—

Motion to my left. I move before looking, skipping back and bringing my weapon up. The Aberration growls and leans forward with gnashing teeth, uncaring as the sword sinks into its decaying flesh. A gasp is torn from my throat and I fall back, losing my balance and sliding to my rear. The hand that snaps out to catch me aches from the force of the fall, but there's no time to worry about a broken bone as the creature presses forward still, nothing more than a ravenous animal held back from its prey.

I dare to throw myself forward, removing my sword and only protection so I can dive into a roll. I hit the monster's legs with enough force that it stumbles, off balance for a precious few seconds. I'm up a moment later, thrusting my sword through its ribs.

Either these creatures don't have hearts like we do or my

aim is off, because the Aberration only roars its fury and throws itself at me, yanking my sword from my grip.

Shit shit shit!

I fling myself to the side desperately, avoiding its wickedly fast downward swipe by a scarce few inches. Stumbling to my feet once again, I palm two daggers and throw with as much accuracy as I can. Not being able to line up a shot costs me, and one dagger buries itself into the Aberration's shoulder, the other merely grazing its sunken head.

Shit.

I only have two daggers left. I can't see my sword at all in the flickering torchlight; it might still be embedded into the creature, or fallen to the bloody ground by now. The chances of killing an Aberration with two daggers is laughably slim. But I grip them anyway, because the other option is not an option at all.

As I try to decide if I should risk another headshot or hope to find its heart, something *shifts*. The moment seems to freeze in time, everything slowing between one breath and the next. I see the Aberration pause, head turning away from me, as if looking for something. The snarls and screams waver, the sudden silence shocking and unnerving. I find myself turning, searching for the cause, and relief bursts like a new morning's dawn when I see the mage wavering on her feet before her ice dungeon. It has grown to completely envelop the shadows inside, but it's all too easy to imagine the swirling vortex, the inhuman screaming, the murderous words that spill from a mouthless entity.

The mage snaps her fingers, and the dungeon collapses in on itself, shrapnels of ice overlapping one another as her prisoner is obliterated.

I turn and throw the dagger. My aim is true, and it sinks into the Aberration's red rimmed eye. It howls, clawing at its own face, but blackish blood seeps from the wound, creating rivulets down the creature's face. I stride forward and grab the thing's neck, pulling down with all my strength until it's close enough to drive my last remaining dagger into its skull.

Ichor, hot and stinking, spurts from the wound to coat my arms and chest. I watch as the creature collapses, unable to find a sense of victory or pride in the defeat. Just relief.

I wrench my dagger free. I need to find my sword. The battle isn't over; the Aberrations have lost their single-minded focus, but they don't retreat with the death of their commander. Master? Whatever the hell the shadow creature was.

Several things happen simultaneously. I find my sword, thrown several feet away. As I approach it, there is a sudden swell of voices, more than before. I look up and find a contingency of Watchers, led by Olivie, flooding our battlefield.

Relief blooms in my chest.

I take a moment to breathe, surveying the field to see who needs the most help, but the remaining few Aberrations are being taken down incredibly effectively.

A new movement catches my attention. A dark figure rapidly approaching, zeroing in on me. It moves with grace and purpose, slinking through shadows until it seems to become one. My heart stutters, seeming to stop, as horror fills my bones.

How can there be another one—

The figure coalesces into a man and I recognize the dark clothes, the gait of his loping run.

Vaen.

My heart resumes and relief I hadn't expected floods me. *He's okay.* I had managed to push his mission to the back of my thoughts, but now finding Vaen whole and alone, Sunillen nowhere to be found, brings a torrent of emotions. Glee, that we did it. Relief, that me leaving him didn't bring disaster. And, finally, that flicker of pride as I look at the dead Aberration at my feet. I did that. I killed it. Just me, no one else. Even Vaen will have to be impressed at that.

But the closer Vaen gets, the more I realize something *is* wrong. The pride flees as quickly as it came as he stops before me. He looks at the battlefield, the mercenaries weeping over their dead brethren, the Watchers coalescing around the mage to ask what happened. Olivie sees us and nods, unsurprised. I give a weak nod back, but Vaen doesn't so much as bat an eye.

Slowly he turns back to me, and the rage that fills his face snuffs out any remaining relief. And I realize there will be no congratulations, no exclamations over my skill, over my help in this field. Not from him.

"You left me." His tone is incredulous. Damning.

I wince and look down. The adrenaline vanishes, leaving me cold and aching, shivering in the wind, in the exhaustion that only comes from a hard fight. Drying blood cracks over my hands, already sinking into the exposed skin.

"I did what I thought I needed to." The words are a whisper. "They needed me."

Vaen is unflinching as he says, "I needed you too, Raylen. We had a plan. And now you've gone and exposed us, destroyed our alibi—"

"I'll fix it," I interrupt. "I'll figure out a story that Olivie will believe."

"You. Left. Me." The words are a snarl, ripped from a place of betrayal. My stomach hollows out at the disbelief, at the hurt and the anger. "I was counting on you, and you couldn't even be bothered to use the calling glass to send me a message."

I close my eyes as shame fills me. The calling glass. I hadn't even thought about it, hadn't bothered to remember we *did* have a way to communicate.

"All you had to do was tell me what happened." There is no pity in his voice, no leniency. I am attacked anew, flinching at each weapon-sharp word. "Instead, you rush off like a battle-happy fool, ready to throw away everything we've worked on because you thought it was the right call."

I can't look at him. I can't bear to see the same damnation on his face as in his voice. But I also can't stop the words that pour out in his fury-wrapped quiet.

"You say it was wrong. And I messed up, I fucked up well and truly. I'm sorry for that. But it wasn't the wrong choice. They needed help. And I do not regret giving it."

The silence stretches on for so long, I dare to look up. Vaen watches me, face smooth and unreadable.

Then, without another word, he turns and walks away.

I stay and talk with Olivie for only a few minutes. She asks what I saw, and I tell the best partial truth I can come up with: that Vaen and I impulsively decided to take a walk around the fields and came upon the attack. I blame it on coincidence with a dash of intuition, and Olivie accepts my explanation without question. The ease at which I lie to her is almost a physical pain, but I don't hesitate.

I don't stay to talk to the mercenaries or help them gather their dead to burn. The Watchers can assist with that. I can't be in this field for another moment, feeling blood slowly trickle down my skin while the eyes of the forest bore holes into the back of my skull.

We might have defeated the monster tonight, but more lurk just out of sight. I cannot be rid of the image of that otherworldly antlered beast, and I know that should I stay, it will call to me again. I don't know if I'm strong enough to resist its siren's song a second time.

I debate going straight to Haith's, knowing that Vaen will want nothing to do with me, but my wound needs to be looked at. I don't dare risk poison like before.

The walk back to The Night's End is almost too much. I overestimated my energy, and by the time I reach the inn, my breathing is unsteady and loud, chest expanding harshly with grating gasps of air. The only consolation is, with our cover blown, I don't have to attempt to haul myself up a rope dangling out of our window.

I wrap myself in my cloak as best I can, trying to hide the worst of the blood splatters, but it's useless. I'm drenched in it almost from head to foot. Keeping my head down, I ignore the calls from the last few revelers and head straight for our room.

Vaen and Lyr are already inside, hovering over something small on Lyr's bed, their voices hushed. The conversation halts as soon as I enter and bolt the door behind me.

I don't look at Vaen. Can't look at him. The shame bubbles and festers, threatening to devour me from the inside out. I keep my eyes instead on the floor near Lyr's boots.

"I'm sorry," I say, the words cracking with exhaustion. "I won't stay. But, um, I was wounded. I don't want what happened last time—"

Lyr's face appears before mine, soft with understanding. The kindness there makes me want to weep. I swallow thickly and add again, "I'm sorry. I didn't—"

He takes my filthy hands in his own clean ones and gently squeezes. "Raylen, if I wanted someone who obeyed all the rules, I would have asked for a knight or mercenary guild member to accompany me. You might have gone about it the wrong way, but you did something right by helping. And, thank the light, everything worked out in the end. Let's forget about it, okay? We can't change the past."

His reassurance banishes some of the coldness that has settled into me. But when I look at Vaen, there is no forgiveness there. I'm not surprised, but that spark of warmth, so recently rekindled, flickers.

"I'm glad you came to me for healing," Lyr continues, a wicked, excited gleam entering his eyes. "It'll give me the chance to try out our new prize."

He picks up the object they were studying. The gem is onyx, smooth and glittering, set into a hexagon of gold on top of a wide ring band. It's not much bigger than my thumbnail, but the quality is breathtaking. The gem is the deepest black, almost mirror-like in the candle's flame.

I manage to crack a smile. "You got it."

Vaen's snort drips with disdain. "Of course I got it."

Lyr shoves his way between us. "Come on, let's get you healed up. Vaen, will you draw a bath? She's filthy."

"I can do it." The last thing I need is for Vaen to have one more thing to hold against me. As it is, there is a terrible feeling of doomed certainty that the camaraderie we have been creating is irreparably broken.

I ignore Lyr's blustering and turn the tap. The water is decidedly less than lukewarm this late at night, but remaining covered in Aberration blood is far worse.

By the time the tub is filled enough, exhaustion and pain have my teeth on edge, pushing modesty straight out the window. I struggle out of my clothes, sucking in a great gasp of air when my shirt sticks to my back and seems to pull the very skin up.

"Stop," Lyr orders. He comes behind me and begins the slow, painful process of pulling the material away from the wounds bit by bit. Whether these gashes are just that much deeper than what I've dealt with before or exhaustion has heightened my senses, by the time the garment is discarded to the floor, tears prick my eyes.

I don't let them fall as I step into the tub, not giving myself a chance to back out.

The coldness sends the last bit of air out of my lungs, and I can do nothing but sit there, miserable and shivering, legs pulled up to my chest in an effort to retain the smallest scrap of body heat.

"Hmm." Lyr takes a washcloth slathered with soap and begins attending my shoulders and back, his administrations straightforward but gentle. "It got you pretty good. I think I could heal it on a good day without an imbued object, but it would wipe me out for a day or two after."

His cloth swipes at the gaping wounds and I close my eyes, forehead falling to my knees.

"We definitely don't have any days to waste." I focus on the words, on each syllable falling from my lips, so I can try to ignore the burning pain radiating over me. It doesn't work.

I risk a glance at Vaen, but he sits on the bed with his clasped hands between his knees, head lowered. I don't know if he's looked at me once. I don't know if I want him to.

"Tell me about the attack," says Lyr.

I swallow thickly, immediately back in that field amid the screams of the scared and the dying.

"All my life, I thought I was prepared for battle." The words burn as they leave my soul. "I listened to stories of the war, I trained countless hours... I was never afraid of fighting. Never. Dying on the battlefield has always been a likelihood, and I accepted it. But tonight... tonight I was afraid." And only now do I acknowledge the fear I had so effectively ignored for the last few hours. It's enough to bring sour bile flooding my mouth.

"I've never seen death like that before." The red mist of the mercenary destroyed by the shadows, the corpses staring with wide, fearful eyes at a night sky empty of stars.

I sniff and sit up, taking another washcloth and scrubbing my face with it, my arms and hands, watching black-red flakes float in the tub around me.

"The shadow Aberration was controlling the others. Olivie mentioned it happening last night, too. It knew which one was the mage and directed the others to attack her." Facts are good. They're not messy like the inside of me. "The shadow was smart and cunning, displaying the skills needed to process multiple possibilities and think ahead. Its death distracted the others, like they felt it. Like it confused them."

I step out of the tub, accepting the towel Lyr hands me. I can't help but look at Vaen as I do, and this time he *is* looking, but not at my body. His eyes find me and pin me to the floor, and there is no heat there, no desire. Whatever he expressed the other night is gone entirely.

And wildly, despite everything, disappointment flares bright and ugly.

I wrap the towel tightly around myself and sit on my bed, turning so Lyr can see my back. Trickles of blood trail down, mixing with bath water to pool in the crevices of the towel.

The bed creaks as Lyr sits next to me, the onyx gripped in one hand. "They're getting stronger."

I nod. And I remember the creature in the forest, watching me with death in its ancient eyes. And I know I should tell them, know they need this information, but the words are sludge in my throat.

"This shouldn't hurt like the last time," Lyr says. "It may not be pleasant because I'm not a healer, but stop me if something feels wrong, okay?" There's a breathless excitement in his voice. I wish I could share his enthusiasm, but I remain tense, unable to banish the memory of pain from before.

He places his hand flat on my back, right over the worst of the gashes, and I have to close my eyes to keep from making a sound. I think of the bed beneath me, firm but yielding, the rough scratch of the warm woolen blanket against my fingers.

For a long moment there is nothing.

Then the feeling of flesh moving, of torn muscles interlacing as a thousand thread-thin strands reach for one another and intertwine. The sensation is uncomfortable, strange, but not exactly painful. I keep still and silent, breath held, waiting for something to go wrong, for Lyr to start cursing, for the frantic pain to beat alongside my heart. But there is only the movement, softer now, abating. Then a breath of relief from Lyr as he removes his hand, followed by a stifled whoop of exhilaration.

"It worked! Look, Vaen, it really worked!" the mage gleefully declares.

Vaen rises to stare at my bare back, and somehow this inspection is more stripping than sitting naked and hurt in the tub. I feel myself shrinking away, making myself as small as I can. Lyr's words from days ago ring in my head: do not make myself less than for anyone else.

I guess that includes Vaen.

But tonight, I *am* small.

"I barely felt anything at all," Lyr goes on, words tripping over themselves in exultation. "I never would have been able to do that before." He draws back, staring at the onyx with wonder and greed. "This... this is incredible." He laughs, incredulous and delighted. "We'll test its true strength tomorrow."

The mere idea of going back into the field makes my belly clench and blood turn to ice. I rise quickly, towel still drawn around myself, and clumsily find the warmest pair of clothes I can.

Lyr frowns at me, clearly puzzled. "Raylen? What's wrong?"

I just shake my head as I pull on breeches and a tunic, wishing my woolen cloak wasn't covered in blood. "I'll see you in the morning," I say, not meeting his eyes. "For whatever you need me to do."

Then, feeling like an utter coward, I flee.

TWENTY-ONE

Without my warmer clothes, I feel half frozen by the time I reach the forge. The front door is locked; it's late, and I never told Haith I would come by, so I'm not particularly surprised. I know the layout of the building well enough by now to recognize which window belongs in his room. I feel bad for waking him, but it doesn't stop me from knocking on the glass pane until he opens it, bleary eyed and confused.

I smile apologetically. "Can I come in?"

He seems vaguely irritated at first, but eventually his features soften and he nods. A few minutes later I'm sitting on his bed, the shivers starting to abate. All I can think about is burrowing under a mound of thick blankets and sleeping until this whole nightmare disappears.

Haith settles down next to me, one hand dropping to my back where he rubs in slow, soft circles. I let out a huff of air, head drooping at the administrations, some of the tension starting to leech out of me.

Haith switches positions when he feels me relax, climbing behind me so his legs slide on either side of my hips. Now his hands dig more powerfully into my shoulders, loosening the muscles. I wait for the ache from my wound, but there isn't even a whisper of pain. I want to be grateful, but the words just echo endlessly through my head instead: *you left me.*

"What happened?"

Red mist floats slowly down, lighting on the ground like a thousand raindrops.

"It was awful," I whisper. I close my eyes but it doesn't help. There is only more blood, faces twisted in horror, the unending screams, so much light forsaken *noise.* "The Aberrations went through the mercenaries like they were nothing but broken toys." An arm wrenched free, thrown to the ground as blood gushes from the man and he screams and screams and screams. His friend, gaping at the wound, only for the creature to lurch forward and bite down in the fleshy gap between neck and shoulder, severing sinew and muscles but not vocal cords or nerve endings or brain function, leaving the man to gasp wildly for life until *crunch* the eyes go blank.

"You've been in battle before." It's a statement, not a question. The reality is biting. Haith knows so little of *me,* our time together minuscule, our conversations even less.

Lyr would understand. Vaen might, too, and I suddenly miss their presence so fiercely it's like a hole has opened in my chest, the skin and bones caving in to create a chasm that aches. Maybe I should have tried harder to apologize. Maybe I should have stayed and forced Vaen to have that hard conversation so we could begin to heal together.

Maybe now it's too late.

The pity wells up no matter how hard I try to push it aside. "Not really," I admit to Haith. "I've fought Aberrations before, and I've sparred practically every day of my life. But a battle? I was just a kid when the war happened. We weren't anywhere near the coast, and my dad wouldn't speak more than generalizations to me." I shake my head, despair and self loathing welling in equal measures. "I was told to leave the Knight's Temple before we could do anything of worth. What happened today was nothing I was prepared for."

Haith pauses. "I'm sure it was shocking," he finally says. His hands resume their administrations. "Not seeing an actual battle before."

I frown, and it takes me a minute to pinpoint why his statement makes my skin crawl. "I'm not horrified only because it was my first time to witness something like that. It was terrible because it was a bloodbath. It's a miracle the Aberrations didn't massacre them all."

"That's battle, Raylen. People die. That's what happens."

The callousness of his words hit me like a hammer. I push away, twisting to remain on the edge of the bed, and face him with incredulousness in every line of my body. "Were you there?"

He blinks at the harshness of my voice and shakes his head slowly. "No."

"Exactly," I interrupt, and there is anger filling the syllables, rolling off my tongue like flames. "You weren't there. You didn't live it. You don't get to tell me what it was like or how bad it was."

Haith cups my face in his hand, shushing softly. "Raylen, it's okay. You're safe now. You don't need to attack me like this."

But it's not right. He doesn't get to tell me how to feel. I go to tell him so, but Haith smoothly says, "Is that why you came here tonight? Because it was so terrible?"

I pause. I can't decide if his statement is mocking, but his eyes are kind, so I answer anyway. "No. Well, in a way, yes. It *was* bad." Haith just nods, like I'm some sort of infantile girl overreacting. Frustrations bites, hard and angry. "I would have stayed at the inn, but Vaen and I had a... disagreement." It hurts to admit even that much. I have enough sense not to go into details about what our *disagreement* actually entails.

The sympathy falls away from Haith. He clicks his tongue, clearly annoyed. "You'd be better off without them."

I blink, completely thrown off by the statement, frustration sizzling into ember warm coals. "That's not true."

"It is. They're dragging you down. You could be doing anything, but you're stuck on a useless quest because your mage refuses to do the right thing."

I'm so confused by this point I can only shake my head. Everything is too much: this night, these mistakes, this conversation. "The right thing? What the hell would that be?"

"Killing Sunillen," Haith says simply.

I'm so shocked I can do nothing but gape at him. "What...?"

Haith shrugs like the answer is obvious. "There's no other mage in Ulingard, Raylen. Well, there wasn't when the creatures started appearing. So unless your mage or the new girl have been hiding and secretly using magic from within the forest, there isn't another possibility. Sunillen is the catalyst behind the attacks. Whether he intended for this to happen or not doesn't matter. He's not doing a damn thing to stop it, and these deaths tonight are on his hands."

Restless with irritation and frustration at his overly simplistic view, I rise and begin to pace. "You don't understand. We can't just accept one answer. Sunillen should have helped. Sunillen should have come to talk to the village, to clear his name if he's not the one behind it. He's made a lot of mistakes, and Sunillen is suspicious, I agree, but the other day, he was actively trying to find out more about the Aberrations. He's spent days in his library, searching for explanations, for weaknesses, for how this could be happening."

"Hiding away while we toil? Very admirable."

I shake my head at the insult even if a very large part of me agrees with him. "How do you know someone from the village isn't pretending?"

Haith's laugh is loud and jeering, stopping my words immediately. "What are you saying? Don't you think we would have noticed? I've lived in this city my whole life, as have most of the people here. How would we not have noticed someone else having magic? But you think you can come in and tell us our neighbors and friends could be harboring this kind of evil secret?"

His words hit me like a sword, striking deep into the core of confusion and shame that threatens to devour me. "I d-didn't mean..."

The words trail off. I don't even know what I intended to say. Because I *do* mean what I said. It's foolish to refuse other possibilities.

But tonight, the weariness drags at my bones. I just want it to stop. All of this. The fear, the death, the smell of blood permanently etched into my skin. The constant questioning of what will happen next. What the next monster will be. Who the next victim will be. It needs to *stop*.

My emotions must be plainly written across my face, because Haith's expression softens. He grabs my wrist and gently pulls me down onto the bed, smoothing hair away from my face. "It's okay," he says, low and comforting. "You're tired. I know you didn't mean anything."

I want to shake my head and roar my rage. But maybe he's right. Maybe, half-delirious from exhaustion and fear, I've overstepped my bounds. Read into things not there.

I am so very tired.

"I just want to sleep." My voice cracks on the last word.

Haith nods, smoothing my hair once more before he blows out the lit candle, plunging the room into darkness. He guides me into bed, under the pile of warm blankets I so longed for, and wraps himself around me until I am cocooned.

Despite everything, sleep is a long time coming, and when it finally does, an antlered monster haunts my every step, staying in the shadows as it whispers my blood will be spilt next.

When I finally wake, I am nearly as tired as when I first went to bed. I lay still for a long moment, feeling the rise and fall of Haith's chest against my back, but the movement brings no contentment.

I came seeking solace, but there is no quieting in my soul. If anything, I feel crushed by the weight of even *more* questions.

No matter how much I might wish Haith to provide answers, last night proved the futility of that.

I slip out of bed, moving carefully to avoid waking Haith. Dawn edges along the horizon, sending rays of pinks, golds, and purples playing across the tops of houses and trees. It's beautiful. A moment of serenity.

The cold outside is biting, but for the first time, I relish it. It drives away the last remnants of sleep, leaving me hyper aware of my surroundings. Of myself.

Frost lines the tops of houses, white glistening on the tips of winter-dried grass. It won't be long before the fields are covered in snow, the people forced inside for warmth and safety. My eyes skitter to the forest always lurking at the edges of Ulingard. Are there wolves in there, or did the antlered creature consume them all?

I will strip the flesh from your bones and devour it to the sound of your screams.

I close my eyes against the memory of violence and terror, but my pulse races, sweat lining my forehead despite the cold. It takes the entire walk back to The Night's End before I can calm the shaking enough to feel like myself again.

The common room is mostly empty, the mercenaries nursing their wounded and mourning the fallen. I can't imagine what they could possibly be thinking today, if there are any thoughts at all beyond a blood stained memory of darkness and fear.

"I wondered when you would be back. If you would come back at all."

I jump at the voice, stomach dropping immediately. Reluctantly I turn to face Vaen, who watches me with dark eyes as steam from his coffee curls around him. His food remains untouched before him. His face is carefully schooled to blankness, but I can see the wariness in his eyes.

"I'm surprised you're even deigning to speak to me," I admit. It takes more convincing than I would like to move my feet forward and awkwardly lower myself to the seat across from him. I've lost count of how many conversations we've now had at this table, in this inn. I would almost be fond of it, were it not for the dire straits we find ourselves in now.

Vaen puffs out his cheeks, eyes skittering across me to land on the small window next to us. He pretends to be interested in a stoutly husband and wife setting up a stand of fresh eggs and herbs, but we both know it's just a facade.

The silence becomes unbearable; although I would like nothing more than to win this battle of wills, I find the words tumbling out of their own accord. "I never would leave, you know. I wouldn't abandon our work. These people." I steel myself. "You." Or Lyr either, but it's Vaen I want to know more about, Vaen I somehow care about impressing, Vaen whose opinion matters to me even though it shouldn't.

Something about Vaen softens, and when he looks to me, there is understanding. As if he sees *me*, knows me. "I know you wouldn't." He directs his gaze back outside even as he continues. "We both made mistakes last night. While you did not do it the right *way*, you did do the right *thing*." He inhales deeply. "I'm sorry for suggesting otherwise."

I can't keep the shock from my face. Vaen is apologizing to me? Never in all my life would I have expected such a thing to happen. It gives me the courage to say, "I'm sorry too. I shouldn't have left you like that. I should have remembered about the calling glass." I want to add more, to further defend my actions: that they needed me more than he did. But I bite back the impulse. We both know the truth; some things are better kept silent.

Vaen offers me a honeyed hotcake from his plate. I take it, along with the peace it represents. The tension that has festered through the night loosens, and the hotcake is the best damn thing I've tasted.

I'm not naive enough to think this has solved all our problems, erased the wound in his trust in me. But it's a start.

"What's our next step?" I ask when the hotcake is nothing but sticky crumbs on my fingers. I lick them off one by one, to hell with manners.

"Lyr wants to help the wounded as much as he can without completely depleting himself," Vaen answers. His tone is overly neutral; he doesn't exactly approve of Lyr's choice, but there's no way to stop him either. "He wants to go back out tonight with the onyx, see if it draws more of them or not."

It's a struggle not to leave the table, find Lyr, and demand what the hell he's thinking. "More of them?" My voice is too high, too loud. Vaen gives me a dark look and I try to lower it even as panic edges my words. "We were sorely outnumbered last night, and he thinks bringing out more is a good idea?"

Vacant eyes staring at a starless sky amid so much red.

No. I shut the image out forcefully. But the memory remains engraved in my bones.

Vaen sighs and rubs the bridge of his nose. I notice for the first time the dark circles, the lines around his face that look just a little bit deeper than the day before. It seems I was not the only one kept awake last night.

"We're drowning," Vaen says simply. "We still have so many more questions than answers. We're not going to figure things out by sitting on our asses."

He's right, of course he's right, but that doesn't mean I'll go quietly.

"Did he say how the Aberrations happened?" I ask.

Vaen frowns.

"It's okay. I didn't realize until this morning either." I lean forward on my forearms. "There were *five* Aberrations last night. Where did they come from? Where did they get the corporeal bodies?"

Vaen sucks in a sharp breath. "Shit. I didn't—"

"They weren't like the others," I continue, ignoring his words. "I didn't get a chance to really examine them, but they were animalistic, wrong in a different way. Less human than Aberrations already are."

His eyes are round and disbelieving. "Like their physical form came from animals instead of humans?"

"Exactly. But that's never happened before, at least that we know. Which doesn't make sense, because there are a lot more animals than humans just wandering around, prone to falling into that excess magic. But Lyr has never mentioned a subspecies of Aberration."

"You think someone is forcing the animals to undergo the Aberrations transformation?"

I nod. "Whoever did this is intentionally creating Aberrations. We always knew that. But this was a direct attack on the mercenaries. Maybe on Ulingard, and the mercenaries simply got in the way."

"So then the question we keep circling back to... is who?"

I scrape at the worn wood of the table, peeling bits of it underneath my fingernail. "I've gone over and over that question all night. Every logical path points to Sunillen."

"Or a hidden mage."

"Which puts us directly back to square one, since we have no earthly idea who it could be."

What I don't say is how long I questioned if it could be Haith. He was so *adamant* last night, insistent on putting the blame squarely on Sunillen. If I were the mage, I would recognize Lyr and Sunillen as the biggest obstacles in my path of destruction. It's almost too easy to frame things just right for everything to fall on Sunillen.

And as for Lyr... well, it would be simple work to woo his companion.

But.

There were many times Haith would have been hard pressed to be in the forest, summoning Aberrations, and make it back to the forge in time to see me. Possibly even impossible.

It makes me sad to think that logistics aid Haith more than his own character.

Vaen rubs a hand over his face, the weariness almost palpable. "We've been distracted, focusing on the onyx these last few days. We need to be roving the fields and forest, trying to find the mage. We need to attack instead of waiting to be found."

The searing eyes of the beast pin me to the spot, promising pain and unending damnation.

It's on the tip of my tongue to say something, to tell him about the creature I saw, the promise of other creatures lurking behind it. What secrets does that forest hide?

"We've been lucky so far." If this could be counted as lucky. I swallow thickly, fear coating my mouth and throat. "If we step into that forest, I don't think we'll come back out alive."

Vaen looks at me sharply, brows lowered. I can't meet his eyes.

"What happened?"

I want to tell him. But the fear is paralyzing, freezing the words as they try to tip out.

Vaen looks down, at the table, and I follow his gaze to see my hands, splayed open and *shaking*.

Horrified, I snatch my hands back and hide them under the table. The damage has been done, but I can pretend otherwise. I can pretend about a lot of things.

What a failure. How can I sit here and proclaim myself brave when the first sight of shed blood reduces me to nightmares and terrors? When the mere threat of something waiting out there terrifies me to the core?

No wonder they discarded me at the Temple.

Knights don't shake in fear after battle. They don't pray for a reprieve, for an answer to come in time so they don't have to face their fears.

They were right all along.

"Raylen?"

The concern in Vaen's voice is enough to rip me from my spiraling thoughts. And maybe this is the coward's way out, but maybe it's also the only way to secure our victory. "We need to determine Sunillen's true alliance."

The abrupt change in conversation is enough to throw Vaen off. I'm safe, for now. Vaen asks, words heavy with trepidation, "What are you planning?"

I shake my head as I help myself to the last of his coffee and rise. "To talk. Nothing more." *For now.* "You should meet with Olivie, see if there is anything we missed last night. Might be good to make sure your name is still in the clear, too." With every word I shove the fear down, locking it in a metal box somewhere deep inside where the key can be lost. By the time I finish, I feel almost like myself again.

I can do this. Tonight is a long way away. All I need to think about now is how to handle Sunillen, and the task is almost laughably easy compared to everything else.

Vaen rises as well, face darkening like a thundercloud. "You should wait for Lyr. You'll just get us into more trouble with that mouth of yours."

"My mouth is good for a lot of things, the least of which is pissing people off."

Surprise darts across his features and I like that I caught him off guard. It helps soothe the fear licking at my heels.

"Relax," I say as I head towards the door. I need to leave before Lyr catches me. "Remember, I'm friends with Nalista. If Sunillen looks to go on a rampage, I'll think up some excuse about needing to see her."

Vaen doesn't look entirely convinced, but he nods once. "Fine. Try not to do anything stupid."

I manage to school my features to hide the truth ricocheting throughout me.

I won't leave until Sunillen agrees to fight for us.

Or one of us is dead.

Vaen would call this a stupid, headstrong mistake. It could destroy the tentative trust I've just started to build back.

But the idea of sitting back and letting Sunillen do what he wills while more innocent people die? That's even worse.

Vaen managed to forgive me once. All I can hope is that he will again.

TWENTY-TWO

The fields are lonely in the day.

I walk quickly, refusing to look towards the gaping forest even though I'm fairly positive these Aberrations return to their hellish home when dawn graces the land.

But the fields — there is no avoiding them, not when I must traverse the expanse to Sunillen's mansion. I try not to look down, but I see the blood anyway, long since dried in impossibly large arcs across the winter-hard ground. I smell it, the air thick with the stench.

Everywhere I turn is red. Death. Is this what my uncle saw looking at the beaches? A constant reminder of what happened, what will happen again and again and again unless he did something?

And now, unless *I* do something.

I take a breath, inhaling the death. Holding it in myself, in my soul, making it a part of every muscle and sinew and thought and belief. And I promise the souls that linger that this will not be the end of it. This will not be their legacy.

I won't let it.

I take their deaths and bind them to myself, and inside is another creature entirely, a creature made of fire and hatred and burning *need*. To protect. To defend. To take back what has been stolen. To make sure it never happens again.

I knock on Sunillen's door with a hand made of steel.

The bondsman looks positively shocked to see me, going as far as taking a step outside to see if Lyr is hiding just around the side of the house.

I smile slightly. "Just me today I'm afraid. Is Mage Sunillen in?" There is no point for false pretenses.

"In the library," the bondsman carefully answers. "Will Mage Lyr be joining you later?"

"No. This business is my own." I step forward confidently, forcing the bondsman to retreat or be run over. He wisely chooses the former.

The door closes behind us, and the sound of the lock clicking buoys me even further. There are no Aberrations in here waiting to tear me apart. The darkness here is caused by man alone.

And I know how to handle them.

I don't wait for the bondsman to announce me, or, more likely, try to persuade me to stay in the kitchens and away from Sunillen. As if this is my own house, I brush past the man and jog up the stairs, every echoing footstep only adding to the fire now filling me.

This reckoning has been far too long coming, and I only wish the mercenaries' deaths hadn't been the catalyst.

No one stops me as I ascend the staircase. The corridor goes off both sides, and I choose the left, where the window was that Vaen used. The corridor is decorated much like the sitting room, with tapestries depicting naturalistic scenes hanging between narrow but bright windows. A spotless carpet runs down the hall, and I almost feel sorry for stepping on it in my muddy boots.

The corridor is almost sacred in its silence. I find myself holding my breath, ears straining for any indication of Sunillen. Or any life at all. There is an aching emptiness here, and I wonder where the children are, where Nalista is.

The first hint of doubt creeps in, my momentum faltering, but almost immediately I spy a half-opened door.

I pad on silent feet to the door and glance inside. The room is not overly large but reeks of opulence. Of power. Each wall is covered with floor to ceiling bookcases; rolling ladders hooked onto rails sit at the ends. Some of the shelves contain leather bound books, others filled with neatly arranged scrolls. The smell of books, oiled leather and paper and dust, lingers in the air.

The center of the room is taken up by a magnificent rug in reds and golds, upon which rests a heavy table, polished till it shines, and a variety of chairs — some hard backed, some cushioned. Lamps and mage lights litter the bookcase edges and the ceiling, unlit candles on the table.

Sunillen sits at the table, hunched over a scroll. There are half a dozen other scrolls and tomes scattered about; the only thing that I have ever seen out of place in this house. The mage himself sits with rounded shoulders, head lowered until his nose almost touches the parchment. Shock cascades through me to find his hair in disarray, his robes creased and loose, as if he slept in them. The entire scene is unlike anything I expected, and some of my bravado falters.

Is this a man torn by guilt? Or one looking frantically for the last missing piece in whatever twisted plan he has enacted?

Sunillen does not immediately move, although how he doesn't feel my eyes on him, I can't understand. It isn't until I edge into the room, door creaking at the movement, that he raises his head. The mage then has the audacity to glance over me, no doubt looking for Lyr.

Finding me alone, he returns to his scroll, but says, "I do hope there is an excellent reason for you disturbing my work."

I enter the room fully and pull the door closed behind me. That gets his attention. Sunillen looks at me, brows lowered and face darkening. He still doesn't rise, though. Still doesn't perceive me as enough of a threat.

It takes everything in me not to draw my sword and attack. This man, this despicable man, thought it was okay to watch all those people—

"It was admirable, what you did."

The words knock the wind out of me in an almost physical way, sending my thoughts into disarray. All I can manage is, "What?"

Sunillen turns in his chair to face me directly. The lines on his face are dark and prominent, weariness that permeates every movement, every look. And even though everything in me wants to place the blame on him... this does not look like the man on the verge of a massacre.

"Helping them last night," he continues plainly. "The mercenaries."

I gape at him. Outrage swells once again, an ocean of bitterness and anger that is too easy to open myself to, too easy to let myself drown in. "If you were there, why the hell didn't you fight?" I find myself shaking and clench my fists to hide it.

Sunillen doesn't rise to meet my anger. I always knew coming here would likely end in a fight, if not a death. But the mage just purses his lips, and although there is a cold arrogance there, it isn't what I anticipated.

"If you didn't fight for them," I say before he can respond, "the only thing I can assume is you were the one to bring the Aberrations."

He shakes his head slowly. Still there is no rage. I flounder in my sea of righteousness.

"I admire your innocence." Sunillen's voice is quiet but sincere. Perhaps the most sincere I've ever heard from him. "To think there is only right and wrong. Hero or villain. I'm sure I was once like you, although I do not remember a time."

I let loose something akin to a growl, frustrated at these word games. "If you are not a hero or villain, what are you?"

The eyes that look at me are haunted. And for a moment, I see myself in them, staring at a battlefield I can't fully comprehend, watching the men around me be slaughtered.

"No one talks about the war truthfully," Sunillen says quietly. "They talk of the heroics, of the victories. But the long years of fighting are brushed under the rug in favor of singular battles, of showcasing our bravery, our resilience. And maybe all that is important too. But what I remember are the still faces, pressed into mud like animals. Carcasses piled on top of one another to let rot in the sun or to burn if we had the energy, if we weren't hiding from the enemy."

Every word leeches a bit more of the fight from me, dripping to the floor as droplets of rainwater. The ocean, gone.

"They don't talk about watching your friend die. Every friend. Of trying to protect your comrades, only to find your magic faltering, giving out, because you've used too much of it, and if you draw even a single bit more, you'll burn from the inside out. They don't talk about huddling behind an outcropping, feeling like a coward, while soldiers are struck down all around you. They don't talk about the guilt of surviving. Of trying to live another day, knowing half your contingent won't."

His gaze captures me, pinning me in place even though his words have already stolen any possible movement.

"And sometimes, you can want to do something with your entire being. You walk to the door, fire at your fingertips. But you hear the screams and howls of pain, and the mere sound is enough to bring you back to the trenches. And you stand there frozen, listening to the battle rage, but you're really in another place, in another time, lost to the memory of death and blood."

I draw in a shuddering breath as he finishes. There is guilt there, and disgust — with the Aberrations, undoubtedly, but mostly with himself. I stare at Sunillen, grand battle mage of the Zuneshan War, and see a tired, worn man who has witnessed more death than I can possibly imagine.

And I realize something perhaps no one else has dared spoken aloud.

"You don't keep your imbued objects because you desire power." The words are slow, quiet. But he hears them. He closes his eyes. "You keep them because each one is a friend who died on the battlefield. For you. For the crown and country. And if you don't remember them, who will?"

Sunillen's head bows. He doesn't weep or shake or break apart — perhaps because he's already broken.

I walk to him slowly and take a seat next to the mage. I stare at the table, searching for answers in the wood and seeing only blood.

"My uncle died in the war," I say around the boulder in my throat. "He was a knight. I was supposed to be too." I swallow. "I'll never be the same after last night."

He nods without pity. "No one is."

We sit in silence for a long time. Never would I have imagined to be comfortable next to this arrogant, cold man, but now there is a strange camaraderie connecting us.

"You did not summon the Aberrations." It's not a question, and I already know the answer.

Sunillen finally meets my eyes once again. "I've spent every conceivable hour searching for an answer. But these words are useless." He sweeps an arm out, sudden and harsh, sending the pages spilling to the floor. I jump at the clatter and stare at the jumble of ink and time-worn parchment.

"Whoever is doing this is using a dark magic I have no knowledge of." He shakes his head, angry. "There is not much magic that is unknown to the conclave. I *thought* we were privy to that knowledge, but I suppose I was wrong in that as well."

"What do you mean?" The gears turn as I struggle to work out his words. "The mage's conclave is hiding magic from you?"

"Or it has been lost to time... until someone found it again." He runs a hand through his hair, further disrupting it.

I choose my next words carefully. "I understand now that you haven't gone out in order to protect your mind's stability. But last night, blood was spilt. The time for hiding is over."

He flinches, gaze dropping away.

"I know you're scared. We all are. But we can't barricade ourselves and wish for the best. Even if the village could protect themselves, the monsters will eventually be here at your door too. There will be no mercy for your servants. Your children. And when you look death in the eye, will you do so proudly, knowing you've done everything you could?"

His silence is damning.

I rise and hold out a hand. "There's still time. Will you join us tonight?"

I never expected to broker peace today. But when Sunillen takes my hand in a grip strong and sure, I can't help but think we might finally have a fighting chance.

Leaving the library is a wholly different experience than entering it. Although I have not been given permission to stay, I do not head out the door once I descend the stairs.

I turn instead to the kitchens and spy the cook stirring a large pot of delicious smelling white soup. Crusty bread cools on the table, still steaming from the oven.

I give a small wave when the cook looks curiously at me. "I'm looking for Nalista and the children?"

The cook smiles, warm and kind, and beckons me to the cutting board. "I was just about to call them in for a morning break," he says. His words are slow and pleasant, rolling in that strange accent, and the euphoric feeling from my successful parley makes this room feel almost like home.

The cook slices thick portions of bread that have my mouth watering. He spoons purple and red jellies into small bowls, then adds a container of soft butter. He clucks his tongue at the rising pile of dishes stacked in the sink.

"Where is your kitchen boy?" I ask, peering around as if he's hiding behind a table.

"Gone." The cook makes a disgruntled noise. "Been missing for a few days now, no word about leaving. Suppose the monsters have scared him away."

To be honest, I'm surprised not more have fled.

"You can take this out to them," he announces, lifting the platter of food and handing it to me. "They're in the gardens."

Their sanctuary.

Nalista crouches before a sea of dark green leaves, studying the plants so intently she doesn't immediately hear my approach. Amilla kneels next to her, a piece of parchment in one hand as she scribbles messy notes next to a painstakingly drawn picture of the plant. The girl's brow is furrowed with concentration, mouth moving as she spells out words.

Thomalen, on the other hand, idly swings a stick through the air, drawing arcs in the half-frozen dirt.

I clear my throat, earning an annoyed look from Amilla. Nalista jumps, nearly falling before regaining her balance at the last moment. She rises with a small laugh, dusting dirt off hands that shake. Concern flickers through me as I take in the ever-darkening circles around her eyes, the strain in her shoulders and mouth. Although she smiles at me, there is little of her normal contentment.

I hold up the platter of food and say, "Cook asked me to bring out some bread."

Thomalen gasps and heedlessly throws the stick. Amilla is quick to follow, staring at the butter with saucer-wide eyes. Nalista opens her mouth like she's about to remind them of manners but closes it as the children fall upon the bread greedily.

Nalista and I manage to take a little for ourselves before we retreat to the nearby table, letting the children bicker over their favorite jams. We sit in silence, chewing the delectable treat, but I can't keep my eyes off my friend. Her entire body seems to bow under some invisible weight.

"Did you hear it last night?" I finally manage to ask.

Nalista looks at me, and the haunting in her eyes is answer enough.

"I have never seen such bloodshed before," she whispers. Her eyes glaze, staring sightlessly down at the bread forgotten in her hands. "I couldn't sleep after. I'm just exceedingly grateful the children were not a part of it."

I reach out and grip her hand. She pauses for a moment, then slender fingers wrap around my own and squeeze tightly. I want, suddenly, to do anything to protect her. "We're going to stop this," I say quietly, fiercely. Perhaps if I say it enough, I'll believe it.

"Sunillen agreed to help us tonight."

Nalista startles at this information. She swallows hard, nervous. "I understand why, but I hate that he has to leave the children." She withdraws her fingers, warmth receding with it, rubbing her arms and pulling her knit shawl tighter around bony shoulders. "I admit, I have found a sort of peace knowing he's here in the house should anything attack us."

"It will be okay," I say with more confidence than I feel. "The Aberrations won't look twice at the manor, not when two mages are out waiting for them." That, at least, should be the truth.

Nalista nods but does not look convinced.

We chat for a little while longer, but conversation is stilted and awkward. Nalista has a hard time focusing, trailing off often to stare at the flowers, the dance of grass stalks in the breeze, the children sitting in relative peace with full bellies and tired eyes.

I excuse myself before too long. There's nothing to do here.

It will all come down to tonight.

"You're going out again?"

I nod, barely pausing between bites. After returning from Sunillen's, I stopped by the shop to invite Haith to eat a midday meal with me. It feels odd, almost more intimate than sex, to sit across the table from him and just converse. Be in each other's presence without any expectations or reason except wanting to. I guess it's my way of apologizing for the mess of last night. And, however immature it might be, I want to show him I was right — that Sunillen is not the villain Haith was painting him to be.

"There's no time to stop," I say, laying my fork down to take a drink of water. Haith watches the movements with single minded focus. "Last night might have been the push for the Aberrations to seek us out instead of waiting to be found. We can't risk them coming into Ulingard."

He acquiesces this point with a nod but still doesn't look

entirely convinced. I can't help a flash of annoyance. I don't have the time or spare energy to uselessly bicker. There are so much bigger things at stake.

A door from the second floor closes, and Lyr jogs down the stairs half a moment later, looking serious but surprisingly spry. He doesn't ask before joining us, sliding in the seat next to me and saying without preamble, "Vaen said you went to Sunillen's this morning?"

I flush with embarrassment when he levels a stern eye at me, but it's not enough to distract me from the downright filthy look Haith directs at Lyr. There is no friendship, not even a pretense of camaraderie. The raw emotion is unsettling, and I can't help but remember his disregard for both my companions during our last conversation.

A part of me wants to reason it away: that he's acting like this out of a strange sense of protection. Of fondness, perhaps. But it sounds false even in my own mind.

"I did," I say carefully, eyes shifting from Lyr to Haith and back again. "It was absolutely enlightening."

Lyr's eyebrows shoot up in clear shock. He chokes back a laugh, accepting a drink from the serving maid as she brings his meal. As she sets the plate down, it clatters against the table, nearly spilling the food into Lyr's lap. The girl's hands shake almost uncontrollably as she pulls them back, stuttering over an apology. Haith gives a harsh laugh, ugly and demeaning.

"It's no problem," Lyr tells the girl with a smile.

"Stop being an ass," I snap to Haith at almost the same time.

Time freezes as Haith looks at me, surprise flitting across his face before fury settles in his eyes. He stands quickly, gaze pinning me to the spot, and it's all I can do not to *flinch*. The serving maid does, shrinking behind my chair before scurrying off to the kitchen with another hasty apology.

Trepidation hammers as I wonder what exactly Haith is intending — what he's capable of. I never viewed him as dangerous before, but now I can't shake the feeling that I may have crossed some invisible line. Perhaps I should be scared. But mostly I'm just *angry*.

"Sit down."

I look at Lyr, surprised at the order, but his gaze is focused on Haith. The mage watches the jeweler calmly, but there is utter authority in his voice. He does not expect to be disobeyed. When Haith doesn't immediately move, merely staring at Lyr with the same fury, Lyr rises with controlled slowness, pushing aside his sleeves so his hands are free.

Panic now ripples through me. We can't afford a fight, not when Lyr needs to save his strength. Not when we still need a place to stay.

"Lyr—"

He raises a hand, silencing the words in my throat. He doesn't look at me as he says, "Raylen is right. You're being an ass. So either sit down and act civilized, or leave and don't bother coming back. Trust me, boy. You don't want to cross me."

He's not a boy by any stretch of the imagination, and Haith's nostrils flare at the derogatory term. Lyr doesn't move. But, to my intense surprise, Haith lowers himself back into his chair.

He doesn't apologize.

Lyr settles back down, picking his fork up like nothing happened. "Tell me what happened at Sunillen's."

I blink, closing my gaping mouth. I don't know what to think, what to feel, beyond relief that Lyr was here, that he stood up for me. For his friend.

I relay in briefest terms what happened, keeping emotion out and skirting around the edges of my own fears. I avoid looking at Haith, who stares down at his plate but doesn't attempt to eat.

When I finish, Lyr makes a humming noise. "I don't know, Raylen. It seems too forced. The famed battle mage, struggling with trauma? I'm not saying it's impossible. But we need to be wary tonight and keep a close eye on him."

"I think he's being sincere." I'm not surprised at his reluctance to believe me, but disappointment still gnaws my gut. I was so proud of myself for convincing Sunillen to join us when no one else could.

"He might be." Lyr shrugs, then smiles. "I'm glad you went. I'm very intrigued to see how tonight unfolds."

"Intrigued is not the word I would use," I mutter.

Lyr chortles, slapping me on the back as he rises. "Let's get some rest. We're going to have a long night."

I nod and go to rise as well but hesitate, looking back at Haith.

He offers a thin lipped smile. Not his ordinary reaction, but it's better than nothing. "Come tell me what happens after?"

"Of course."

But I don't know if I will.

Haith returns to the shop, and Lyr goes to check on the mercenaries once more before sleeping. I start to follow him up the stairs, but a hand grabs my elbow, stopping me.

I turn, confused, to find the serving maid staring at me with dark, haunted eyes. She swallows hard before saying in a harsh whisper, "Don't trust him."

I blink. "What? Trust who?"

But someone calls from the kitchen and she just shakes her head and retreats, giving me one more wary look as she disappears behind the door.

More confused than ever, my steps are heavy as I ascend the stairs.

She heard our conversation — we didn't even attempt to keep our voices down. Which begs the question: is she warning me against Haith... or Sunillen?

I can feel it watching me.

I don't look at the forest, no matter how much my instincts beg me too. I turn my back to it, because if I can't see the antlered monster, it doesn't exist. I'm still not even sure it existed in the first place.

"You're sure about this?"

Sunillen scowls at the question. He was waiting for us at the city edge, surly and quiet, ignoring Olivie and the other three Watchers who volunteered for this battle. I'm honestly surprised any of them agreed to come at all, but I suppose the same sense of dread that hovers over me also lingers in them. We all know the end is coming, and the best we can hope for is to stem the tide while we still can.

"If I wasn't excruciatingly positive, I would not have come," the mage answers Lyr dryly. There is a taut tension in our entire group that only heightens the longer we wait.

My skin crawls. I lock my muscles, refusing to give in to the temptation to look over my shoulder. To remember the hellish eyes promising my death.

"I'll go into the forest," Lyr says casually, like it's a stroll through the gardens and not the looming threat of death.

My stomach plummets. It was already made perfectly clear I would be the one to stay with Lyr, and Vaen with Sunillen. As Vaen rationally pointed out, Lyr is the important one to protect, and the better swordsman needs to stay with him. But the plan was to be here, in the fields, drawing the Aberrations out while Sunillen and Vaen comb the forest for the perpetrator.

Sunillen snorts loudly. "You will not. I am the more skilled mage." He says it without boasting, as merely fact. And it's true, especially since he is unaware Lyr has the onyx. "Your scribe here has shown to have far more stealth than your lumbering knight."

I bite back the impulse to bare my teeth and rage. Sunillen meets my eyes, and I'm surprised to find no animosity there, no dismissal. "You have already tasted battle," he says, more quietly now, the words meant for me. "You know what to expect."

"I will go with you," Olivie says to Sunillen. While her tone is level, without warmth, there is no fight in it, her disdain for him momentarily held at bay. She has a job to do, same as the rest of us. Petty differences and disagreements will not help us survive the night.

I have the terrible feeling we will not all survive.

Sunillen says something else to Lyr, but I am distracted by Vaen coming to stand at my side. He stands close, almost too close, but his warmth relaxes me.

He speaks quietly, without looking at me. "Keep Lyr alive. No matter what else happens, he needs to survive."

I huff a little, nerves making my annoyance bitter. "I know that. It's been the same since the start of this whole thing."

I glance at Vaen and see not a mercenary or thief or queen's guard, but a tired, strained man who has seen too much since coming here. Just as we all have. I see my ally, my sometimes-rival, my... friend.

And the thought of him going into the forest, facing that *thing*, terrifies me to the core. I regret, now, never saying anything, never voicing my sightings. Of giving in to my fears. What if my warning could save him?

Sunillen motions sharply, and Vaen turns to go. Panic seizes me, sharp and unrelenting, and I grasp his arm before he can leave me.

"Don't die."

I don't look away from his gaze, trying to impart everything all at once. To be careful. To watch out for himself first.

To come back to me.

He gently dislodges my hand from his sleeve and brings it up to his lips. I don't dare move as he turns my hand over and kisses not the back, but my palm, soft lips pressing into the callouses with infinite tenderness. My breath catches in my throat, and I stare at him, coherent thoughts scattering like broken stars across a silver dusted sky.

"I don't plan on it." He releases my hand, giving me an absolutely smug smirk, and follows Sunillen before I can gather my shattered self together enough to reply.

And finally, *finally*, I turn to face the forest, watching as my friends slip into the dark abyss, blending seamlessly into shadows that seem to bend and twist unnaturally.

I hold my breath, scanning for twisted bones, moon white eyes.

I barely have the time to be relieved at its absence when the first whisper floats across the field, so faint to be nearly inaudible. Then again, accompanied by the familiar coldness stealing over us.

"Get ready," Lyr says, gripping the onyx tightly as he looks around with wild eyes.

I draw my sword just as the edge of the forest explodes in gnashing teeth and rending limbs and whisper-fast shadows.

And a promise, slamming into us with the force of a monsoon, unrelenting in its ferocity.

You will be ripped apart and fed to the creatures of the abyss, and finally we will be free.

CHAPTER
TWENTY-THREE

"Don't you dare listen to that piece of shit!" Lyr yells, never looking away from the oncoming creatures. I count at least six Aberrations, but it's hard to tell in the tangle of limbs and surging bodies as they hurtle towards us. "No one is dying today!"

I don't believe it for a minute, but it's a nice sentiment.

"There were five yesterday," I confide in a soft voice. "And twice as many mercenaries to hold them off. And they were almost wiped out." Not to mention the shadows darting between the creatures, ten times more dangerous than these foot soldiers.

Lyr looks at me, calm and assured. "You didn't have me yesterday."

"Brace yourselves!" one of the Watchers shouts.

But I'm staring at Lyr. He raises his onyx-ringed hand high above his head, and there's a light-forsaken *grin* on his face. I blink, and a wave of magic races out, like a mist upon the grass. I stare, open mouthed now, as Lyr fractures, body splitting and reforming a few feet to either side of him. Two more Lyrs, identical in every way.

The Watchers cry out in surprise, and I echo the noise a moment later when I see *myself* standing a foot away. The fake Raylens' faces twist in fear and shock, no doubt a parallel to my own reaction.

"They move as you do," Lyr says, quick and just loud enough for us to hear. "They won't stay at your side and they'll dissolve if hit, but hopefully this will confuse the Aberrations enough to destroy them quickly."

There's a howl of animalistic rage and hunger. I look away from Lyr, nearly missing his last words — "Pay attention to yourselves, not your doubles! You'll never survive watching someone else." But the monsters are almost here, cresting the last hilly knoll that lies between us and them.

My heart pounds, blood racing to my ears and filling my head. There are screams everywhere, the wails of the wounded and dying, and the smell of blood fills my nose. Voices I don't recognize beg me to do more, do something, *help them.*

It's too late for that. But not to save those around me now.

The first Aberration reaches our group, a snarl ripping free as a Watcher slices into its head. It's not enough to kill it, but the Watcher dances back, avoiding a blow, and dips to the side where one of our doubles waits. The monster lurches forward, ichor black teeth bared to dig into its head, but of course it's merely an illusion, and the Aberration is left snapping at thin air. The Watcher takes the opportunity to come from behind, severing the head clean from its shoulders with an arc of dark blood.

The blood falls like rain onto the unforgiving ground, darker than a human's, the stench of it eye watering.

Too weak to do anything.

No. That's not true. I shake myself, tightening my grip on my sword. The whisper is nothing but the Aberrations playing mind tricks once again.

I have slain them before.

I brought Sunillen into the fields when no one else could.

I am strong. I am fast. I have the blood of warriors in my veins.

I see the Aberrations and the steps I need to take to hurt, to kill, to survive, all in razor sharp detail. But then the battle blends together, monsters melding into one, until I can't tell where one ends and another begins.

I don't look at the projections except for how to use them to my advantage. Neither do I concern myself with any shadow Aberrations — that is Lyr's battle to fight. I stay near the mage and focus on making sure his path is clear, that nothing can possibly get to him. He uses magic I never would have thought him capable of, sending ice shards the size of my forearm into the enemies, lightning sparking from his outstretched palm to zigzag between targets, fire blooming to light the night.

Deer explode from the brush, leaping over each other and the bushes, bounding in front of an Aberration who cannot do anything but stumble to a stop, staring dumbly as a fawn leaps right through the Watcher who sidles up to slide a blade into its neck.

I move and slash and cut and stab. Over and over and over, as ichor and blood run free into the soil, soaking into my boots, staining my clothes and skin, splattering like paint across my face.

One more, just one more. There is always one more. One more monster, one more move, one more attack to drive them back again. A great roaring fills my ears, blocking out whatever sounds hammer against my skull, words both real and not. I don't look to my companions. I don't see how they fare. I don't look to the forest, to see whether the antlered creature has emerged from the trees and stalks to kill me at last.

I just fight.

And then... it's simply over.

The Aberration goes down in front of me, unable to howl its fury around the gaping hole in its neck. I back up a step, gasping for breath, and turn to find my next quarry, but there is none. The soundless roaring at last subsides, leaving an aching silence broken only by our battle-weary pants.

An icy breeze freezes the sweat sliding down my face and neck. I do my best to wipe my blade on a clean bit of my cloak, looking around at our ragtag group as I do.

Miraculously, we have all managed to survive, although one Watcher slides coughing to his knees as I watch. He clutches his side, face white with agony, as blood drips between his gloved fingers.

"Don't bind it," Lyr orders, striding past me to the Watcher. The mage kneels next to him, and I catch the wobble in his movement. The onyx may have given him far more power than he could ever achieve on his own, but he's drained nearly all he can use. Reaching too far will cause burnout, rendering a mage at best unconscious, at worst dead, not to mention create a new Aberration from the backlash of magic.

I have had enough Aberrations to last me a lifetime.

I join Lyr, pressing one leg lightly against his side. He leans his weight into me as sweat beads on his forehead, slipping down into his eyes, but he doesn't flinch. His hands are steady as they hover over the jagged edged wound, drawing the poison out inch by inch.

The Watcher handles it better than I did, muffling his scream into his leathered bound forearm. I don't envy him the pain, the memory of it all too easy to recall.

Lyr finishes a moment later, falling back onto his heels with a grunt. I catch him under the arms, lowering him until he's sitting on the ground.

"Couldn't heal it all the way," Lyr says between gasping

breaths. His voice is pitched high, syllables choppy, and panic shoots through me.

I kneel next to him. "Hey, you okay?"

Lyr meets my eyes, offering a thin lipped smile that does nothing to reassure me. "I've been better," he admits. He grips my arms, wincing at some invisible pain. "It's been a while since I've struggled like this."

"You did too much." I run my tongue over my dry lips, hoping he can't see the worry painted plain on my face. "We need to get you back to town."

"That's all I need," he says. "Just a day to sleep it off. No permanent damage."

I can't quite bring myself to believe that.

Weariness thrums in my muscles as I stand, gently pulling Lyr to his feet. I hand him off to the two Watchers. "Get him back to The Night's End, or the Watcher's tower if he can't make it that far. He needs food and rest. You two do, too."

The Watcher Lyr healed looks at me with a frown. "Are you not coming with us?"

I shake my head, eyes skipping over the bodies littering the field around us. The stench of blood and rot is nearly over-whelming, but one thought remains clear.

"The others are still in the forest."

If we had six Aberrations, plus however many shadow crea-tures Lyr fought off, how many more did Sunillen's group have to face? I can only hold out hope that we proved enough of a distraction to let them flit through the forest without engaging in battle. Hope they managed to find the villain in this tale. The fact there is not a second wave of Aberrations spilling from the forest helps fan that spark of hope into a flickering flame.

I wait for the Watchers to start towards Ulingard before facing the forest and beginning my own journey. My eyes scan the edges of the trees, jumping from one shadow to another. My antlered demon does not rise from behind the mossy tree trunks, and the hope is now exploding in my chest like fireworks. Excitement dares to new strength to wearied limbs, and I quicken my pace.

My foot breeches the barrier between field and forest for the first time, but before I can think to react, there is a crackling of sticks, tree limbs brushing against each other as *something* charges directly for me.

I step back, sword halfway drawn before my mind makes sense of what I'm seeing.

"Vaen?"

I shove the sword back into its scabbard, reaching out just in time to catch the thief as he stumbles from the forest. His weight slams into me, nearly bowling me over, but I manage to steady myself before we both tumble to the ground.

His harsh gasps fill my ears, and the hands that grip my elbows are so tight it borders on painful.

The scent of burned flesh hits me a moment later, curdling whatever joy remains like sour milk.

"What happened?" I ask, unable to hide the desperation from my voice. His hands grip my elbows tighter, as if holding me helps keep him together.

Vaen takes a minute before he pulls away, and the bleakness in his face tells me whatever the truth is, is far worse than any nightmare I could dream up.

"Olivie is dead," he whispers. His voice doesn't shake, but the hollowness in it is somehow worse. "Torn apart by the creatures. She tried to hide, tried to flee, but they found her. I couldn't save her in time."

My heart fractures. Olivie was my friend. I knew there would be casualities in this war, but never did I think it would be her. It was one thing to see the mercenaries torn apart. But trying to save a *friend* and failing? It rips my heart, and I wasn't even there to see it.

"Why didn't Sunillen stop them?" It's the only thing I can think to ask even as my eyes flicker over Vaen, looking for wounds.

I find the burns, scored across his left side from hip to chest, his clothes tattered and blackened, at the same time as he speaks.

"Sunillen is gone."

I want to touch him, help him, to put something on the burns, to ease the unbearable pain they must be causing. But his words, and the darkness that hovers behind them, draws my attention away from the wounds.

I ask my question carefully, softly. "What do you mean, gone?" My heart begins to hammer with an unknowable dread.

Vaen stares at me, the hollowness deepening, blurring with the remnants of disbelief, of despair.

I can't breath, can't swallow, can't look away, can't—

"Nearly as soon as we entered the forest, Sunillen disappeared." My heart bottoms out, a screaming ravine that splits me in two. I know what's coming next, but I still shake my head, willing it not to be.

"I did my best to track him, but he knows this place much better than I, and Olivie needed me." Vaen swallows thickly. His hands, still on my arms, twitch with the memory, and when he speaks again, his whisper is hoarse and broken. "He attacked us, one by one, from the cover of the trees. I don't know if he got the other Watcher or not."

Each word is a dagger driving deeper into the gaping wound in my heart.

Sunillen attacked them. He disappeared as soon as they got to the forest... when the Aberrations appeared. Right as they appeared.

Olivie is dead... because of me. Because of my foolish, blind trust.

I was wrong. Sunillen has been the villain all along.

The room is cold and silent. A single candle burns on the table, red-orange flame flickering, sending formless shadows onto the walls. There's a small brazier in the corner waiting to be lit, but I haven't gotten the strength to find kindling.

Lyr sits on his bed, knees drawn up to his chest, a blanket wrapped around him like a cloak.

I dip trembling fingers into the small pot of burn salve, unable to look Vaen in the face as I spread it as gently as possible over the wound. It looked worse in the night than it is, but his entire side is still bright red, the edge nearest his chest spotted with white blisters. He hisses in pain as I work, his entire torso locked tight with the strain of staying still.

Tears burn my eyes as I trace the hard, muscled planes of his body as carefully as I can.

It's my fault he's hurt. My fault Olivie is dead. If I hadn't trusted Sunillen, if I had believed what everyone else was saying, what Haith had said from the beginning, none of this would have happened.

I forced the confrontation. I engineered it, brought it to its bloody conclusion.

And now Olivie is dead, Lyr's magic is completely drained, and Vaen is wounded without a mage to heal him.

I thought I knew what I was doing. I thought I knew better than everyone else, thought I could see something they couldn't. I believed I could figure it out on my own, gather the clues and draw the correct conclusion.

Me. A farm girl, too idealistic for the Knight's Temple. Too simple to see the truth. Too eager for someone to share my trauma, that I greedily bit into the first offering fed to me. Sunillen told me what I wanted to hear, read me like the opened book fool I was.

Lyr lets his breath out in a soft sigh, the usually quiet sound now abnormally loud. "We need to get to sleep. Tomorrow we have to meet with the Watchers and discuss what the next step is." He winces. The idea of going to the tower without Olivie waiting for us there is unimaginable. "I'm sure the city council will be wanting to speak to us as well." They have been mostly silent during this quest, taking their cues from Olivie, but too many are dead for them to continue to put their hope in strangers.

I slowly screw the lid back onto the pot of salve. I can't look at either of them in the face.

"I'm sorry."

The words are a broken whisper. I keep my head down so they can't see the tears that roll down my cheeks. This is the first time I've cried since I left the Temple, every cracking piece threatening to shatter into oblivion.

A hand, rough with calluses and still stained with flecks of blood, tilts my chin up until I'm forced to look into Vaen's somber face. My bottom lip trembles as he scrutinizes me.

"Did you wield the weapon that struck down Olivie?"

I don't want to reply. I press my lips close together. He doesn't give in at my silence, and finally his silent pressure draws the word between strained muscles.

"No."

"Did you send a blast of fire into my side with magic?"

"No."

"Then it wasn't your fault."

I draw back, his hand sliding from my chin, fingers trailing for just a moment down my neck. "Of course it is," I protest, the word sharp as broken glass. "I'm the one who went to Sunillen and convinced him to come with us tonight."

Pieces of myself splinter into a dark abyss I am too afraid to name. I want to lay down and cry, to go back and somehow *fix this* but there is no changing the story. It has already been written. All there is to do is forge ahead and hope there is enough to salvage.

Even that seems an impossible task.

"You can't take the blame of someone else's actions," Vaen says, still quiet, still unwavering.

I can, I absolutely can, and they are not just his actions, they are mine as well. I aided in his path whether or not I wielded the fire.

"He's right," Lyr says, voice weary. There is no blame there, no shame. But my heart can't accept it. He lays down, eyes already half-hooded with sleep. "Sunillen chose this path. All we can do now is hope to catch him before he causes any more harm."

It seems a lofty goal when so much harm has already been inflicted.

"Rest now." A giant yawn cracks Lyr's face. "Hunt tomorrow."

Tomorrow. One way or another, this will end tomorrow. I know it in my bones.

I don't say anything else as I shrug out of my grime encrusted clothes. Vaen, wincing, positions himself on his good side, his shallow breathing the only indication of his pain. I hope Lyr can heal him tomorrow, but judging from the snores already rising in the room, that possibility doesn't seem likely.

"I'll bunk with Lyr," I say quietly as I go to blow out the candle. "I don't want to hurt you in the night."

Any more than I already have.

Because despite their reassurances, I know the truth.

If Vaen replies, I don't hear it, my ears filling with an endless buzzing as I curl up against Lyr's back. His warmth offers no reassurance. They might have survived tonight, but Olivie didn't. And what of tomorrow? There is never a guarantee any of us will live to see the next sunrise, but now the chance of survival seems slimmer than ever.

Your fault your fault your fault your fault your fault

It is a long time before I fall asleep.

Lyr looks moderately better come morning, and he scarfs down food like a starving child. He does not offer to heal Vaen, however; an unspoken admittance to not being at his best yet.

What follows is an excruciating morning of waiting. Lyr departs for the city council with stern orders not to leave the inn's property or do anything even remotely suspicious. Vaen is confined as well, and we spend the time mostly in silence, taking turns washing the blood from our skin, the dirt and debris from our hair falling like ash on to the water. I apply more salve for him, then we grab our weapons and retreat to a sunny spot near the inn's door, where we can see Ulingard's town green and keep an eye on the coming and goings of the inn as well.

Every time I see a Watcher, harried and marked by dark circles under their eyes, I feel another pang of guilt. Another barb digging under my skin, burrowing until I'm infested.

This poison is far worse than any an Aberration can inflict.

Midday comes and goes before Lyr stumbles back to the inn. Our weapons have long since been cleaned, sorted, and sharpened, and the last hour has been spent in strained silence. I can't find the words to apologize again, or talk of other matters, all of which are too trivial now. The prattling words, usually dancing off my tongue whether I want them to or not, have gone quiet.

Every sinew and muscle tenses as Lyr slides down next to me, the exhaustion clear in the shaking lines of his body. He lets his head fall onto my shoulder, the weight comforting. I take his hand because it seems like the right thing to do, and he squeezes back tightly. I suddenly realize how comforting this has become. His presence, his mannerism, the way I can read his emotions before he voices them. Lyr has become woven into my life, stitched together with me intrinsically until I can't see how to unwind us. And I don't think I would, even if I could.

Vaen is there too, perhaps even more so than Lyr, despite the tension always lingering between us. Either from disdain or disagreements or something else, something more, something I'm not sure I can put words to or even want to.

What happens tomorrow? The day after? When this is all over, what do we do?

I finally manage to work words from my dry mouth. "It wasn't good news, was it?"

Lyr's whole body rises and falls in a gut-deep sigh. "No, it wasn't. We're effectively under arrest."

Panic prickles, but I keep silent, letting him continue.

"The council is stuck in a damn hard place. Until they can find Sunillen and ascertain his guilt, all mages in Ulingard are ordered to their place of residence and advised not to leave until the all clear is given." He gives a dry chuckle devoid of humor. "Since we were all out of the city last night, you two are under orders not to leave either. The Watchers at the gate have been alerted to use force if necessary."

Vaen snorts in disgust. Disbelief and the faintest tint of that familiar anger war against the void that has swallowed me the rest of the day.

Nothing about this is right.

"What do you mean we can't leave?"

I'm too loud, too angry, and Lyr sits up, his hand tightening on mine in what I imagine is a show of sympathy. I bite back the urge to shake him away.

"You're possible accomplices," Lyr says with a small shrug.

"Do they really think you could be behind it?" Vaen interrupts before I can formulate a response.

"I think I'm the next likeliest person after Sunillen." This is a simple fact for him, an objective statement. Nothing to get his feelings hurt over.

I want to rage at the council, demand they issue a formal apology. After everything Lyr — and Vaen and I — has done for them, they're attempting to cast blame on him?

I could perhaps forgive that of them. They're scared, they're desperate. It's not right, but covering their asses is better than letting a potential enemy roam free. What I cannot forgive, however, is their utter lack of foresight for protecting Ulingard.

"They're sentencing the city to death," I state flatly. "If they refuse to let a mage out there to defend them, they're opening the gates and welcoming the Aberrations inside."

Out of the corner of my eye I see Vaen clasps his hands together tightly, pressing his forehead into his knuckles. He knows I'm right.

Lyr does too, if his shaky exhalation is any indication. "They're bringing out the full battalion of Watchers," he says quietly. "They've sent word for aid from the next closest cities."

"It won't be enough."

He doesn't say anything. We all know it's true.

After several long moments of silence, I push myself to my feet, dusting my worn breeches off as best I can.

"Where are you going?" Lyr asks, watching me carefully.

I nod towards the jewelry shop. "Haith has been a part of this community for his entire life. He might not be on the council, but he's a strong member of Ulingard in good standing. Maybe he can vouch for us, convince the council to at least let us stand with the Watchers tonight."

Stand at the gates for the slaughter.

It's undoubtedly not enough, but it's all I can think to do. I am suddenly overwhelmingly grateful for whatever the hell Haith and I are.

Lyr doesn't look convinced. "I don't think the council will be swayed, Raylen. They were pretty adamant."

I spread my arms wide, desperation making my words clipped and short. "It's better than nothing. I have to at least try."

Try to fix this. Try to fight. Try to protect the ones I can.

The pressure is overwhelming. I'm angry still, so furious at the injustice. But I am also, to my very core, so very tired. It pulls at my limbs, drags down my heart until I almost cannot bear it. I ache from so many days fighting, countless bruises and strained muscles coalescing into one throbbing mass I call my body. I would like nothing more than to crawl into my bed and sleep for days.

But the war isn't over yet.

"I need to tell the others." Lyr runs a hand over his face, looking suddenly older as he pulls himself slowly to his feet, Vaen a hairsbreadth behind. "Check in on them."

He grips our shoulders briefly before he leaves.

"I'll let you know if Haith thinks anything can be done," I say to Vaen, turning to go as well.

His hand catches my elbow before I can finish my step, pulling me to an abrupt halt. It's a measure of how tired I am that I actually stumble a bit. But his fingers are warm around my arm, steadying me effortlessly, and I look up into his face, now so near to my own, the question dying on my lips as I stare.

He looks at me, grim and serious but also... worried.

"You need to be careful around Haith." He has never once bothered to dull his words or intentions. I've come to appreciate that about him.

The automatic response rises. "He won't hurt me. He's not a bad person."

Vaen's expression doesn't change, and he doesn't release my arm. "You don't know him, not really. But we both have seen his temper, haven't we?"

The anger at me for speaking against him. The uneasiness when he has to be in the same space at Vaen and Lyr. His words, damning them, calling them useless and beneath me.

Vaen isn't wrong. I'm not stupid enough to pretend he is.

"He's my only chance at doing something," I say. "I have to try."

Finally he releases my arm, and I immediately wish he hadn't. Vaen takes a single step back, nodding at me. "I know you do. All I'm saying is, be careful."

I try to give a reassuring smile, but I doubt it's anything more than a grim slash across my face. "I will be."

I think about doing something, saying something else. Gripping his hand in a show of companionship. Embracing him, even. Saying how glad I am that we're friends now, or asking if I'm still just an annoyance.

I don't think I am.

But it all seems too trivial in the moment. So I don't say or do anything at all except turn and start down the path towards my last real hope.

TWENTY-FOUR

The shop is closed, door barred tight, no sign explaining Haith's absence hanging over the door.

I try to peer in through the window, but everything lies dark and quiet inside. It's no true surprise, as the town green is quiet as well, the usual daily tasks under a pallor in the wake of last night's upheaval.

I go to the forge next, entering without knocking, slipping through the unlocked door as little more than a shadow.

The forge is cold and quiet and empty. The kilns are dark, no fires billowing, no lingering warmth in coals. There is no semblance of activity, the very air heavy and silent around me.

I scan the space carefully, searching for threats, eyes flitting from one familiar object to another. Every sense is alive and alert as I wait for something to jump out. The familiar feel of my hilt at my fingertips lends a fraction of peace, but it's not enough to dispel the dread that crawls through me.

I am so tired of this dread. Peace seems a fleeting, unattainable notion nowadays.

I wait long enough that if there is someone in the forge prepping an ambush, they have the patience of the earth itself. I check shadowed corners and behind the kilns quickly before silently treading to the door of Haith's living quarters.

I place my palm flat on the wood and listen, breathing as shallowly as possible. But there's nothing that indicates anyone is on the other side, much less a threat. I push the door open slowly, wincing when the hinges squeal in a cry for oil.

"Haith?"

He sits at the small table in the corner with a bowed back, resting his head on one hand while the other cradles a mug I doubt very much holds tea. He confirms my suspicions when he looks up, eyes faintly bloodshot and unfocused.

I take a step into the room, gently closing the door behind me. This is uncharted territory, but whatever his personal crisis might be, the safety of the city supersedes it.

"Are you okay?" I ask, keeping my voice low and soothing, as if he's some kind of wild animal.

Haith blinks at me, awareness returning slowly. He straightens a little, wiping his mouth on the back of his rumpled sleeve. It looks like he slept in these clothes.

"I don't know," he answers, voice little more than a hoarse croak. He clears his throat, takes another swig of his drink. I watch his hand tremble as he lowers the mug.

I cross the small distance to the table and sit carefully, eyes never leaving Haith. "What's wrong?"

He shakes his head, squeezing his eyes tightly for a moment. "It was never supposed to be like this," he whispers, words broken and choppy.

"What wasn't?" I can't think of anything else to say.

"No one was supposed to die." He looks up, finally directly meeting my gaze. The brokenness there feels like a reflection of my own soul. "Things like that don't happen here. Not in Ulingard. We're just a quiet little city of loggers and shepherds. We're not meant for the ramifications of magic." He spits the last word out like it's a curse, upper lip curling in disgust.

"I'm sorry," I say, because even if it didn't start with me, we were the catalyst. Guilt sits like a rock in my throat. "I wish it never would have happened. I'm so sorry for Olivie, too."

He nods, gaze dropping back to his drink.

I lean forward, daring to reach out and lay my hands atop his. "Haith, I need your help."

He just looks at me, eyes shadowed, and I take his silence as permission to continue.

"The council put us under city arrest. We can't leave, not even to help guard against the Aberrations. With Sunillen out there unchecked—" My throat closes over and I stop, struggling past the mantra beating through my head. *Your fault your fault your fault.*

"I know our fault in this, and I understand why the council is hesitant to let Lyr out into the fields, but we *need* to be there. We need to be combing the forest for Sunillen. And if they won't let us do that, we need to stand with them tonight and try to help hold back the tide that will come." My fingers dig into his hands, undoubtedly painful, but he doesn't flinch or draw away. I stare at him beseechingly, praying he sees the honesty there.

"It's going to end tonight," I whisper. "One way or another. If we're down there, maybe we can help. It's a small hope, but it's all we have right now."

Haith doesn't speak after I finish, staring down at our interlocked hands. Then, slowly, he frees his fingers and sits back, arms crossed over his chest, his entire demeanor closing off from me.

"Why do you think they'll listen to me?" he asks at long last.

"You're an important member of the community. Surely that carries some weight."

He shakes his head, impatient and annoyed. "Everyone knows I'm involved with you. They won't take my word as without bias."

The hope flutters, dips. "You won't even try?"

Haith stands so suddenly my instincts surge and I stand, too. I look at him and can't quite quell the shock when I see disappointment.

"You got into this mess on your own, Raylen."

My body goes hot and then cold as his words hit me, one by one, daggers to cut into my heart. The overwhelming hurt that washes over is almost as surprising as the words in the first place.

Haith shakes his head, lip curling in disgust, and the look he gives me now... it is from a stranger, not the man whose bed I've shared the last week. "You insisted on going to Sunillen, even when I warned you against it. You refused to listen to any sort of reason. You don't even *know* anyone in this village, but you act like you're some kind of light-sent savior, clear eyed while the rest of us stumble around blind. Well, guess what. You were wrong."

And he laughs, harsh and jeering. "I would never help someone like that. Figure out your own mistakes, sweetheart."

The harsh use of an endearment makes me snarl. And even while I accept my own wrong doings *your fault your fault* how dare he put the entire blame on me? How *dare* he?

"I might have sped things up, but I sure as hell didn't make Sunillen summon Aberrations and fucking kill Olivie."

I draw myself together, head up, chin high, meeting him heated glare for glare. He will not make me feel small. He doesn't have the fucking right.

"Looks like I put my trust in the wrong man twice. I just never expected *you* to be the coward." And I curl my lip, just like he did, before turning to walk away.

He moves like a snake, sliding in front of me so quickly I never would have believed it if I didn't see it. His arm rises before I can react, the back of his hand connecting full force with my face.

All the breath rushes out as I stagger, pain pulsing at the impact, and I swing wildly, blindly, but feel my strong fists make some contact, hear him cough in surprise, then a second blow comes to the side of my head before my eyes can clear. My body is spun, feet slipping out from under me. I land on my knees, the impact nearly as painful as the blow, one hand snapping out to catch me from falling face first as the other scrambles for a dagger.

But my head is spinning and blackness sparks in my vision and my fingers are too big and clumsy and I can't free the weapon in time before the next blow comes, his elbow driving into my back, all air gone, sparks of pain dancing down my nerves. My precarious balance gone, I fall forward, unable to stop myself this time. A fourth blow to the back of my head, and my forehead connects with the ground, hard enough to shake my teeth. The world goes dark.

 It can't be but a few moments before the darkness recedes and awareness comes rushing back. There is no slow awakening this time. This is not rising from sleep, but a violent realization that I'm laying on the floor, head pounding unbearably, and hands are at my waist, hoisting my hips up. Jumbled words float piecemeal between my scattered thoughts, taking an unbearable time to make sense.

"I am no fool. I will not allow... bitch... mocking me."

The understanding that my breeches are around my ankles comes at the same time as Haith slams into me, cruel and strong and uncaring.

The pain that rips through me is nothing compared to the screaming in my head, the disbelief this is happening, *why why*

why why, and the fear and hatred rise like a tidal wave to sweep me under, obliterating the useless voice that begs him to stop.

I try to fight, but the room spins and my limbs don't want to work right and he leans forward to place a hand on the spot between my shoulders, his blacksmith-trained strength keeping me effortlessly pinned.

There's a roaring in my ears, blotting out the sounds of his harsh pants, my own pained whimpers, the light damned begging I can't seem to stop. It obliterates everything, stealing the strength from my shaking body, eventually stealing my words as well, words that fall on deaf ears and carry no meaning any longer.

All I can do is wait for him to be done, and I hate myself for it, almost as much as I hate Haith.

When he finally does finish, he picks me up like nothing happened, bringing me to his bed where he wraps a blanket around the both of us. My mind screams for me to get the hell up and run, but my body refuses to obey. It's disconnected, belonging to someone else. Someone weak and pathetic and small.

It takes entirely too long for me to realize Haith is talking, even longer to make sense of the words.

"I'm sorry, Raylen, I didn't mean it. You know I have a temper, everyone knows it. I was just so mad at everything, but it was too much, I know that now. It won't happen again."

He actually sounds like he believes himself.

He traces a hand down the side of my face and I flinch away so violently blackness threatens the edges of my vision again.

He continues to apologize and try to explain his actions away until the alcohol and fading adrenaline catches up to him. He falls asleep with my name on his lips.

As soon as I'm sure he's well and fully asleep, I slide out from his heavy arm, falling bonelessly to the floor. My head pounds with every beat of my heart, vision sparking if I move too quickly. My shoulders ache with the promise of a magnificent bruise, and I can't even think about the rest of me, the split lip and forehead, the incessant ringing in my ears, the blood that has dried sticky on my thighs, the reason it's there.

I take my time, making sure I can breathe before pushing up, then waiting until I'm steady on my feet before attempting to move. I stare down at Haith, face smooth in his sleep, and think about how easy it would be to kill him. The dagger is in my hand, the weight more reassuring than a thousand consolations. It would be so *easy* to slide the blade into his neck, watch the blood pool into his pillow while he gasped for breath and begged me to stop.

Like I begged him to stop.

It takes more willpower than I thought I had to slip the dagger back into its sheath and step away.

Killing Haith would be satisfying, but it wouldn't erase what happened.

But more than that, there would be no question who did it. The Watchers would find me in a few hours. Haith has plenty of friends who would notice his absence. I would have to leave Ulingard to escape a life of prison.

I would have to leave Lyr and Vaen alone, on the cusp of war.

And in the end, I can't do that.

So I slide my dagger back into place and pull my clothes back into order and leave.

A sense of loss slams into me as soon as I step onto the cobblestone street. I stand still for a minute, listening to the whispers of movement around me. The entire city is blanketed by fear, words and actions muffled and small. No one tries to approach me, and I watch them scurry, securing food and water and gossip, clutching their friends tightly as they wonder what Sunillen will do.

He's going to kill them, that's what.

Everything is just too *much*. The urge to flee, to run away, rises high. But where to? I can't go to the Watchers and tell them what happened. I can't go to Lyr or Vaen — the idea is so horrifying, sour vomit rises to coat my throat. The inn—

I stop and stare at The Night's End as the pieces *finally* click into place. All those warnings, those fearful glances... My body turns, begging to go there, find the serving maid, sob together at our shared injustice. Thank her for trying to warn me, even if understanding came too late.

But I don't move. Returning to the inn is too risky. Hell, standing in the central green is too risky. Haith could awaken any moment and I sure as hell am not waiting around to see what his version of peace looks like.

I don't think I have the resolve to not kill him a second time.

So I pay a few coins to a soft eyed woman selling cheese, cured meats, and water. Essentials. She doesn't question me, doesn't even try to make awkward side talk about the ever present winter wind. Sees my bruises, looks away. The aura of waiting darkness, as if the whole city is holding its breath, is too tangible.

I take my sparse supplies and head blindly off into the city, weaving aimlessly through residential streets and closed door shops until I find a corner of peace. The garden is wedged between the shoemaker's shop and an ever present lumber front. Most of whatever has grown here before is gone, wilted by the winter frost, but there is still a patch of scraggly grass. It's tucked back between the buildings enough that I don't feel on display.

I curl into the back of the garden, in the corner of the buildings, and begin to plan.

Going into the forest and confronting Sunillen, council verdict be damned, is the obvious, and only, option. Begging the council for leniency in helping was the best case scenario, but now that that has been shot to hell, my resolve is not weakened.

It's a suicide mission, plain and simple. I don't *want* to die. There is so much more life to live — so much more I could do, so many places to see...

I never got to say goodbye to Liseah.

The thought nearly destroys me, so I abolish it. I don't have time, room, for weakness, for sadness. I have spent enough of this day being sad, being stripped down and torn apart and told I was nothing more than dust on a forgotten shelf.

I may not live through the night, but I'll be damned if I end it as an abandoned husk.

I know what I have to do. The chances of me killing Sunillen are incredibly small. But creating a distraction? Projecting his position loud and clear to the waiting Watchers, to Lyr who hopefully will wait by the gates ready to defend even without me there, orders be damned. If I can weaken Sunillen, slow him down, garner his attention so others can get close... that will be enough.

It has to be enough.

I expected it to be near impossible to wait for twilight, but somehow I manage to fall into an uneasy sleep, propped against the cold masonry. When I wake, blinking owlishly in the dim light, my body protests the harsh sleeping position but my head feels better. Less painful, more clear.

I don't think about the rest of me. The broken pieces, the sharp edged glass lining every thought, ready to shatter at a moment's notice.

Instead I take that fear, that sadness, and wrap it around

myself like a cloak. I force it protect me, force it to become something more. Dangerous. Angry.

How *dare* Haith think he has the right to my body? How *dare* he speak to me like that, like I am nothing but a foolish, simpering fool? A *woman*. Lesser than. Someone to be controlled, someone to mock and use and throw away. Sunillen did that too, seeing my terror, my weakness, and using it against me. He forged a bond that never really existed, trying to reduce me to just another fool.

All my life I've been told my temper is too much, too fierce, unneeded. But now I see it for the gift it is. I step into the anger, relishing the way it lights my bones on fire, ligaments and muscles burning from the fierceness. I *am* the fire, and Sunillen will regret ever underestimating me.

I move with purpose, shoving the last of the food and water into my mouth as I shake off the lingering stiffness with a few simple stretches. Then, body alight with anticipation, I head out.

As I hoped, the southern gate is virtually unguarded. The majority of the Watchers are gathered at the north, ready for their stand against the Aberrations. There are only two guards left here, young and green and clearly annoyed at missing their shot at the glory. They're too wrapped up in their daydreams to realize there will be no glory for anyone tonight. If we even manage to survive, the losses are likely to be insurmountable.

They don't even see me coming. I feel bad for disarming them so swiftly, delivering jarring blows to their heads. And I worry that this is all a mistake, that I'm leaving a vital part of the city undefended. But in the end, it's a risk I'm willing to take.

I slip through the small door near the gates, shoving debris around it to try and mask the entrance as best I can. It wouldn't fool a human, but an Aberration? Very possible.

While the evening steadily darkens around me, I make my way to the north of the city as quickly and quietly as I can. I keep close to the wall, arm brushing against it as I move. Any time there is a suspicious sound, I stop, eyes roving the growing darkness, wary for both creatures and Watchers. If anyone has noticed my absence there is no sign of it, no patrols out here looking for a runaway. If they notice at all, I'm sure I'll be quick to be called traitor, but that is one more despondent thought I can't bear to consider. All that truly matters is getting to the forest and finding Sunillen as quickly as I can. Of doing the most good with the small amount of time I have remaining.

I slow even further when I reach the northern wall. I take the extra time and avoid the light from the flickering torches on the wall, crouching low into the brush and scratchy brown grass, keeping to the shadows as if I too were one of the creatures. Voices from the wall drift down, but I don't bother trying to listen. Their tone is steady, not raised in alarm, and that is all I need to know.

By the time Sunillen's mansion comes into view, it is almost fully dark. We are still hours ahead of the normal time of the attacks, but I wouldn't put anything to chance today. I stare at the looming house for a moment, imagining how quiet the halls are. Are there guards there to protect the remaining staff? Protect his imbued jewels from further abuse?

What do his children think?

Do they even know yet of their father's treachery?

He is lost to them now, like their mother, but not even the memory of him can hold an ounce of comfort.

I huddle in the shadows near the mansion, staring at the expanse before me, empty but for the echoes of battle, of blood.

Nothing stares back at me from the trees. Not yet. But it will come find me before the night is over, of that I am certain.

Somehow, impossibly, I make it to the edge of the forest without a single cry of warning from Ulingard.

It is so much darker even here, just teetering on the border. No matter how hard I stare into the trees, I see no sign of movement. Nothing stares back at me. There are no snapping twigs, no snarling creatures, no whimpering forest animals fleeing for their lives. Everything is.... silent.

It is far more terrifying than facing a charging Aberration.

You can do this.

I'm not sure I can. The fear that grips and twists is stronger than any courage I contained on the journey here. The longer I look, the more bitter the fear becomes until acid coats my throat and I can't shove it aside. I turn and vomit.

When my stomach has stopped roiling and I can breathe again, I straighten and face the nightmare once more.

If you don't do this, the death will be worse. You have to try.

My hands shake. How am I supposed to be strong enough for this?

Haith didn't think you were strong. Sunillen used your own weakness to manipulate you. Are you going to let them win?

Going into the forest won't erase what Haith did to me. But it will sure as hell tell the world I didn't lay down and wilt away. Let my weakness consume me.

I can't let them win.

Before my nerves fail again, I step forward. Then take another step. And another.

The trees are close together but their branches do not form a complete canopy, allowing moonlight to filter through. It is faint but enough to illuminate not scattered bones and exposed flesh, but the utter ordinariness of the forest. A ground of leafy loam and fallen branches and scattered rocks. It smells like pine and frost and winter. There are no ominous shadows, no scent of blood lingering in the air.

None of it releases the tension radiating through me, the knowledge that something is *wrong*, that I'm missing something important.

It takes a while, but I finally realize what drives the sense of wrongness.

Silence.

No birds call to one another, no squirrels scurry and chitter and dig for acorns. There is no *pat pat pat* of elongated rabbit feet as they dart for their burrow. No echoing owl hoot to wind through branches and warn the scurrying mice to hide.

Everything is silent. Holding their breath, waiting for what is to come.

I move deeper into the forest, aiming for the center as best I can. Trying to watch the ground for tracks, the foliage for broken branches, and the surrounding forest for threats is damn near impossible. A more skilled tracker would undoubtedly spot clues I pass over, and I find myself wishing I had paid more attention to Vaen's lessons on the road. Anything to help.

Still, I know that I'll reach him, quickly or not.

The changes come slowly. The air thickens like before a storm, dragging at my lungs, sliding down my throat in a slimy coating. I start noticing broken branches, trampled tracks that would be impossible to miss.

A sharp, copper tang hits me, so fiercely I gag.

Blood. Lots of it, and close by.

My eyes can't catch everything at once. I crouch down, legs shaking from the strain, gripping two daggers until my knuckles turn white. Better to throw them fast and try to get a hit in before going in with my sword.

I slip through the foliage, which is getting increasingly rocky as the terrain becomes more treacherous. It's as I maneuver over a fallen log that I see her.

Her body slouches over the back of the log and for the

briefest moment, I think she's simply resting. Then the details hit, one after another, and the scream builds in my throat, kept back only by sheer will.

She's missing half of her left leg. It's just simply gone, torn off below the knee, ragged pieces of flesh draped over bloodied muscle and bone. Her stomach was ripped open, exposing rope-like intestines that pool in her lap, grotesquely purple and putrid with stink. Half of her face is burned, the skin blackened and melted so her eye dangles from the socket.

Still, there is no doubt it's Olivie.

Rotting death burns my nostrils, and I retch into the soil, body shaking as it tries and fails to bring up anything more than sour strings of bile.

I want to cover her, bury her, show her the mercy and reverence she deserves.

But there is no time.

Instead, I touch her boot and whisper, "I'm so sorry, my friend."

A thousand regrets pile high, just as foul as the corpse I have to leave behind.

Rage blinds me, overtaking me, filling me until I can't seem to breathe because of it. I turn and stumble away, not caring to keep quiet any longer. Let him hear me come and know I carry death with me.

It isn't long before a sound pierces the forest, absolutely startling not because of its volume, but because of its very presence. I stagger to a stop, ears straining to hear it again, every bit of my body taut and alert. Gone are fatigue and fear and horror. The gaping hole left by them is only filled with the ferocious anger, the need to *fix this*.

It comes again, lilting and light, carried on the breeze that worms between the stitches of my cloak to worry at my being.

Every bit of me freezes as I make out what the sound is.

Crying. Someone, a girl, crying softly.

A child, crying.

Panic and anger vie for dominance as a thousand thoughts rush through me.

Sunillen is here. And he has a child, probably ready to sacrifice for some perverse reason.

It is probably his own child.

I explode into motion, head cloudy with the need to move, all my surroundings fading until I can only focus on the sound and which way I need to go to draw closer to it. My heart pounds along to each footstep, urging me on. *Closer closer closer.*

The trees open before me, dumping me into what has to be the heart of the forest. I get a brief impression of a rocky outcropping to one side, a slow moving brook cutting across the glade, separating me from the others here. The moonlight pours into the small area, illuminating the scene in ghastly detail.

Amilla kneels on the ground, weeping into the dirt.

Sunillen lies bound hand and foot before her, blood running from a fresh wound on his forehead, eyes wide with panic and warning.

"There you are," says the figure at the front. "I was wondering when you would join us."

Nalista turns and greets me with a familiar smile, a glittering diamond dangling from her bloodied hands.

TWENTY-FIVE

A void opens beneath me, filling my ears with roaring wind as my stomach bottoms out, mind scrambling to process the sight before me.

The villain is Sunillen, was always Sunillen, everything pointed to him—

But he lies bloody and broken before me, covered in dirt and old wounds, staring at me like some kind of cracked doll begging me to understand, to see the big picture, to *figure it out*.

"You tried so hard, I'll give you that."

My head snaps back to Nalista, who watches with a faint, mocking smile. I am nothing more than a child, facing a problem too great to comprehend.

My lips part and somehow words make it past the shock, the desert in my dry mouth. "This isn't right."

Nalista's laugh is high and cruel yet somehow still *hers* and what little remains of my soul shatters into shining pieces.

"Of course it is, my dear. You were just too narrow-minded to see it."

She glances down at Sunillen, nudging his side with the toe

of one mud encrusted boot. His eyes roll trying to find her, seething hatred dripping off him in waves.

"It's okay, Raylen." My name is poison on her tongue. "I fooled everyone. You weren't the only one to miss it."

Faced with undeniable truth, the pieces come flying back, snapping together one by one. All those dark circles under her eyes, the haggard exhaustion I thought was purely from comforting scared children night after night while monsters raged. Her distance to Sunillen, the unwillingness to try and bridge the gap between them. The countless times she mentioned hesitations, worries, downright dislike, sowing seeds of doubt into my subconscious with every needle sharp word.

A single mention of going away to schooling, staying with her aunt.

It was Haven. Not some random city, but the birthplace of mages.

Nalista grins as the understanding seeps across my face. "There it is. Too little, far too late."

She squats down, body still angled towards me, and grabs Sunillen's hair at the back of his head, pulling so he arcs painfully off the ground. She studies him for a moment, then, for no apparent reason beyond her own amusement, she slams the butt of the dagger into his temple. He drops, eyes fluttering on the verge of unconsciousness, while Amilla's weeping grows louder. The girl kneels unbound, eyes round and glassy, shock keeping her locked and stiff while she stares at her father. Her mouth parts slightly, lips moving soundlessly. Praying for help.

"It's not entirely your fault you missed it." Nalista rises, the dagger held idly in her hand, eyes never once straying from mine. "No one ever expects much of so-called lesser magics like mine. Like Lyr's. The crown is only concerned with the flashy bits, lightning and growing things and *fire*." She looks back down at Sunillen, clicking her tongue. "They forget we have power too. They don't understand how important it can be, twisting perceptions just *so,* just a minuscule amount so you don't realize it's outside interference. If I could only manipulate without touch, I would have been the most sought after person in court."

There's something I'm missing, something important, but it dances just beyond reach.

"It was so *easy* to work with you, Raylen. You made it almost too simple. You were already primed, aching for a friend, for another woman to bond with." There is no female gentility in her now. "A nudge here, a push there... you were practically begging to be my friend."

The understanding that it was manipulated from the start is both a staggering blow and, strangely, a relief. It is easier to think I was, at least somewhat, influenced to like her rather than jumping in blindly with my whole self.

Still, the quiet truth is I probably would have done it anyway.

The mercenaries died because of her.

Olivie died.

I need to keep her talking. Because if she's not talking, she's acting, and I don't know how to stop her yet. I need time.

I nod to the diamond dangling from its chain wrapped around her wrist. "Is that how you've been able to do it? Stealing Sunillen's imbued objects?"

Her grin grows, a violent slash of twisted amusement so out of place with the demure governess I know. Knew.

"Of course it is. It's why I came here in the first place, same as Lyr, same as the others over the years." She nudges Sunillen again, then draws back her foot and lashes out, boot connecting solidly with his stomach. He groans, coughing, trying to curl around the spot as Amilla cries over him. I flinch at the action but do not move. Not yet.

"So that's it? It was just greed?" My voice breaks, betraying weakness, but all that matters is keeping her attention.

Nalista stares at me, head cocked to one side slightly, as if viewing a wounded animal. Her grin slips bit by bit, and the somberness is somehow worse.

"No. It's not greed at all."

She steps back, gesturing to a rock face in the sharp incline of a hill behind her. Deep cracks mar the surface, more than nature could wrought, criss crossing and jagged and dark and I know without words that this is where the Aberrations come from, this is their birthplace, this is the twisted fountain of dark magic.

"When my son died, I thought my life was over." Her voice is bleak but calm. "I was ready to kill myself. I wasn't a strong mage, so the crown didn't need my services. My family had already thrown me away. No one wanted to marry a grieving mother, and I wouldn't have them even if they did. Kallum was my world. What was the point of staying here when he was no longer with me?"

The hairs rise on my neck. I don't look away from her, afraid of what will happen when I do.

"I was ready to die. Instead, I found salvation."

A beauteous grin breaks over her face.

"He told me what I had to do. To come north, where I wouldn't be caught as easily. To find work with Sunillen and gain access to his magnificent collection of objects. It took me two months to use up the first one. I didn't even know the magic would run dry eventually, but I suppose even souls are finite."

She looks down at the diamond, a frown tugging at her lips. "That was the problem. No matter how much I used, I still could only channel so much at a time without being ripped apart. And no matter how much I tried, I could never get those cracks to open up the whole way."

She points to the rock and I stagger forward, daggers up. Nalista laughs at my reaction, tutting softly as she lowers her hand once more.

"Jumpy little thing, aren't you? Stupid girl."

I blurt out, desperate to keep her on track, "But why? Why do you want the Aberrations here?"

"It's not about bringing them here. It's about going *there*." Wild eyes swing back to the stone for a moment, and I almost do it, I almost fling myself forward, but she looks back too quickly, as if sensing my sudden decision, and the movement dies with the shifting of my toes.

"What do you mean, *there*?"

Nalista shrugs her delicate shoulders. "Another realm. Parallel to our own, just out of reach, where magic lives untamed. An infinite amount of power, right there. Tantalizing, taunting. You could do *anything* with that power. Destroy the world and create it anew."

Sweat beads and drops down my forehead, stinging my eyes. I can't keep up with my frantic thoughts. "But mages can only handle so much power at once."

Her face darkens in sudden fury. "Because of those damn Crystals. They gift us magic and choose who deserves it and how much they are given. For what? Why do they get to decide? Why are *they* the rulers of this material plane?"

Her anger is searing, unbearable, and she's wrong, that's nothing what I've learned of magic, but she plows on, fury raising her voice to beat at the night.

"Those inanimate *objects* think they are gods? That they are good enough to determine who is powerful?" She is wild, a creature untamed, full of her own mistaken fury.

"So why didn't you go to one of them?" I ask. My desperation reeks.

She scowls, utter disdain in every syllable. "I would be caught. There are too many mages there, too many blind to what I'm doing." Her gaze drifts back to the rock and the countless cracks, and, against my better judgement, I look too. "But here... there are remnants of magic here. Old magic. Older magic than these fools think to wield. Once upon a time, creatures passed between the two realms freely. Once upon a time, they brought magic back to this realm and set up gateways."

"Who did?"

She ignores me, perhaps doesn't have a true answer. Her eyes are glazed as she says, "In there, the possibilities are limitless. Everything has to return to its source eventually. Our physical bodies to dust, our souls to the beginning of their creation. The beginning of all things."

My head spins, struggling to keep up. "Are you saying our souls return to this other realm?"

The reality hits and I finally understand.

"You're trying to reclaim Kallum's soul," I breathe.

Her smile is gentle, and that is the most frightening of all.

"Of course I am. He's my baby. A mother would do anything for her child."

Fuck, *fuck*. I finger my dagger, thinking of throwing it, but as if sensing my intentions, Nalista moves next to Amilla, hand resting on the girl's head. The child shudders, tears finally breaking into great gasping sobs that fill the quiet clearing with their desolation.

"The thing is, I never could get it quite right." Nalista moves closer to the outcropping, eyes traveling along the marring lines. "I tried and tried and tried. The power created pockets, turning unwary shepherds into my monsters, infecting the very forest creatures."

My breath catches, but it's not the antlered thing she speaks of but the loping, animalistic Aberrations. The antlered monster is no mere Aberration wrought by mortal magic.

"And things could get out, could slip through the cracks I created, but they weren't the *right* things. I knew I needed to open it the whole way. Needed to send a live being inside to find what I needed." She smiles down at Amilla, soft and gentle. Like a mother.

"But when old Sunillen here was looking through all his scrolls, I was too. And he finally found it — the answer. Only he didn't realize it at the time. You see, the most powerful type of magic is when it's released at death. It's why imbued objects are so valued."

Her eyes find mine, focused and razor sharp and entirely intelligent. "Blood for blood," she whispers. "Blood and magic to call to magic. A live soul to bring back a lost one."

Her hand snaps out and gusts of wind surround me, so strong they push me to my knees, shove themselves down my throat to choke back the words, pleas, threatening to spill out.

She strides forward, gripping Sunillen and hauling him to his feet with supernatural strength. Amilla screams, long and loud, begging for her to stop, words pouring out like water from a sea, a torrent to pull us under.

Nalista doesn't blink as she grips a dagger, hilt sparkling with shards of precious stones, and slides the blade across Sunillen's throat. He spasms, blood splattering across the rock, pouring from the wound to drench the soil at his feet.

Amilla screams and I do too, leaning against the wind with all my strength, I just need to raise one arm, one dagger, I just—

The diamond, coated with blood, swings from Nalista's hand as she directs the outpouring of magic at the rock face. I can feel it, hot and humid and too great, too much, pressing against my skin, and there is no doubt that anything between her and the stone lies dead now. The dozens of cracks emit a soft white-silver light, pulsing in time to the blood still pooling around the forgotten corpse of the once-great battle mage.

And just like a doorway opening, the cracks coalesce to form an entryway, crooked and slanted and *wrong* but entirely there nonetheless. The void beyond is filled with gray fog that slithers and slides from the entryway, enveloping Sunillen within a moment, rolling over our feet to fill the forest. Beyond is darkness, impenetrable from where we are but seething with a sense of evil that shakes me to my core.

Nalista turns, eyes wild, features alight with triumph. She never breaks my stare as she grasps Amilla and hurls her into the otherness.

The child's scream cuts off abruptly, sound swallowed by the darkness.

Whether she is weakened from the monumental magic or distracted, or the horror that engulfs me is enough to lend me unknown strength, I'll never know. But my arm rises and a dagger flies through the night, embedding itself true into the mage's shoulder.

She hisses in pain and surprise, the winds stuttering before dying away completely. I move before they're gone, the second dagger flying out to graze Nalista's cheek. My hands are shaking too much to aim properly, thoughts flung out in every direction.

Nalista howls her rage, nothing more than one of the dozen Aberrations she's pulled from this hell, but that sound too vanishes the moment I hurtle myself, unthinking, into the void.

I stumble as I exit the archway a heartbeat later, immediately hit with the scent of decay and wet mildew. I have a vague impression of a very large creature moving very quickly towards me and throw myself into a side roll. My shoulder hits a half buried, jagged rock, sending shards of pain through my arm, but it's a momentary concern, quickly forgotten as my vision clears and I see what lies before me.

Four stumbling Aberrations jostle each other as they try to shove themselves through the glowing archway. They look identical to the ones we've seen, with their strange melted skin and dark bone teeth and poison in their blood.

I nearly stop breathing, trying to make myself as small as possible, but I came into this realm reeking of fear and desperation, not trying to be quiet, and I know they've seen me. They couldn't not have.

But, despite the logical impossibility, they don't look at me. The Aberrations are wholly focused on the gateway, drawn to whatever magic opened it. Blood magic.

Shadows dart between the creatures, whispers filling the silence of the space, wordless noise that I can't focus on.

Eyes never leaving the sight before me, I slowly rise to a crouch. Still no acknowledgement. Hands shaking, I ease myself backwards, and although the movement is quiet, I'm completely exposed. I am nothing but a mouse waiting for the owl's piercing grip.

Somehow it never comes. The four Aberrations disappear, cloaked by their shadow comrades, and I am left alive and whole not twenty feet away.

As soon as the last trace of them is gone, I stand and rotate in a slow circle, trying to take everything in at once.

The landscape reminds me of our own world: fields, trees, rocky hilltops, even a mountain in the distance. But the colors are darker, muted, everything dulled to grays and blacks with the barest hints of blue and green. Veins of sharply bright silver light, the same that erupted when the doorway was created, snake across the ground and through the landscape, giving enough light to see. There is no moon or sun; looking towards the sky, I'm only met with more darkness. It feels as if there is no ending, no change between one space and the next, and staring upwards too long makes me feel untethered to the very ground.

I snap my gaze back down, focusing on my ears now, straining to hear anything beyond my own labored breathing.

There is no wind, no creatures chirping or mewling, no babbling water or snapping of sticks. Just... emptiness.

But where is Amilla? Did she have the sense to keep quiet and run and hide? Or did something already take her?

I have to find her.

Nalista believes this realm is where souls end up once their physical bodies have died. But, staring at the barrenness, I don't see a whisper of anything remotely human. Would a soul even look like our physical bodies?

Light above, this is too much, this is an impossible task for someone like me. I'm not a thinker, not a philosopher, not a fucking mage. I'm just a swordsman. I should have stayed and fought, should have tried to subdue Nalista before she did even more harm, but condemning Amilla is not something I could live with.

Vaen will be so upset when he realizes I've left him again.

I close my eyes at the thought. I can't even fathom his anger. And if — when — I don't return? He'll have been proven right. But I somehow think there won't be much victory in that.

I wish, achingly, I could apologize. Find a way to just say one more thing, to explain—

My breath catches.

Hands shaking, I pat my pockets. And there, snug in the inner pocket of my cloak, the cloak I haven't worn since the first battle, is a hand size piece of smooth glass, perfectly intact.

The contact shard, charmed to convey one single message to the person holding the other piece.

Oh please let him have it.

Every ounce of me vibrates with trepidation and *hope* as I run my finger around the edge three times, just as Lyr said to. The glass answers with a soft white glow, almost blindingly bright in this dim world.

I don't know how long of a message it will convey, so I try to speak quickly, words entirely inadequate to the thoughts hammering at my head.

"Sunillen dead, Nalista real mage, has imbued jewels, in center of forest. Looking for Amilla, don't come after me." My voice breaks. "I'm sorry. Please don't die."

The glass shimmers, light slowly fading. I close my mouth, heart beating impossibly fast, and pray it's enough.

It has to be enough.

I slip the glass back into my pocket. There will be no return message, so I shut the thoughts away. There is no point to dwell on them any further.

Now it's time to hunt.

I know, in my own soul, the creatures living in this realm will begin to notice my presence very soon. There isn't much time left if I want to save Amilla, much less myself. There will be more Aberrations drawn to the gateway, more perhaps drawn to my own life force.

And I think of the antlered creature with eyes like death, and I know it will try to find me tonight. I have entered its domain, and it will not allow me to escape unscathed.

The expanse before me is so very large and daunting — where would Amilla even go? I rotate slowly, trying to imagine myself as a small, scared girl who just watched her governess cold heartedly murder her father, but the reality is too unbearable.

Adrift in a sea of uncertainty, I start forward, away from the gateway, hoping I can somehow find my way back. I fall into a steady jog, sword drawn and ready, eyes flitting from surface to surface and ears pricked for any sound.

The landscape doesn't seem to change, but when I look over my shoulder, the gateway is already a fading light. It still emits a glow brighter than the surroundings, although there is no way to say how long it will last.

If Vaen kills Nalista, will the gateway vanish as well?

By sending the message, have I doomed myself?

I pick up the pace, panic threatening to send me into a full out run, but somehow I manage to rein it in. Crashing through this strange netherworld will certainly spell my doom.

The strands of silver, which I can only assume are pure forms of magic, mark my path. Some lines grow thicker and branch off in different directions, creating a cobweb network on the ground to light my steps. I follow the thickest clump of magic strands, hoping the attraction of light would have drawn Amilla as well, but make sure never to step on or touch the strands. Who knows what touching raw magic could do to someone, much less someone without an ounce of magic of their own.

Although it seems I've been running for miles, I feel barely winded, suggesting it hasn't been nearly as long as I feel. Time is meaningless here; surely it must pass differently for Amilla to have hidden so thoroughly from me already.

Unless something else found her first.

Desperation grows, and I realize I have no choice. My cracked lips part, her name just a whisper as it slithers out of my throat. Not nearly loud enough. I clear my throat and try again. "Amilla?"

No response.

A little louder this time. "Amilla?"

Still nothing.

This was a death wish. An impossible task. Tears build as everything that's happened since this morning — was it only this morning? — comes crashing down. I threw away my life for nothing.

No.

No, that's not true. Trying to save even one innocent person is never the wrong thing to do.

I turn again and again, tears blurring the trees until they're nothing more than a gray painting left in the rain, leaves and bark and roots blending into one dark mass.

"Amilla!"

A scream this time, scared and angry, so very angry. Not at her, never at her, she's being a clever girl. But at the world. For taking her, stripping her of her innocence in a quest for power, for answers when fate has already spoken. Anger at every person who dared to tell her she wasn't worthy of her own life. For every person who took bits and pieces of her, stole them away for their greed.

And maybe it's really for me, too.

And again, "Amilla!" Voice cracking, every sense jittery, my body reacting to what it knows is wrong, telling me to stop, to be quiet, to hide.

Not this time. Not anymore.

I will never hide again. I will never let someone else dictate what I do, who I am, what I am capable of, ever again.

"Amilla!"

And this time, a mouse soft voice answering, "I'm here!"

I whip around, relief pouring through me, and see her emerging from the shadow of a tree. Tearstained, blood splattered, shaking. But alive.

All the breath leaves me in a great gasping sob, and I run to her.

So does the shadow.

It peels itself off the tree, sentient eyes finding me, a slash of a mouth opening in the darkness to grin with wickedness and teeth and death. The Aberration skitters to the ground, flowing like water, gathering more to itself as it goes, smaller shadows scampering to add to its mass.

"Get down!" I roar to Amilla and she obeys, self preservation sending her sprawling on her hands and knees. I send the dagger over her head, straight to the shadow, but it passes harmlessly through it. I choke on my sob, readying another anyway even as my long legs eat the distance between us.

I reach Amilla before the Aberration does, pulling the child behind me and bringing my sword up just in time to parry a swipe from dagger-like claws. My sword catches on them, sending the strike away, but when I swing it back, the blade once again slices through nothing but air.

Fuck fuck fuck.

What am I supposed to do without Lyr? Without magic?

As if sensing my horror, my desperation, the Aberration laughs, a horrible mocking sounds that rends through the air. Amilla screams and claps her hands to her ears, sobbing, "Stop it, stop it! No more, please!"

I slash out with my sword, but it sinks into the Aberration, blade swallowed by the darkness. I gasp, tugging the hilt, but it's stuck fast, the monster rapidly consuming the weapon bit by bit. I let go before I lose my hand and backpedal, dragging Amilla with me.

How is it possible? Are they stronger here, in their birthplace?

"Run," I breathe to Amilla. It's our only chance.

We turn and start to sprint back towards the silver aura just barely visible, but the Aberration cuts in front of us, that mocking laughter surrounding us like a cocoon.

I see, over its shoulder, another Aberration. Hear the low moan of a third behind us.

The shadow before us grows, towering over me now, so great it seems to meld with the sky and draw the darkness into itself, becoming the very night.

Amilla grips my hand, fingers frigid with cold. Her sobs have died away. "Thank you for coming for me," she whispers, looking at me with clear eyes. "I'm sorry you have to die too."

The snarl rips my face in two. I'm not going to let her die. This netherworld will not be our graveyard.

Magic. We need magic. It's the only thing that will stop them.

A vein of silver breaks the land only a foot from me.

The thought strikes, the idea taking root, and I know there isn't another choice. Not daring to think of the consequences, of whether this will only lead to a faster death, I kneel next to the vein and plunge my hand in.

The reaction is immediate and visceral. The magic clamps onto my hand like it's a lifeline, burrowing into the skin, slamming up my veins and through me and into my heart and brain and filling every ounce of my being until I can't think or breathe, until all there is, is magic.

It burns and rips and tears with a pain unlike anything I've felt before. I scream and scream and scream but it doesn't help, doesn't dull the blazing inferno trapped within my skin.

I'm going to burn out, it's too much, far too much, there is no possible way to contain this firestorm, this maelstrom, this never ending agony—

But through the haze someone is yelling, begging me to keep going, to keep trying, and I'm not sure if its Amilla or Liseah or Olivie or the magic itself, my own twisted mind, but it gives me the distraction I need to yank my hand away from the burning flood.

The pain dulls, but not by a lot. Amilla is yelling at me over and over again, words meaningless in the tempest in my head, but the tone is clear.

Save me.

Getting to my feet is the hardest thing I have ever done. My body burns with a thousand aching welts, bones melted into liquid. I raise my head and see the child, eyes wide and frightened, the Aberration looming over her.

Instinct raises my hand, palm out, fingers spread. I call to the magic using my body as a host for its power, and it answers.

A fireball of pure light rips from my hand, searing the skin in its ferocity, barreling straight for the Aberration. It dosen't have time to hide or defend itself, the agonized shriek deeply satisfying as the light consumes it, burning brighter for an instant as the darkness bursts into ashes.

More.

Another light blast, and the second falls. I turn, muscles weeping, and the third dies before it can take a step.

More more more.

The magic begs to be used, begs to be released and channeled until it destroys the world.

That's not right.

I came to save the world, not destroy it.

If moving my body was an impossible task, caging the magic is earth shattering. It screams and flails and roars, a silent battle coursing through my body, but I am relentless too. I imagine an iron bird cage and shove the magic inside until I can breathe around the storm within.

"Go," I croak to Amilla, and she takes off towards the gateway.

If our presence wasn't noticed before, it is now. Aberrations shamble from all directions, eyes gleaming with greed as they single-mindedly focus on me. There is everything we have faced before, shadows and broken once-humans, and new things my brain can't wrap around, giant hovering insects with stingers that drip viscous poison, bear-like monsters that roar until blood drips from my ears, things with shards of bones protruding from their chests like a second set of teeth.

I have the presence of mind to notice them stepping through the veins of magic seemingly unaffected. They cannot absorb more magic into themselves, but still crave it like a life source.

One by one they come, and one by one they fall.

Amilla has to take my hand halfway through to guide me.

Running steps turn stumbling, and soon it's all I can do to drag one foot over the other. Everything burns, my skin tight and hot to the touch, and my skittering thoughts know I can't keep this up.

"Come on," Amilla pants, half dragging at my slowing body. "We're almost there, come *on*, you're so close."

I look up, expecting it to be nothing but a placating sentiment, but she's right. The gateway stands open before us.

The relief is almost enough to wash away the pain of the magic. I grip Amilla's hand and try to push back my hunched shoulders, lift my feet a little higher.

The antlered king of Aberrations steps around the gateway, skewed head and broken bones and white eyes just as terrifying as the first time.

It stops before us, directly in our path, and grins at me, ichor dripping from its fanged mouth.

I knew you were special, the voice hisses through the still air of the netherworld, far more coherent than any Aberration has the right to be. *I knew you would be a worthy vessel to slake my thirst. You, the best of the warriors, the one with a clear heart. I craved you the moment I stepped into that world, and now you will be mine.*

I sob and raise my hand but I know it's not enough, it won't be enough, I will die if I channel more and this monstrosity is faster than me anyway.

I never would have succeeded. But nonetheless, I have to try.

I raise my other hand. Maybe, at least, I can give Amilla a chance to make it.

I open my mouth to warn her, to sound my last defiant cry, but another's roar eclipses my pathetic sounds.

It's a roar to shake the very bones of the earth, a sound so inhuman and magnificent I can barely comprehend it. I look up, towards the sound, just as a monstrous beast with wings of starlight crashes into the ground before me.

It stands larger than a house, with a grand sweeping tail with angular fins at the end, a tail that whips around wildly just inches from our forms. Leathery wings that glimmer with fine silver dust flare out, transcending the light of the gateway. The entire creature is covered in night-dark blue iridescent scales — and threaded through those scales, shimmering with their now-familiar light, are veins of magic.

The creature raises its head, looking at me with an intelligent amber eye.

I would leave if I were you, Raylen Starstealer.

The voice is deep and bone chilling in its power. I want to fall to my knees. I want to demand an explanation. I want to ask a thousand questions.

I can't do any of those things. The antlered Aberration growls its rage, shadowy tendrils of power whipping out to try and ensnare me. With a soft chuckle, the scaled creature turns back to the monster and opens its massive mouth. Fire, white and scalding, boils within, steam hissing from between teeth.

Go!

I jump at the order but manage to grab Amilla's hand.

We skirt around the creature, unable to tear our eyes away from the battle. Fire against shadow. Light against darkness.

Then we're at the gateway and step through it once more.

CHAPTER
TWENTY-SIX

We stumble out of the gateway in a flurry of tangled limbs. Sound hits immediately, too harsh, too loud, and Amilla shrinks back against my side with a muted cry. People are shouting, the ground shaking with the stomp of their boots, screams crashing into each other in the air above us.

I can't make out the words. I am so very, very tired. All I want is to sleep.

I lay my head on the scratchy forest floor, the smell of wet earth filling my nose. It smells good. Like home.

"Raylen." Amilla shakes my shoulder, whimpering, but I can't open my eyes.

"Just a minute," I mutter to her, words slurring together. "I just need to sleep a minute." Just long enough for my skin to cool, my innards to stop boiling.

Someone yells, a high pitched scream of anguish and fear. So much fighting. It needs to be over. I ache for peace.

I should be more worried about the sounds. I should stand up and see what is happening and get Amilla to a safe place. But I just *can't*.

"Raylen!"

A different voice this time, one I would recognize from across the realm. The fear and desperation in his tone is new. Something truly terrible must have happened.

I force my eyes open, put all my strength into one arm to start and prop myself up, but he's there before I can make any headway.

Vaen's body crushes into mine, strong arms engulfing me and pulling me tight against his chest. One hand finds the back of my head, fingers tangling in my hair as he presses me to him, face in the crook of his neck. He smells like forest and blood and sweat, but I breathe it in deeply. Somehow my arms manage to loop around him, fingers shaking and weak, and he grips me tighter, like he's worried I'll fade away.

"You're alive," he whispers into my hair, voice thick with relief and awe.

For a moment, absolutely everything stills. The noise fades, Amilla's shuddering body next to mine ceases to exist. Even the magic intertwined with my blood is of no importance. There is only Vaen's arms, solid and warm around me, and his whispered assurances that it's going to be okay.

For the first time since this morning, I feel absolutely, utterly safe.

Tears threaten, but I swallow them down. There will be time for crying later. Once I know the gateway is closed and this long nightmare is finally over.

I don't pull away, unable to bring myself to face such a monumental task yet. "We need to get Amilla someplace safe," I say. It hurts to talk. My throat is raw from so much screaming in the netherworld.

He doesn't try to rise yet, but leans back enough to look me in the face. Those familiar eyes flicker over me, taking in dust and blood and weariness. What does he see in mine? What darkness lies there? I feel encompassed by it, by the knowledge of everything that's happened. By what I was willing to do to survive.

I wonder how long I can survive now, until the magic kills me.

"Are you okay?" His voice is a whisper, hand cupping one side of my face.

I tell the truth. "No. I'm not. But I'm alive."

He studies me a moment longer, then nods. Now is not the time to discuss what happened in that dark, cold place. What happened before, here in this clearing. In the forge. The thoughts threaten to overwhelm me, so I shove them down once again, in that iron cage with the magic. Cover it with darkness, pretend it doesn't exist. I can't fall apart now. The night is not yet over.

I finally manage to look around. The clearing is full of Watchers, mercenaries, and, shockingly, citizens of Ulingard, wielding what weapons they could find, standing in clumps together as they fend off the Aberrations. There has to be a dozen of the monsters, and more lay dead on the ground. There are humans there too, corpses mixed together to create a graveyard.

The mercenary's mage darts between fights, skating on a slick river of ice that melts with every step, icicles that rain down from the treetops, that bloom at her fingers to deliver blow after blow.

But where—

Finally I see them, at the far end past the brook. Lyr and Nalista dance around one another, shards of energy lashing out from outstretched hands. Two more Lyrs peel off from the mage, surrounding Nalista, who only laughs as she dodges one and destroys the other with a flick of her wrist. Lyr uses the momentary distraction to send a whip of burning energy at her, but she twists away, the end of it merely scoring her cheek instead of beheading her.

"My message went through?"

Vaen slowly stands, bringing me with him. He keeps one arm looped around under my shoulders, and I lean into him, unable to find the strength to take my own weight.

"It did. It gave us enough warning to gather the forces and meet Nalista before the Aberrations could attack the town." He gives me a tilted grin. "Glad you finally remembered to use the glass."

I try to smile back, but my lips won't work right. I look instead to the gateway still crackling with energy behind us.

"How did you get the town to let you come?"

I feel his chuckle reverberate through my skin. "Lyr gave a very impassioned speech — using magic to project his voice so the entire city heard it, waking them from their sleep. Many of the citizens were very upset with the council for keeping them in the dark. Much to the council's surprise, the city chose to join the Watchers and protect their land." He chuckles again. I like the sound. "It was really something to see."

I can only imagine, and I'm rather sad I missed it. But the feeling is fleeting, and my attention remains riveted to the gateway. Vaen notices my stare and turns to look as well.

"We need to close it," I say. It takes far more effort than it should to move my feet in that direction.

"Do you know how?"

I shake my head. "Blood magic opened it. If Nalista dies, perhaps the outpouring of magic will be enough to seal it."

It's a tenuous hope at best, but it's the only hope we have.

I turn my eyes towards Nalista and Lyr, still dueling. Almost matched in power from their imbued objects. I have to do something.

I grip Vaen's hand. "Don't leave me."

His eyes are open and honest as he looks back to me. "I just got you back. I will never leave you again."

Something in me both breaks and heals with that. I'm torn apart and put back together, piece by agonizing piece, and it's enough to give me the strength to push myself taller, to stand on my own two feet. Two strong feet that have carried me across hell and back, who have held me up time and again when I thought it would be too much. When I thought it would be the end. Somehow, through it all, I've survived.

I will survive this night, too.

I take a moment to find Amilla, hovering just behind me, eyes wild and scared as they take in the scenes of battle.

"Protect her first," I tell Vaen. He looks about to protest, but I add, "It won't be much longer."

He hesitates, nods. Trusting me.

I look to Lyr and Nalista, neither of whom have noticed our return yet. How long has it been — five minutes? More? The Aberrations, miraculously, seem to be falling steadily, the people of Ulingard gaining a tenuous upper hand. But it won't last if we don't seal the gateway and end the stream of abominations.

I hold myself straight and tall, ignoring the pain, the exhaustion. My voice rings clear across the battlefield. "Nalista!"

Heads whip towards me, surprise dotting their expressions, before they swivel back to their engagements. Lyr gives me a broad, triumphant grin, nodding as if he knew all along I would return. He had more faith in me than I did in myself.

I guess that's what friends do.

Nalista stares at me, shock scrawled across her features, followed quickly by a shadow of despair. Her eyes dart, looking for a whisper of spirit that was never there.

"You have been lied to this entire time," I shout. "There are no souls there, beyond this realm. Only the tainted, twisted creatures you have let loose upon our world. Your son is not there."

Her lips twist in a silent cry even as anger hardens her features once more.

"Please," I continue, words rushed now, trying to salvage the moment as it quickly slips away. "Please, help us to close the gateway before more die."

Her face is haughty and hard as she glares at me. "If a thousand of you have to die to bring my son back, then so be it."

She opens her arms, power rushing to her, the very air sucked into the whirlwind forming before her.

I open myself up to that river of magic once more, and it eagerly rushes to fill my being until I am nothing but a vessel for power. Is that what all mages feel? Is this power their every day existence? No wonder they are prideful, when the ability to create and to destroy lies in their fingertips.

I sense the Aberrations pause, turning to me as the power swells and calls to them. Vaen's quick, indrawn breath is the only sound I hear from him, echoed by Lyr's widening eyes, mouth forming a perfect O of shock.

Nalista doesn't have time to be surprised. She's too focused on her own building power, on trying to salvage this desperate, lost plan.

I point, and the light flares once again, bright as the sun.

As the stars.

Starstealer.

Lyr adds his own magic to my ray, and a third joins a moment later from the mercenary. All of us have been touched by Nalista's deviousness. It's only fitting.

If I could, I would give Amilla the right to the kill. She deserves it more than anyone.

Nalista doesn't crumble into dust like the Aberrations in the netherworld did. She freezes, face contorting in shock, body going rigid as the magic works its way through her system, killing off nerves and severing muscles, parting bone from bone. It destroys her one piece at a time, until she can do nothing but slump to the ground, mouth still open and eyes staring sightlessly at the night sky above her.

The stark reality of her death should bring a sense of victory, but I only feel hollow.

"What the hell happened in there?" Vaen whispers.

I try to look at him, but my eyes skitter back to the gateway, breath held in hope. The magic surges around us, stronger than a moment ago, as Nalista's body releases its last energy. I swear I can almost see it, a delicate haze that dances through the air.

I reach out a hand, eyes on the motes, and think with all my might of seizing them and sending them into the gateway. Of channeling my own roaring power, using it to grip the edges of the gateway and bring it back into itself, sew it up so no one can ever set foot in that realm again.

The gateway shimmers, undulating like sudden waves upon a still lake, but does not shrink in size. I pull again, hard, sending out ropes of magic, frantic to shut it before anything else comes through. It's time for this to be *over*.

But nothing happens except a growing buzzing in my head, wordless noise that builds and builds and builds until it's all I can hear. I'm only vaguely aware of the beginning of true pain, of fire that licks my stomach and scratches my chest, begging to be let out.

Someone grabs my shoulders, shaking me hard and sending myself back into my body, the roughness just barely enough to make the buzzing recede. "You're burning out!" Lyr yells, his face a mere few inches from mine. "For the love of light, you need to stop!"

But the gateway is still open. I feel like I'm close, like I'm missing something, that last extra piece that will tie everything together and make this possible.

You need to ask.

The words force themselves in between my own jumbled thoughts. They're amused, utterly lacking the panic that grips us. There is no sinister hatred in this strange otherness, no greed for our blood, and I know who uttered the thought.

I still, listening hard, but nothing else comes. Feeling utterly ridiculous, I send a tendril of magic out, questioning, and the response that comes back is immediate and forceful.

You cannot do this alone.

"Then help me!" I shout back down that tendril, locking the words behind gritted teeth.

I cannot use the magic myself. But I can give you and your fellow mage more.

I hesitate. More will kill me. I already feel like I'm deteriorating into whatever bits and pieces compose us.

I did not name you Starstealer for nothing. Prepare yourself, mortal!

There isn't time, so I do the only thing I can think of and grab Lyr's hand tightly in my own, stepping away from Vaen, should the magic seep into him as well.

"Together," I shout to Lyr, who stares at me with wide, confused eyes.

The magic hits us at the same time, quick and powerful and wonderful and terrible all rolled into one. I want to cry and scream and shout for joy. Lyr gasps next to me, choking on his cries even as he sends out ropes of magic to join my own. I can see the remnants of the power, the web of magic that connects us to the gateway.

I spin strand after strand, pulling the thread tauter each time. And with every breath, the open doorway shrinks. Bit by painful bit, while the magic pours through us, aching vessels just begging for relief. For an end.

When the gateway is nothing more than a pinprick of light, a pleased hum fills my head. *Well done, Starstealer. You've proven yourself a worthy vessel. I will see you again one day soon.*

There are a thousand questions I long to ask. Who are you? How can you be made of magic, but unable to channel it? What is the netherworld, and who is trying to force their way inside?

How can I steal the stars?

But Lyr sends out one final strand, and the gateway seals shut, the light immediately doused.

With it, the remnants of the gifted magic dies as well. The shock of losing it is like a slap to the face, leaving me cold and aching despite the power that still hums beneath my skin.

I take a step back and the world rushes to meet me. Darkness claims me, but this time, there is hope within its depths.

We won.

I sleep.

There are moments of consciousness, but they come rarely and are clouded with confusion and pain. Sometimes Lyr is there and sometimes Vaen, offering water to parched lips, cold compresses against fevered skin, soft words that this won't last forever. I never have time to reply to them before the darkness claims me again, filled with red eyes and teeth and pain.

When clarity finally does come, it is immediate and overwhelming. There is no slow remembrance, no gradual coming to. The memories come one after another, pummeling me like physical blows. I feel my breathing speed up, my hands on top of soft blankets beginning to shake.

"Hey, hey, it's okay. You're okay."

The voice is not Vaen's or Lyr's and threatens to send me further into a panic. I stare wide eyed at the young woman, struggling to put the pieces together. Her eyes are big and dark and calm, the hand on my arm comforting. I finally realize who she is.

I relax into the soft bed, eyes steady on her as the panic fades into a quiet sadness.

"I never asked your name."

The serving maid's face softens. "It's Wrenna," she says, voice light and sweet.

She offers me a cup of water and helps me sit up to drink it. My throat aches — actually, every part of my body aches, but it's better than the blinding pain that came with the magic.

"Where are Vaen and Lyr?" I ask when I've drained the cup.

"They had to meet with the council. They didn't want to leave you alone, so they asked me to stay for a while." She offers a shy smile and starts to rise. "I'll go get you a cup of broth. Master Lyr has told everyone at the inn to be ready for a ravenous appetite when you wake."

Now that she mentions it, my stomach is achingly empty. I want to eat more than I ever have before in my life. I give her a grin. "I don't think a cup of broth will be enough."

She laughs. "To start with."

For a moment, it almost feels normal. To sit with another woman, laughing about something innocuous. Like the entire city wasn't just under attack. Like we don't have a shared trauma bonding the two of us.

She's almost at the door when I manage to say, "I'm sorry. I'm so sorry for you." My voice breaks. "And me, too. I'm sorry I was too blind to hear you."

She turns, eyes welling with unshed tears. She lifts her chin, lips trembling but face set. "Don't you dare apologize to me. I should have worked harder to warn you. I should have yelled it to the city the moment it happened. But..."

"You were scared," I finish for her.

Wrenna nods, shame clouding her features. "It's a terrible thing, to be so cowed by a man's power you lose your own importance."

I scowl. "That's the thing about men like Haith. They thrive on power. On controlling others. It becomes the thing they crave."

Wrenna's face is firm and unwavering as she says, "I'm not going to let it happen again. Tomorrow, I go to my father. He'll help present my case to the council."

I don't know if I can stomach the thought of joining her, should the council call for more evidence.

"It may not do any good," she continues. "Haith is a strong member of the community. My claims may not be taken seriously, and he may not be punished. But I have to try. So maybe it won't happen again."

I barely know this woman, but my chest bursts with pride. "Don't let anyone tell you that you aren't strong, Wrenna. You may be the strongest person I know."

Wrenna blushes prettily, back straightening a bit. "You are too, Raylen. Thank you for saving us. We all owe you our lives."

I go to protest, but Wrenna slips out the door before I can.

I'm halfway through my second full plate of food, Wrenna gone to return the dishes of my first, when Lyr and Vaen finally return.

Vaen comes in first, immediately spotting me sitting upright, and gives me a small, knowing smile, as if fully confident the entire time that I would be all right.

Lyr, on the other hand, rushes past Vaen and nearly knocks

me over with the fierceness of his embrace. I lean into the warmth he offers, suddenly so very glad to be alive.

"You absolutely stupid girl," he says when he finally holds me at arms length. He looks me over, apparently satisfied with what he sees. "Do you realize how easily you could have died? You *should* be dead right now."

"But I'm not." I blow out a heavy breath. "Somehow, none of us are."

Vaen takes my tray and leaves it outside the room, gently closing the door behind him. The lock clicks into place, and he nods to Lyr, who mumbles something under his breath and slowly waves his upheld palm throughout the air.

"We're safe," he says. "No one can eavesdrop now, although I can't think of anyone who would want to."

The mage turns to me, placing his hand on top of mine. Vaen sits on the other bed, arms braced on his knees, hands clasped between them.

"Do you still have it, Raylen?"

There is no question what *it* is. Neither is there any need to consider my answer. It's been shimmering this entire time, tantalizingly out of reach, begging me to wield it once more.

"Yes," I whisper. "I still have magic."

Lyr lets out a breath, scrubbing a hand through his hair, turning it wild and unkempt.

"Can you tell us what happened?"

His voice is gentle, but the imagery that immediately assaults me leaves me cold with fear. As if I'm back there, in that colorless world, enemies on all sides, hopelessly searching for an answer.

"I did what I had to do," I say, and there is no shame in those words, no regret in me. I would do it again if I had to. No matter that I have no idea what this means, for a magicless girl to suddenly become a mage.

I tell them everything — once I decided to leave Ulingard. I gloss over the details with Haith, saying only that he refused to help, the cruel words he spoke. The assault is too intimate, too raw, for me to speak of yet. One day perhaps I will. But not now. Not until I figure out how to piece myself back together first.

I tell them of the forest, of confronting Nalista and her twisted reasoning for this entire ordeal. Of diving into the gateway after Amilla — who, Vaen briefly interrupts to say, has asked about me every day and is being looked after with Thomalen by her father's staff until family can be found.

I describe the netherworld in as much detail as I can remember, although the moments seem to blur together now that I look back. What is crystal clear is the plunging my hand into the vein of magic, and the appearance of the creature.

Lyr remains silent the entire time, a true testament to his willpower. When my voice grows hoarse from talking, Vaen brings me water, fingers hesitating for just a moment as they brush against mine.

When I finish, the room falls silent for a heartbeat. Lyr's face is blank, eyebrows furrowed as he thinks.

"What does it mean?" I finally ask, unable to stand the quiet, the gnawing voices inside me.

"I don't know." Lyr shakes his head. "Nothing like this has ever happened before. The only way to receive magic is to be chosen by the Crystals. But this creature... it was almost magic incarnate. That netherworld must be its home. Perhaps it's the home of all magic."

He sighs heavily, rubbing his hands over his face. "We need to go to Haven. They'll have manuscripts to study. Perhaps some of the elder mages have heard of this before, although I can't imagine it being kept this secret. Besides, you'll need to start training. I have no idea how you'll manage not to burn out, with the amount of magic you seem to contain, but I'll be damned if I let you die after everything."

"It seems Nalista was not the only one involved in this search for another realm," Vaen adds. "She was being manipulated. If we want to keep this from happening again, we'll need to see if we can root out the true culprit."

My head spins with the enormity of the road before us. Things were supposed to be done after Ulingard. It was never supposed to get worse.

So I don't drown, I focus on the one recurring thing they both said. "We?"

Lyr looks downright insulted. "What, did you think we would let you go off and figure things out on your own?" He snorts in derision.

"For better or worse," Vaen adds, eyes locked on mine, that all-too familiar smirk upturning his lips, "we're together in this."

It shouldn't be enough. The odds are stacked against us in every single aspect. But, somehow, peace drapes over me, and I can breathe a little easier.

"All right then." I nod, the decision made, surety settling into my being like an old friend.

Together it is.

Acknowledgments

Writing a book is no small feat, and I would be deeply remiss to not give thanks to the many people in my life who helped make this is a reality.

To my parents, Curt and Diana, who first gifted me a laptop at twelve after many weeks of completely taking over the family computer to write the ideas pouring from my head. Your unwavering support means more to me than you could ever imagine. From those first few years of teenage enthusiasm to the current countless rounds of edits, you have never once doubted me.

To my loving husband, Jake, who hounded me for each new chapter, listened to my wild ideas, and worked through plot holes with me, thank you. I wouldn't want to be on this journey with anyone else.

To my children, thank you for bringing constant joy to my life. I wouldn't know the meaning of true happiness without you.

To my faithful D&D group, thank you for letting me stretch my writing wings once again. Your characters may never recover, but that's a sacrifice that must be made.

To my alpha readers, Miralis, CJ, Lindsay, Olivia, and Stephanie — thank you for wading through the unedited mess, giving suggestions, and rooting for not only my characters, but me as well. Sorry for all the cliffhangers.

To my cover artist and dear friend, Shannon, thank you for collaborating with me and bringing this vision to life.

To everyone else who has supported me, held me up when imposter syndrome threatened to take me down, and quietly whispered love — I thank you from the bottom of my heart.

About the Author

Ruth York has been writing stories nearly as long as she's been breathing. Pre-pandemic she was a children's public librarian, and has a BA in English and a master's in library science. Besides writing, she enjoys board games and Dungeons and Dragons, where her role as DM gives her many chances to creatively torture various characters. She lives in Texas with her husband, three children, and five cats.

ABOUT THE AUTHOR